PENGUIN CRIME FICTION

CRIMES OF THE CITY

As a journalist, Robert Rosenberg (who has reported for *Time*, *The Jerusalem Post*, and *Playboy*) covered the investigation of a double murder that horrified Jerusalem.

Crimes of the City is Rosenberg's fictional reimagining of the true crime. Currently at work on his second Avram Cohen mystery, Rosenberg lives in Tel Aviv, Israel.

CRIMES of the CITY

Robert Rosenberg

PENGUIN BOOKS

PENGUIN BOOKS
Published by the Penguin Group
Viking Penguin, a division of Penguin Books USA Inc.,
375 Hudson Street, New York, New York 10014, U.S.A.
Penguin Books Ltd, 27 Wrights Lane,
London W8 5TZ, England
Penguin Books Australia Ltd, Ringwood,
Victoria, Australia
Penguin Books Canada Ltd, 10 Alcorn Avenue, Suite 300,
Toronto, Ontario, Canada M4V 3B2
Penguin Books (N.Z.) Ltd, 182–190 Wairau Road,
Auckland 10, New Zealand

Penguin Books Ltd, Registered Offices:
Harmondsworth, Middlesex, England

First published in the United States of America by
Simon & Schuster, Inc., 1991
Published in Penguin Books 1992

1 3 5 7 9 10 8 6 4 2

PUBLISHER'S NOTE
This is a work of fiction. Names, characters, places, and incidents either
are the product of the author's imagination or are used fictitiously, and
any resemblance to actual persons, living or dead, events, or locales is
entirely coincidental.

THE LIBRARY OF CONGRESS HAS CATALOGUED THE HARDCOVER AS FOLLOWS:
Rosenberg, Robert.
Crimes of the city / Robert Rosenberg.
p.   cm.
ISBN 0-671-70222-X (hc.)
ISBN 0 14 01.6686 6 (pbk.)
I. Title.
PS3568.07878C7 1991
813'.54—dc20   90-49671

Printed in the United States of America
Designed by Laurie Jewell

AUTHOR'S NOTE

THIS BOOK would never have been written without the encouragement of Silvia Cherbakoff-Rosenberg, my best critic and my best friend, who always wants to know the end, first; and my father, Norman "Bob" Rosenberg, may his memory be blessed, who taught me the meaning of remembrance.

Thanks also to Michael Eilan, Roy Isaacowitz, Margery Greenfeld-Morgan, Ze'ev Chafets, Harry Wall, Ellen Barie, and Helen Kaye. At various times their advice helped me over hurdles I had never expected. The unflagging enthusiasm of Lisa DiMona and George Hodgman combined to make their friendship as valuable to me as their professionalism.

Most of all, I thank my daughter Amber, for putting up with my absences—especially when I was at home; and of course, I thank all those watchmen at the gates of Jerusalem who still put as much faith in people as others put in gods.

I

ITWAS WINTER'S END in the holy city, cold enough to turn shouts into steam. Demonstrators chanted demands for the prime minister's resignation as they marched through a gauntlet of government loyalists. Policemen struggled in the breach.

"Traitors!" screamed an unshaven man, clutching a fist-sized chip of the limestone from which almost all Jerusalem is built. A mounted policeman grimaced. His horse snorted and knocked the man backwards. The stone fell from the man's hands, and his curses turned on the cops.

"Fascists!" sneered a teenaged girl, her arms linked with friends and strangers marching on the prime minister's office. A parade marshal hushed her, repeating the instructions laid down from the start of the rally—"No provocation, no incitement."

It was a season of hatred and fear in Jerusalem, a worrisome, tiring season for Avram Cohen. Old enough to remember goosestep marches outside his bedroom window in Berlin and yet young enough to be commander of the Criminal Investigations Department for the Jerusalem police, Cohen was wise enough to know that ideals can be rusted by politics.

So he watched the demonstration from the passenger seat of the white police Ford Escort, seeing his own tensions reflected in the face of his lieutenant, Chief Inspector Nissim Levy, at the wheel. Slowly they rolled up and down the hilly streets behind the moving crowd, listening to the droning voices of sector commanders reporting to a mobile temporary headquarters parked outside the prime minister's office, already under siege by the front ranks of the protesters. They followed the marchers out of the downtown triangle, across King George Street and down Bezalel Street on the eastern slope of the Valley of the Cross. The street was lit by the last of the marchers' torches and the blue revolving lights of police cars. Photographers' flashes caught faces twisted in anger. The limestone-block walls of the four- and five-story stone buildings refracted the lights into crazy colors.

Straight across, on the hilltop across the dale, they could see the lights of the Knesset's security perimeter and a chopper's beam grazing the park. Cohen's weary eyes stared out the window, squinting against the flaring light. Levy's impatient fingers tapped on the steering wheel, setting a deliberate counterpoint to the chants.

Cohen had read both secret and published reports leading up to the demonstration. Although he had confidence in Operations Commander Yosef Schwartz, calm on horseback at the front of the police troops struggling to keep the march and gauntlet from turning into a riot, Cohen that night feared more than mere fisti-cuffs and tear gas in the holy city.

"It looks like the sound and light show at the Old City walls," he muttered, "showing the tourists how the city fell to the Ro-mans." The chanting outside the car changed from *"Two states for two peoples"* to *"Stop killing, Start talking,"* and Cohen's voice, raspy from too many cigarettes, fit with its own rhythm into the phrasing of the slogans.

"I wonder which version the tourists get," he added, thinking about history, half aware that with his comment, the tapping stopped and that the junior officer, ever ambitious, was straining silently to decipher his meaning. "Do they get Josephus Flavius' version or do they get the rabbinical version?" Cohen continued, wondering aloud, thinking of the Judean general who first fought the Romans and was celebrated by them for writing the history of how the Jews turned their fight against the empire into a civil war of atrocity and inevitable defeat.

Levy's knuckles relaxed as he turned to Cohen with the answer Cohen already knew. "The rabbis say that Josephus was a traitor,"

Levy said matter-of-factly, his reedy voice tinged with cynicism about the rabbis.

Cohen rubbed at his arm. The eczema rash, just above the pale purple tattoo of his Dachau number, was both annoying and familiar. It sometimes seemed to him as permanent in his life as the city's pull at pilgrims and their passions. "Josephus was a pragmatist," he answered Levy. "He made sure he was on the winning side. And he knew that once the Jews started killing each other, they were bound to lose."

Levy turned off the four-lane boulevard from the valley and onto the five lanes that pass the Knesset. The chopper beam's erratic sweep caught them for a moment, long enough for Cohen to remember the searchlights of the camp. The prime minister's office, five hundred meters ahead, was the last of the Kirya government-complex office buildings. Demonstrators packed the entire width of the avenue all the way to the ivy-covered building where the cabinet was in emergency session, debating the latest peace proposal. Cohen could hear the unintelligible echoes of a speech blaring from a loudspeaker.

"You make it sound like a Likud-Labor debate," Levy finally said in response to Cohen's sarcasm. The chief inspector grinned in expectation of a crack from Cohen about "bloody politicians."

But before Cohen could answer, there was a sound that momentarily silenced the monotonous staccato of the police radio and turned the booming echoes into the squeal of feedback. It was a noise Cohen had long expected with dread. But despite his expectations, he was surprised when it finally came.

"Grenade!" Cohen shouted, and a split second later, he was out the door, running toward the sullen silence already turning into screams.

The bomb squad worked all through the night, taking advantage of the light of the TV crews beaming their pictures of Jerusalem's strife around the world. Every scrap of metal found in a hundred-meter radius from the explosion was collected.

One piece starred the back window of a minister's car, parked in the lot outside the cabinet office. Another flew all the way to the outdoor windowsill of the cabinet room itself. But it was a sliver, barely half a centimeter wide and twice as long, that made the headlines. It was found embedded in the brain of a paratrooper reserve captain.

One dead, 12 wounded in grenade attack on Jerusalem peace rally, the world press announced. The prime minister's office issued a statement saying that until it was proven otherwise, any implication that a Jew might be responsible for the attack was a blood libel. The statement raised cynical smiles amongst those who remembered the prime minister's youth. An extreme nationalist, he had never hesitated to assassinate those he regarded as traitors to his underground movement's fight against the British mandate and Arab nationalist claims to The Land. And one of his aides told a curious reporter that the ministers' meeting had not been affected by the explosion. "The cabinet room is soundproofed, of course," was Cabinet Secretary Ya'acov Nussbaum's straightfaced explanation.

Cohen took it more personally. He kept the reconstructed grenade in his own office safe rather than consigning it to the clutter of the national police headquarters' evidence stockroom. It was the murder weapon, and the dead man was a martyr to half the country, a traitor to the other half, and in Cohen's mind, a victim of that division.

Civil war was on everyone's lips. But Cohen could not use the term officially, although it was his greatest fear. As a policeman he was supposed to be impartial in the partisan debate that pervaded everything. In that season, even the mention of the possibility of civil war was a violation of the professional neutrality he had sworn to uphold.

So, he began with the weapon. Within forty-eight hours, it was identified by the experts in the police bomb squad labs. From the Sidra 13 series, it was developed by Israel Military Industries for hostage situations. The army wanted a grenade that would knock out a terrorist but release little shrapnel in a contained area. Sidra 13 was experimental and a failure; it released too much shrapnel. But the bureaucracy processed a production run of 12,000 before the series was halted.

Major Ehud Gozani, who was Cohen's liaison at military intelligence in the Central District Command, reported that grenades had been distributed throughout more than a hundred army units ranging over six divisions during the past five years. As many as 120,000 people had access to the weapons during those years. They were packed in Styrofoam cases of ten grenades each, and the army began the painstaking accounting of each of those cases. Army computers, the computers from the Sherut Bitahon Klali, the secret counterintelligence and counterespionage police known as the Shabak, and the police force's more primitive system of human record keepers all poured out lists of potential suspects. Soldiers with relatives in the underworld, soldiers with records of losing equipment, soldiers suspected by the military police of stealing for profit or fun were on these lists. Convicted felons were not allowed in the army, but soldiers known to associate with criminals were to be questioned, as were the criminals. Known political extremists from the right wing were also on the list of potential suspects that grew from day to day.

But Cohen and his people had to be careful. Sources in the prime minister's office told the press that investigators could not rule out the possibility that Arabs were responsible. "Provocateurs," the sources said, "trying to turn Jew against Jew," was their explanation for the attack.

"The prime minister should know," wrote one partisan columnist. "His followers often used the exact same methods when he was fighting British occupiers and Arab nationalists." Cohen put down the newspaper when he read that, as uninterested in opposition politics as he was in coalition crises. He found no thrill in partisan debate and regarded the prime minister's political opponents with the same disdain he had for all the politicians who turned ideology into idolatry.

Officially Cohen had two hundred men and women working in uniform and plainclothes for CID in Jerusalem. But the Palestinian *intifada* surged and ebbed in rhythm with international terrorism and diplomacy, army crackdowns and rumors of atrocities, drawing resources from the underbudgeted police force. Arab East Jerusalem, in Cohen's purview, was an almost daily set piece of rock-throwing, strikes, and tear gas. Of late, someone was torching Israeli cars, distinguished by their black-on-yellow license plates, and Cohen already had a dozen men on that case alone. Another two dozen were on assignment as temporary commanders of police units brought in from other parts of the country for riot control duty. And the usual crimes of any capital city, from pickpocketing to drugs, from burglary to underworld murder, went unabated.

So, in the choice between a quiet East Jerusalem and an all-out investigation for the person responsible for the grenade attack, the fifth floor of national police headquarters knew how to please the prime minister. The top priority was an end to the rumble of *intifada,* especially in the capital called eternal by the prime minister.

Hobbled by politics, Cohen began the race to find the killer or killers. He was determined to win, even if it took him a year. But he didn't have a year.

A week after the grenade attack, in a cloudy dark dawn of a Friday morning a few hours before the Moslem prayers, a Wakf gardener mulching a flower bed just behind the Dome of the Rock on what the Jews call the Temple Mount and the Arabs call Haram al-Sharif, found an IDF-issue knapsack buried in the dirt. Inside were a dozen more of the Sidra 13 grenades, prepared as a time bomb set to explode at noon.

If not for a drowsy policeman pouring his tenth cup of over-night-duty coffee in the tiny police station on the Mount, the grenades might have ended up in the hands of Islamic fundamentalists with whom the gardener was acquainted. But glancing out the window, the cop thought it strange that an Arab was running across the empty plaza from pillar to fountain wall, clutching something heavy to his belly as if to hide it. The policeman pulled at the handle of the window, shoving it open to the cold morning air and shouted "Stop!" at the frightened man. When the Arab continued running, the cop gave chase. Though tired, the policeman was much younger and faster, and he caught up with the Moslem at the steps that lead into the tunnel to the Street of the Chain. The Arab was out of breath from too many cigarettes. The policeman was grateful for his Saturday afternoon football games.

And half an hour later, bomb squad experts, along with a team of detectives under Cohen's command, were combing the area, looking for other hidden explosive devices. There was only the one bag. But the grenades had been wired together for a single blast, with a simple timer set for noon, just when Friday prayers would have peaked and tens of thousands of devout Moslems would have been bowing southeast toward Mecca. On their knees, foreheads to the ground, dozens, if not hundreds of people could have been killed. Irreparable damage might have been done to the gilt-domed mosque covering the rock from which the Moslems believe their prophet Mohammed rose heavenward.

The bombing would have been like pouring gasoline onto the already hot coals of the *intifada*. As it was, the news of the discovery turned that day's prayers into seventy-two hours of rioting throughout the territories. Rumor and counterrumor were like wind to a flame. Seventeen stone-throwers and Molotov-cocktail ambushers were shot dead by soldiers along the roads between Arab and Jewish villages in the territories. An express bus from Tel Aviv to Jerusalem was forced off the mountain highway by a Gazan who grabbed the steering wheel away from the driver, plunging the bus into a ravine. Fourteen Israelis and a tourist were killed, and another twenty-five were crippled for life. The Gazan fundamentalist miraculously survived the crash. From his hospital bed he told interrogators that he had expected to reach heaven when the bus finally reached its resting place at the bottom of the hill.

As far as the Moslems were concerned, the hidden grenades could mean only one thing: another Zionist plot to drive them out of their holy place. The mayor worked around the clock to calm the Wakf council of *kadis,* themselves under pressure from extremists to turn the next week's prayers into a call for jihad, an all-out holy war. The mayor promised that the police would do their utmost to capture the saboteurs—"whoever they may be"—insistent on that wording in his statement to the press. It angered the right wing that the mayor was ready to imply that Jews might have been involved in the attempted sabotage. From the prime minister's office again came leaks to the press explaining how Arab provocateurs could easily have been responsible for both the attack on the rally and the attempted sabotage on the Mount.

"Bloody politicians," Cohen found himself mumbling more often than ever before as he worked over the files. The men and women brought him their handwritten notes of interviews with AWOL soldiers and weepy mothers' explanations that their boys were really good. Shmulik, his liaison in the Shabak, sent over his own daily sketches from *shtinkers,* the informants from the muddy alleyways of Palestinian refugee camps; and Ehud's computer lists piled high on Cohen's desk.

Sometimes during that chilly season, after sending Levy home late at night, Cohen found himself staring at one too many pieces that fit nowhere into the puzzle. He'd open the bottom right-hand drawer of his desk, stained with cigarette burns, to pull out a bottle of cheap brandy and a small Pyrex glass more usually used in the police station for muddy Turkish coffee. It would take a half-glass, sometimes two, before he could tilt back in his high-backed chair and remember that he had once believed that he could help the city to fulfill its name by being one of the watchmen at the gates, preventing criminals and the insane from infiltrating the city of peace.

2

T HE MAN WALKED SLOWLY, knowing that he would meet no one. In the thick fog of Ein Kerem, the streetlamps quickly receded. The damp leaves and fir needles muffled his footsteps as he made his way to the convent high above the village in the valley.

He did not walk through the convent's large green gate, nor pause at the small chapel decorated with ancient icons and lit by bare bulbs. He climbed higher, above and around the compound of whitewashed buildings and red woodwork. He picked his way along a narrow path that he had been told had been forged by shepherds during centuries of leading flocks along the mountain's slopes.

Above him was the highway to Hadassah Hospital. Due east was a large stone house, where a group of students lived. He could hear music, and he thought of it as an angelic choir showing him the way around the wall surrounding the compound.

He was looking for a place he knew, a small rift in the mountainside. There the stone wall was low enough for him to make a silent jump. On the other side he picked through the damp leaves to the stairs. Worn smooth during nearly two centuries of use, the steps were made from the same soft white stone used throughout the city. They glistened in the chilly humidity of the night fog. He moved quickly, his breath catching once as he started to slip. But with a twist of his torso, he regained his balance. With a fling of an arm, he seemed to fly down the flight of stairs.

The requiem had faded into the backyard, and now he heard another music, the droning of women singing in responsive chant to a man's methodic rhythm. He listened for a long minute but did not turn toward where the Russian nuns prayed in a raw yellow light of candles and naked low-watt bulbs.

Instead he chose to move into the courtyard where the nuns lived in pairs beneath the brick-red tiled roofs of tiny one-story houses. He knew the two nuns he was seeking. One was much older than the other, the younger one much too beautiful to be sequestered in the habits of the convent. The dusty hem of her black robes swayed as she walked. He knew that rhythm well. It made promises, and he remembered those vows as he stepped silently from one single-room house to the next.

Through the window of the fourth house he saw the yellow basket that the older nun always carried when she shopped in the grocery store in the valley. The light from his flashlight shone through the weave of the basket, checkering the wall with squares. The light flickered over the painted faces of two gold-haloed women in an antique icon. The gilt of the illumination flashed in the yellow rays, and the eyes of the painted women stared back at him.

Quickly he moved to the door. It was unlocked and he stepped through, taking care to close the thin panel behind him. He moved deliberately and knowingly, searching the room. First to the closet, where two black habits hung from wooden hooks and a cardboard and vinyl suitcase stood. It was empty except for two pairs of sandals.

With his hand he gingerly explored the shelf above the habits, freezing with the discovery of a shoe box filled with handwritten letters. The letters were tied with a pale blue ribbon, which he broke with a yank. The letters fell to the floor. After scooping them up, he sat on the narrow bed. He rifled through the letters, holding the penlight in his mouth.

Underneath the letters he found a single black-and-white photograph, which had long ago faded to pale browns and yellows, almost the same colors as the icon above the bed. In the photo he could see a decorated soldier, a tall man standing beside a young woman holding a baby. He held the picture up to his eyes, the light shining so close that the brightness reflected from the scratched emulsion back into his face. He knew the woman in the picture, recognizing the oval face of the older nun in her youth. He marveled at the resemblance to the younger one, whose swaying walk had first caught his eye.

The thought made him aware that the circulation in his thighs was being cut off by the taut thongs holding his two knives. He untied the weapons, smiling as he released each one.

For the third time, there was music. A woman was humming. A second woman murmured something in response.

His body tensed. Clutching the knives, he rose from the bed. The yellow light from the lamp above the unlocked door cast a golden shadow across their white faces as they stepped into the room. He moved toward them, as fast as the accusation of recognition in the younger woman's eyes. Her last sight was the blades flashing in the light. Sinews bulging, he drove the blades deep into their necks, a powerful drive through the flesh, slicing the jugular veins, cutting cartilage between the vertebrae, severing the spinal cords. Neither had time for a sound to issue from their open mouths before the knives plunged. The younger heart pumped a full beat longer than the older woman's. Her chest heaved out the last of her life in a long spurt of blood.

With both knives in one hand, he gathered up the photo and the letters—all but one page, which had fallen under the bed. He surveyed the scene, feeling the eyes of the two faces in the icon staring at him. With one slam of the knife handles against the antique wood, he smashed the painting, splitting it along the grain, separating the two holy mothers forever.

Before he stepped out the door, he turned to look at the bodies one last time, his long gaze finally interrupted by the itching of the dampness of the blood on his cheek. He rubbed absentmindedly at his face with the back of his hand gripping the papers, and with two quick strides he was swallowed up by the fog.

His footsteps stained the pale stone path. But by the time he reached the wall, the traces were gone, except for a single deep footprint in the soft soil of the garden. Inside, the two nuns lay side by side, their mouths frozen open in eternal prayer.

3

LEVY DROVE. Cohen barked commands and demands into the radio: the mobile forensic lab should meet him at the scene; Ziv, the Jerusalem police press spokesman, was to keep reporters away; spaniel trackers were needed; a jeep-load of Border Patrolmen to secure the convent perimeter was essential. And, Cohen emphasized, no delays, no excuses.

With the microphone in one hand, he used the other to grab a box of plastic surgical gloves from the shelf beneath the dashboard. He yanked out two pairs, stuffing the plastic bags into the pocket of his windbreaker.

Levy sped and slowed, flicking the siren on and off to clear traffic. Cohen braced himself each time Levy reached for the siren's switch. As the car slipped back and forth between the two lanes of Gaza Road, Levy cursed under his breath, braking or swerving to avoid cars that moved too slowly out of the way.

"I know you took the driving course," Cohen said paternally. "You don't have to prove it. A minute more or less in getting there won't change anything now." He glanced over at his aide, who was grimacing in concentration on his driving. Cohen smiled at the perfectionism Levy applied to every endeavor.

Levy was in his mid-thirties, Cohen twenty years older. They were dressed almost identically in gray twill trousers and white shirts, with winter's addition of windbreakers and Cohen's navy blue V-neck sweater over his shirt against the cold. Cohen had kidded Levy about the flattery of adopting Cohen's personal style after being picked as Cohen's aide almost five years before. But Levy was not embarrassed and certainly never hid his ambitions. For a year he had been chafing for a promotion and for a year Cohen had postponed the inevitable, needing the younger man's talents as an administrator. Cohen knew the postponement was selfish. But glancing at his aide, whose short curly black hair was already graying, Cohen knew that Levy would be the first to admit that he still had a lot to learn from his mentor.

The chief inspector sighed silently before flicking off the siren and slowing the car imperceptibly. Cohen pursed his lips and turned to gaze out the side window. Outside, the air was crisp. A short downpour followed by a brisk wind had cleared the skies an hour after dawn. But it was still too early in the spring morning for the eastern wind to carry any of the eastern desert's heat to the mountain city. The glass window was cold on Cohen's cheek, and he tried to use the chill to calm his concern.

Two dead nuns were the last thing he needed. There were still hundreds of people to question about the grenades, the *intifada* raged, and the holy city was also a growing city, with a crime rate increasing faster than fundamentalists' eager compliance with the biblical commandment to be fruitful and multiply. But what most worried Cohen as Levy waited impatiently at a red light was the fact that Gorny, the Russian Orthodox convent in Ein Kerem, was Red Russian, run from Moscow, and thus a mystery all to itself.

Taking the shortcut through the Mt. Herzl parking lot outside the fir tree–shaded national cemetery, Levy sped past the entrance to the Yad Vashem Holocaust Memorial and Research Institute. The tires screeched as he turned the corner overshadowed by a rust-red stabile by sculptor Alexander Calder that looked westward over the one-lane road that dropped into the Ein Kerem valley.

As Levy sped down the twisting hill, Cohen stared into the steep drop into the forest of the valley. Across it, he could see the outline of the main building of the Holocaust memorial. He shifted in the car seat, crossing his arms. "What do you know about the convent?" he suddenly asked, without looking at Levy.

"They're Red Russians, of course," said Levy, snatching a glimpse of his passenger just before entering the road's sharpest curve. Cohen hung onto the hand-grip above the window.

"This side of the Green Line," said Levy, "they're Red, on the other side they're White." Green was the cartographers' color for the line that divided Jerusalem, indeed the entire Holy Land, between Israel's war of independence in 1948 and the end of the Six Day War in 1967. Since then, more colored lines marking military retreats and advances had been drawn. Cohen had no doubts that more lines would have to be drawn before peace would be possible. He only wondered when he gave up believing it would happen in his lifetime.

"Why?" Cohen prodded.

Levy was silent for a moment, twisting the wheel to keep the car on the asphalt as he passed a school bus coming up from the village. Cohen could hear the children singing about the blossoming of almond trees signaling the arrival of spring. He was hard on Levy, certain that affection from a commander is not always the best way to train a future commander. Cohen also felt that Levy was the closest thing he'd ever have to a son, and that if indeed Levy had been his son, he wouldn't have treated him any differently.

"After the war of independence," Levy recited, showing off his knowledge, "Ben-Gurion thanked the Russians for their help by returning the properties the British had expropriated from the communists. I've heard that the government pays rent to the Russians for our offices at the Russian Compound." He glanced at Cohen, wanting something more than approval. He wanted recognition as an equal. Both men knew that he had a long way to go before he'd win it.

Cohen knew that the downtown complex of rambling government buildings dominated by a gleaming church that towered over the gravel parking lot was indeed owned by the Soviet Union, built by Russian aristocrats on pilgrimage to the holy city long before the 1917 revolution. In addition to the main Jerusalem police station, the complex included the Supreme Court, the Agriculture Ministry, some Hebrew University extension school offices, and a small museum dedicated to Jews who had been hanged by the British during the years of the Mandate.

Levy continued, trying to find something that Cohen didn't know. "The Jordanians inherited the White Russians from the British Mandate," he said. "And ever since '67," he added, "we've had them all. Red and White Russian, Ethiopian Copt and Egyptian Copt. You name a church and we've got one, divided."

"Just like the Jews," said Cohen quietly, more to himself than to Levy. Neither man said anything more until they reached the bottom of the valley, where Levy paused briefly before Cohen directed him onto the small road that led past the spring for which Ein Kerem, the Spring of the Vineyard, was named.

Once the spring served village farmers growing grapes on terraces delineated by low walls painstakingly made from the limestone boulders and stones that filled every empty patch of earth in Jerusalem. Canals took the water from a small fountain spilling from a spout into a pool, to the farmers in the lower valley. Up until the mid-1920s, the fountain had been the only source of fresh water in the village, where even now, a few families owned horse-drawn carts to lug supplies back and forth between the village and the city. But most of the houses of the village were inhabited by professionals, and it was more likely to find a brand-new European sedan than a horse-cart parked outside one of the houses. The spring still spilt into the cut-marble pool, but it drained into a pipe that led to the city's reservoir.

"Anything else?" Cohen asked as Levy worked the gears to get the car up the steep hill of the one-lane road lined by orchards, groves, and ivy-covered outer walls hiding homes built around courtyards.

"What's that?" Levy asked, concentrating on the road.

"The two churches. What else do you know?" Cohen quizzed his aide.

"They fight," Levy said, smirking. "I've heard you once personally broke up a scuffle between two of their priests." He jerked at the wheel when he discovered a stretch of steep hill ended with a sharp right-hand turn that immediately gave way to another climb. He down-shifted, and for a second the rear tires spun on some wet leaves before the car lurched forward.

"Archimandrites," Cohen corrected his lieutenant, snorting a laugh at the memory of the dusty brawl of nuns and priests outside the Gethsemane basilica at the foot of the Mount of Olives. It was a week after the two halves of the city were reunited in the '67 war. The brawl was a sign that the divided church had rediscovered its ideological arguments about communists, czars, and saints

"Anyway, it's just another convent," Levy continued. "They're all over the place here. Convents, monasteries. *Yeshivot* for *goyim?* No?"

Cohen smiled to himself. Levy was an Israeli, a *sabra* born into the fact of Israel and thus absolved of religion by the rhetoric of Zionism. For Levy, religion was a quarrel between the politicians and the *haredim,* the ultraorthodox who study Torah instead of going to the army and live off their wives or charity, which in Israel amounted to government handouts. Levy had little patience for the *haredim,* regarding their draft deferments as blackmail money paid by politicians who needed the political support of the religious parties. Like many of his generation, Levy regarded religion at best as arcane ceremonies of folklore, and the political influence of the religious was just another reason to regard political rhetoric as meaningless.

Cohen's own belief in God was taken away a year before his bar mitzvah, stolen in one gory night by the same people who torched the Berlin townhouse of his childhood and marched him to the trucks that took him to the train that deposited him at Dachau.

"No, not quite," said Cohen knowingly about the difference between a yeshiva and a convent or monastery. He rolled down the window as they reached the final turn and the wide green gates of Gorny. There were two men standing beyond on the open gate, and Levy's theological curiosity evaporated quickly with the task at hand.

"There's Yaffe," said the inspector, looking down the long dusty driveway to where two men were standing in the middle of a gravel parking lot. Cohen looked ahead as the car bounced down the rutted path. As usual, Meshulam Yaffe was dressed elegantly in a beige suit, his white hair neatly cut.

"I wonder if *I'll* ever get a chance to see a barber," Cohen complained, jolted out of his thoughts by the car's bouncing down the dirt road. Instinctively he pushed his silky salt-and-pepper hair off his forehead.

Yaffe was chief of the small police unit that specialized in the delicate relationship between the police and the diplomatic and church missions in Jerusalem. He handled everything from parking problems to vandalism, demonstrations to terrorism; Yaffe stepped neatly between the coarseness of the Israeli police bureaucracy and the rituals of public gentility required by international diplomacy. He loved his role and how it gave him access to secrets and therefore power. A gossip at heart, Yaffe loved the intricacies of the cocktail circuit. Cohen often thought of Yaffe as a fool, but even Cohen could appreciate the value to the police of a devoted gossip in a city small enough for politicians and plumbers to have played together as schoolchildren, yet internationally magnetic to presidents, prime ministers, and popes.

"Go past them slowly," Cohen ordered. "Take your time parking."

"Who's that with him?" Levy asked as he followed Cohen's order, making a wide turn in the lot. "A priest?"

The man was much younger than Yaffe, taller and strongly built. He had longish wheat-colored hair that hid his ears, covered his collar, and fell across his forehead. Indeed, at first glance, the black shoes, trousers, and turtleneck jersey made him appear to be a church functionary. But the black trousers had the cut of jeans and were worn tight. No white collar peeked out from beneath the black jersey. From up close, Cohen could see the black shoes were ankle-high boots zipped up on the side, and the hair had a fashionable cut that wasn't done by any central bus station barber. The man's powerful build and cocked hip made him look more like a fashion model than a monastic who had taken vows of poverty.

Cohen shook his head slowly. "Meshulam will introduce him to us as the driver and official translator for the convent. But he's not a very typical driver. Or translator." Levy looked at Cohen with surprise as he turned off the car engine. "I haven't taken a look at him since he arrived in the city, a long time ago," Cohen continued, "but he looks pretty much the same."

He could hear the footsteps in the gravel of the two men approaching the car parked in the shade of a grand cedar tree planted a hundred years before by a Russian pilgrim who brought the sapling from Lebanon. "I don't understand," said the junior officer, removing the rechargeable walkie-talkie from its dashboard slot. "Who is he?"

"That fellow out there is Alex, the KGB baby-sitter for the Red Russian Orthodox church mission in the Holy Land," said Cohen, grinning. "Come on, you're about to meet a spy. Not a very important spy, but a spy nonetheless. And remember," Cohen added, turning away from the door to speak directly to Levy, "he's been trained by the very best in the business. And we're here to find out how it happened that such a professional was unable to prevent two murders from taking place here."

He grinned once again quickly, a tic familiar to Levy. The smile had nothing to do with humor; it was more to prove a point than to punctuate a punch line.

Cohen opened the door to Yaffe's offered handshake. By the time Cohen was out of the car, Yaffe had made the formal introductions. Cohen was Commander Cohen, chief of investigations. And the man in black was Alex, "driver and translator" for the church mission.

Alex smiled as he reached out his hand to Cohen. "Your reputation precedes you," he said to the policeman in an elegant Hebrew that Cohen immediately found condescending, too obvious an effort to prove credentials as a translator.

Cohen smiled back. "My condolences," said the detective, automatically. "About the sisters," he added, deliberately using the Christian term.

"Thank you for your sympathies," Alex answered, no less formal and sincere than Cohen.

Formalities over, Cohen turned to Yaffe. "So. What do we have?"

"The two nuns were mother and daughter," said Yaffe, glancing with slight disdain at Levy, who began taking notes for Cohen in a small yellow pad. "The mother, known as Miriam, was here since 1960. A widow. The daughter, known as Helena, came in '77. It seems the mother became religious after her husband died and her daughter was born, and ended up here. The daughter followed her mother into the order. Anyway they were noticed missing at prayers at dawn, and afterwards, one of the nuns went to look for them. She found the bodies. Alex tells me that she says she didn't touch anything except the handle to the door when she opened it. She vomited just outside the door. And then she screamed. The other nuns came running and . . ." Yaffe was about to continue, but Cohen motioned for silence.

"What time was that?" asked the detective.

Yaffe began to speak, but Cohen had spoken directly to Alex, silencing Yaffe with a quick look.

"I got here at 5:15," said Alex. "I sleep at our mission office. Not far from your own headquarters, behind the supreme court chambers."

"I know where the office is," Cohen said impatiently.

"I have to admit I may have broken some speed limits getting here," Alex added with a cloying smile that Cohen found inappropriate.

"But what time were the bodies found?" asked Cohen.

"The archimandrite informed me at 5:00," Alex said forthrightly.

"Then why did I only hear about it now?" demanded the detective, looking back and forth between Yaffe and Alex.

Just then the blue jeep carrying the mobile forensic lab pulled into the parking lot. Cohen signaled to the two technicians inside the jeep to pause alongside him. "Can they drive to the scene?" Cohen asked. Yaffe looked toward Alex, an indication to Cohen that Alex had so far prevented Yaffe from visiting the scene of the crime. Alex shook his head. Cohen waved the technicians on to the parking place beside his own car, apologizing through the open window that they'd have to lug the heavy boxes of equipment.

"All right, so why do we only know about it now?" repeated Cohen after the jeep passed. He looked at his watch and added with a glare, first at Yaffe and then directly at Alex, "almost two hours later." Yaffe began to respond. Cohen snapped his fingers to silence the liaison officer and looked to the Russian for an answer. But Alex turned away from Cohen, toward the archimandrite standing in the shade of the first of the white plaster and red woodwork buildings that made up the convent.

"He wanted to calm down the women," said Alex. "You surely know how women can be. Especially about a matter like this." His voice was surprisingly high pitched, and again there was that genteel condescension that annoyed Cohen. Alex's arms were folded against his chest, but Cohen thought the posture had more to do with a presentation of the Russian's biceps than with protection from the chilly breeze against his coatless torso. Cohen thought for a moment about telling Alex off, right there. Yaffe's face, full of worry that Cohen would do exactly that, made Cohen change his mind. At least formally, Cohen would continue pretending that Alex was exactly what he said he was—a driver and a translator. For now, he wouldn't give Yaffe the satisfaction of complaining about him once again on the fifth floor of national headquarters. There was no time for an argument that Yaffe would report back to the fifth floor, where too many conspirators were waiting for Cohen to fall, hoping to replace him. The progress on the grenades case had been slow. Cohen's detectives had still not finished the first rounds of interviews. Indeed, the lists of potential suspects was still growing instead of shrinking. The politicians were looking for a scapegoat, and Cohen's credit margin at national headquarters was close to overdrawn. So, though he anticipated the confrontation with Alex, for now, he held back.

"All right, let's go see," he ordered. Led by Alex, they walked through the compound, followed at a respectful distance by the archimandrite and a woman Alex identified as Sister Elizabeth, the mother superior of the convent. Nuns peered through curtains and from doorways. Men, particularly secular men, and certainly Jewish and Moslem men, were never to be found past the chapel where the tourists and pilgrims congregate. Tourists come to see pilgrims touch and kiss the chapel stone, marking the birthplace of John the Baptist, who came into the world a few months after a fateful meeting between the Virgin Mary and Elizabeth. The stone has been worn shiny and smooth from more than a hundred years of kisses. Only three men—Alex, the archimandrite, and the convent gardener—were allowed beyond the chapel and its holy stone.

Levy walked with the technicians, behind Alex, Yaffe, and Cohen. The men occasionally changed direction according to Alex's instructions, turning at forks in the path. Gradually they were forced into a single file by the narrow pavement through the simple gardens. Alex led the way, Cohen directly behind him, thinking that there was too much confidence in Alex's manner for a security officer who had just discovered that two of his wards had been murdered. Cohen was annoyed by Alex's swagger, so much so that he realized he was relieved when he could finally take charge again when they reached what Alex indicated was the scene of crime.

They were at the last little house of the convent on the mountain slope. From the tiny patio, Cohen could see all the way to the clouds over the coastal plain. Beyond, he thought he could see the blue of the sea. But haze blended into the sky, making it impossible to see the sharp line of the horizon where sky and sea met.

"Before we go in there, there's something I want to ask you," Cohen said to Alex, breaking the silence. Levy pulled up short, notebook ready.

"Anything," answered the Russian, "whatever you want to know."

Cohen stood half a head shorter than the KGB officer and was suddenly conscious of himself as out of shape and old, much older and thus probably a lot slower than the Russian, who Cohen guessed was even younger than Levy. "Did you do any investigation at all on the scene?" Cohen asked. "Did you question anybody, touch anything, remove anything?" He had no doubt that Alex had done something, but he wanted witnesses to the query as well as the answer. For the record. "Did you play cop?" he asked, certain that the KGB man had done just that.

The wind gusted, carrying the whisper of a bus shifting gears on the road to the hospital complex above them. Alex kept his eyes on Cohen. "Commander Cohen," said Alex, insistent on using Cohen's full rank. "I asked what happened. I looked inside here," he added, motioning toward the dead nuns' room, "and I called my friend Yaffe. I did not, as you so colorfully describe it, play cop." Alex's Hebrew was deliberately High, full of obscure conjugations that seemed to test the listener's own command of the language.

Cohen felt his cheeks blush, the broken capillaries of his face camouflaging the evidence of his anger. Yaffe put his hand on Cohen's shoulder. Cohen reflexively shrugged it off. He returned Alex's stare and then nodded, first to Alex and then to Yaffe. Cohen's eyes moved briefly to Levy, expectant and poised.

"You also arrived in 1977, didn't you?" Cohen said, suddenly turning back to the Russian. "That's the same year as the daughter."

Alex said nothing, just nodded slightly. But Cohen was certain that he saw a slight twitch in the corner of the Russian's eye before he turned to the task at hand.

4

PEOPLE WHO routinely encounter dead bodies, especially the bodies of murder victims, develop private ceremonies. Some take deep breaths before approaching, this halting the rising nausea. Some finger crosses concealed in coat pockets or *mezuzot* hanging around their necks on silver chains. Some mouth silent prayers and some seem to will themselves into a sort of trance, distancing themselves from what they are about to confront.

Cohen always paused at the doorway for a long moment, rubbing slowly at the rash on his arm, taking in the whole view first and then gradually the details. Starting with the walls, the floors, the windows, he worked his eyes around the room carefully before finally confronting the bodies. His pause was more than getting used to the scene or choosing its details. Like any prayer, it was a meditation that eliminated all the rest of the world and focused his mind on the thing at hand. The long years as a teenager in Dachau taught him well how to live with death. Almost forty years as a policeman taught him well how to study a body. But after all the bodies, all the scenes of all the crimes he had seen, every time he saw a corpse he remembered, even if only for a moment as fleeting as the stroke of a starling's wing, the first dead body he ever saw: his grandfather lying on the floor of the entrance to his family's Berlin townhouse, jeered by the brownshirts marching past the body into the house.

He could hear the hum of the flies inside as he slipped on the surgical gloves. Levy, familiar with his teacher's patterns, blocked the doorway to prevent Alex or Yaffe from following Cohen into the room. The two bodies were lying on the floor, but with two steps, Cohen was past the corpses, standing in front of the open wooden closet. He reached into the closet, carefully brushing the habits aside, thinking of the nuns' vows of poverty and the distance they had traveled from Russia to Jerusalem in order to live with one change of clothing and one pair of shoes, in the name of a God who had not protected them. He ran his hand along the shelf, smiling at their neatness when his fingertips turned up dustless. He thought of the fastidious nuns and of the technicians who would look for fingerprints. And he thought for a moment about Alex. He turned away from the closet and glanced at the doorway where the Russian, a head taller than Levy and almost two heads taller than Yaffe, was watching with his foxlike eyes. He wondered how long it would take before he would have to ask Alex for his fingerprints and how Yaffe—and others on the fifth floor—would react when Cohen demanded Alex's hand for the inkpad.

Cohen turned to the two narrow beds, head to head. He noticed the rumpled blanket of one and the pristine tautness of the other. He approached the rustled bed, inspecting the wrinkles on the faded gray wool. He stood quietly, gradually lowering himself into an almost-sitting position on the bed, and studied the room from that position. Without actually sitting down, he remained in that position for a moment, looking around. Then he bent over to look under the beds and spotted a piece of flimsy paper that had come to rest leaning against the wall under him.

All the while he dictated a description of each detail to Levy, who concentrated on keeping his notes accurate and legible. And all the while, Cohen thought of the mother and daughter. He weighed the senselessness of their deaths if they were in fact innocent against the mystery of their deaths if they were not. Most of all, he thought of the sorrow of foolishness of their belief in Jerusalem as a city of peace. Still, he didn't look at them.

He rose from the awkward posture, feeling his thigh muscles ache from the effort. He swatted at a fly that had discovered the eczema below his elbow, and he pulled his jacket sleeve down from where he had shoved it up past the rash in the warmth of the rising sun during the walk to the house. Casting his eyes across the spotless floor marred by the blood pooled around the bodies, he looked beyond the bodies to the smashed icon on the opposite wall.

"Who are the two women in the picture?" he asked. The question was directed at whoever could answer, but Cohen expected Alex to speak.

"The mothers of Jesus and John," came the now-familiar voice.

"You must pardon me," Cohen said, working hard at maintaining his politeness. "Which one is which?" he asked, looking toward the doorway where Levy kept the entrance blocked.

The KGB officer snorted. "The one on the left is Mary," he said, his tone implying to Cohen that the information was obviously irrelevant to the investigation. "You people call her Miriam. The one here on the right is Elizabeth, whom you call Elisheva. The founder of this convent called herself Elizabeth, and so have all the superiors of this convent. We had an Elizabeth who led the revolution here, in 1917. She was a great leader. She brought the sisters into the revolution. This was the first of what you call Red Russian convents." Cohen heard pride in Alex's tone and grinned as he realized he was wondering about Alex's attitudes toward Gorbachev. Levy smiled for the moment it took for Alex to realize that no joke was behind the grin. The Russian turned away from Cohen's quickly bared teeth.

Cohen turned back to the broken icon, leaning forward over the bed like a connoisseur in a gallery studying the details of a painter's brush strokes. "Was it broken yesterday?" he asked aloud, keeping his eyes on the picture. Alex shrugged.

"Ask one of the nuns out there," Cohen commanded in response to the silence. Alex looked back at Cohen for a moment and then yelled in Russian toward the spot where three of the braver nuns had taken up positions at the edge of the tiny garden. Sister Elizabeth answered the Russian.

"No," said Alex. "She says it was fine." He paused for a moment and then added, "It's worth a lot of money, so it seems that theft had nothing to do with this crime."

"I don't suppose it was insured?" Cohen asked, his sarcasm making Yaffe wince.

"Well, yes, I presume so," said Alex, disarmed by the question. "I'll have to check. I guess."

"Yes, you'll have to check," said Cohen. "I guess," he added, not hiding his mimicry of the Russian's tone. Again, the twitchy grin forced Alex to look away.

Cohen remained peering closely at the icon for a few moments. He held his finger close to the break in the painting, tracing the split in the wood. "I want the technicians to take this in," he said, certain that Levy had already made a note of it. "I want to know what broke it."

He turned abruptly away from the icon, finally moving toward the bodies on the floor. His first impulse was to try to determine how the bodies fell and where they were standing when last alive. He imagined a succession of photographs of the bodies, dozens of them taken from every angle. Later, he would mark the photographs with grids, asking for enlargements of certain details. He would sit for hours with the photographs, studying them like a rabbinical student looking for a new nuance in an ancient text, searching for an inconsistency that might have been overlooked. But all that would come later.

"The wounds are in the necks," said Alex from the doorway.

"I thought you said you didn't do anything," Cohen shot back, shifting his eyes from the bodies to Alex at the doorway.

"I could see from here," the Russian said over Levy's head.

Cohen looked back at the bodies. Their heads were almost touching. They were face up, eyes still open, the blood a flat red halo around their heads. The edges of the skin where the knives had pierced each neck were white and bloodless. The blood drained so quickly that dehydration had already begun, a puffy distortion of the shape of the gaping faces. The younger nun's habit had ridden up the side of her leg, revealing an unexpected shapeliness. It surprised him to realize that he was embarrassed momentarily by the sensuality abandoned for an innocence he had not known for a long time.

He leaned back on his heels after bowing over the bodies. None of the hands clutched at anything. The robes were not torn. He recited to Levy's notebook, and then suddenly he was finished. He rose painfully, the cartilage of his left knee remembering the pain of a guard's club.

"Are you ready?" Levy asked from the doorway.

Cohen nodded. Alex stepped out of the way of the two technicians, one ready with a camera, the other lugging the large box containing all the tools needed for fingerprinting and collecting evidence.

The archimandrite remained at the doorway, mumbling in Russian and clutching his cross, a necklace of silver and semiprecious stones. Outside, three nuns stepped closer to the doorway. The priest suddenly turned to hush their whispers.

Cohen looked down one last time at the bodies and then took one stride to the door. The people at the doorway moved aside for him, and he went out to the garden. Stretching, he looked upwards. Far off above the Mediterranean Sea, sixty kilometers away, he saw the contrails of two fighter jets in mock combat.

Running his hand over his forearm, he pushed the windbreaker sleeve back up above the elbow as the morning sun rose higher into the sky. Levy materialized at his side and immediately began reading back the notes he had taken in the palm-sized notebook. It took several minutes, and then done, Levy slipped the yellow pad into his shirt pocket. "Just what we needed," Cohen muttered. "The press is going to go crazy with this, and that means the politicians will go crazy, and . . ."

Cohen could smell Yaffe's aftershave approaching and fell silent. But before Yaffe could speak, Cohen spotted Raoul, the coroner, coming up the path toward the little house. "Raoul," Cohen called out, his voice an abnormal boom in the quiet of the breeze-stroked garden, "I'll need to know as much as you know."

"You always want to know as much as I know," the coroner laughed. "You always want to know *more* than I know. Why didn't you become a pathologist instead of a policeman?" Raoul was an Argentinian who left Buenos Aires in the early '70s to escape the right-wing death squad that had shot his son and daughter-in-law down in the street outside their home.

Cohen laughed, enjoying the thick Spanish accent of the doctor's Hebrew as much as what he regarded as a compliment. "Because I hate the sight of dead bodies," the detective said.

Raoul smiled. *"A philosoph,"* he said.

Cohen cocked his head gratefully, holding it that way for a second as he listened to a siren rushing along the highway above to the hospital. "How soon?" he asked, his tone pleasant but insistent.

Raoul knew that Cohen always wanted everything yesterday. "A few minutes. Here, I can give you some basic information. But you want an autopsy. That takes time."

"Time of death? Sexual assault? I didn't move the bodies, but the wounds seem exclusive to the neck." Cohen listed his immediate concerns.

"A few minutes, please," Raoul smiled, shrugging helplessly. "Let me at least see the bodies . . ."

Cohen raised his palms in retreat. "Go ahead, go ahead," he said, sending Raoul into the house. Cohen stepped away from Yaffe and Levy, taking a seat on a boulder in the lacelike shade of a gnarled olive tree on the terrace looking north out over the valley to the Mt. Herzl military cemetery. He lit a cigarette and asked Levy for the walkie-talkie to send a perfunctory message explaining the situation to Abulafia, Jerusalem's chief of police. In turn, he knew, Abulafia would message the southern district commander, who would send his own message to the inspector general. But he wasn't expecting the answer he received barely fifteen minutes later.

Cohen was wanted at the prime minister's office to brief him on the homicide. It was an unprecedented summons, and Cohen's astonishment gave way to self-approbation when he realized that his first reaction was to calculate whether he would have enough time to get back to the office to get the commander's uniform that he wore only on ceremonial occasions. Usually the uniform was left hanging in the plastic dry cleaner's bag on a hook on a wall in his office. He chose to forgo the uniform in favor of a few more minutes with the archimandrite and the mother superior, Sister Elizabeth.

Alex interpreted as Cohen asked for information about the two dead nuns. The archimandrite was apologetic as he explained that he had nothing further to add to what Yaffe already reported. The nun remained silent, her eyes darting back and forth between Alex and Cohen.

"But if General Cohen could arrange it," the priest said, his eyes lowered, looking neither at Alex nor at Cohen, "a guard, yes a guard might help ease the fears of the women." Yaffe, standing to one side, nodded.

"We'll also need help," said Cohen gently, negotiating a deal. "We'll have to question all the people of the convent."

The archimandrite grimaced as he grasped the meaning of the request in translation. "You cannot think that one of the nuns . . ."

"We're a poor police force," said Cohen, applying pressure. "You are translating this properly, aren't you Alex?" he added, keeping his smile aimed at the priest.

His intention did not match the tone in which the words were spoken, and Alex's answer was no less a coded response.

"It is my job, no?" Alex said, matching Cohen's smile. "But I think you understand, the mission members have immunity, and to interview them all, well, I am not so sure. The archbishop will have to be consulted. And considering that such a thing has happened, I am not certain that the Israeli authorities, who are responsible for our safety here, are going to be considered exactly trustworthy by our poor sisters."

"I'm surprised they find you trustworthy after what happened," Cohen said, still smiling, still looking for a reaction in the Russian security officer's face. "You, after all, were responsible for security inside the convent," Cohen added pointedly.

"I am a driver," Alex answered angrily, "and a translator."

Cohen chose to ignore the statement but was glad he had brought the issue out into the open. "Where is the archbishop?" he asked. But in light of the answer already given, he knew the question was futile.

"In Damascus, of course," said Alex, in a tone that gave Cohen the feeling that the Russian would have liked to have added, "far beyond your reach."

Yaffe stepped forward, ever eager. "Let me suggest something," he said, conciliatory and with authority in his tone. "I'm sure that Commander Cohen can find a uniformed officer to be on patrol here for a while, and I'm sure that my friend, his holiness the archimandrite, would like to help our investigation. Avram," Yaffe said, his eyes searching Cohen's face, while Alex interpreted monotonously for the archimandrite. "I'll finish the interview with his holiness," Yaffe concluded.

There was nothing Cohen could do. Yaffe's responsibility for the diplomats and churchmen in the city gave him bureaucratic authority in the situation. He'd report to Cohen. But Cohen never had much confidence in Yaffe's ability to differentiate facts from speculation or intelligence from gossip. Cohen wondered if Alex was aware of the undercurrent between the two senior officers.

But Alex merely translated, and from the archimandrite's answers, seemed to be doing an accurate job of it. The archimandrite unctuously offered thanks and a promise of cooperation. Sister Elizabeth bowed slightly to Cohen and then backed away to join the curious nuns standing at the edge of the garden outside the house. The four men stood silently for a long moment, each waiting for the other to break the tension.

Then Cohen saw Raoul coming out of the house. *"Nu?"* asked Cohen, relieved for the chance to step away from the sour breath of the nervous archimandrite.

Raoul shook his head. "Ten hours, maybe more, maybe less. I'll know better when I open them up. No sign of struggle. No sign of sex. But again, I'll know better when I open them. And yes, one wound apiece." He slapped shut a black notebook and stuffed it into his black bag.

"Thanks," said Cohen, "I'll be down to see you on Sunday morning."

"Commander Cohen . . ." the doctor said plaintively, conveying the need for more time.

"I'm sorry, Raoul. It gives you almost forty-eight hours."

"Through the weekend," the doctor noted unhappily but with no surprise or resentment. "Never take a job from Cohen on a Friday morning," he mumbled to himself as he walked away. "It always ruins the weekend."

Before Cohen left, he instructed Levy to wait for the spaniels, which would search for the killer from a footstep discovered in the garden by the technicians. "The rains probably washed away any scent," Levy offered.

"For the files," Cohen ordered. Files were Cohen's commentary, piled as high in their brown cardboard folders on Cohen's desk as a rabbinical scholar's books of Talmud and commentary.

Cohen informed Levy that Yaffe would handle the interviews with the nun who found the bodies. "You take notes," he instructed the inspector.

"What about Alex?" Levy asked, accompanying Cohen part way down the path back toward the parking lot.

From far away, they heard an army chopper coming from the east. Cohen glanced up at it, guessing it was on its way to the hospital on the hill above, carrying yet another *intifada* victim to emergency surgery. After a moment, the helicopter appeared over the valley and then quickly over their heads on its way to the hospital.

"Everything has its season," Cohen sighed. "You'll have yours. He'll have his," he added, before sending Levy back to the photographer's snapping, the flies buzzing, and the sightless eyes of the dead nuns.

5

COHEN HAD OFTEN WATCHED political demonstrations from the roof of the ivy-covered building. But he never had been inside the prime minister's office. There was a small sitting area, with a sofa and four comfortable armchairs all upholstered in the same beige wool. The curtains were closed and the wood paneling on the walls added to the darkness of the room. The only light came from a lamp, illuminating the papers spread out on the prime minister's large desk. All Cohen could see of the elderly prime minister was his bald head, lit by the lamp as he bent over a document.

Cohen was shown to a standing place along the opposite wall from the prime minister's desk by the cabinet secretary. Cohen knew that Ya'acov Nussbaum was a baby-faced historian plucked off the rewrite desk of the country's only newspaper to endorse the prime minister's policies. Yaffe had told Cohen that Nussbaum's mother won the job for her son by reminding the newly elected prime minister that Nussbaum's father had been a loyal member of the underground. Cohen smiled as Nussbaum raised a finger to his lips for silence and officiously sent Cohen to stand meekly alongside Shmulik, his opposite number in the Shabak, the domestic secret security service.

"Welcome," whispered Shmulik, whose brief covered counterterrorism and counterespionage in the capital. The Shabak was an investigative and operative service with no powers of arrest, so often Shmulik called on Cohen to provide arresting officers. Cohen was nearly a decade older than Shmulik, yet in the political hierarchy of Jerusalem, Shmulik was senior to the detective.

"What does he want?" Cohen answered, his voice even lower than the hum of the air-conditioning that had made him shiver slightly when he stepped through the doorway into the room. As Shabak, Shmulik was a regular visitor to the prime minister's office, for the secret service was under the PM's direct command, and the former underground commander loved to handle the secrets the Shabak collected for him.

"To survive," Shmulik murmured. Cohen raised an eyebrow at the response and fell silent, watching the other invitees file in. All the while, the prime minister studied the document on his desk, oblivious of the gathering men.

Nobody sat down. They waited for permission like schoolboys called up before an unpredictable principal. Cohen had a sour taste in his mouth, hating himself for falling in with the other anxious sycophants. He was already looking forward to a cigarette after the meeting. He strained his eyes to no avail, trying to see at least the title of the document the prime minister was so painstakingly studying.

Finally, Nussbaum checked his watch and approached the desk. He spoke softly to the prime minister, who raised his head, the light making a white reflection in his thick spectacles as he inspected them lined up before him. "Mr. Nussbaum suggests that perhaps I would be more comfortable in the cabinet room," said the prime minister. "I am less concerned with my comfort than with yours, so please," he said, gesturing with a liver-spotted hand toward a door to his right. Cohen had heard of the prime minister's manners and his adulation of officers in any form of military service to the state.

The inspector general, the chief of the Shabak, Shmulik, Cohen, Ehud, the military intelligence liaison to Jerusalem, Nussbaum, a stenographer, and the prime minister's bureau chief, all filed past him, into the cabinet room. Again they waited by their chairs, standing at attention around the long shiny table, in which were mirrored the double row of fluorescent lights hidden behind translucent panels in the ceiling.

The PM moved slowly and seemed much thinner than he appeared on television, Cohen thought, sitting down with the other officers only after the prime minister took the center seat at the long table. The PM was nearly twenty years older than Cohen, who couldn't help notice that the prime minister's face was pale and grayish, like the car-exhaust-stained limestone of the city's downtown commercial district. He thought for a moment of the bloodless bodies in the darkness of the black plastic in the back of the truck taking them to the Abu Kabir forensic labs.

"Gentlemen, I have been informed," began the prime minister, "that two Russian nuns were found murdered this morning. I would like to know why this has happened and how quickly the murderer will be apprehended. Please," he said, looking at the man known to Cohen only as Dovik, the chief of the Shabak, the most senior of the officers present.

Beyond that, the prime minister said little during the meeting. Sometimes, in fact, he closed his eyes as if dozing or listening to something else entirely. Cohen studied the PM.

The anxiety was in his hands. He had long slender fingers, a narrow palm and angular wrists. He began the session with his hands on the table, flat in front of him. But after a while, his hands began to fidget, clasping one another, shifting to his lapels, adjusting his tie, always straightening his tie. Despite the air-conditioning, Cohen realized, the prime minister was sweating. Nussbaum, pretending to be warm, suggested turning up the air-conditioning. Cohen wondered if he had been wise to doubt newspaper columnists who had been reporting that recent foreign visitors to the prime minister had come away describing his state of mind as a pendulum shifting between euphoria and depression. But he shoved the thought away as the discussion veered across the political spectrum, through categories of possible suspects.

Specific groups of Jewish zealots of both religious and nationalist ideologies were named, as were Moslem fundamentalists and Palestinian nationalists, which the assembled men referred to as terrorists. Cohen noticed that with each mention of another category, the prime minister's interest seemed to briefly ignite and then just as quickly fade.

"Commander Cohen?" the prime minister suddenly spoke up, breaking a round of commentary on Moslem fundamentalist attitudes toward Christians.

"Sir?" Cohen answered, surprised. The PM had remained silent during Cohen's report on the scene at the convent, nor had the gaunt man said anything in response to Cohen's own catalog of possible suspects.

"These inquiries you want to make among our fellow Jews. They are absolutely necessary?"

The tone of the question rankled Cohen, who found no pleasure in the fact that Jews might be responsible. But he answered forthrightly. "Unfortunately, yes. Sir," he said.

The prime minister sighed. "You will be discreet," he commanded. "It was bad enough that there was that other defamation, the assumption that a Jew could be responsible for those bombs . . ." His voice faded and he looked down at his hands. For a long moment there was silence. Cohen glanced to Shmulik on his right, but the Shabak officer was studiously making notes on one of the yellow pads on the table.

Cohen had been surprised by the call to the prime minister's office. No such meeting had been held when the grenade exploded outside his office, nor when the grenades were found on the Temple Mount. Certainly those events posed much greater dangers for the state than the murders in the convent, Cohen thought, no matter that the convent was Red Russian. The Temple Mount was the heart of the conflict, the source of all the fundamentalist fervor in the city. On the Moslem side, there was always an undercurrent pulling toward a jihad to eradicate the Jews. On the Jewish side, Cohen knew, there were the fanatics and the foolish who were preparing for the construction of the Third Temple. The *haredim* insistence that the messiah's presence was required for the construction of the Third Temple fell on deaf ears amongst the most extreme of the nationalists, who sought every opportunity to prove Jewish dominion over the site of the ancient temples. Indeed, Cohen knew that the prime minister's fragile coalition was a delicate balance between those opposing strains in Judaism. For every member of the Knesset eager for a photo-opportunity tour of the Mount— often provoking Arab demonstrations—there was an MK who regarded treading on the Mount as blasphemy, a violation of the holy of holies.

Cohen thought of a memo that had reached his desk a few days before. It was a report of an official request from two leaders of a group calling itself "The Organization of Temple Builders." They wanted police permission for a demonstration that would include laying a foundation stone for the Third Temple. Some in the force regarded the group as marginal, but Cohen had suggested vetoing the request on the grounds that it would require hundreds of policemen to safeguard the demonstrators from angry Moslems fearing Jewish designs on the Mount. The two leaders signed to the form were among the two thousand members of the central committee of the prime minister's political party. The Temple Mount movement was drawing more people at every holiday, when the groups would unite for demonstrations at the Mograbi Gate, waving flags and blowing shofars, demanding entry to the Mount. To Cohen, at least, the grenades—if indeed they had been planted by Jews—indicated that to some, shofars and flags were not enough. But the prime minister seemed unconcerned by the magnetism the Mount seemed to be exerting. Asked about the movement, his office issued a statement saying that "every Jew aspires to see the Temple rebuilt. Meanwhile, the status quo," the official statement said, referring to religious freedom for Moslems on the Mount and an Israeli police station as evidence of Israel's sovereignty over the site, "will prevail."

But the status quo was built on the assumption that reason would also prevail, Cohen thought, and there was growing evidence that that assumption was shaky at best.

Another report had recently crossed Cohen's desk. It came from the district psychologist, who described what he called a "syndrome." There were growing numbers of outbursts of individual madness in the city, mostly by tourists, said the psychologist. A dozen cases were cited of tourists dressing up in white robes and trying to throw the money changers out of downtown banks. He calculated that he had seen nearly one hundred people a year who were afflicted by delusions of being either the messiah or the prophet announcing the messiah's imminent arrival. There was nothing new in pilgrimage, and Cohen would have tossed out the report if not for the psychologist describing some other, much more dangerous symptoms of the syndrome. The best example, the report said, was the Australian tourist who had tried to burn down El Aqsa mosque on the Temple Mount in 1968 and, when caught, had explained he was trying to make room for the Third Temple.

And now, the report said on its penultimate page, the syndrome was infecting residents and not merely tourists disappointed that Jerusalem was not a religious Disneyland in which people lived as they had two thousand years before. "In America," the psychologist had explained, "they have psychosexual crimes. We are beginning to witness psychomystical crime."

It was no worse an explanation than some of the others Cohen had heard about why fundamentalism was sweeping through the city like a fire in a field of summer-dried thorns. The secret report was controversial in the tiny circle in which it was distributed, for the psychologist implied that extremist political rhetoric could be a trigger for the syndrome's susceptible loners, who sought purpose to their lives.

Shmulik took the prime minister's view, regarding the doctor who had prepared it as "another self-hating Jew looking for ways to embarrass the government." But Cohen wasn't so sure and therefore had to be careful before answering the prime minister's request for discretion, indicating that the PM wanted no police activity that could antagonize the delicate coalition with the religious right wing.

Cohen looked down the table to the prime minister, who was watching him with hooded eyes behind the thick spectacles. "All the avenues of investigation are open, sir. We'll do our best to be careful," Cohen said. "But, of course it depends . . ."

Cohen was about to continue "on which way the investigation leads us," when he was interrupted by the arrival of the chief of the Mossad, whose manner indicated his indifference to protocol. His seniority to all present except the PM excused his tardiness— at least in his own eyes.

Introducing him only as Nahum, the PM perked up with the Mossad chief's arrival, turning away from Cohen and toward the late arrival, who took his seat without apology. Nussbaum passed him the same material that all the others in the room had received: two pieces of paper, photocopies of the visa applications from the two nuns. "The Interior Ministry provided these, at my request," explained Nussbaum, attempting to impress the Mossad chief with his thoroughness. Cohen thought it would have been more worthwhile to come up with Alex's visa application, or for the Shmulik to have shown up with the Shabak files on the Russian. But he kept quiet, waiting for another opportunity to explain that he could not exclude Jews from the investigation. He made a mental note to ask Shmulik for those files after the meeting and wondered if he'd get the full version or a sanitized one.

Nahum plunged into his own report. "It's important to keep in mind the changing of the guard at the Kremlin," he said after a cursory glance at the two documents, giving Cohen the impression that he had no interest in the lives the two pieces of paper represented. Again, Cohen imagined the bodies of the two women in the black plastic bags in the back of the truck on its way to Abu Kabir. The intelligence chief droned on a few minutes about convoluted circles of conspiracy that currently determined the shape of Soviet action on the face of the globe. The prime minister's interest in this part of the discussion lasted longer, especially when his spy chief became specific, mentioning the withdrawal from Afghanistan, *glasnost* and *perestroika,* and commenting on nationalist turmoil in the various provinces of the Soviet Union. At one point Nahum leaned from his seat to whisper something into the prime minister's ear. The PM nodded and smiled, and the Mossad chief continued.

As far as Cohen was concerned it was an interesting but irrelevant lecture. He watched impatiently as the Mossad chief inspected the two visa applications. "We surely have to know more about who these two were," the chief said. "These," he added, in a scoffing tone that made Cohen want to smile at Nussbaum's discomfort, "tell us very little." He dropped the two pieces of paper onto the table in front of him, dismissing the humble effort.

Cohen broke the silence. "Actually," he said, "the documents do tell us something. Maybe it's too early to know what it means, but they tell us something."

"What do you mean," Nahum demanded, surprised that he could be contradicted, especially by a policeman.

Cohen looked down at the two pieces of paper. "Well," he said, "it's strange that Miriam, the older nun, makes no mention of a daughter in her original application to us for residence." Papers shuffled as attention turned to the documents. The prime minister was the only one not to look, and Cohen was aware of his stare.

"What could that mean, Commander Cohen?" asked the prime minister.

"I don't know, sir. It may be completely irrelevant. The victims may have been chosen totally at random. But perhaps there is significance in it. Perhaps it was supposed to remain a secret that they were related. Maybe it was a secret to the Soviets when the application was made. But if it was a secret to us, it's been known to the people at the convent for a long time. They made no effort to hide the fact of the relationship when I was there today. Unfortunately, so far that's about all we were able to learn about the two women from the mission officials."

"That's a lot of maybes," said the Mossad chief.

"Let him continue," said the prime minister, surprising Cohen and the Mossad chief both.

"Now," continued Cohen, moving down his mental checklist of points to consider, "it's true that nuns do change their names when they join a convent, like converts to Judaism change their names. But to hide the fact from the authorities that they were mother and daughter, well . . ." Cohen turned to the stone-faced Mossad chief, "that's something that maybe only your people will be able to find out for us. We'll try here, of course, but it would be helpful, for example," Cohen said to Shmulik, "if you could help with the files on the driver."

"We know that he is KGB," interrupted Dovik, Shmulik's boss, making Cohen wonder what secrets the Shabak would try to keep from him. "But at most he's a glorified mission guard, a security apparatchik," he continued. "We have no evidence of any significant espionage. He's their baby-sitter."

"He's KGB trained," the Mossad chief reminded Dovik, taking Cohen's side.

Nussbaum interrupted. "If he was conducting espionage," said the cabinet secretary, trying to display his acumen in matters of intelligence gathering, "I assume you wouldn't arrest him."

"He could lead us somewhere," confirmed Dovik.

"Or he could be burned," the Mossad chief added dryly, "turned around to work for us."

Cohen was interested in Alex, but it was one of many worries he had about the case. The murders were a step beyond everything he had known in the city until then. He knew about zealots and terrorists, about fanaticism making people choose martyrdom—or trying to arrange it for others. He knew about gang wars, struggles over territory that included booby-trapped cars of underworld figures.

But there was something about the simplicity of the murders, the presumable innocence of the victims, and most of all, the prime minister's interest in the case, that made Cohen feel it all as a great personal burden.

It meant pressure—from the press, always hungry for a mystery, and from the politicians. For the reporters, it would soon be a headline with something for everyone. The police spokesman was already desperate for a briefing, the police reporters had heard the bustle of police radio activity and were already sniffing for the story, with Israel TV's top crime reporter insisting his viewers had a right to see the scene of the crime that night on the news. A statement would have to be issued in the next hour, and Cohen had nothing yet to say that would advance his cause. So speculation would take over. Nuns are always mysterious to Jews. These nuns, from the land of Cossacks and pogroms and, of course, Moscow, the superpower ally of Israel's enemies, were especially exotic, Cohen thought, an invitation to the politicians to get involved. The PM's extraordinary interest in the case was no less a mystery to Cohen than the murders themselves. The secrets of the case extended far beyond what the nuns' sightless eyes had seen just before they died.

Thus Cohen knew from the start that, more than anything else, pressure would become part of the inquiry. Nobody would ask him to pin it on someone innocent, but there would be none of the official patience that accompanied the Sidra 13 inquiry.

That, of course, was left unsaid in the prime minister's office. So, when the prime minister finally lifted his hands from the desk to signal the end of the meeting, Cohen had the feeling that before the case was over, he'd have to explain to the prime minister what he had tried to explain just before the chief of the Mossad came in late to the meeting. In a holy city, even saints can be suspects.

6

THAT FRIDAY NIGHT, Judge Ahuva Meyerson listened to Cohen as she did her witnesses, her head resting in her hands, which were cupped beneath her chin, her eyes probing but sympathetic. But she was not in her courtroom.

Ahuva Meyerson was the only person Cohen could absolutely trust, and he was the only person she had never felt cause to judge. Because of their careers, their relationship as lovers had to be kept secret, lest they step into conflicts of professional interest. In any case, they avoided the argument between her representing the imperfection of justice and him demanding an absolute moral order. Yet, precisely because of that unwinnable argument, their relationship was all about everything except their work.

"Our time together," she had once said to him, "is like being on a desert island or in a beautiful oasis surrounded by hundreds of kilometers of sand."

Cohen thought of it as an escape for both of them from the loneliness of their respective positions. They spent every Friday night together. Cohen cooked, each week trying to surprise her with a new dish of his own invention or one discovered in one of the cookbooks he collected. When feeling particularly romantic, he would try to recreate one of the meals they had enjoyed most during their annual week-long trip to Florence during the summer court recess.

Usually he was in the kitchen when she arrived. But that night she found him in the living room, sitting in the chair that looked out into the garden below, his cat, Suspect, asleep in his lap. He had said nothing when she entered, and at first she thought that all her fears about his health had come true. She stroke quickly to him, placing her hand on his neck, feeling for a pulse.

He opened his eyes and smiled at her.

"You frightened me," she said, almost angry, relieved.

"Sorry," he said.

"What's wrong?" she asked, peering into his weary eyes.

"Nothing, nothing," he said, pushing the cat off his lap and rising to embrace her. "I was waiting for you," he said.

"You're depressed," she said. The cat pushed itself up against her nylon stockings. She picked it up, held it to her breast, and stroked it.

"Nonsense." He was moving toward the kitchen, pausing for a moment to study a print of a Crusader-era map of Jerusalem that she had given him two years before.

She dropped the cat onto the sofa and moved toward him. She moved lightly across the room to him, and reaching him said, "I've never seen you depressed." She put her arms around him, her head against his.

"The situation's never been like this," he admitted without taking his eyes off the print but enjoying the whisper of her breath in his ear. "But I'm not depressed." He stepped out of her embrace and faced her, realizing that he had spoken with a surprising vehemence, as if he was trying to defend himself.

"What are you talking about?" she asked. "What situation?"

"A drink," he offered, trying to ignore her question, knowing it opened up into subjects they had long avoided.

She shook her head, turning down the drink. But he filled half the glass balloon with the pale amber liquid for himself, and then turning to her, he held the bottle out and asked, "Are you sure?"

She shook her head again, remaining silent in an expectant pose he had first noticed when she was a brilliant state prosecutor a decade before and he had been as drawn by her contained sensuality as by her incisive arguments.

"We can't talk about it," he said. "Work," he added, disappearing through the kitchen doorway, just beyond the dining table that was set as it always was set on Friday nights. It was the magic word in their relationship, a boundary they could not cross. She remained in the living room, watching the flickering of the two candles on the table. Elsewhere in the city, candles were lit on Friday night to welcome the Sabbath. In their oasis, the candles were lit for romance. The silverware and china were neatly laid out. His wife had brought the tableware as a dowry years before and was killed in a car accident barely a year later, just after his graduation from the police academy's officer training course.

Ahuva pirouetted away from the table and went to the long low rack of stereo equipment, records, and cassettes in the built-in floor-to-ceiling bookshelf that covered the windowless wall facing the kitchen doorway. She ran her fingers along the cassettes in the rack, smiling at the consistency of his fluid handwriting neatly labeling the cassettes recorded from the radio or from LPs. But she made no choice, furtively glancing into the kitchen to watch him as he moved back and forth from the refrigerator to the gas stove, working on the meal in the tiny kitchen.

Catching one of his own stolen glances, she went to the kitchen door. "Avram, we promised each other a long time ago not to let anything that happens to us in our work interfere when we are together. Ten years, we've kept that promise. Now, something has happened. Something obviously very serious. Maybe it's time to break the promise. What is it?"

Behind her, the flickering candles illuminated her red hair, and he thought of the halos of the two women in the broken icon on the wall in the convent. For a moment the only sound was the city just beyond the window. From a tiny synagogue behind Cohen's apartment, they could hear odd Balkan melodies welcoming the Sabbath queen. She approached him, her hand outstretched gently to touch his barrel chest. He was standing with the pot in one hand and a serving spoon in the other. The sauce was pale orange, with a rich citrus aroma. "Really, I'm fine," he said. "Why don't you put on some music and I'll be right in. I've made something wonderful. Veal, not chicken breast, for the schnitzel, and steamed cauliflower, and this sauce. Here, taste," he said, offering her the tip of the spoon. She pursed her lips, blowing to cool the steaming sauce. He watched her pale green eyes closely for the reaction, grinning as they widened with pleasure.

"Grapefruit and turmeric," she said, scoring perfect on his taste test. He smiled and turned toward the stove.

"So?" she said to his back, refusing to give up the subject, as insistent as she had been as a prosecutor. "Are you going to let work ruin what I'm sure could be a marvelous meal?"

He turned and let out a deep breath before finding the excuse of lowering the flame to break the look between them.

"All right, all right," she said. "I understand. You don't want to talk about it. We won't talk about it," she said, backing out of the room. A moment later he heard her pluck a cassette from the rack, and he smiled when he heard the first bars of the music she chose.

"Complicated music for a complicated situation," he said as he came out of the kitchen carrying two neatly prepared plates of food.

"Bach has a way of showing there's a solution for everything," she said in a sprightly voice.

"Maybe we should talk about it," he conceded as he put down the plates. He took his seat opposite her, remaining silent until he had finished pouring the wine. "We'll start with a toast," he said, "to the prime minister. May he orbit in outer space for many long years to come." He drained his glass.

"Avram, really," she said with a slight mocking tone.

"I was in his office today," he explained. "That's right," he said to her surprise. "I haven't seen him from so close since he was in the opposition and still carried his own groceries."

"What did he want?"

"Two nuns were murdered in a convent in Ein Kerem."

"Yes," she said, "I heard on the radio. Horrible. Horrible. But why did he call you in?"

"Well," said Cohen, rubbing at his brow. "That's the thing. I've never known him to ask for a briefing about the crimes of the city."

"What did he want to know?" she prodded.

"Not much—except that we find a suspect and fast, and as you can well imagine, he'd rather we don't find a Jew was responsible."

"That sounds like interference in the investigation," she said.

"No, not really. He was careful. He didn't say anything to mean that. He just wanted to make sure that the investigation wouldn't become embarrassing. Discreet, he wants a discreet inquiry." Cohen snorted at the thought, wondering if the fifth floor understood the meaning of the word.

"Embarrassing to whom?"

Cohen shrugged. "To him. To us. To the Jews." He could feel the wine softening the colors and brightening the candlelight. "He didn't call us in when someone threw the grenade into that crowd," he said, unable to keep the bitterness out of his voice. "He didn't call us in when those grenades were found on the Mount. Maybe he thinks that's normal. But two murdered nuns. For *that* he calls us in."

"He has his own considerations," said the judge.

"He has his considerations. I have mine. The problem is that he's obviously not well. And the people around him pretend that he's fine."

"What do you mean, he's not well?" she asked, concerned.

"He's looking older than ever," Cohen said.

"Well, he must be close to eighty," Ahuva said, "He *is* old."

"You read the newspapers," Cohen tried to explain. "You've seen what they're hinting. That he's depressed, apathetic . . ."

"Newspapers," she said, her tone implying a general disrespect for the professionalism of journalists. "You know how they are . . ."

"That's what I thought," Cohen admitted. "But I saw him. I saw what he's like. He's not present. That's the only way I can describe it. He's not present. Except for a few questions to me about questioning Jews, and a bit of interest in Soviet intentions, he seemed asleep most of the meeting."

"He's under a lot of pressure," she suggested. "Maybe he's just tired."

"I thought so. But afterwards I asked Shmulik. He said he's been like that for weeks."

"I don't see how it affects your work," she said, "you've worked under political pressure before."

"Don't you see?" he said, surprised by the sudden vehemence that burst from him. "Things are going out of control, but he seems to be in his own world, as if he's apathetic about it all. He's not in control . . ."

"Well, you are," she said emphatically.

He poured another drink for himself as he spoke. "The fact that he called the meeting means that I'll have him on my back the whole time."

"You said he's not in control. Now you say he'll be watching your every move. Make up your mind." She said it forcefully, demanding clarity.

"Not him. The fifth floor. If he's interested in a case, they're interested in a case. They're desperate for a budget increase. He can give it to them. So they'll want whatever he wants."

"You'll manage," she said. "You always have managed," she added.

But for the first time, he wondered if he deserved that confidence in his ability to maneuver through the political minefields that dotted Jerusalem's landscape. But before he could voice his doubts, she made her own surprise announcement.

"I have news. I'm going to New York," she said, beaming.

Cohen put down his forkful of veal with surprise. "When?" he asked.

"The day after tomorrow," she said, "I know it's the last minute. There's a conference on women and the law, and you know Knesset Member Rachel Glazer, well, she was supposed to go, but her husband had a heart attack, so she had to cancel her participation and suggested that they invite me instead."

"How long are you going to be gone?" he asked gruffly, resentful of the journey, jealous of her career and the way it kept them apart.

"The conference starts on Wednesday and runs through the weekend. I spent the entire day rearranging my schedule so I could stay on. I've already spoken with my sister in Chicago. I haven't seen her in two years. And shopping. Glorious shopping . . ."

She stopped suddenly. He realized that his expression must have given away the sense of abandonment that he felt as soon as she said she was going away.

"Well," she asked, "aren't you pleased for me?"

"Yes, yes, of course," he said. "It's an honor, of course. It's just that . . ."

"What?"

"I don't know," he said, honestly. "I feel you're leaving me behind."

"Poor Avram," she said with a loving mockery. "Of course, you could come with me . . ."

She was joking, but he took it seriously for a moment too long. He studied her face for a moment. She was close to forty but had the skin of a woman ten years younger. She wore little makeup on her lightly freckled face, and her pale green eyes were brightened even more than usual by the candle flames. It was her eyes that first appealed to him. There was always an excitement in her eyes. She reached for his hand, and her warm touch made him suddenly feel all the desire he had for her from the very first time he had seen her. It had taken him almost six months to offer her dinner, and when he did, she asked him why he had taken his time. Cowardice, he had said then with a smile, and her laugh chimed, appreciating the irony of the star detective of the Jerusalem police force describing himself as a coward.

"Maybe it's time, Avram," she said suddenly. "You're a year past retirement. We could finally have our lives. No more secrecy. No more oasis. Just to be two normal people living together. The King David Hotel wants you. You know that. It's a good job. Head of security. A good salary. And we could be together. Really together."

"I have a job to do," he said simply. "I can't give it up now. Especially not now."

"Why not?" she asked, boring in with a simple question.

There was anguish in his face. "I see what's going on and I have the feeling I'm the only one who sees it. The grenades. These murders. The uprising. The hatred. There's madness out there."

"It's been like this for years, Avram. For years. No worse. No better. And despite everything, we both know that the system could manage without either of us."

"Can I ask you to give up your job?" he asked with the same vehemence that had surprised him earlier. He adjusted his tone. "Can I say to you, No, don't go to New York, stay here, get off the bench, have a child with me. There's still time for that, but there won't be in another few years. Can I demand that of you?" He searched her eyes, half-hoping that she would offer to resign, too, knowing well that he couldn't ask her to end her career that way. "No, I can't ask you to do that," he continued. "So why can you tell me that it's time for me to quit? Because I'm older than you? That's not good enough. Not good enough." He was sad, not angry, but his words had driven deeply, and he regretted it immediately when he saw the pain cross her face. "I'm sorry," he quickly added, "I'm sorry." He grasped her hand across the table. For a moment her hand was limp, but then he felt her squeeze back.

"You're right. You couldn't ask me to resign. I can't ask you. But still, think about it while I'm away. It's only a couple of weeks," she said. "And I'll make up all that time," she added with a smile, "starting tonight."

Later, he woke beside her sleeping body, the sheen of their mingled sweat glistening on her moonlit skin. He lay silent, remembering how he rose with all his love and strength and entered her. Her eyes had first widened and then closed in the familiar pleasure, as did his. But when he opened his eyes, looking down at her again, he had seen not Ahuva, his beloved, his friend. Instead, the pale alabaster face of the young nun in the convent was staring back at him with a look of recognition frozen into her eyes.

7

COHEN'S SHADOW cast a silhouette over the T-shaped table. It was early Shabbat morning in Jerusalem, the sun barely higher than the walls of the Old City three blocks away from the Russian Compound. Beyond the window, the Jewish city was at its most serene, still drowsy. On the other side of the city, Arab Jerusalem was already awake and at another work day. At noon, the daily *intifada* strike would shut down the Arab businesses and the schools. An hour later, the walkie-talkie on its shelf beside Cohen's desk would start rapping out *intifada* reports.

The special investigating team, called in on what normally was their day off, sat around the table. But none of them had complained when they were ordered into the office. These were not normal times.

Levy was in his usual place and to his right was Cohen's Russian expert, Shvilli, who had immigrated from Soviet Georgia, lured to Jerusalem not by the city's myths but by the tourist girls of Ben-Yehuda street. Yaffe sat across the table from Levy, and farthest from Cohen, at the end of the table, two empty seats between them and Yaffe, sat the Twins. Their very choice of seats betrayed to Cohen their feelings of self-importance. They never forgot their special status as agents of the Shabak. Cohen was unhappy but not surprised to see them as Shmulik's appointed delegation to the team. He had complained in the past to Shmulik about their interrogation techniques. They relied too much on threats, he believed, using methods that were often useless in court. While efficient at getting confessions, such methods, Cohen knew, did not always guarantee the truth would come out.

"Either he's giving them to me to set them up, or he's given me to them to set me up," Cohen thought about Shmulik, as much competitor as friend, as much an antagonist as a partner in the struggle to keep Jerusalem sane. He pressed his fingertips to his forehead, watching the Twins smirk at Larrybird, an extraordinarily short policeman whose job was to deliver tea and coffee throughout the Russian Compound police headquarters. Larrybird was a fanatical basketball fan, which won him his nickname from Cohen, who was bored by the sport and the little policeman's long and convoluted descriptions of games. But while he sometimes cut short the endless play by play, Cohen never patronized Larrybird, who at this moment was having trouble setting up a blackboard twice his height. Cohen shrugged at Levy, who rose with a sigh to help the small man maneuver the cumbersome device past the piles of cartons and cardboard folders. Collected evidence gathered like Jordan River waters in the Dead Sea of Cohen's office.

Once the board was set up, Larrybird left the room, Cohen calling after him to rustle up some aspirin to bring back with the coffee. Levy's eyes questioned his commander silently, but Cohen always kept his private pains a secret from Levy.

He lit his tenth cigarette of the day and rose painfully to go to the blackboard. The chalk squeaked as he wrote the list.

Crazy.
Nationalist right wing.
Arab terrorists—embarrass Israel.
Anti-missionaries.
Anti-Soviets.
Personal reasons?
Specific targets; someone wanted them, in particular, dead.

Under this heading, he added:

Something in their past. Something they knew or had seen.
KGB spies? Double agents?

"Look at all the reasons for killing two nuns," Cohen said as he turned away from the blackboard. "It would be a lot simpler if it was Avi Hakatan and Gidi Hagadol," he said, referring to the current two underworld kingpins in the city.

"Nobody promised life would be easy," said Shvilli.

Cohen smiled and took his seat.

"I think it's obvious," Cohen continued, ignoring the pounding in his head, "that we won't have a motive until we have a killer. So we're going to need luck."

The lab reports on the footprint and the fingerprint cards from the nuns' room were expected only the next day, but fingerprints—if indeed they were the killer's—would be useless without a suspect to match them against. The plaster casting of the footprint left in the damp soil near the wall might be useful. Shoe stores could be canvassed until it was known what type of shoe the killer was wearing, and if the shoe was uncommon, it could become a lead. The forensic team might even be able to identify whatever it was that broke the icon.

"First. The vermin." Cohen never used the word in public when referring to Eliahu Ben-Yehoshua, the American-born rabbi whose extremist right-wing politics, imbued with racism and totalitarianism, were carried out in the name of the Bible. It would be unbecoming for an officer of the law to refer to a Member of Knesset that way, no matter that even the prime minister refrained from seeking Ben-Yehoshua's support for the fragile coalition because of the rabbi's tactics.

"You deserve him," he said to the Twins, "and he deserves you," he added with a grin. Levy chuckled, and Shvilli's guffaw began to bray again but was quickly stifled by a glance from Yaffe.

"No hands," Cohen ordered, as he continued laying down the assignment. "I don't want any violence," he added gruffly, using his voice as a threat, wondering if they would heed the command. The Twins had no more affection for the vermin and his followers than they did for Arab terrorists. Their interrogation methods were often abhorrent to Cohen, yet he knew that the Supreme Court had ruled that in certain circumstances, "a reasonable amount of violence," could be used for the questioning of terrorist suspects by the Shabak, if innocent lives were immediately at stake. It was a decision that Cohen hoped he'd never have to test himself.

"His people have harassed church delegations before. Maybe someone among them has gone over the edge, maybe Goldstein decided on some independent action," Cohen said. Nahum Goldstein was chief operations officer for the extremist politician, running the political organization and often leading the way in brawls, vigilante attacks, and harassment of Arabs, peace movement demonstrators, and anyone who he decided was an "Arab-lover." Hatred of Christian missionaries was second only to hatred of Arabs on the group's agenda. The convent did not proselytize, but nuance was not a strong point in Goldstein's circle. Moreover, anti-Soviet feelings, despite the freedom of Jewish emigration promised by *glasnost,* were still rife among the most extreme of Israeli nationalists.

Goldstein had been called in for questioning about the grenades, but it was only a formality. Goldstein himself was leading a counterrally that night outside the premier's office. If he had known about the grenade attack, he would hardly have spent his evening within the hundred-meter radius of the grenade's explosion.

The Twins promised they would use caution with Goldstein, but Cohen remained doubtful. Nonetheless, he sent them on their way, telling them he expected to hear from them within forty-eight hours.

"It's Shabbat," one of the Twins pointed out to Cohen. "Should we wait?"

Cohen knew that the arrest of a religious Jew on Shabbat could become politically controversial. He knew that the PM was generally displeased with Ben-Yehoshua, who claimed to be the direct heir of the PM's original ideology and accused the PM of selling out to the power brokers. And he also knew that the religious ranks would close on the issue, even for Goldstein, if he was picked up on Shabbat. He considered the dilemma for a moment.

"Saving a life defers even the Shabbat," he said, enjoying the irony of the Talmudic quote.

"So?" asked the Twin.

"If you find him today, question him today," Cohen ruled, wondering if he made the decision for the nuns' sake or his own.

Levy started to protest, but Cohen silenced him with a wave of the hand. The Twins left the office, chuckling.

Yaffe was also freed early for the rest of the day. Cohen asked him for a full written report on the tensions between the Red Russian and White Russian churches. The assignment pleased Yaffe. It was the kind of job at which he excelled. It didn't really occur to him that to Cohen, the report was only busy work, designed to keep the little man out of his way for a while. Cohen knew that the less Yaffe was around, the less the politicians or the diplomatic cocktail-party circuit would know about Cohen's doings.

Thinking of Alex, Cohen turned to Shvilli. "I'm going to need you," he said, "so meanwhile, I want you to listen. But before anything else, I have to know something. Does Alex know you? Have you ever met? Maybe at that Russian restaurant where you're always trying to drag me?"

Shvilli thought for a moment, frowning before shaking his head. "I've seen him once. Somebody pointed him out to me one day across the street. But I don't think he knows me or knows that I'm a cop. Maybe. They know a lot about us, you can be sure of that. Do you think that the organs," which was one of the cruder ways that Shvilli, like many former Russians, referred to officers of the Organ of State Security, "didn't send people with us, disguised as immigrants? So maybe even here, inside the police there are now organs. Maybe even inside the services," Shvilli said. "Maybe even them," he added with a gold-toothed grin at the Twins' empty seats. Cohen smiled at the thought of the two Shabak officers, so confidently sabra, as Soviet moles. But he also thought of Alex's loneliness as a KGB officer who had failed in his job, at a time when the KGB was going through the upheaval of *glasnost*. He has reason to be afraid, thought Cohen, knowing too well how loneliness, combined with fear, can lead to paranoia.

He held onto Shvilli as a wild card, wondering when he would need to use the Russian-speaking detective but already certain that it would be necessary. "I'll need you later," he said to Shvilli, "but most important right now—stay out of Alex's sight. Stay out of sight of any Russians. And Shvilli, most of all, stay out of Ein Kerem." With that he released the junior officer, asking him only to translate the tiny feminine handwriting on the piece of paper Cohen found underneath the bed in the convent.

"Next," he added, "crazies."

Cohen wanted all the mental hospitals in the country contacted. Releases, escapes, vacations, holidays—"anybody with any kind of history of violence. And against Christians in particular," the detective instructed. As he spoke, Levy marked the blackboard.

"Maybe the same for recent prison releases," said the young detective, "and suppose we get a computer check correlating psychiatric treatment of convicts, so we can find out about any weird political or religious views and behavior." Cohen nodded, and the junior officer began making notes for the memos he would send to government and private hospitals.

They worked down the list, Cohen all the while rubbing at his temples as he thought. He had swallowed four aspirins with his coffee and was chainsmoking filtered Noblesse cigarettes from the crumpled green package on his desk. The smoke made a pale blue ladder in the sunlight streaming through the horizontal blinds. Larrybird scuttled in and out of the room all that afternoon, bringing glasses of mint tea to Levy and Turkish coffee to Cohen. They made a list of twenty officers who could be pulled off other cases, if necessary. As soon as the media started carrying the news of the murders, the police would be inundated by phone calls from people who wanted to confess or report that their next-door neighbor had been acting suspiciously the night of the murders. Every phone call had to be checked out, the way every call reporting a suspicious object that might be a bomb had to be investigated.

Cohen thought long and hard about whether to send detectives to canvass the village far below the convent. Canvassing door to door in Ein Kerem would bring the media, doubling the political attention on the police procedure. That would be dangerous, more dangerous than Cohen could yet risk. Cohen needed quiet as he worked, not the roar of a watching crowd. Any remarkable action by the police would fill the stands with an impatient audience, already made skeptical about the effectiveness of the police who had failed to keep the *intifada* out of Jerusalem and seemed helpless in the face of the rising rates of property crimes.

He made charts as he worked, lists and tables of names and cases and questions he wanted answered. The charts listed his paths, the routes into the darkness. One road was the plaster cast of the footstep in the garden. One route was the nationalist fringe. One avenue was Daniel, his undercover man in Mea Shearim. Yet another was Shvilli's knowledge of Russian. Each was a territory for which there was no cartography except Cohen's own imagination. Levy copied Cohen's finished pages onto a large plastic sheet, a map of the imagined world they would have to penetrate. As he completed the last page, he taped the chart on the back of the door, his arms raised above his head. He noticed the time and cursed under his breath.

"It's three o'clock. I missed my football game." Levy played goalie every Saturday afternoon with friends he had known since elementary school.

"Sorry," said Cohen. His hangover was almost gone. He had fought off the rheumatism of the mind with which he had begun the day, and now he was exhausted. He leaned back in the executive chair with its missing ball bearings and a lopsided tilt that only Cohen could find comfortable. His arm was outstretched, and using the fountain pen Ahuva had given him when he was promoted to commander in chief of criminal investigations, a year after she was elevated to the bench, he doodled on a scrap of paper. "Of course, that means you can drive me to Ein Kerem," the senior detective added, not looking up from the nonsensical drawing. It was a picture of two knives made into a cross.

"To Alex?" asked Levy, eager to learn more about the KGB officer.

"No, not Alex. Not yet. Alex is more complicated. We need more information about him before we can move."

"That's what you have planned for Shvilli," said Levy, "isn't it?"

"Everything has its season," Cohen said. "We're going mountain climbing."

"Are you sure you're in shape for that now?" Levy asked gently, realizing it was the wrong thing to say just as he said it.

"What are you talking about?" Cohen snapped at his aide.

"I don't know. I just saw, this morning. The aspirin. Maybe it can wait. Maybe I could go. You look like you didn't get enough sleep last night."

"Before you were born I was going sleepless," Cohen said, his voice a low rumble of power that reminded Levy of his place.

"Sorry, sorry," Levy quickly apologized. "I didn't mean to pry."

"There's nothing to pry at," Cohen snapped. "I'll be right down," he added in a businesslike tone, sending Levy down the stairs to the parking lot.

A moment later, Cohen was already regretting his outburst. When he went downstairs he found Levy waiting in the driver's seat, the car engine running. "Nissim," Cohen said gently, "by the time all this is over we're all going to need some rest." He knew that Levy would understand that it was the closest Cohen could come to an apology.

8

I T WAS A STONE HOUSE with huge eaves that hung over the square stone walls, making a shade in which the ivy flourished. A low jungle of wild flowers and perennials lined the pathway, grabbing at the early spring's warm arrival. Before they reached the front door, it opened, and a young, bespectacled woman wearing a long dress opened it. Cohen introduced himself and Levy, and for a moment the woman disappeared back inside to call together the other residents of the stately house just above the convent.

The six students, three men and three women, gathered in the garden, offering Cohen a weather-faded wicker chair, answering his questions with the pleasure of true believers given a chance to explain themselves. "We're not couples," said Uri, who was older than the other five. "We're futurists," he said. They had made their separate peace with the world and were making plans for better times. "We meditate every day," Uri explained, "and if more people meditated, it would help bring peace."

Levy raised an eyebrow; Cohen grinned at the explanation and then took the conversation down the paths that interested him.

On the night of the murder, they agreed, they were listening to Mozart's *Requiem*. Cohen loved Mozart and asked which recording they heard. "Bernstein conducting in New York," said the student known as Yehuda, going into the house to bring out the record.

They waited in silence until the student returned.

"How loud was it?" asked Levy suddenly.

"Well," smiled Yehuda, stroking at his mustache and with a glint in his eyes, "you see, one of the reasons we like living up here, so far from anything else, is that we can play the music at the right volume."

"How loud is the right volume?" asked Levy again.

"This loud," said Yehuda, taking the record from Cohen's hand and going back into the house. Again they waited in silence. Cohen watched Yehuda disappear around the corner of the house. As his eyes came back to the garden, he noticed a pair of loudspeakers tucked under the eaves.

A moment later, the loudspeakers came to life, the rising chords of the opening bars blew into the garden, and for a moment, it seemed to Cohen, the music rolled deep into the valley below. Yehuda came out and shouted, "This loud," but his voice could not be heard over the music.

"Are the outdoor speakers always on?" Cohen asked, raising his voice.

"That's one of the reasons we live up here. No neighbors to complain about noise," Uri explained. He confirmed that the loudspeakers were on the night of the murders, and then signaled Yehuda to lower the music. Cohen made a mental note to pick up a copy of the same version of the *Requiem*. He wanted to hear what the murderer had heard.

From the garden, Cohen could glance down onto the red tile rooftops of the convent below, and beyond to the woods of the national military cemetery across the valley. He admired the view and asked about the nuns and whether Alex had ever made contact with the students. He offered no characterization of Alex other than to call him the convent driver.

"He seemed all right to me," said Uri. "I met him once. I was out that way," he explained, pointing westward into the woods of the slope. "I had been meditating, and we met on the path. We talked for a couple of minutes, and when he learned I was living here, he asked about us, what we're studying. When I told him we were living as a commune, he seemed interested until I told him that we were not interested in the Communist Party. Oh, I did invite him to visit, but he never did," Uri concluded.

Levy wrote it all down, as Cohen prodded. His questions turned from Alex to other visitors to the mountainside.

"Are there any regular hikers? People who come up here often?" asked Cohen, noticing that the question made Yehuda glance toward Uri, bearded and silent behind his frameless spectacles during the conversation.

"No," said Uri, not letting Yehuda or any of the other students answer.

Cohen studied Uri's face for a moment and then surprised Levy by suddenly announcing that it was time to go. He rose from his chair, asking Uri for permission to look at the students' record collection. Uri nodded, and the two men went into the house, Cohen telling Levy to wait for him at the car.

Like Cohen, Levy had noticed Yehuda's reaction to Cohen's questions about regular hikers. The junior officer walked with Yehuda out of the garden toward the front walkway and the car.

"You wanted to say something before," said Levy.

"No, I didn't."

"My boss asked about regular hikers and your boss said nobody comes up here and you started to say something but stopped." Levy spoke matter of factly, like one overworked laborer to another.

"We don't have bosses up here," said Yehuda, offended by the suggestion.

"Well, your platoon commander," said the detective, using the acronym *Mem-kaf*, familiar to anyone who had been through the army.

Yehuda smiled. "Yes, he sometimes behaves like the outstanding soldier in the tent. Always trying to be best, always trying to be in charge."

"I know you, don't I?" Levy said suddenly.

The student shrugged.

"Where were you in the army?" Levy asked.

"Seventh brigade."

"That's it. I used to be a regimental commander in reserves there," said Levy. "Who was your *Mem Peh?*" again using the familiar acronym for regimental commander.

"Zvika Applebaum," said the student.

"Right," said Levy, "I trained with him. Give him regards,

next reserves. I've been out of there a while," he added, "because of this job."

The student nodded.

"Look," Levy said, "we really need help on this. Are there any regular hikers?"

They had stopped walking and were standing at the edge of a grape arbor that had begun to sprout. The sun was unusually strong for spring, and Levy could feel its heat beating into his scalp.

"There are people. Nobody in particular. Your usual hikers. Weekend family *tiulim*. There are a lot of historic sites around here. Churches, stories, tourists. Sometimes they come knocking on our door thinking we're on view, too. Like a museum. We don't pay much attention, as long as they don't actually march into the garden or living room."

"Maybe someone who you've seen hiking at strange times. Late at night, or something like that?"

"Well, that's the thing. This is a murder case, right? That's why I want to help. We all want to help. There is someone. I don't know anything about him. He doesn't come in here, but we see him."

"Which way does he come from?" asked Levy.

"I don't know. He just sort of appears on the hill . . . and disappears. He heads in all different directions. He doesn't seem to have much direction."

"What makes him so special?" asked Levy.

"Well, he's a foreigner. I suppose that shouldn't mean anything, I mean, I don't have anything against foreigners."

"Have you ever spoken with him?"

The student's eyes drifted nervously from Levy's face to the other students at the end of the path.

"No. None of us. None of us speak with him. He stays away from our land," said the student.

"Nobody is going to get into trouble if they didn't do anything they shouldn't have done," said Levy.

"I mean, well, maybe Uri should have said something."

"Why didn't he?" asked Levy.

They were both looking down the flagstone path to where Uri and Cohen were talking. Uri suddenly turned away from Cohen to look at Levy and Yehuda.

"Never mind," said Levy, "I'll ask him myself."

"Wait," said the student as soon as Levy took the first step down the path.

"This really is important, isn't it. Much more important than other things. I mean, if I told you we did something that's really not legal . . ."

"The foreigner's a *nafas* contact," Levy said, easily guessing that hashish had something to do with what the student was trying to say.

Yehuda shrugged sheepishly. Levy's instinct had been right, and Yehuda's apology had rushed out of him so now all he could do was admit the rest. "He always seems to have *nafas*. But we don't go looking for him. It's just when he comes by. None of us know where he lives, where to find him. But sometimes if we see him in the hills, one of us will go over, and he'll give us some *kef*, a piece of fun."

"Can you describe him?"

"Long hair, skimpy beard. The kind of beard that only covers the chin and where the mustache goes. A sixties refugee. You know the type. There are lots of them around nowadays."

"Of course. You never spoke with him? Have any of you ever spoken with him? What's his name?" asked Levy.

"I don't even know. I don't think any of us know. Uri found him one day, smoking up higher on the hill, and I guess they talked a bit. Since then, well, like I told you, sometimes if we ask, he gives us a piece."

"Did he ever mention the convent? Did you ever see him go down toward the convent?"

"No," said the student, "the last time I saw him, it was more than two weeks ago, that's for sure, he went up there," pointing up the hill toward the crest where the highway to Hadassah twisted and turned down the long hill that led to the end of the valley.

"Does he come from the valley or from above the valley?" asked Levy.

"I don't know," said the student.

"Anything to identify him by? Does he have a limp, a scar?"

"Only the beard, I guess. It's one of those like that Knesset Member, you know, the one with the paintbrush on his chin."

Levy laughed. "Anything else?" he asked.

"Not that I can think of," said Yehuda.

Levy turned away and started to walk toward Cohen. "Wait," said Yehuda, "are you going to make a big deal out of this? I mean us using *nafas*."

Levy looked into the student's eyes. "How much do you do? A month? A week? A day?"

"Very little."

"How much is very little."

"A couple of fingers a month. Maybe three a month. Maximum."

Levy laughed. "You made it sound like you're doing three sacks a week. If we had time for every person smoking a joint in this city, do you think we'd have time for murder?"

When Levy got into the car, he was still smiling to himself.

"What's so funny?" asked Cohen.

"I forgot about being a student. That one I was talking with. I noticed he had wanted to say something when you asked about hikers and Uri said they never saw the same person twice. Well," said Levy, "he said that there is someone . . ."

"A hippie," Cohen interrupted in a matter-of-fact tone. Levy was startled and ceased his struggle with the wheel.

"How did you know that?" he demanded of Cohen.

"Uri told me," Cohen said, aware that once again he had taken the wind out of Levy's sails.

"Did he tell you that sometimes they get their *nafas* from this hippie?" Levy tried.

"Of course," said Cohen.

"Well, does he have a name?" Levy prodded.

Cohen was making notes on the back of an envelope, leaning against the dashboard. He was silent for a moment, and shook his head.

"He has a funny beard," said Levy, "that's what Yehuda said. 'Like the MK,' he said. A goatee." He offered the information as matter-of-factly as Cohen had mentioned his own awareness of the hiker.

"Good," said Cohen, "very good."

"Just so I feel I'm doing something . . ." Levy mumbled to himself.

Cohen smiled to himself and leaned back in the seat as Levy

took a curve on the bias. First the left tires rustled the dirt embankment of the road and then the right tires, as Levy kept the car on as straight a line as possible. Cohen awaited Levy's next question.

"Do you believe him?" Levy asked, as they came into the small plaza in front of the village fountain.

Cohen nodded. "It's a small town. I know him. I believe him."

"Why didn't you say something?"

"If he had wanted the rest of them to know that he knew me, he would have said something when we came in. He wanted to speak to me in private. That's all. He's all right. He'd tell me if he had a name for this hippie."

"He's crazy, if you ask me," said Levy. "A separate peace. Futurism. Meditation. Nonsense. Bunch of hash-heads. And he's the biggest of them all."

"He has the right to make a separate peace," Cohen said knowingly. "How old do you think he is?"

"I don't know. Like the others. Mid-twenties."

"He's older than you."

"You're kidding," Levy said.

"You didn't notice his right hand?"

Levy swallowed. "No."

Cohen shook his head, displeased with his lieutenant. "Three fingers burnt into one. That's how I recognized him. He was a sapper. Years ago on the police bomb squad. He was lucky to be able to grow that beard. Underneath his face is a mess. He's lucky to be alive."

"I didn't know."

"You should have noticed," Cohen snapped. "It's your job to notice things."

"He sat with his hands folded. I didn't think of it . . ."

"Watch," said Cohen. "Listen," he added, and Levy knew what was coming . . .

"Think," the inspector recited. "Think," he repeated. Cohen smiled and leaned back in his seat, looking at the passing terraces and groves.

"So what now?" Levy asked, as they reached the bottom of the mountain and drove through the village in the valley and started heading back up the hill to the main road to the city. "How do we look for this hippie with the funny beard?"

"How many hippies are there in the city nowadays?" asked Cohen.

"Who knows?" said Levy. "A thousand? A few thousand? Maybe he's gone by now. And who's to say what's a hippie? Someone with long hair, someone with a beard? Everyone dresses funny here."

"How many tourists do you think we'll have for Pesach?" asked Cohen. The holiday was barely a month away.

"If there's no big troubles? If nothing nasty is in the international press and if the tourists don't cancel at the last minute because their friends say that there are bombs in Jerusalem? A quarter of a million, maybe? And if there is something—and at the rate things are going, who knows what else might happen—maybe a quarter of that."

Cohen thought for a moment. "We can't pick up every foreigner who looks like a hippie and every foreigner with a funny beard. And even if we could, what would we have? All we know is that a goateed foreigner takes hikes in the woods and sometimes has *nafas* for sale. I'll tell you what, get something on paper to Shahar," Cohen added, referring to the head of the Jerusalem drug squad. "He should let us know immediately about any hippies picked up for drugs. Any foreigner arrested, we want to know about immediately."

"We could put someone on the hill," suggested Levy. "We're putting someone into the convent, we could find someone to put on the hill."

Cohen snorted. "I put a warm body in a uniform in the convent. You saw who I had to put there. Yerahmiel," a semiretired policeman whose wife believed that if her husband was forced to retire, it would kill him. He was used when the presence of a uniform was all that was required from the force. Putting a round-the-clock team of competent investigators on the hill was no less a pipe dream than Uri and Yehuda's futurism. Cohen didn't have enough investigators for his ongoing cases. He'd need half a dozen men to work the mountainside, all for a suspect who was no more than a vague description. And anything short of a complete undercover operation would scare away anyone suspicious, making the entire job meaningless.

"Who do you want me to put up there?" Cohen said bluntly to Levy, "Larrybird? Patrolmen in uniform? Who? And for what? All we can do about this hippie is let Shahar know we're looking for him. Uri said the hippie sometimes wears a vest. That's something."

As they reached the top of the road, Cohen asked Levy to stop. The view was clear all the way to the sea, where the sun seemed to be hanging from a purple band of clouds. Cohen got out of the car and crossed the asphalt to the western side of the road, and stood there, arms crossed over his chest, a slight breeze ruffling his graying hair.

Levy turned up the volume of the police radio loudspeaker, listening to the city's pace pick up with the end of Shabbat and the beginning of a new week. The bomb squad was checking out a suspicious object in an alley behind a café on the Ben-Yehuda promenade. A Border Patrol squad reported some stone throwing at the Damascus Gate. Two teenagers had been arrested.

Cohen stood on the ridge of the mountain until the distant gradations of purple along the profiles of the clouds grew too dim to see any longer. He returned to the car.

While they moved through the streets, Cohen used the radio to order Shvilli back to the office with the translation of the handwriting on the flimsy notepaper Cohen had found under the bed in the nuns' room. Shvilli handed Cohen his own handwritten translation:

> . . . apartment and move but there are problems of course there are problems is there nothing in this place without problems? I always think about you and about being with you and how to arrange it I have spoken with father and he says that it could be done but it might take time not only the paper but for decision not my decision or his decision but their . . .

"Who's the father?" asked Cohen.

"Well," said Shvilli, "maybe it's the girl's father, but it also could be a priest."

"And the 'decision'?" Cohen continued, and Shvilli suggested it was Helena's decision to go to Jerusalem. "Or maybe to join the order," he added, "to join the convent to go to Jerusalem."

Cohen accepted Shvilli's analysis without argument, listening and learning. The interior ministry documents on Alex were due in the morning, and Shmulik had promised that Shabak papers on Alex would reach Cohen's office by the end of Sunday. Cohen had no expectations that the bureaucracies involved could keep their promises. But he needed to know more about the lives of the two women before they became nuns. It could be just as important as who they were after they became nuns. Yet he couldn't rely only on the paper, on the documentation that churned slowly through the bureaucracies—his, Shmulik's, the Mossad's, Nussbaum's. He let Shvilli go, once again warned to stay clear of Ein Kerem and Alex.

Alone, Cohen thought some more about the KGB man. He had been arrogant, condescending, strangely unmoved by the killings. But there was something else, something deeper in the way Alex had reacted when Cohen remembered the fact that the KGB officer arrived in 1977, the same year as the younger nun.

"He promised cooperation, but he's done nothing. You'd think he'd be investigating. Something," Levy had raged in the car. Cohen had to agree. But he also had to be careful. Any move toward Alex would be a move onto Shabak territory, for by definition, any move on Alex was counterespionage, Shmulik's concern.

Under those circumstances, it was impossible for Cohen to predict what might happen. He remembered the Mossad chief's comment, "He could be turned." They were capable of making a deal with Alex. But as far as Cohen was concerned, if Alex was the killer, Alex should pay.

9

O N SUNDAY MORNING, Cohen and Levy drove from Jerusalem to the medical forensic laboratories at the Abu Kabir morgue in Jaffa where the coroners worked.

"Two knives, one killer," said Raoul, even before Cohen could take a seat. The tiny office was halfway down the corridor that ran from the surgery where the corpses were cut to the morgue where the bodies lay chilled in stainless steel drawers. Many times Cohen had stood with Raoul over a body in the cold room, each time noticing how soundlessly the drawers slid in and out of the refrigerator, each time anticipating the cigarette he would need as soon as he left, to clear his nostrils of the chemical smell that pervaded the place.

Raoul's office was cluttered with foreign medical publications, piles of official forms, books, and pieces of bodies kept in large jars of chemicals. Two aged mannequins were propped against each other in a corner.

"What kind of knives?" asked Cohen. He held an unlit cigarette in his fingers, turning it absentmindedly around in his hand like a cardshark playing with a deck of cards.

"Hard to tell precisely," Raoul said. "Straight blade, for sure." Cohen's eyes were drawn to the mannequins, to the graceful curve of the plastic necks. "Maybe fifteen centimeters long," he continued, making Cohen remember the deep wounds on the necks of the nuns, "maybe a little longer or shorter. Very sharp, narrow, too. The cut is only one and a half centimeters wide," Raoul said. Cohen's eyes moved back from the mannequins to the coroner.

Raoul said he believed the killer was "adrenaline strong."

Levy jumped in. "He was emotionally involved with them," guessed the detective.

"Don't jump to any conclusions," said Cohen, silencing Levy with a raised palm. Turning to Raoul, he clarified. "The killer was very strong, very coordinated." And then he added, "Hyped?"

"Yes, yes," Raoul confirmed. "The way he managed to strike both women nearly at once. They died almost instantly, though the younger one's heart held out slightly longer. She bled more than the older one, too. But I have no way of knowing if he was drugged."

"They were killed simultaneously," Cohen said thoughtfully after a moment's thought. "It was one movement. There was no struggle."

"That's right," Raoul said, nodding vigorously. "They were both standing when they were struck. The killer was taller than both of them."

In great detail, Raoul explained the physiological consequences of the knives penetrating the skin, cutting through the jugulars, and striking the spinal cord. "There's a scrape on the old woman's fourth vertebra. But otherwise, the conditions of the entry are very similar. Both were dead by the time they actually fell. Look, I can show you." He took two rulers off his desk, and clutching them in one hand, tried moving one of the two mannequins to the center of the room.

"Help him," Cohen instructed Levy, who had been leaning casually against a bookshelf. Levy shrugged and moved to the other mannequin. Raoul stood with a ruler in each hand in front of the mannequins.

"Watch," he said. "He was standing in front of them and must have raised his arms like this." Standing on either side of the two dummies, Cohen and Levy watched Raoul stretch out his arms high and wide above his head. The coroner brought the two rulers down, the tips touching the place where neck and shoulder meet invitingly.

"You see," said the pathologist, smiling. "It could be done." Levy took the two rulers from Raoul and tried the movement.

"I believe he might be left-handed," said Raoul suddenly. "You see, the older woman was on the left, and the cut was both deeper and a full vertebra lower than on the younger woman. He had more strength in his left arm."

"Was it luck or knowledge?" Cohen asked. "Did he know where he was hitting them?"

"He'd probably have to be practiced," said Raoul. "Trained."

Cohen thought for a moment. Raoul started to continue, but Cohen held up his hand. "Wait a second," said the detective, "I want to make a note."

Cohen took one of the palm-sized yellow pads out of his pocket and unscrewed the cap to the fountain pen he wore in his shirt pocket. He wrote for a moment and then looked back up at the coroner, noticing Levy looking at him with curiosity.

"Anything else?" asked Cohen.

"They were mother and daughter," Raoul commented with a half-questioning tone that indicated he wanted confirmation.

Cohen nodded.

"Well, that explains the older woman. But I'll tell you something, where I come from, a nun is supposed to be a virgin."

Cohen was surprised. "What do you mean?"

"The younger one. She was not a virgin. No sign of recent sex, but she was definitely not a virgin. Of course," he quickly added, seeing perplexity in Cohen's face, "she might have lost it some other way."

"Is there any way of telling?" Cohen asked.

Raoul shook his head slowly, leaving another mystery in Cohen's hands.

Levy spent the entire hour of the drive back to Jerusalem wondering what Cohen had written in his notebook, knowing that if Cohen meant for him to know, he would have said something, wishing that once and for all, Cohen would let him know everything. At the entrance to the city, Levy moved into the left-hand lane, preparing to take the shortcut to the Russian Compound through the religious neighborhoods.

"Drop me off on Emek Refa'im," Cohen ordered.

"I thought . . ."

"I have some errands to do," Cohen said.

Levy jerked the wheel angrily and immediately had to jam his brakes to avoid hitting a taxi that had moved up on his right. The

CRIMES OF THE CITY

cab driver yelled "maniac" at Levy, who raised his hands apologetically and mouthed "my fault" back. The driver muttered something, and Levy allowed him to pass.

"It's okay, you can go," said Cohen calmly, looking over his shoulder into the right-lane traffic.

When they reached Emek Refa'im, Cohen asked Levy to drop him a block away from his house, by the commercial center, five small shops on the ground floor of residential buildings. "I'll work from home for a while," said Cohen, "keep the car, I won't need it."

Levy pulled over, and Cohen got out. "Find out from Yaffe what time the nuns' funeral is tomorrow, and make sure we'll have at least one of our own photographers on the scene," the detective instructed.

Levy drove away watching through the rearview mirror, his curiosity turning to jealousy of Cohen's free time. Meanwhile, the senior detective stepped into the doorway of Moise's, Cohen's favorite butcher shop.

Cohen sat on a wooden stool beneath a wall fan that swung on a hinge, back and forth across the room. There were three customers in the shop, and Cohen waited until they were gone before he began to talk with the butcher.

"Avram Cohen! You haven't been in here in a long time," said Moise. "What can I give you? I got some nice duck, you like duck. I remember. Nice duck I got. Nice."

"Moise," said Cohen, "I have a problem, maybe you can help me."

"Yeah, sure, what's the matter? I'm always ready to help the police," said Moise.

"How accurate can you be with a knife?"

"What do you mean?" asked Moise.

"How precise can you be? You know the vertebrae," said Cohen, pointing at chicken necks piled up in a corner behind the glass wall of the counter refrigerator.

"You need some chicken necks for your cat, eh?"

"Yeah, sure, give me some necks. But that's not why I'm here. Look, I'll explain. Do you think you would know exactly where to put a knife so that with one cut it would go right between the bones, right into the neck?"

Moise used the handle of his knife to scratch at his cheek, tilting his head and frowning.

"Look," said Cohen, pointing to a large section of cow ribs hanging from a hook behind Moise. "You see how there's a space between the ribs. Well, there's a space between each pair of vertebrae in the neck. Do you think you'd be able to cut through a neck with one try. With a knife. Not a cleaver."

"Sure," the butcher said. He opened the stainless steel door of the refrigerator behind him, reached in and took out a thick section of beef. He laid the meat down on the wooden counter, and selected a long sharp knife from a rack on the wall. "Which vertebrae?" he asked Cohen, holding the knife in his hand.

"Doesn't matter," said Cohen.

"Watch," said Moise. He raised the knife and with one blow drove it all the way through the meat into the wood. "Now, look," he said. He took out a large cleaver and in a motion too quick for Cohen to see, cut through the beef, perpendicular to the knife. The meat split into two pieces. On the right-hand side, the knife had slipped in between two vertebrae in what Cohen suddenly recognized as the neck of a cow.

"This is the fourth and fifth vertebrae," said the butcher. "I show you again?" he added, but Cohen stopped him.

"That's okay, I believe you. Now I'll ask you something else," said Cohen.

"Yes?" Moise answered expectantly.

"Could you do the same thing if the neck was smaller, if it was, oh, this big?" Cohen asked. He held out his hands, holding the tips of his thumbs and his forefingers together, making an oval. Moise looked thoughtfully at Cohen's hands.

"You mean a person's neck, don't you?"

"Yes," answered Cohen, "a person's neck. Could a butcher, somebody with experience, know how to do that?"

Moise thought for a moment. "Yes. Sure. It's possible. Why not? A good butcher, strong, maybe he'll miss, the knife might slip a little. But it would still go in. You need a strong, sharp knife. Very strong, very sharp. You need a strong butcher. You got a case? You got somebody who did this terrible thing?"

"You've been a big help, Moise," said Cohen, ignoring the

butcher's last question. "So what do you say? Are you going to let me have that duck?"

Cohen added butchers to his list of possible suspects. Some worked in slaughterhouses, others had their own shops. Cohen wanted them all checked out, particularly those living or working in Ein Kerem. And while he was at it, he added a list of anyone arrested during the last decade during anti-Soviet demonstrations. There wouldn't be too many on those lists: Most of the anti-Soviet rallies held in Israel were sponsored by official organizations demanding free Jewish emigration.

There was one other thing he learned from Raoul, something that worried him even more. The killer had faced his victims, yet there had been no struggle. They may have known the killer. He wondered if Alex was proficient with a knife.

T HE NUNS WERE TO BE INTERRED in the afternoon, in a private ceremony at the convent, where their bones would eventually be removed from the ground and stored in a cellar storeroom containing the bones and skulls of all the nuns who had ever served the Lord in that place. But first, there was a public ceremony on the porch of the gleaming white church of the Russian Orthodox mission in the heart of the Russian Compound.

Cohen stood at the side of the lot, avoiding the attention of anyone who might ask him about the case and watching Yaffe play his favorite role as the designated police representative to the affair. Cohen smirked as Yaffe worked the crowd, shaking hands with the dignitaries, turning a noble profile to the cameramen. The police and press photographers worked the funeral, taking pictures of everyone from the cognac-breathed archimandrite in his dusty black robes to the various officials from government ministries. The milling of the large crowd raised a cloud of white gravel dust over the parking lot, but gusts of a warm eastern wind blew it away, salting the black robes of the clergy gathering for the funeral and the black robes of the lawyers on their way to and from court. The clergymen ignored the dust, Cohen noticed, while the lawyers tried to brush the powder out of their own black robes.

The entire Red Russian church delegation attended the service, but there were also clergymen from other churches including—to the surprise of those who understood the intricacies of church politics—the mother superior of the convent attached to the White Russian Church. The mayor regarded the public ceremonies and the impressive attendance as a public relations triumph that displayed the freedom of religion in Jerusalem.

Gorny's mourning nuns were quiet as the coffins were carried out of the mission offices through a side door of a small fir-shaded building behind the Supreme Court. Priests from the Russian Orthodox monastery near Tiberias carried the coffin across the cramped gravel parking lot to the terrace in front of the white cathedral. The mission had no money to maintain the church, but the archimandrite led the prayers on its marble steps facing the entrance to police headquarters. From the side, a knot of Arab women and children watched the ceremonies. Usually, they were the only people to use the church, sitting on the steps while waiting for the daily visiting hours of prisoners in the police station's holding cells across the street.

The two dozen nuns of Gorny crowded together, their dark habits blowing silently in the gusts of warm wind. Clustering together in the brilliant whiteness of the morning sunlight, the nuns tried but failed to stay clear of the prying lenses of the photographers. There were no tears, no hysterical weeping, no muffled sobs. Their faces were solemn, respectful, and composed. But as Cohen looked into their eyes as they filed past, he also saw their suspicion of all about them. Cohen was used to a different sort of funeral: burial ceremonies for young soldiers killed in war, innocents killed by terrorists, criminals killed by other criminals, and policemen killed in all the ways policemen can die. He was used to noisy funerals full of outbursts, mothers or wives or fathers or sons trying to hurl their bodies into the grave, screaming to heaven for pity and cursing revenge on those blamed for the death.

But no trace of emotion emerged from the nuns' faces as they followed the two coffins. They watched silently as the boxes were loaded into the back of a black van for the drive to the convent and the small graveyard at the far western end of the property.

Alex was dressed in black. But Cohen had come to realize that Alex always dressed in black. From a distance, he watched the Russian lounging in the driver's seat of the van, waiting for the handshaking and condolences to finish so he could drive the coffins back to the convent.

"Cooperation," said the policeman, placing his hand on the open windowsill of the black and dusty van. "I'm still looking forward to your cooperation."

"Of course," said Alex, looking down at Cohen from the high seat of the van. "But there's much that I have to do nowadays. I'm sure you understand. The funeral, arrangements . . . I told Yaffe that I'll make myself available to him as soon as I can."

"Reports to write," Cohen suggested. "Yes, I can imagine you're busy nowadays." He was looking away from Alex toward the crowd. He smiled, watching the indefatigable mayor move from one church dignitary to another, sharing condolences, politicking, as always, to keep the tinder damp. Cohen spoke softly. "Yes, you must have a lot of explanation to do about the quality of security at the convent."

"You're the authorities," said Alex, taking a stick of chewing gum from a packet on the dashboard. He unwrapped it deliberately and studied it before popping it into his mouth. "You're responsible for security." He looked into the rearview mirror and stroked his hair back over his ears, then turned back to Cohen and smiled.

"Outside the convent," said Cohen. "Inside, you were responsible," he added, turning down Alex's offer of a stick of gum.

"If you won't take this," said Alex, smiling, "perhaps you'll take a word of advice."

"I'm listening," said Cohen, his eyes again scanning the milling crowd.

"Don't make the same mistakes that the politicians make."

"Which mistakes? They make so many," Cohen said.

"Don't assume."

"What shouldn't I assume?"

"That I am your enemy in this matter."

"Prove to me that you aren't. Tell me why you took so long to let us know what happened. Tell me what you know . . ."

"I'm sorry," said Alex, "truly I'm sorry. But there's nothing more I can tell you. There's nothing more that I know."

The familiar smell of Yaffe's after-shave was in the air. "What did you want to know, Avram?" asked the liaison officer, stepping up to Cohen from behind.

"I was asking Alex to tell me when he would sit down with

us to tell us about the convent, about the nuns, maybe even about himself," said Cohen.

"Am I under arrest? A suspect?" The KGB man smiled at Cohen. "The women are not yet even laid to rest, you have nothing except a footprint, and already you are blaming me?" His tone was accusatory but not hostile. Cohen scowled as the Russian performed for Yaffe, adding, "I knew these women. Maybe I, too, deserve a bit of consideration for my grief."

"Of course, of course," Yaffe stammered, "I'm sure that Avram did not mean to accuse you."

Cohen ignored Yaffe. "Come on, Alex, tell me why it took you two hours to let us know about the murders."

"I told you at the convent. The archimandrite wanted to say prayers to calm the sisters," Alex answered and then demanded of Yaffe, "Do I have to answer these questions, right here? Now? I have a funeral to attend to."

The crowd was dispersing, and Cohen was aware of the archimandrite and Sister Elizabeth watching them.

Yaffe turned to Cohen, desperate. Cohen continued staring at Alex. "If not now, perhaps some other time," Cohen pressed. "Of course, if I knew you were trying to help, well, things might be different between us. But you haven't told me anything, have you?"

"Avram, he has to go . . ." said Yaffe.

"That's okay," said Cohen, "I'm sure he won't be leaving the country, maybe not even the city, for a while. Unless his *church* wants him elsewhere. Home, perhaps . . ." Cohen watched Alex for a reaction to the emphasis of the use of the word "church." There was a slight clenching of the jaw, and then the Russian leaned forward to turn on the engine of the van. Yaffe stepped back, but Cohen left his hand on the door's windowsill. "Alex. I'm going to have to find out, eventually."

"I am not your killer," Alex barked, losing his temper. He jammed the van into gear and lurched forward, using his open palm to spin the steering wheel to make the turn out of the parking lot.

Striding briskly away, Cohen spat out at Yaffe, "You really are an idiot, you know that."

Yaffe struggled to keep up. "Avram, Avram," said the white-haired officer, "wait!"

Cohen halted in the middle of the parking lot. "What is it?" he asked impatiently.

"Look, I'm sorry, but there are things you don't know, things going on. God knows I'm the last one who would try to hurt one of your investigations. And God knows I want this case cleared up quickly. But there are things going on, and . . ."

"*Nu?*" Cohen prodded. "What's going on?"

"You know I'd tell you if I could," said Yaffe.

"Tell me something, Meshulam," said Cohen, "were you like this before the job, or is it the job that makes you like this?"

It took a moment for Yaffe to react. "Cohen, just be careful, that's all. Be careful. You can't talk to a diplomat that way. And as a churchman, he's here on diplomatic status. He's not some kid from the streets your men and you can browbeat or sweet-talk into a confession."

"I never said he was a suspect," said Cohen, "I just want to know if he's going to help us. That's all. And you come along and . . ."

"Don't give me that," said Yaffe, holding his own. "I heard you. Really, Avram. These things are delicate. And I'm on your side."

Cohen wasn't at all sure that Yaffe wanted to help—if help meant complicating the relationship between the police and the diplomatic and church communities. And he was certain that Yaffe was only on Yaffe's side. As far as Cohen could tell, Yaffe would have been happy with any solution that kept things quiet, unruffled, and smooth. But, more adept than Cohen on the obstacle courses laid out by the politicians, Yaffe could also be dangerous, with an insider's knowledge of political maneuvering.

"Forget it," said Cohen. "Tell me something I don't know. Tell me something that will help me." They resumed walking toward the police station across the parking lot, pausing for traffic in the street that cut through the compound from city hall to the Street of the Prophets. "Tell me about the convent," Cohen suggested.

Yaffe smiled and launched into a lecture on the history of the place. He mentioned that Orthodox nuns sent to Jerusalem rarely leave.

"You mean they never get to leave, never go home?" asked

Cohen, as they started up the wide, worn steps of the ivy-covered police station.

"That's right. Once here, they stay," said Yaffe.

"Like emigrants. Refugees," said Cohen.

"Well, they think of the convent as their home. It's not temporary. They're here to take care of pilgrims . . ."

"But there aren't any pilgrims any more," said Cohen, "not from Russia, anyway."

"Yes, well, there's the convent to maintain and other properties. I saw a report. It said the property is worth at least half a billion dollars on the real estate market."

"How much?" asked Cohen, astonished.

"Half a billion dollars. They own the only private beach on the Kinneret. They own half the parking lots downtown. What am I talking about? They own your office. The Russian Compound. The government leases it. It was Ben-Gurion's idea. The British expropriated the property, and when Moscow recognized us, Ben-Gurion gave it all back."

Cohen strode up the stairs two at a time, Yaffe on his heels. "I know all that," said Cohen, "tell me something I don't know."

Yaffe continued, "Since '67, we've been paying rent into a blind trust. Of course, it serves them right, for cutting relations with us in '67. Anyway, there's not much in there," he laughed. "Inflation ate it all away. But the rumor at the Kirya," said Yaffe, and with the word "rumor," Cohen slowed down to listen carefully, "the rumor is that the Russians want to improve relations in part for the sake of the foreign currency they could be earning from the properties. So you see, the PM's interest in this matter . . ."

"Yes, I know about his interest," said Cohen. "I know too damn well about his interest."

They reached Cohen's office. Yaffe took a seat at the T-shaped desk, while Cohen began to scan a stack of internal mail that Rutie, the secretary he shared with Schwartz, had handed him when he walked in.

He scowled when he saw the documents were all administrative memos dealing with budgetary matters. He dropped them into Levy's tray.

"Look," he said, turning back to Yaffe, "if I have to talk with Alex, I'll talk with Alex. If he's in my city, I can talk with him, diplomatic immunity or not, KGB or not. If he knows something I have to know, then I'll do what I have to do in order to know it. And as far as you are concerned—if there's something you know that I have to know, you better let me know it now, and not after I find out from someone else."

Yaffe went to the door, looked out it once at the broad second-floor landing, and closed it. "The PM," Yaffe whispered, "he's working on something. With the Soviets. A big deal. That's all I know. I can't say anything more."

Cohen rolled his eyes. "That's the big deal? That's the big secret? Every day in the newspaper I read about the PM making big plans for a big deal with someone. But meanwhile, nothing much has happened has it? All his big plans turn into arguments about a comma here, a word there. There's always an excuse. So now it's the Soviets. So?"

"So, it's not a good idea to rock any boats nowadays. It's not a good idea to mess around with Alex."

Cohen's grimace made Yaffe wince. "Meshulam, Meshulam, let's take things a step at a time. I'm not messing around with Alex, I asked him some questions. He might have told me something—if you hadn't stuck your finger in. I want to talk with him. That's all. And you screwed it up. Now, as far as the PM's plans are concerned? I'm not worried about diplomacy. I'm worried about two dead nuns and a lot of other things as well. Look at this," he said, slapping his hand on one of three stacks of cardboard folders that reached waist high on his desk. "I've got all this to worry about."

Yaffe knew the files for what they were, the unsolved cases of the city. Most were the petty crimes of any city, but he recognized the different priorities of cases according to the different colors of the folders. More than half of one stack were the yellow folders containing "serious crimes" meaning anything involving life or limb, drugs or weapons illegally obtained. In Jerusalem, that category included crimes that might be applauded by some, even if not many, as a proper approach to a problem of national significance or religious importance. At the very top of the pile, was a folder with the words "Sidra 13" written in large block type.

"So now, if you'll let me be," said Cohen, "I have work to do."

Yaffe left the office, leaving Cohen alone in the chair, turning pages in the folders, making notes on the edges of reports, passing some on for action, leaving others piled high on his desk. He opened the first Sidra 13 folder and, for what seemed to him the one hundredth time, began reading from the start. The interviews with the potential suspects were getting nowhere. Leads that had seemed promising had dried up like wadis in summer. Of the 12,000 grenades in the series, the army had been able to account for nearly 11,000. More than half had been used in practices. A few thousand more remained in brigade munitions stockpiles. An eyes-only note from Ehud of military intelligence reported to Cohen that the missing 1,000 grenades would be most difficult to account for. The grenades had been trucked to Lebanon as part of a major munitions depot set up in the south soon after the start of the invasion three years before. "And as you well know," said the note, "in that chaos, anything was possible. We're still on it," Ehud had scrawled beneath the typed note. "But we need some luck."

The police photographer came out of the darkroom that afternoon with a stack of pictures of all the mourners. Many of the faces were known to Cohen and his team. There were representatives of the Religious Affairs Ministry, a pair of attachés from the Romanian Embassy, which handled Soviet diplomatic affairs in Israel, and several Eastern Europe desk officers from the Foreign Ministry. All ninety-seven nuns and priests were to be matched to their visa applications. Of more than five hundred people at the funeral, forty-seven faces were unknown to any of the police officers and were to be located for future questioning.

They made two separate piles of pictures, tourists and locals. Sometimes it was obvious which group the face belonged to; other times, Cohen had to rely on intuition. Dark skin and curly hair meant somebody local. A scraggly beard could mean either religious or a tourist, except a religious man would be wearing something on his head, a hat, a *kippa*.

Two detectives were sent out into the Ben-Yehuda mall and the Jaffa Gate with postcard-sized enlargements of the photographs. They would scout the tourists, showing the pictures to buskers, who arrived in spring from Europe to play music on the streets, and youth hostel receptionists, visiting pubs frequented by travelers. At the Jaffa Gate they would sit at the cafés where hashish deals are routine, looking for the faces. They would go to hotels, from five star to flophouse, asking about the people in the photographs.

Levy went back to the students in the Ein Kerem hills with a similar stack of pictures, but none of the students recognized anyone.

Two other detectives began touring old-age homes and the small boulevards of the city where old people sat on park benches. Cohen didn't think the killer was an old person; too much strength was required for these murders. But Cohen was interested in everyone who came to the nuns' funeral. He wanted everybody identified.

Jerusalem is a mosaic of closed communities whose members are immediately recognizable to each other. Arabs recognized Arabs; the *haredim* recognized *haredim;* secular university people knew familiar faces from the two campuses; and government officials knew each other from the Kirya. It would take time, but Cohen was certain that eventually a name would be attached to every picture. But meanwhile, despite all the ongoing legwork, there was no overall strategy for the investigation. As far as Cohen was concerned, he was still laying groundwork. Nonetheless, the unusual phone calls had already begun.

"The inspector general is taking a personal interest," said the national CID chief in a phone call before the funeral.

"Don't give me that nonsense," Cohen said angrily. "He hasn't taken a personal interest in anything except his retirement since he became IG. If I screw this up, he won't have his ambassadorship. That's what he's figuring. He's under pressure and I know from where."

The prime minister, secure behind the curtains of the American sedan that shuttled him between his office and his official residence in Talbieh, said nothing in public. Nussbaum released a regular statement saying that the PM and the entire government had confidence in the police. But Cohen had his doubts.

"The public sees a cop show on TV and thinks that we can also solve a case in forty-five minutes," Cohen mumbled to himself when the first hints of disapproval began showing up in the press reports. It wouldn't take long, he felt, before the pack moved in, and the questions would begin in the Knesset. The left would demand to know whether the government was interested in progress and charge that the prime minister or his henchmen were impeding the investigation because Jews were probably involved. The right would say it was all the work of Arabs and charge that talk of Jewish terrorists was the talk of self-hating Jews and weak-spined Zionists. If the police wanted to make an all-out effort on something, they should focus on the *intifada*.

So the "bloody politicians" would push. They wanted a suspect and fast. Cohen wanted the truth and didn't care how long it took.

II

THE TWINS didn't find Goldstein on that first Shabbat, to Levy's open relief and Cohen's private relief. They searched for Goldstein in the drab apartment blocks of Kiryat Arba, the first of the Jewish settlements over the Green Line in the West Bank. They chased after a tip that he was inside the barbed-wire perimeter on the rooftops of houses in the Jewish Quarter settlement in ancient Hebron. They took the long drive to a settlement of three mobile caravans serving as temporary housing at the end of a long, dusty trail on a hilltop in the Judean desert, and they raced to a political meeting in a basement yeshiva at Joseph's Tomb in Shechem, the Arab town of Nablus. They tried three government-funded *yeshivot* placed in the name of security and nationalism in the heart of the Moslem Quarter of Jerusalem. Everywhere, they just missed Goldstein; everywhere, he seemed to be a step ahead of them.

Their street names were Rafi and Danny. They were recruited out of the same army unit at the same time. They had been through the training courses together and shared a sprawling, high-ceilinged apartment on Street of the Prophets, a few blocks away from the Russian Compound police headquarters. They were called the Twins because they looked alike, stocky and rusty blond, with dark brown eyes. After years of working as a team, they even stood alike, and both had the slight scar tissue of broken noses.

"He's like Arafat," Rafi said to Danny at the end of their long Sunday chase, "never sleeping in the same bed twice."

"Probably claims it's for security. More likely nobody can put up with him for more than a day," Danny said.

Shmulik called Cohen at the office on Tuesday morning. "My boys haven't found Goldstein yet," he reported. "They said you expected to hear from them today, but they're still looking for him. They asked me to call to let you know."

"Probably were scared to tell me face to face," Cohen grumbled. "Tell them to try the People's Guard museum. In Nahlaot."

"They said something about going there next," Shmulik offered.

"They should have gone there first," Cohen complained.

"They're not used to chasing after Jews," said Shmulik.

"I'm afraid they're going to have to get used to it," snapped Cohen, adding for spite, "but I'm sure they'll find out it's no different from chasing Arabs." With that he hung up, not waiting for Shmulik's response.

The People's Guard had a four-room apartment in Nahlaot, a neighborhood of rambling courtyards and 100-year-old buildings. Half the neighborhood seemed to be about to collapse of age; the other half was being gentrified by Jerusalem's yuppies. The People's Guard museum, known as "The Museum of Future Jewish Victims," was housed in a three-story apartment building at the edge between the poorest section of Nahlaot and the wealthy neighborhood of Rehavia. It was a first floor flat, with a glassed-in rear porch overlooking the Valley of the Cross. The offices of the museum and The People's Guard organization consisted of two desks, an imported Rolodex file with the movement's four hundred official members, and piles of leaflets promising that the Arab-owned villas of East Jerusalem would one day be owned by the Jewish poor of Jerusalem.

The walls were painted black. The first room was decorated with anti-Semitic wall posters. Flea market folding tables held piles of anti-Semitic literature in many languages. The second room was wallpapered with newspaper pages taken from American neo-Nazi periodicals; portraits of Hitler, Ku Klux Klan literature, and posters showing hooknosed Jews and thick-lipped blacks being stomped by whites.

The third room was a memorial to "The Jews who will die, if they don't awaken to the threat." The memorial was like a small altar. A print of the famous photograph of the little boy being led out of the Warsaw ghetto, arms raised under a stormtrooper's rifle, was pasted to a piece of Masonite and propped beside a large Bible open to the description of Pharaoh's troops being washed away in the flooding waters of the Red Sea.

Rafi and Danny passed through the three rooms before reaching the back porch, where two young men were stuffing envelopes. A young woman was seated in an overstuffed chair that needed reupholstering. Even sitting down, the woman looked tall and ungainly. She was dressed in a long skirt made from blue jeans and wore a gray pullover that had once been white. Her hair was tied into a ponytail. She was crocheting a *kippa,* her fingers moving fast through the motions. She didn't have to look at the *kippa* to do the work, and she stared at the two strangers as the round piece of growing material moved around and around in her hand.

Watching the Twins suspiciously, the two other People's Guard activists stood straight. One was in army uniform. The other wore a large *kippa* into which somebody, perhaps the girl, had crocheted a series of Uzi submachine guns alternating with Stars of David.

After their fruitless searches up and down the country, the Twins had no patience for any small talk. "Goldstein," Danny demanded, like a customer in a shop knowing exactly what he was seeking. The three people in the room looked at each other and seemed to pass a silent signal amongst themselves. They remained quiet.

"Where's Goldstein?" Rafi barked, stepping inside the room to cover Danny who had walked in farther, closer to the table covered with leaflets and the envelopes. Still there was silence. The woman's eyes shifted nervously to a set of green cabinets that formed an interior wall inside the room. Danny took a step toward the lockers.

"Yes, who wants him?" From behind the lockers came a short fat man, his white shirt stained with coffee, his trousers faded to a colorless gray. The fat man's breathing was labored, asthmatic, and rumbling.

"You can call me Rafi," said the Twin. "We'd like to have a word with you. In private."

"Shabak," said Goldstein, smiling.

Danny kept his eyes on the uniformed soldier. The young man looked back defiantly.

"Goldstein, let's go," said Rafi.

"What do you want from him?" asked the soldier in a Hebrew heavily accented by American English.

"Goldstein, once more, I think you should come with us," said Rafi, still ignoring the soldier.

The fat man stepped forward. "You can talk with me here. If you show me some ID."

"I don't think so," said Rafi. "Not here." He had moved close enough to the table to rest his hand on a pile of leaflets. "I think," he said, and his hand moved quickly, scattering all the leaflets and envelopes onto the floor, "I think that it's a bit messy. That's not very conducive to conversation. Don't you think?"

"You can't do that!" the civilian People's Guard member shouted in English. "We have rights!" He stepped forward toward Rafi, and suddenly Danny's grip was on his shoulder, yanking him backward off his feet.

"Listen, you," said Rafi, looking down at the civilian. "This isn't America. This isn't a game. And you," he said, pointing his finger at the soldier, "I want your name and ID number. You're in uniform and that means you have nothing to do here. Nothing."

"And I want to see your ID," Goldstein said.

But for the moment, Rafi ignored him. The soldier swallowed. "They can't talk to you that way," the young man on the floor said. "This is a free country. You're not breaking the law."

"Tell him," said Rafi.

"As long as I'm a soldier I'm not supposed to be involved in politics," said the soldier, meekly.

"Well I'm not a soldier and they can't do this to me," said the civilian, getting to his feet. "I want to see your identification."

Danny sighed, flipping open his wallet to display the government card. Rafi was less polite. "You'd be surprised what we can do," he said. "Go back to America, kid, you're in over your head here. You don't know what it's about here."

"Go back and fight your what you call it your Ku Klux Klan. Your demons are there," said Danny, finishing Rafi's thought.

Goldstein lifted a sports jacket from where it was hanging on the back of a chair. "Let's go," he said resignedly to Rafi.

Danny waited in the room until Goldstein had squeezed past. The soldier and civilian stood in the middle of the room staring. The girl had continued her crocheting throughout, not saying a word. "Sweetie, you're gonna wear out your fingers doing that." Danny grinned and left.

"They usually take me to the Russian Compound," Goldstein said with slight worry in his voice, as Rafi sped past the Jaffa Road turnoff to the police station.

"Oh, we're not usual. Not at all usual," said Danny.

"Where are you taking me?" asked the fat man.

They were heading out of town, past the Mount of Olives cemetery on the road to Jericho and the Dead Sea. "We're taking you someplace nice," said Danny. "We want to take you on a *tiul*, a nice day trip. To learn the country."

The Twins rolled down their windows, the hot wind cooling their faces as they drove. Goldstein discovered the handles of the windows in the back seat had been removed, and quickly he began to sweat, the drops rolling dark down his forehead, collecting grime. It was hot in the desert mountains at noon, and the sun's glare dulled the eastern horizon. They passed an army base built on a plateau, a Bedouin encampment in a valley, and the turnoff to a new highway built to shorten the distance between the coast and the Jordan Valley.

Just after a small stone marker announcing SEA LEVEL in English and Arabic, a relic from the days when the Jordanian king raced sports cars from Amman to Jerusalem, Rafi turned right off the main highway.

There was no pavement, but there was a road of sorts, created by centuries of Bedouin leading flocks and decades of army jeeps, British, Jordanian, and Israeli, heading into the mountains. The Ford sedan bounced and jolted along the dirt road. When the muffler scraped the ground the first time, Danny said, "It's Goldstein's fault. He should lose some weight." The second time, Rafi suggested that Goldstein should pay for any damage.

"What do you want from me?" Goldstein whimpered. His white shirt was dark damp from the sweat. He held a white handkerchief that had turned gray by the time they had driven through the hills for half an hour.

Around them the landscape was littered with rusting jeeps.

Old tanks, treadless and turretless, dotted the sides of the wadi.

"Where are we?" Goldstein asked, his acrid sweat filling the car like a pair of used sweatsocks.

"Just a firing range," said Rafi. "It's okay. The shooting doesn't start for an hour. It stinks in here," he added. "Let's get some fresh air."

He stopped the car. They were in a wadi, and in every direction there were hills. The valley floor was pockmarked by small craters made by exploding shells. There was no horizon, no view for more than two hundred meters in any direction. Danny opened the door for Goldstein, who cowered inside. "Come on, get out of there," said the Shabak agent, reaching inside and pulling at Goldstein's shirt. Rafi had a canteen of water. Goldstein struggled to get out of the car.

"We know you aren't well, so we figured a walk in the fresh air would be good for you. Isn't that right?" said Rafi, his tone perfectly reasonable as he asked Danny the question. Danny nodded.

"What do you want to know?" Goldstein whined.

But the Twins ignored him, making him even more nervous.

"The day will come when we'll make sure there aren't people like you in government service. One of these days we'll take care of people like you," Goldstein suddenly changed his tone. "Why aren't you out there getting some terrorists?" He spat the word. "Leftists!"

"You a leftist?" Danny asked Rafi.

"Communist. I vote Communist," Rafi confided with a chuckle.

"I vote for the Aguda," said Danny, with an equally straight face. "They're the only ones who know what they really want." The Aguda was the *haredi* party that traded support for the government in exchange for special budgets for their religious schools.

"C'mon," said Rafi, yanking at Goldstein's shirt to pull him along to the easternmost hill in the mountain cul de sac.

"Where we going?" Goldstein asked.

"A *tiul*. That's all, a little walk," said Danny. "Come on, it will be fun."

"I'm not supposed to do this sort of thing," Goldstein said meekly.

"It's healthy, very healthy," said Rafi.

They headed up the slope, trekking through the natural gravel

formed eons ago by earthquakes and the departing seas that once
had filled the entire Jordan Valley. Stones skittered backwards,
causing tiny avalanches that were the only sounds apart from Goldstein's heavy breathing. The white polyester shirt, shiny under the
sun, stuck to Goldstein's skin and the rolls of fat on his stomach.
He stumbled often as he climbed. There were tears in his eyes.

"I'm not going any farther. I can't," he gasped. "I can't. What
do you want from me? What?"

Rafi reached the top of the hill. "We'll wait for you up here,
Goldstein." Danny was halfway between them, looking down at
Goldstein. "Come on, it's not so far. You had to do more in the
army, didn't you? As far as I know, you once walked more than
a kilometer, all along the main street of Ramallah, didn't you?
That's much farther than we've walked today. And you were carrying a hammer that day. Smashing car windows. Today you aren't
carrying anything. Except yourself."

Goldstein looked up at Danny. The Shabak agent stood with
his back to the sun, and Goldstein's eyes squinted as he tried to
make out the Twins. "I need a drink of water. Let me have a drink.
Please!"

"Goldstein," said Danny, speaking like a father to a son, but
with threat instead of love. "Goldstein, Goldstein, Goldstein.
What's it gonna be? How are you going to be a hero, how are you
going to fight Arabs if you can't even climb a little hill. Now, I
think you ought to join us up here on top of the hill. We'll wait
for you. And when you get here, we'll have some nice cool water
for you."

Danny turned and scrambled up the last two dozen meters to
the top of the hill. When he reached the summit, Rafi passed him
the canteen and Danny took a long drink, ending it with some
water in the palm of his hand, which he rubbed onto his face.

Goldstein watched. He looked back at the car, parked far away
at the bottom of the hill. He struggled to get up and started running
and stumbling down the hill.

A loud crack echoed through the air. A few meters in front
and to the left of Goldstein a rock split in two. Goldstein fell to
the ground. The gunshot echoed thrice through the hills.

"Gold-stein," called Rafi, coolly studying his pistol. "You
really ought to join us."

"What do you want from me?" Goldstein cried out.

"You come up here and we'll tell you," Danny answered.

The fat man rose to his feet again and slowly made his way to the top of the hill. Every few steps he stopped to rest and catch his breath. By the time he reached them, his eyes were red, his legs shaking. Rafi held the canteen out but didn't let the fat man take it. "I'll hold it, you drink." Goldstein barely had a sip before Rafi took it away.

"Okay, Goldstein," Rafi began slowly and quietly. "We want to ask you about nuns. Do you like nuns? You ever fuck a nun, Goldstein?" His voice rose through each taunt until he was shouting, "You ever want to fuck a nun, Goldstein? A Russian nun?" Danny sat on the ground, his eyes half-closed, his face aimed upwards like a lizard barking in the sun.

"The nuns," said Goldstein, finally realizing why they had picked him up. "You think we had something to do with the nuns." Goldstein was silent for a moment. "I'll tell you something. I didn't mind at all when I read about it. Serves 'em right. Goyim. Russian goyim. Cossacks." He was silent again.

Rafi laughed, loud and long. "Cossacks. That's good Goldstein. That's real good."

Goldstein looked up at Rafi, who had risen to his feet. "Yeah, fuckin' Cossack whores." He spat on the ground and smiled up at Rafi. His teeth were crooked.

Rafi stopped laughing. His voice changed. "Not funny Goldstein, not funny at all." His foot caught Goldstein in the belly. The fat man rolled a few meters down the hill. Rafi turned to Danny. "It wasn't funny," he said, almost apologetically.

Danny walked the few meters to where Goldstein had fallen flat on his back. The Twin's shadow fell darkly over Goldstein's face.

"Listen, Goldstein. Let's make this easy. You know what's going on with your crazies. You're crazy, too. We know that. But you're a big shot with those crazies. You're Goldstein and everybody listens to you. Even that maniac rabbi of yours. If you ask me, I don't know why. But you know what they're up to. I'll tell you what. You tell us who did the nuns and we'll take you home. Right to your door," said Danny.

Rafi shouted down, "Of course, if you don't tell us, we'll have to leave you here." He looked at his watch. "We'll let you have the canteen, of course, but we'll have to be leaving soon. In another twenty minutes, they start shooting here."

"And when they find you," Danny added, "when they come down to see how well they shot, they'll say, 'Oh, that Goldstein, such a lover of the Land of Israel, he went for a walk to listen to the Land and God.' Of course, you might survive the shelling. But I can't imagine you walking out of here. So, think of it as a martyrdom. Your friends will say Arabs did you, and that will give them a good reason to go beat up some kids half their size, and then there will be a knifing, and I'll have work to do. So, you know what Goldstein, I suggest you tell us what we want to know."

Goldstein stared at the Shabak agent. He looked up at Rafi, who was holding the canteen to his forehead, and then looked around at the smashed old jeeps and trucks scattered on the hillsides.

"Okay," he said after a long minute. "Okay. Look. All we did was some graffiti. One of the boys, he did some graffiti. And some letters. We sent some letters."

"Who'd you send those letters to, Goldstein?" asked Danny. "What kind of letters?"

"They were letters, you know, they said 'Get out,' you know, 'Russians go home,' that sort of stuff. But I read about the killings in the newspapers. That's all. I swear. I swear to you."

"Don't swear to us, Goldstein, swear to God," shouted Rafi. "You don't swear to us. Swear to your God. Whoever he might be."

The sweat was evaporating in the dry heat almost as fast as it was pouring out of the large pores on Goldstein's nose. "I swear, swear to God, I swear on my father's grave. I swear. None of us had anything to do with it. None of us. I swear to you. I read about it. Knives. We don't do that sort of thing. Not knives." He shuddered, shivering in his fear. "Please, some water, please," he begged. Danny stared down and then slowly moved his head back and forth, believing what he heard and disgusted by it.

"You know what," said Danny, "I believe you, Goldstein. I believe it. None of your types would have the guts to kill somebody you could see die in front of you. None of you would have the guts. You'd have to do it from far away. A gun. A bomb. But look at you. Especially you. You don't have it, do you Goldstein? You know Goldstein, you're not serious. So tell me, what about the grenades? What do you know about the grenades?"

Goldstein's eyes opened wide with fear.

"You know," added Rafi, "on the Temple Mount. You're always demonstrating there, aren't you. You must know something."

Goldstein's sobs were hollow and quickly became a sore cough. "I know nothing! Nothing!"

Danny rose to his feet. He waved to Rafi who was standing on top of the hill. As he walked past Goldstein, he dropped the canteen beside the fat man, who grabbed for it, guzzling the last few swallows inside. When he looked down, the two Shabak agents were already at the bottom of the hill.

"Wait! Wait for me!" he cried and rushed to his feet. He ran down the hill, falling and rising, falling and rising. He caught up with the two agents just as they reached the car.

"You're lucky, Goldstein," said Rafi. "This time you were lucky. But we don't want to have to see you again, Goldstein, do we?" said the Shabak agent, turning to his partner.

"No. I don't think we want to hear from Goldstein again," said Danny. When they reached the main road, they could hear the first of the incoming shells, a distant vague thud way off behind them. Rafi and Danny smiled. Goldstein looked out the back window and shivered.

The fat man was silent all the way back to the city. When they pulled up in front of the Museum of Future Jewish Victims, Goldstein started to open the door.

"Remember, Goldstein, we really don't want to hear from you again," said Danny.

"Or see you again," added Rafi.

"I promise," said the fat man. "I promise."

"Can we trust him?" Danny asked Rafi.

"We really can't trust anybody, can we?" answered Rafi.

"You can trust me, I promise," said Goldstein. "I'm a Jew, you're Jews, you can trust me."

"Actually, I think of myself as an Israeli," said Danny, as Rafi put the car in gear and drove away.

12

THERE WAS NO FREE TIME ANYMORE. The paper had suddenly piled up like a winter rain filling a wadi with water overnight. Every action was duly recorded, no matter how futile. Butchers were questioned—so far nothing. The footprint cast was studied to the useless conclusion that maybe the shoes were American, maybe Italian, or maybe knockoffs from the shoe district behind the Tel Aviv bus station. The reports on phone calls that came in after the news of the nuns' murder were all dead ends, turned into paper for the files.

With no breaking developments, the media were left with only news features ranging from portraits of the divided Russian church to rehashed accounts of the anti-Soviet graffiti scrawled on the convent walls. The reporters knew nothing yet of the prime minister's interest in the case. And they knew nothing of Alex. Cohen hoped it would all remain that way. But he wasn't optimistic.

Despite all the paper—five days after the murders, two and a half yellow folders were filled—Cohen found time twice to hike up and down the hillside of the village.

He went once early enough to catch the morning bread truck, delivering hot loaves to the village's two grocery stores. The fog from the changing temperatures at dawn had turned into a day-long drizzle.

As usual, Cohen wore his sneakers, gray cotton twill pants, and a white cotton shirt under his windbreaker, and as he set off from his parked car at the lowest point in the village, he noted the time on his watch. Then, taking a deep breath and pressing the play button on his Walkman, he started off, heading up the winding road to the convent. Mozart's *Requiem* soared in his ears as he climbed higher and higher above the valley. He stayed off the road but close to it, breathing heavily as he climbed. Soon his legs began to ache, and then there was a stitch in his side. He tried bending at the waist to drive it away and worried that he was moving slowly, too slowly. I'm getting too old for this, he said to himself, hearing his voice from inside his head, realizing he had spoken aloud over the sound of the music. He removed the earphones for a moment to listen to the sounds of the woods. But all he heard was the sound of his heavy breathing and the echo of Ahuva's voice extracting a promise at the airport the night she left. "While I'm gone," she had said, "try to cut down on the smoking," and then added, "and the drinking."

He would have smiled at the memory of the last-minute phone call from the airport, but the pain in his side from the hike was twisting his face. He waited for a couple of minutes until his breathing returned to normal and then resumed the hike, the earphones firmly back in place.

Finally he reached the top. Just inside the green gate, Yerahmiel, the pensioned policeman, was sitting on a chair, sunning himself in the spring light. The policeman jumped to his feet when he saw Cohen approaching. "Avram! How are you?" asked the policeman with the familiarity of thirty years. "My wife told me to send you the very best regards. Here, she made me some nice honey cake for a snack up here. Why don't you have some?" The policeman scuttled back and pulled a plastic bag out from underneath the wooden chair.

Cohen was speechless, once again out of breath and silently cursing himself for not taking better care, but he couldn't help but smile at the policeman's patter. "She said to me, Yerahmiel, you be sure to tell Avram Cohen that he's always welcome at our house, and that if he ever needs a place to go for dinner . . . Well, I told her, I said to her, Avram Cohen's a great cook. A gourmet, that's the word, isn't it? And she said . . ."

"You tell her that it's very kind of her to invite me," Cohen said, finally able to speak. "But no, thank you, no cake," he added.

The thought of dry food almost made Cohen gag. "If you have some water," he asked.

"Better, I have tea. Here," said the old policeman, uncapping a thermos bottle. "You don't look well. Why not have a seat?"

Cohen shook his head with the thermos cap still held to his lips. When he finished gulping the sweet tea, he handed the cup back to the policeman. "No, I have to get back down below."

"Avram, we're not so young as we used to be, are we?" the uniformed man said. "We have to learn to take care of ourselves. You have to take care of yourself."

Cohen nodded and smiled, but he wasn't paying attention. He was calculating the time it had taken him to make the climb. Twenty-five minutes. A younger man could have done it in half the time. He felt disgusted with himself.

The second time, Levy drove. Cohen motioned him past the usual turn-off to the village, and they drove toward Hadassah Hospital. High above the village, on the short stretch of highway, Cohen said, "Stop." It was a steep drop into the woods of the slope.

"I am not an invalid and I am not an old man," Cohen insisted, when Levy suggested that it might be easier for him to make the hike.

"Tell me what you're looking for, I'll look," said Levy, and that only irked Cohen more.

"If I knew what I was looking for," he said, "I wouldn't have to go personally to get it, would I?" He could see the disappointment in Levy's face.

"Look, I'm sorry," said the older detective, "I didn't mean to snap at you. Just do what I told you to do."

"It's just that I want to do something more than fill out forms and take notes. I want to feel I'm doing something that moves the case forward."

"You want to be a cowboy," Cohen snorted, but he quickly changed his tone. "Nissim," he said, as always using the officer's first name to indicate appreciation of Levy, "If you want to help, please, do as I say." Not waiting for Levy's response, he lifted an old strand of barbed wire that had once lined the edge of the small forest and ducked through the gap in the rusting fence.

Levy held a pair of binoculars to his eyes, scanning the view.

It took almost half an hour, but then Cohen appeared in the plaza by the fountain way below. It took several minutes for Levy to make the drive along the ridgetop highway to the Calder stabile overlooking the valley and then down to the fountain. There Levy found Cohen talking with a small boy wearing a red knapsack full of schoolbooks.

"Chief Inspector Levy," said Cohen in a grave official tone that made Levy smile. "I'd like to introduce Mr. Shuki Mizrahi, who has explained to me in great detail how that spring over there has a hidden tunnel. Mr. Mizrahi has visited it on several occasions."

Levy extended his hand to the boy, half his height. The child's eyes widened at the sight of Levy's pistol, a Baretta .22 in a holster tucked into the waistband of Levy's pressed blue jeans.

"Pleased to meet you," said Levy, in a tone as grave and official as Cohen's. The boy proudly extended his own hand and they shook.

"Mr. Mizrahi has helped me in my inquiries," said Cohen. "He says that he has found things back there, in that tunnel. He said he once found an old knife back there."

"Really?" said Levy, impressed. "Well, we'll have to take a look, won't we, sir?" Levy climbed onto the wall surrounding the fountain and worked his way around the pool until he could duck his head into the marble shelf that led into a cave behind the fountain spout. He jumped lightly down and went to the car, from which he took a flashlight. Cohen and the boy watched.

For a few moments they could see the light's reflection on the dark waters in the pool, but then the tunnel must have taken a turn, for there was sudden darkness.

"I only go in there with my father," the boy said soberly.

"I can understand that," said Cohen. "It must be scary."

"A little, a little scary. But with my father it's okay."

Levy came out after five minutes. "It goes for about thirty meters but becomes too small for somebody my size to go any farther."

His sneakers and trousers were soaked dark with water. "There are ledges. And there are things. A doll. An empty packet of cigarettes. People have scratched their names into the walls. A few different languages. No knives."

Cohen turned to the boy. For a moment, the boy thought the detective was going to be mad. "Well, you can't always be lucky, can you?" said Cohen, and he smiled as he reached out his hand to shake with the boy.

"I once guessed twelve games right in the football pool," said the boy. "That was lucky. My father put the money in the bank, and when I finish the army I'll be able to go to the university."

"Yes, that was lucky," said Cohen. "I never get more than five or six games right." There was a pause, and then the boy stuck out his hand to shake with Levy and Cohen in return.

"Well, we have to go," said Cohen. "Thank you for your help."

"No problem," said the boy, his cockiness making Levy grin.

The boy watched as they got in the car and drove away. Then he walked toward his house, a rambling stone building shared by three families, a few doors down from the grocery store.

Neither the boy nor Cohen nor Levy could see the goateed man wearing a golden-green velvet embroidered vest over his bare chest. He had watched them through the thick white and pink blossoms of the oleander bushes that walled off the Ein Kerem inn next to the spring. He had no trouble seeing them.

13

COHEN WORKED THROUGH THE REST of the day and night at his desk, first reading from the files and studying the skimpy paperwork on Alex that Shmulik finally sent over. There was nothing particularly revealing, except for one date that sent Cohen scrambling backwards to the first folder: the visa applications for residency of the two nuns.

It wasn't merely that Alex and the girl had arrived in the same year. They had arrived on the same flight.

But the information was not enough, not anything more than a bureaucratic convenience—"Moscow got a package deal from its travel agent," Shmulik had scrawled on the notepaper clipped to the file, with an additional P.S. apologizing for the delay in transferring the documents.

Cohen grumbled as he tore off the note and began reading. At midnight, he got a second wind and continued plowing through the case files, signing what he had to sign, notating detectives' reports and sending them back for further action. He had a bottle of cognac in the lower left-hand drawer, and by 2:00 A.M. he had drunk three short glasses and opened his third pack of cigarettes of the day.

By 3:00 he was leaning back in his oddly tilted chair, asleep.

The phone rang at exactly 5:45, Cohen made a note of it, as soon as he began to absorb the message coming from the other end of the line: "There's been another knifing," said Rotem, the dispatcher, calling from the basement switchboard of the police station.

"Where?"

"A used-book store, off the Ben-Yehuda promenade," Rotem said, "Dorot Rishonim street."

"I know the place," Cohen barked back, shaking off the sleep by raising his voice. "Send a unit, get Levy on the phone, I'll be on channel four," he commanded, grabbing the walkie-talkie from its recharger on the shelf beside his desk. "I'm on my way there."

It was a three minute drive, including the time it took for the cold engine to start. At the bookstore, he found the white-haired woman who ran it waiting for him.

"You there," she commanded as soon as he opened the door. "Are you the police?"

"Yes, I am," said Cohen.

"Extraordinary," said the woman. "All these years I hear from people that our police are not very quick. Finally I call the police about something, and look how quickly you arrive. Marvelous."

"I understand that . . ."

"Yes, right over here, come, look. I have seen many people die and I have seen many people die terribly, but I have never seen anything like this," said the woman. "I was in the Battle of Britain, you see. We were lucky, we got out of Poland. And then here, all the wars here. You remember the bicycle bomb? It was right over there," she said, pointing like a tourist guide to the café at the end of the street where a bicycle packed with explosive in its frame had exploded three years before. "It was also terrible. But nothing like this. Remarkable."

Cohen wasn't shocked by her patter. Many in Jerusalem had a familiarity with violent death. But Cohen had no time for the woman's memoirs.

"My good lady," he said, using a formal expression that he intuitively knew she would appreciate. "If you could please show me . . ."

"Yes, of course, of course," the woman said, flattered by the officer's respect, oblivious to the slight tone of mockery that tinged Cohen's address. "Of course, please come." She led him out the door. "Right over there," she said, pointing. Cohen's eyes followed her finger.

It would have been easy to miss, perhaps just a pile of old clothing discarded in the alley between two Jerusalem buildings, beside the trash containers. An old overcoat, two plastic bags stuffed with other plastic bags beside it. But as Cohen approached, he could see the blood, and when he bent over the gray shapeless form, he could see how even a woman who had survived the Battle of Britain and a bombing that killed six could have regarded it as remarkable.

The face had been slashed over and over again, the nose practically cut off, the throat cut, the eyes punctured, the whole face a mass of cuts. The overcoat, too, was cut and slashed, but as Cohen looked without touching, he noticed that none of the cuts went very deep. The beggar had bled to death, Cohen guessed.

"Every day," the woman was saying, "every day I gave him a black bread and yellow cheese sandwich. For years, really, for years. And you know, I don't even know his name. Nothing about him. Nothing at all. Really, astonishing."

Cohen heard it all and nothing, his eyes taking in the sight, his ears hearing her words, but his mind thinking back to those lost years when he had seen people turn into the most brutal killers imaginable, all for the sake of a bowl of soup made from rotten potatoes. He stood, staring down at the slashed face, looking into his own past.

The siren of the patrol car on its way began to echo down the canyon of the promenade, and with its gradual approach, Cohen, too, returned to the scene. He could hear windows opening in the few residential flats in the upper stories of the mostly commercial neighborhood.

Levy showed up a moment after the patrol car. He was dressed in a sweat suit and woolen slippers that zipped up the front.

"He was a beggar," the woman was saying. "You know how beggars can be. I don't know why he chose my alleyway," the woman was saying, her babbling voice suddenly disgusting Cohen.

"I want the body out of here as quickly as possible, and I want an autopsy by this afternoon," he said. "If there's not enough time for Raoul to be up here within the hour, I'd just as soon one of the hospital pathologists does it."

"They'll bill us, through the fifth floor," Levy warned, "and we're not even halfway through the year," he added, fulfilling his most important function for Cohen—reminding him of bureaucratic constraints.

"Make whatever arrangements to get the autopsy report on my desk by four o'clock this afternoon," Cohen insisted. Then turning to the woman, who was explaining to the patrolman how she had heard the police never arrived when they are needed, Cohen introduced Levy. "He'll take your statement," he said.

He tossed Levy one of his quick grins and left on foot, walking back to the office. If someone had asked him right then what he was thinking, he would only have been able to say, "I'm confused."

Stabbings were relatively rare in Jerusalem.

In the Old City, a year before, there had been a stabber, an Arab who struck from behind, targeting religious Jews or tourists, motivated by hatred. He was caught after three victims by some of Shmulik's men who were working on a case involving an Islamic fundamentalist cell.

Now, in less than a week, there had been three stabbing victims. The nuns were murdered with strong, single strokes. The beggar was also murdered with a knife, but Cohen's cursory inspection of the body assured him that the wounds were inflicted by someone much weaker than the murderer of the nuns.

It didn't feel right, it didn't look right. There was no match between the two killings. Yet the fact of the knife gave him no choice but to link the two cases in his mind.

He started a new yellow folder with this notation: One thing was clear, "the killer of the beggar wanted to make sure that the dead man was unrecognizable."

Hours later, when Levy finally hand delivered an autopsy report prepared by a pathologist at Shaare Zedek hospital, Cohen sent his assistant to Yad Vashem, the Holocaust research institute overlooking Ein Kerem from the north, for help. The only identification found on the body was a concentration camp tattoo number, differing from Cohen's own by 10,000 numbers in the serial. Another Holocaust survivor might have been able to decipher the number's secret, known the code, and been able to say when and where the person had been tagged by the Nazis. But Cohen had never wanted to know more about the camps and their systems than what he had learned while he was in them.

At Yad Vashem, Levy sat with a sweet-smelling Danish convert who had taken the name Rachel. They poured over tomes of names and numbers, lists both handwritten and computerized. By the time they had determined that the beggar had probably survived Birkenau—a lead that could be followed up amongst survivors' organizations—Levy decided he preferred to know a lot more about the girl who had given up the Danish farm country to join the Jewish people than he wanted to know about the camps.

14

ONE OF MEA SHEARIM'S nameless beggars slipped quietly out of the neighborhood and headed toward the *Kotel*, the Western Wall. The man appeared to be one of the many poor men who wandered the alleyways of the small *shuk* beyond Agadot Shlomo, the bastion of Jerusalem's most militant *haredim*, the most orthodox of Judaism's believers, the most zealous in their protection of their traditions. His black overcoat was dusty and his black trousers tied with a rope at the waist. He wore sneakers, in the fashion of religious Jews at Yom Kippur, when they are in repentance, denying themselves the luxuries of leatherwear. His hat was cocked on the back of his shaven head, and he strode quickly down the Street of the Prophets, through the Damascus Gate into the Old City. To any Jerusalemite he was just another of the pious, on his way to prayers at the foot of the ancient remains of the Temple.

But the beggar was Daniel, Cohen's spy in Mea Shearim. He had grown up in the *haredi* world of the mystic city of Safed in Galilee. He was one of the few who had given up the security of absolute religion after being born into it. In the Holy Land, many more streamed toward God than away. When Cohen had heard about the new recruit's background, he immediately adopted him as a student and follower, combining a paternal attitude with the knowledge that Daniel could fit in perfectly as an undercover informant inside the *haredi* world. The religious world wrapped newcomers with warmth, giving them direction. But for those who left the religious world, life could be lonely, as their families turned their backs on the skeptics. So Cohen did everything to make Daniel feel appreciated and handled him directly instead of assigning him to another senior officer.

Daniel's job was to keep Cohen informed of the goings on in the neighborhood. His reports were always brief, usually concerning demonstrations being planned or a new conflict between one or more neighborhood factions. In Mea Shearim, 200-year-old theological debates had a way of transforming themselves into fisticuffs and riots, pitched battles between the followers of various rabbis with differing interpretations of the same Talmudic passage.

Sometimes Daniel would be able to tell Cohen in advance about these impending battles. Sometimes he'd report on a rare moment of unity when the entire *haredi* community—growing faster than any of the other demographic tiles in the city's mosaic—was likely to join forces for a demonstration against the secular forces in the holy city. Daniel knew of protests against restaurants open on Friday nights, actions against boutiques selling indecent women's clothing too close to Mea Shearim, and attacks on movie theaters where the *haredim* believed the Biblical injunctions against graven images and adultery were brazenly broken in public. An aged rabbi's mumbled mention of such "abominations" often resulted in arson, a smashing of shop windows, or a sudden demonstration by hundreds of angry yeshiva students. Often Daniel could name the person behind the action—though no rabbis would likely ever be arrested for incitement or conspiracy as long as the Aguda wielded its political power.

Cohen's information from the secretive neighborhood hidden in its own courtyards reached him on those alternate Sunday mornings when he would meet Daniel at their usual place, a tiny landing in a dead-end flight of stairs just off an alley halfway between the Damascus Gate, the Old City entrance closest to Mea Shearim, and the *Kotel,* the last remnant of the First and Second Temples.

Cohen and Levy waited almost twenty minutes before the beggar appeared on the landing. Usually he would smile when he saw Cohen and Levy waiting. But on this Sunday morning, his face was troubled, his eyes shadowed by sleeplessness.

"You have to get me out of there," Daniel said, even before he reached the landing where Cohen and Levy were waiting.

"Easy, easy," said Cohen, "what happened?"

"My father, my father is in the neighborhood," said Daniel, his voice tight and tense. When Daniel cut off his *payot* sidelocks, a sign that he no longer was able to work the tension of his doubts into a greater faith in the existence of God, his father had sat in mourning for seven days, burying his son in his mind. Cohen immediately understood Daniel's anxiety.

"Has he seen you?"

"No. But I've seen him and I want out. Now. If he sees me, he'll never be able to understand . . ."

"Why is he here? In Jerusalem?"

"I don't know, but he's here. He's studying at the Ungrin Kollel."

Cohen knew the yeshiva, a large rambling building overlooking the main intersection of Mea Shearim. The place was known as Shabbat Square, named for all the demonstrations and riots that the *haredi* community had held there to protest sabbath violations sanctioned or condoned by the secular authorities of Jerusalem.

Cohen looked at Daniel for a moment and then turned to Levy waiting on a step below the landing of the alley. The early spring *hamsin*—the heated wind from the east—was dry, parching his lips. "Nissim," he asked, "would you mind getting us something cold to drink?" He knew Levy would mind, but he ignored the flash of resentment in his lieutenant's eyes. He wanted a few moments alone with Daniel.

"Now," said Cohen, turning back to Daniel, "will he recognize you?"

"Yes. No. I don't know. It's enough I recognized him. If he sees me, I don't know, if he sees me and recognizes me . . . I'm not worried about the job. I'm worried for him. If he were to think that I went back, that I am a beggar is bad enough, but that I went back without telling him . . ."

Daniel's words were running ahead of him, his voice was rising and falling in rhythm, in an almost cantorial melody. He looks like he's praying, thought Cohen.

"Okay, okay, relax. Tell me about it," Cohen said.

"You see, don't you? You see what's happening," said Daniel. "I don't know who I am anymore. What's happening to me?"

"You'll be fine," said Cohen. "You've done so well, so well. You've been excellent." He had to keep the man in place, and more, had to keep him motivated. "A little more time, Daniel," he said, trying hard to keep pleading out of his voice. "Just a little more time," he repeated, his voice deliberately low and easy, like a trainer with a thoroughbred. "One special assignment. One more thing to find out. That's all," Cohen said.

Just then he spied Levy at the bottom of the steps, returning with three bottles of orangeade. He signaled Levy with a slight hand motion to stay back.

"I can't," Daniel said, "I'm afraid for my father. If he sees me . . ."

"Have you heard anything about the nuns?" Cohen asked.

"The nuns?"

"The Russian nuns," Cohen said softly. "Maybe Keshet?"

"I've told you about Keshet," Daniel said angrily. "It's a bunch of kids. Kids, like I was a kid, carried away by belief. They hate the *Tzionistim*, the blasphemy of a state without the messiah, so they spray paint on Herzl's grave. They burn a few bus stops. But kill somebody? Cohen, I hate to tell you this, but boys like that couldn't even be in the same room as two nuns. It would be a mortal sin."

"They bombed that kiosk," said Cohen, referring to a Mea Shearim newspaper stand where an elderly man had sold newspapers for years. A year earlier, a Molotov cocktail decimated the shop. Wall posters appeared the next day promising the same punishment to anyone else who dared sell blasphemous Zionist papers. The posters were signed Keshet, an acronym that even Daniel was unable to decipher authoritatively.

"Maybe you're right. I don't know," said Daniel, exasperated by his dilemma, conceding the point. "I'm trying. Really, I'm trying," he insisted, and at that moment, Cohen knew that Daniel was still in place, at least for a little while.

"We want you in there. We need you. You're the boss out there. But give it some more time. Maybe something will turn up. Maybe you'll hear something about Ein Kerem. Dead nuns in Ein

Kerem. Rumors, whispers. Anything." Cohen nodded to Levy to come up the stairs.

Levy offered one bottle to Daniel and passed a second to Cohen. "Now drink," said Cohen, "it will help relax you." For a moment there was silence as all three men drank the too-sweet drink. The silence suddenly brought the bustle of the bazaar a few strides away much closer.

Daniel drained his bottle and then held it to his forehead, as if trying to cool a fever. "There are rumors," he said suddenly. "Not even rumors. People are talking about prophets. False prophets. True prophets."

"Who are these prophets?" Cohen asked.

But Daniel could only shrug. "I don't know yet, but prophecy is not a province of the mortal. Not since the Temple. But there's talk. Of prophets. And sacrifices for purification."

"The red heifer," said Cohen knowingly.

"What's that?" Levy asked.

"The ashes of an unflawed red heifer are used to purify priests," Daniel explained. "It has been forbidden since the days of the Temple."

Levy rolled his eyes. But Cohen understood the significance of such efforts for purification. "Only the pure can build the Temple," he said, thinking aloud. "They're aiming for the Temple. Whoever they are, they're after the Mount."

"I don't know . . ." said Daniel.

"You'll find out," said Cohen with encouragement, hoping to impart confidence without betraying his own uncertainty. "You're the only one who can help us, the only one."

"Okay," said Daniel after a long pause for thought. "But I swear, again I swear to you," he said, clenching the bottle like a weapon in his hand, "if my father sees me, recognizes me, if anything happens to him, I swear to you that will be the last you'll see of me. I'll walk right off the force. I'm not ready to handle that."

"You'll have to talk to him one day," Cohen said gently, "you'll have to try at least."

"Maybe, maybe. You're probably right. I'm just not ready."

"It's up to you. But for now, scour the neighborhood, listen for clues. Anything at all out of the ordinary."

15

FROM THE START, Levy had kept after Cohen, demanding some field assignment of his own. "I need to feel I'm contributing, that I'm doing something of consequence," he insisted.

At first Cohen resisted Levy's requests for field work. "I need you here," Cohen said, tossing another stack of administrative memos into Levy's in tray. "I need your brains." Levy would grumble but give in to Cohen's authority. He juggled manpower schedules and motor pool logs; he read every piece of paper that came into the office before passing it on to Cohen. He was privy to everything except what Cohen kept in his own notebooks and secret from all. But his most important function, as Cohen himself had defined it, was to serve as a buffer between the fifth-floor politicians and Cohen. Levy was Cohen's administrator and excellent at the job. Cohen would soon have to let him go, watch him move upward in the system. But more than ever before in the five years they had worked together, he needed the junior officer at his side.

After the meeting with Daniel, Levy's demands for some field assignment were insurmountable. "All right," Cohen said, giving in early one morning when Levy had proved to him that he had completed all the paperwork for the coming week and was not going to give up. "Here's a list of slaughterhouses that still have to be checked," he said, slapping a sheet of paper onto Levy's desk. "You can do that, but I want you back at this desk as soon as you've finished."

"What if I find our man?" Levy asked with a smile.

"Get out of here," Cohen snapped, but he shot Levy a smile before the inspector headed out the door.

Levy started with the southernmost of the slaughterhouses in the Shuafat industrial zone of north Jerusalem, next to a refugee camp along the highway to Ramallah. The first two yielded nothing. Few of the men had even heard of the murder of the nuns. Those few who had heard of the murders were ignorant of any motive for the murders, let alone possibly a suspect. It was late afternoon when he reached the third slaughterhouse.

He walked with the owner of a meat packing plant through the cold room. At one end of the factory, cows cut in half with huge electric saws hung headless and tail-less from hooks attached to an overhead system of tracks that moved the carcasses around through the factory. Almost all the cutters on the floor were Arabs, mostly residents of the nearby camp. After twenty years of experience with the Israeli cops and other authorities, they had instincts.

Levy was not dressed unusually—sneakers, jeans, a checkered flannel shirt, and a white cotton coat that the factory manager had loaned him before heading onto the noisy cutting floor. The coat hid Levy's gun, a .22 Baretta with eight bullets in the magazine, tucked into the back of his waistband. But word went out in a flash that there was an authority—maybe a policeman, maybe a Shabak man—on the floor. The working men gazed warily as their boss walked through the cold room with the stranger. The beef hanging from the hooks was gathered at one end of the long room, waiting to be pushed down the center aisle through the various work stations. At the sides of the room were the cutting tables where the workers used axes and electric saws and then finally long sharp blades to cut, trim, and slice the meat for packaging.

Levy and the manager passed a long counter where three men were making steaks from large clumps of raw beef. The butchers were quick and graceful with the long thin knives. The shiny blades rose and fell with precision, and Levy was distracted—by the cold, by the manager's droning explanations, by the speed with which they worked. He didn't notice the tall Arab staring at him from the next counter. As Levy watched the steaks flying from the butchers' hands to the plastic sheets in which they were wrapped, the man from the next table moved into the center aisle and started walking quickly away.

"Abed!" one of the other men at the counter shouted out to him. "Come back here. You haven't finished." Abed pointed his thumb to his mouth, a sign that he was going to drink some water. The factory manager turned to see who was shouting, and Levy turned as well.

When Levy turned, Abed panicked and broke into a run. Levy followed, his right arm already reaching for his gun. "Call the police," Levy shouted, "ask for Commander Cohen," he yelled as he followed Abed behind a row of hanging beef. The man was tall, much taller than Levy, who was slender and agile. And the butcher had the advantage of surprise and knowledge of the slaughterhouse floor plan from the very start of the chase.

After a few quick turns through the rows of meat, Levy realized that the big man with the knife in his hand had disappeared. Shoving aside another heavy carcass, Levy spotted a door made of three sheets of thick vinyl. Pushing through it into the bright sun and the sun's shocking heat, he saw no sign of Abed. Then he sensed something and turned. He caught sight of his prey ducking behind a large shed at the end of the loading ramp.

Levy ran down the empty dock, his gun drawn, his breath short and painful. Within seconds, he was slowly inching around a corner of the shed. But Abed had moved to the field beyond, a long upward slope of brush and rock. Beyond the ridge, Levy knew, was the refugee camp, a maze of adobe and tin where the butcher could easily disappear. Levy ran.

Abed stumbled twice. Each time Levy was able to gain slightly. Finally they faced each other at the lip of the hill where it plunged into a steep drop. Beyond, Levy could see the camp. He could see the knife in Abed's hand. Levy had the Baretta, a small handgun with a small caliber. Beyond Abed, Levy could see some children playing with slingshots, aiming at a lonely tree on the hilly slope, and he worried that if he had to shoot, a stray bullet might hit one of the children.

"Why. Did. You. Run?" Levy gasped, each word coming out separately, slowly.

Far beneath them, a police car and a Border Patrol jeep pulled into the parking lot. The plant manager pointed up the hill, shouting.

"In blood and fire I redeem Falastin," Abed shouted, lunging at Levy. The policeman fired three quick shots into Abed's belly, but the butcher didn't stop. Levy backpedaled, taking aim and firing another shot into the Arab's leg. Still the Arab advanced, knife aloft.

Once more Levy fired, trying to take aim at the butcher's knee as he ran backwards. He stepped back one more time, tripping. Abed's shadow fell over his face. The detective fired a final shot and immediately on hitting the ground, tried to roll aside.

Another shot fired. Abed's head exploded. His body fell directly onto Levy, the knife plunging deep into the detective's shoulder, a few centimeters from Levy's throat.

He woke in the hospital, Cohen sitting in a chair at the side of his bed. There was a yellow case folder on Cohen's lap.

"How long have I been out?" Levy asked.

"A couple of hours," Cohen said. "You need a bigger gun," he added with a gruff smile.

"Now you tell me," Levy said, wincing with pain as he tried to sit up. "What happened? I shot at him and he kept on coming. I thought I was about to die. Why did he run? Who was he? Was he the one? What happened?"

"Now you see why I wanted you at your desk?" Cohen said, ignoring the questions for the moment.

"It wasn't my fault," Levy said with defensive anger. "I shot him three times."

"Four," Cohen said, automatically correcting the junior officer.

"Three, four, what does it matter? Was it him? Is he the one?" Cohen shook his head.

"So? Why did he run?"

"PFLP. A member of a cell. At least that's what Shmulik says. He panicked," said Cohen. "He thought you were some kind of cowboy. He didn't know you're better with a pen than with a gun."

Levy closed his eyes, once again disappointed by Cohen.

There was a brief silence. Then Cohen spoke again. "One of

the Border Patrolmen finally took him down," he explained. "But he fell on top of you."

Levy's eyes opened, and he glared at Cohen. "It wasn't my fault," he insisted. "He started to run, and I assumed . . ."

Cohen nodded. "You assumed. That's the point. That's what I've been trying to tell you all along. You can't assume."

Levy began to protest again, but Cohen held up his hand. "You did it right. You did fine. But now you're going to be out for a while. And I needed you." It was an admission difficult for Cohen to make. "Yes, I needed you. In the office. Not in the hospital. But you had to be a hero. A cowboy. I don't need cowboys. I have plenty of cowboys. Too many, if you ask me. I need you for your brains, for your ideas, for your . . ."

"Administrative abilities," Levy interrupted, with sarcasm.

"That's right," said Cohen, angrily, "that's right." He paused for a moment, and then, half to himself and half to Levy, he muttered, "I knew I shouldn't have let you go out there. Certainly not alone."

"I'm not complaining," Levy said.

"I know," Cohen said gently. It was as close as he could get to conceding his affection for Levy. He admired the young officer's effort, even if he had distaste for the calculated personal ambition that motivated it. Cohen had never sought promotion. It was the outcome of his efforts, not his goal. But Levy was of the new generation. He had a career, not a calling, and sometimes Cohen thought that in that distinction between his view and Levy's was both the success and failure of Zionism.

Levy struggled to sit up. His shoulder was wrapped in a tight bandage, and his arm was in a sling. In his every movement, Cohen could see flashes of pain cross Levy's face. He moved to help him.

"I can manage," Levy insisted, trying to maintain his dignity.

"Sit still," Cohen ordered.

"I have to get out of here," Levy shot back. "I have paperwork to do," he added bitterly.

Cohen suddenly felt like laughing, enjoying Levy's stubbornness. Instead he repeated his order for Levy to sit still. This time he didn't know if it was the pain or his command that made Levy obey, but he suspected Levy was secretly grateful for the order to sit still. The doctors had told Cohen that Abed's knife had grazed the collarbone, and Cohen knew about the pain of damaged bones.

He moved to the end of the bed. On a low table beyond Levy's eyesight, he picked up the bouquet of flowers he had bought in the lobby. He shrugged, embarrassed, as he showed his offering to Levy and looked around for something to put them in.

Levy shook his head, discovering that the motion caused pain to soar along his shoulder and up his neck. "Have the nurse give them to someone who doesn't get visitors," he weakly told Cohen.

Cohen grinned. "Sure. Why not. Listen, I've got to go. The weekly *intifada* meeting." It was a staff meeting of the top brass in Jerusalem to discuss strategies and tactics against the rioting. Levy usually attended as a stand-in for Cohen, who from the start hated the endless sessions that inevitably ended with a speech by Abulafia about how if the army had taken real action right from the start, the uprising would have been over before it even started. Cohen's attendance was not really necessary, but it was as good an excuse as any to get out of the hospital room, to get away from the embarrassment of his feelings toward Levy.

Levy smiled, telling Cohen that the minutes from the last *intifada* meeting were in the top right desk drawer. Cohen realized that Levy was helping him in the pretense of getting to the meeting in time.

"Don't worry about it now," said Cohen. "Get your rest. I'll be back to visit tomorrow."

"Do me a favor," said Levy as his boss reached the door to the room. Cohen expected a crack, but Levy's expression was serious. "Call my flat. Let Rachel know where I am."

"You didn't tell me she's staying in your place," Cohen said, surprised.

"I'm allowed secrets, too," Levy said, beaming as he finally closed his eyes to rest.

16

COHEN INVENTED AN EXCUSE to get out of the *intifada* meeting before Abulafia's usual fire-breathing speech. An hour later he met with Shmulik in a small garden restaurant hidden behind a stone wall, a block from the prime minister's residence in Talbieh. They often met there to sit over coffee, sharing information, bemoaning what they knew or didn't know.

Shmulik had already ordered coffee when Cohen arrived. Shmulik signaled to the barman to bring another longo, the local slang for a double espresso.

"How's your man?" Shmulik asked, already informed about the incident in Shuafat.

"Tough enough," said Cohen, "He's more serious than the wound." It was the highest compliment of all in the security services. To be called "not serious" was the worst insult.

"And you?" Shmulik asked.

"Fine, fine," said Cohen, automatically.

The waiter brought the coffee.

"I wanted you to see that they got results," Shmulik continued, and Cohen knew he was talking about the Twins.

Cohen started to protest.

"Now wait, don't get me wrong," Shmulik continued. "I don't want torture and I don't want beatings or cold showers in the middle of winter. I don't like seeing my men standing like effendis over a row of squatting men. But it's not the same anymore, it's not the way it used to be. It's twenty years we're out there," he said, raising his arm and pointing out the front door of the open restaurant, eastward toward the Old City walls and beyond to the territories. "And we've been to Lebanon and back. Times have changed. We've changed."

Slam went Cohen's hand on the table. "Don't lecture me," he ordered. Shmulik was startled by Cohen's reaction. "Don't start lecturing me on what's changed. I know what's changed. We've got Jewish terrorists at work now."

"We don't know that for sure."

"Don't kid yourself, Shmulik. Don't kid yourself," Cohen shot back.

Shmulik sighed. "You've changed," he said.

"What are you talking about?" Cohen snapped.

"I don't know. Something's changed in you. You're blaming the politicians, for one thing. You used to just call them bloody names and that was it. Now you blame them as if *they're* the criminals. And something else. I think you're afraid of something. I've never known you to be afraid of anything."

When Cohen didn't deny it, Shmulik bore in. "That's it, isn't it? You're afraid of something. What is it? What?"

"I'm afraid of us," Cohen snarled. "Of what we're becoming. Abulafia wants a tank. Can you believe it? He wants to put a tank at the entrance to the Damascus Gate. But I don't know why I'm surprised. I saw the PM. If the PM's in that kind of condition, why shouldn't the chief of police in Jerusalem think he can solve his problems with a tank. And you. You know about the PM but you aren't telling anyone. A great secret-keeper you are. All the state secrets in your head, including the biggest secret of all. The prime minister's catatonic."

"Avram, I'm warning you, he's not out of it. Not at all. You'll find out soon enough, if you keep this up."

"Keep what up?"

"Raving and ranting about the politicians."

Cohen scowled. "Why? They aren't exactly grooming me for the fifth floor, are they?"

"They won't if you start talking about Jewish terrorists. Anyway, you wouldn't take it if they offered it to you on a silver platter," Shmulik said mockingly but with respect.

Cohen shook a smile away. "That's not the point. The point is that they're not exactly doing everything in their power to calm things down."

"They're our masters."

Cohen fell silent for a moment. A pair of young tourists, who Cohen guessed were newlyweds, held hands across the table on the other side of the restaurant. He thought of Ahuva at her conference in New York and hoped she would call soon.

Shmulik interrupted his thoughts. "You buy that syndrome story. As if it was our fault," said the Shabak officer.

Cohen closed his eyes, leaning back to let the midday sun warm his face. "Everybody wants the city, and nobody likes the fact that the Jews have it. The churches don't like it, the Americans don't like it, the Arabs and the Russians, everyone doesn't like the idea that Jews have the city." He opened his eyes. "Our masters. Ha! They'd let the city explode rather than give up their ideologies—or their seats in the cabinet room."

"Now look who's lecturing," said Shmulik.

Cohen conceded to Shmulik's reprimand and moved the conversation to its real purpose—dealing. "I've heard the Russians are going to bring up the nuns in the Security Council." It was a bare hint of information, which he expected Shmulik already knew. But it was the kind of hint that indicated Cohen knew more, and in their relationship, information was the most important kind of help each could provide the other for what still remained their common cause—the peace of the city.

Shmulik thought for a moment and then made his own offer. "I'm not supposed to tell you this. We don't think it's KGB. We have them covered, and we haven't got anything to show that they had any reason to go after the nuns," said Shmulik. "So, we're working on the cousins," he said, using the slang that came out of the Biblical story of Abraham and his sons, to refer to the Arabs. "Maybe fundamentalists, maybe PLO. But not the Russians. Believe me."

Cohen sighed, mumbling to himself, "Belief without knowledge."

"What's that?" asked Shmulik.

"Nothing, nothing," said Cohen, shaking his head.

"I sent you my file on Alex," Shmulik said, conciliatory.

"It's not very helpful," Cohen said, "just some Interior Ministry documentation about his arrival, a couple of early reports following him. Not much else," said Cohen. "But I happen to know that you've put some watchers on him," he added, "and were planning to tell me something." He smiled at Shmulik after laying down the card.

"There's nothing to tell," Shmulik insisted. "He doesn't seem to do very much. He hasn't done anything extraordinary since the murders. The same as always. He keeps track of the Soviet citizens here, the clergymen, a few others whom we also keep our eyes on. Maybe, and this is a big maybe, he has contacts with agents planted among the immigrants. But we haven't found anything of that sort. He stays out of the territories. He's never been spotted anywhere east of the Green Line. I'm telling you, the KGB worries are a little overblown," Shmulik explained. "The Russians learned from the Americans. They use technology. Ships, satellites. True, they've always had their moles here, and we've always somehow managed to uncover them. Sometimes in time, sometimes too late. But we find them. No, they wouldn't use Alex for spying. He's a babysitter, that's all. Maybe a dangerous baby-sitter for his wards, but a baby-sitter. Nothing more. Anyway, it's the Americans who have the most activity. They go wherever they want and find anything they want to know, they throw a party and get a couple of ministers drunk. And Alex? Since the murders, he's been either in the convent or at the mission offices. Nowhere else."

"So why's the PM pressing so hard?" Cohen pressed. "There must be more to it than diplomatic maneuvering."

Shmulik shrugged, and for the second time in less than a week, Cohen found himself wondering if Shmulik's silence was a result of ignorance or a secret that Cohen was not supposed to know.

Cohen leaned across the table, grim and purposeful. "There's something strange about this Alex. You can't tell me that a KGB officer posted alone, abroad, wouldn't do his own investigation. If you ask me, that's what's suspicious. And I'll tell you something else, if the PM's office is wondering about the KGB, for whatever reason, I'll wonder about the KGB."

Shmulik laughed. "And you're the one who says, 'Fuck the bloody politicians.' "

"Yeah, fuck 'em," said Cohen. "Before they fuck you." He

poured the last dregs of the coffee down his throat. "Look, all I'm asking is for anything you have about Russian and Arab contacts that are relevant. I'll offer a deal. It's what we do best, isn't it Shmule?" There was a sardonic trace in his voice. "So here's my deal. You guys turn up a *shtinker* who can tell us something, even if it's something that proves that Abed or any other Arab or Russian had nothing to do with it, and I'll owe you."

"What can you do for me?" Shmulik interrupted cynically. Automatically, Cohen's reports went to the services, but it was largess on Shmulik's part to send Cohen copies of the reports that Shmulik thought might interest Cohen.

Cohen had one card to play and had to be careful. "It's what I won't do."

Shmulik fell silent for a long pause. Cohen watched him, knowing what was going through his mind. The threat was to do what the Shabak hated more than anything else: to violate the secrecy that veiled their entire operation. Military censorship and the intelligence service's inherent distrust of the press kept almost any mention of the service out of the newspapers.

Shmulik slowly raised his coffee cup. It was empty, and he put it down with a scowl. "You're playing a dangerous game, Avram. You're ready to expose us for what? For two dead nuns? I can't believe Avram Cohen would do anything to threaten state security."

"I don't want to, Shmule," Cohen said sincerely, "but I need help and I'll do whatever it takes to get that help. Besides, state security has nothing to do with some of the things I know. You want an example, I'll give you an example. What does state security have to do with the Shabak protecting the biggest hashish producer in south Lebanon?"

Shmulik shot back. "He's powerful. And his enemies are our enemies. He's well-informed. We need the information. It's that simple. You used to understand such things."

"No," said Cohen emphatically. "Such things didn't exist before. I didn't have to understand them."

"It's a dangerous game you're playing," Shmulik repeated.

"We've been playing dangerous games for years, haven't we Shmule?" Cohen said. He stubbed out his fifth cigarette since his first sip of the coffee, waiting for Shmulik's response.

"All right," the Shabak officer conceded, "I'll press on the espionage angle. I thought we were on track of all the Soviet agents at work. Maybe we missed something. But these things take time. And they have to be done delicately."

"That will be my problem," said Cohen, rising from the table. "Just help me out when I need it. That's all. You know I'd do the same for you. After all, what are friends for?"

Shmulik smiled. For a moment, Cohen remembered the Shabak officer's first year as the agency's Jerusalem commander. They had spent hours together, Cohen as teacher, Shmulik as student. Those days were over, too, thought Cohen. As they left the restaurant, Cohen turned down Shmulik's offer of a ride.

He preferred to walk, down Talbieh's tree-shaded streets, into the brightness of Liberty Bell Garden, and then back into shade on the tiny dead-end street off Emek Refa'im where he lived in the Germany Colony.

He needed sleep. An hour, maybe two, he thought, as he walked into his apartment, turned on the *Requiem* on the stereo and went to the bedroom. He wasn't sure whether he could smell Ahuva's perfume or maybe it was his memory of the perfume, but that's what he was dreaming of when he awoke in the deep darkness of night, alone in his flat, with only a distant siren to punctuate the sound of his speeding heartbeat.

17

AT THE FULL MOON, there are special prayers to be said to thank the Lord for the cycle of seasons. But for a small band of men in pure linen robes and slippers made of sheepskin, the full moon required more than special prayers.

Their rabbi's lessons were full of promises about their election to the priesthood of the Temple. They were the select, and they followed him, a blind man whom they trusted implicitly.

He had been teaching them for years, and they learned his lessons well—there was little else to do in the jail cells that he now called his years of blossoming in the desert. Some had been with him in that desert and knew by heart his words.

"I was blind though I had eyes before I was taken. And even while I lost my eyes inside that place, I learned to see."

Others had found him there and in his sightless eyes had seen their reflection, finding meaning in his echoing words.

Now there were almost twenty, and all knew his directions: *"Beyond the spring of the vineyard, below the pilgrims' press. Above the grove of the prophet, behind the branch of the bay."*

So they followed the passage, taking turns leading the goat, and went out to their hilltop for prayers and his commentaries, listening to his promises of coming glory, first standing and then sitting, first together and then apart.

As always, a bonfire began the evening outside the cave that held their greatest secrets. The teacher spoke of the abomination that prevented the descent of the Lord's palace. He spoke of the Lord's messenger and the salvation of the message. And when the time came, he pulled the curved knife from a hidden pocket inside his robe, a signal that the goat's time had come.

It was just before dawn, and the honor of holding the goat for the prophet's knife had fallen to a young man with a pox-scarred face and teeth yellowed by smoke. The teacher clutched the knife in one hand and raised the other heavenward, as the bleating goat was forced to its knees before him.

"*You see,*" he sang out, at just the instant that the first brightness of the sun rose over the farthest hilltop, and the city shone and glimmered on the distant peak. The knife flashed in the same shock of light, and the blood sprayed from the severed throat— the bleating turned into gargling. The teacher rose up, and two men lifted the dead animal, tossing it onto the flames. Soon the smell of cooking flesh billowed with the clouds of smoke.

"*You see now, and you shall one day see from here, the permanence of that light. For the Temple will be God's dwelling, and you shall be his servants, living in that infinite glory. We are the chosen ones, and we shall lead the way. Let this beast be a symbol of the sacrifices we are preparing to make for that cause.*"

It was a prayer they would keep in their hearts, a secret that they would preserve. For he had taught that prayers could be made to materialize, that even the blind could see. It was the new month, and they began their walk back to the city with their faces shielded by the hoods, lest their eyes look into the newborn sun.

Shortly after they were gone, a man in a green-gold vest and carrying an empty sack over his shoulder stepped into the clearing where they had prayed. He kicked at the bloated body of the dead animal lying in the dying embers. The black form of the beast disintegrated into ashes.

Then he turned and walked through the clearing in the olive grove terrace below the hill's ridge. He shoved aside a large thick branch of bay, revealing the opening of a cave. After a few minutes he came out, the sack weighed down by its contents.

18

THE BURDEN GREW LARGER. Every night, Cohen read from the yellow folders until the sun came up. The files contained the Twins' report on Goldstein; a thick sheaf of flimsy bureaucratic forms describing the prison and psychiatric hospital release suspects who had already been checked; photographs from the funeral, autopsy reports, photographs of the scene of the crime, the nuns' passports, a fingerprint chart, photos of the bloody footprint, the scrap of letter found under the bed.

The other files on Cohen's desk also were growing fat. Sheets of paper as flimsy as the information they contained, were laced into the fat folders titled "Sidra 13." Cohen's detectives had interviewed nearly three hundred people, and Ehud's memos kept arriving with more names of people to be questioned.

On each page of each folder, Cohen's initials were carefully inscribed in the lower corner, with the date of the signature indicating the time of arrival of the information. Other pages in the folders were filled with Cohen's exacting script in the black ink from the fountain pen Ahuva had given him years before. She was his lover, his friend, and she was still far away. He missed her comforting touch, he missed their oasis in the night.

When those long nights of loneliness would end near dawn and the handwritten files would begin to look more like Sanskrit than Hebrew, Cohen would allow himself sleep, knowing that Rutie, his secretary, would wake him when she came into the office.

Paper was the great rationalizer of the system, which had turned creaky and cranky, a morass of bureaucratic entanglement. Cohen had endless patience for the paper of the files and almost none for the administrative work.

Cohen knocked at his junior officer's door on the fourth floor of an undistinguished Kiryat Yovel apartment building.

"You can work with your arm in a sling," Cohen said gruffly, offering Levy a plastic bag when the junior officer opened the door.

Levy chuckled, taking the bag without asking what was inside. "I was due back tomorrow," he said.

"Well, are you inviting me in?" Cohen asked, with mock offense taken at Levy's lack of hospitality.

Levy backed away from the door and pointed to an old metal cot with sagging springs that was covered by an Indian batik. "If it's comfortable for you," he offered Cohen.

They were needling each other deliberately but with an affection that neither could admit directly to each other.

"I haven't been here since you moved in," Cohen admitted, trying to find a comfortable position on the cot.

"That's okay," said Levy, softened by the same realization. "It makes the visit special."

Cohen grinned quickly at Levy and then fell silent as he looked around the room.

"So, when do we go after Alex?" Levy continued, putting Cohen's plastic bag on a red-painted packing crate serving as a coffee table.

"You're not doing anything about Alex. You'll be desk-bound for a while."

Levy pouted momentarily. And then his eyes fell on the bag.

"The paperwork is driving me crazy," Cohen admitted.

Levy laughed. Cohen opened the plastic bag he had carried from the car and pulled out a sheaf of the mimeographed administrative memos from national headquarters. They sat on the sofa, across from a wall decorated with inexpensive prints of Israeli art. Levy's books from his on-again off-again studies for a law degree were lined up neatly on a single shelf that ran completely around the room at eye level. It's a student's flat, Cohen thought, and he had no doubt that in the refrigerator there was not much more than the milk needed for the bad instant coffee that Levy offered.

Cohen rose with difficulty from the low sofa, to go to the toilet. On the way, he glanced down the narrow corridor through the open door of Levy's bedroom. On the way out, he went into the kitchen to pour a glass of water—and check the refrigerator.

When he came out of the kitchen he was smiling. "I see she's brought more than a brassiere. You actually have some food in the fridge."

Levy blushed, looking up from the papers. "Is that a hint? Are you hungry?"

"I wouldn't let you cook for me even if you were in perfect condition," Cohen chuckled. "There's no need to be embarrassed," he added.

"I don't know. I like her. She's serious."

"Yes, I know about that," Cohen said, aware as he said it that his voice carried a sadness that he didn't want to explain to Levy, who knew about Cohen's relationship with Ahuva but never spoke of it. "Look, I have to get going," he said, suddenly businesslike. "You can bring those in tomorrow morning."

"I'll have them ready by tonight," Levy offered, recognizing the shift in tone and subject as a camouflage of Cohen's feelings. "They're easy. Manpower is asking about overtime shifts, and the quartermaster's office wants a report on repairs made to equipment. The evidence storeroom is asking for a weekly signed confirmation from you that you still have items in your safe. There's a list here. I guess you'll have to do that yourself," he said, handing the memo to Cohen. "But the rest is no problem."

"Thanks," Cohen said.

"That's okay. It's the job."

Cohen was embarrassed. "Look . . ."

"No, it's okay. But I wanted to ask you something."

Cohen nodded.

"Are you planning to put Shvilli undercover in the convent?"

Cohen laughed out loud. "You see why I need you beside me," he said. "You know what I'm doing before I do it."

"I would have wanted to go in there."

"You wouldn't have been any help inside there. You don't know Russian, and Alex has seen you. It would be stupid to put you in there."

"Yes, well, I know that, I understand that. I just wanted you to know that I understand."

"It's all right, Nissim, really. Look, we'll see how things go. Maybe you'll get your field work. Maybe. But meanwhile . . ."

Levy held up the sheaf of papers. "Yes, I know," he said, "by seven tonight. You come back for them and we'll have dinner. The three of us. Rachel does know how to cook."

"There are some beautiful avocados in there," Cohen admitted. But then he added, "I'll have to see how it goes. Ehud's promised some names from units that were in Lebanon with those last 1,000 grenades. I want to go over the list."

"Call if you can make it. But I'll have this ready by seven tonight."

"So it's done by the time Rachel gets back from work," Cohen guessed.

Levy was still smiling as Cohen closed the door.

19

THE PRESS LEAKS were from national headquarters, reported carefully in the serious press and badly in the tabloids. One report said that the inspector general had already picked a new, fifth-floor investigating team to take over the case. Cohen had to interpret the news reports, for he had heard nothing directly about new staffing from national headquarters and had not been called back to the prime minister's office. But he knew it all as pressure and that the origin of all political pressure in the land was the prime minister's office.

Cohen knew there was nothing as direct as an explicit instruction from the PM to the IG. Instead it was roundabout. The transportation minister, known to be one of the prime minister's favorites among the younger generation of politicians, suddenly announced his office had plans for the establishment of an independent highway patrol unit to fight the growing number of road accidents. The last thing the fifth floor wanted was another police force to compete for the Treasury's limited resources. So, from the fifth floor came the demand for results, to prove that they were on top of all their responsibilities. A sensational arrest was just what they needed, and Cohen was at work on a sensational case.

The press reports therefore were part of the pressure on him. He understood the newspaper reports to mean that there were whispers in the corridors. It would be hard to run a whisper campaign against him, Cohen knew, but this case was different, too different from cases of the past. The permutations of the case—nuns and Russians and nationalism—had given the case front-page treatment since the start. It overshadowed the grenades case, to which Cohen wished he could give all his attention. Meanwhile Cohen felt lucky that he had managed to avoid the press entirely since the case began. It kept the reports in the realm of the fifth floor, which meant the reporters would concentrate on the talk instead of trying to follow Cohen's moves. And he was planning his most important move so far.

The second day Levy was back at work, they were going over a list of detectives who could be taken off other cases in order to press ahead with the grenades interviews when a tall, slender man with a graying beard, a large knitted skullcap, and a jackal's grin of yellowing teeth walked into the office.

"You are Cohen?" asked the man, and to Cohen's nod, announced, "I am Member of Knesset Eliahu Ben-Yehoshua," as if Cohen did not know.

"Well, you certainly trumpeted your arrival," said Cohen. Outside, in the street below, half a dozen of Ben-Yehoshua's followers were noisily cursing the policeman at the main gate. Goldstein led the chants.

"Why are your people harassing my people?" Ben-Yehoshua demanded.

Cohen looked at the Knesset member with disdain.

"What do you want?"

"To find out whether your people had anything to do with the murder of two Russian nuns," said Cohen, honestly.

Ben-Yehoshua laughed. His eyes were rheumy, with deep half-moons of darkness beneath each eye. "Well, you found out that they didn't. So stop your harassment."

Cohen had not put anyone else on the People's Guard group. But Shmulik said that he had wanted to keep tabs on them. Cohen conceded nothing to Ben-Yehoshua. "I'll do what I have to do," he said simply.

"Well, I'll do what I have to do," Ben-Yehoshua said, threateningly. He turned to leave.

"Stop!" Cohen demanded.

"Am I under arrest?" asked Ben-Yehoshua.

"Not yet," said Cohen.

"I want a lawyer," the Knesset member responded.

Cohen laughed.

"What are you laughing about?" Ben-Yehoshua exclaimed. "I have the right to a lawyer."

At that, Cohen's fist slammed onto the table, and he rose from his seat. His body seemed to grow larger and wider, and when he spoke it was in a low voice that seemed to rise with each word, yet at the end of his speech, Cohen had not raised his voice higher than ordinary conversation.

"This is not America. I can't hold you, that's true. You're an MK. But I can hold any one of your people for forty-eight hours. I can arrest them for forty-seven hours, let them onto the street, and an hour later arrest them again for another forty-seven hours. I can hold them in a room with nothing but a faucet and a hole in the ground. I can do whatever I want. And I'll tell you something. I'm waiting. Waiting for a chance to do it. Not to them. To you. No lawyer. The first time you make a speech that I decide sounds like you're inciting anyone to violence against anyone and you're in here, with a request to the attorney general that he ask the Knesset to lift your immunity. The first time I catch one of your people beating up on an Arab, beating up on somebody they don't like, they're going into one of my suites here, on conspiracy to murder charges. I'm sure you're aware that there are plenty of your fellow parliamentarians who would love to see you so charged and would be happy to strip you of your immunity if we had the case. No. This isn't America. No lawyers. Not yet. They come later. Much later."

By the end of Cohen's speech, Ben-Yehoshua's smirk was gone.

But he remained standing, staring at Cohen. "That's okay Mr. Policeman. Because I'll tell you something. Your policemen, your men, they're with me. I just say what they already think. I ask them, why do they protect Arabs who would knife them. I say what they wish they could say but you won't let them. So I'm going to be the one with the truth and even you, one day, will recognize it."

Cohen took a step around his desk and faced Ben-Yehoshua, who reflexively backed away.

"Don't count on it," said Cohen. "Now get out of here. The next time you're here you'll be under arrest.

"Show Mr. Lifshitz out of here," said Cohen, using the name that appeared on Ben-Yehoshua's American passport.

"I'm Rabbi Eliahu Ben-Yehoshua," said the man, still facing Cohen.

"As far as I'm concerned, you're vermin," said Cohen. "Out."

Ben-Yehoshua left the room, smirking at Levy. "You'll see it too," he said, looking at Levy.

As soon as Ben-Yehoshua was out of the room, Cohen yanked open the lower left-hand drawer of his desk and pulled out the bottle of Extra Fine brandy he kept for emergencies. He half filled the empty tea glass on his table and shot the drink down his throat, grimacing with the liquid burn.

He shoved his anger aside by forcing himself to think about Alex. The Russian security agent had made no mention of the threatening letters about which Goldstein had confessed to the Twins. It must mean something, he thought. Why wouldn't the Russians, always looking for opportunities to embarrass the government, protest the threatening letters. Why didn't he? *Glasnost?* Warming relations? Secret deals? There must be a reason. There must be a pattern.

Alex's silence. That's the pattern. At least it seems to be a pattern. Remember, Avram, remember. Go over the notes, think, think.

Alex's routine had not changed. From mission offices to the convent and back, every day at the same time. Once every three days, he loaded the van with the cheapest of the vegetables on sale in the open *shuk* and brough the food to the convent. Shmulik's men were keeping a round-the-clock eye on the Russian, but their reports revealed nothing.

Cohen was convinced that the KGB agent was hiding something. It was time to put Shvilli to work. Levy located the Russian detective in the compound lounge, chatting up a busty traffic cop.

"Whatever you want, boss," Shvilli said when he reached Cohen's office.

He was tall and yet seemed stocky, muscular and partial to clothes tight enough to display that strength. He had long black hair falling down his forehead, a gold tooth at the edge of his smile, and large hands that ended in chewed fingernails.

He had been a young boxer in Jerevan, just across the Turkish border from Mt. Ararat, at the tip of which Noah's ark was supposedly petrified. A Georgian Jew, the youngest in a family of twelve sons, he had moved south with his family into Armenian Russia when he was ten. Seven years later he arrived in Jerusalem. He ended up in the military police, which he liked, and afterward volunteered for the police. He had been on the force nearly ten years.

Shvilli had a way of submerging his own identity into the languages he spoke. He's a good actor, Cohen thought about him, making him perfect for undercover work.

The two men, the former boxer fluent in seven languages and the aging detective fluent in the language of patience, sat alone for hours in preparation, while Levy sat outside the office as a guard, a silent loyalist protecting an inner sanctum. The three of them were the only ones who knew about the plan. Cohen needed Shvilli's absolute trust, and Shvilli would need Cohen's absolute protection.

"You do nothing compromising, nothing at all. Just listen. No questions. No talk. No flirting. You go in and you listen. And most important. Absolutely. You have to be out in forty-eight hours," Cohen instructed, "so we don't have to go into court." The two days were the amount of time he could hold someone without having to bring the suspect before a judge, and thus into open court and part of the public record.

"What if I learn that . . ." Shvilli began more than once during the conversation.

And each time, Cohen stopped him to say "No. No what ifs. The only if is if anything goes wrong, if you have the slightest feeling of trouble. You're out of there. Immediately."

Cohen wanted to be absolutely clear about that. One wrong move by Shvilli and the entire case would come crashing down around all of them. "And Shvilli, forty-eight hours. A minute longer and the cover will come apart. This is the most important thing of all. No matter what, you are out of there. Forty-eight hours. Remember that. It's all the time you'll have. If you're not out by then, we're both going to be in big trouble." The entire operation depended on that time limit, for Cohen's plan was a step beyond the limits. If the mission failed, the speculation in the press about a change in the staffing of the investigation would become true.

So Levy sat outside Cohen's door whenever Shvilli was inside, and when the time came for Shvilli to leave, Levy would make sure that nobody saw his departure. There could be no leak in the system about Cohen's plan for Shvilli. Levy flirted with the secretaries and gossiped with detectives who came by. But mostly he remained silent, reading a case file on his lap and slowly turning the pages, looking for the missing connection between one piece of evidence and another. When Larrybird came by, Levy would knock on the door and open it slightly, announce the arrival, and then take the tray from the sergeant to personally carry into the office. After a moment he'd come out, carrying empty glasses, and hand them back to Larrybird.

Then, three days after Cohen first told Shvilli the plan, they came out of the office shortly before 2:00 A.M.

Cohen patted Levy on the back. "Come," said the commander. Levy followed Cohen and Shvilli down the wide and worn stone steps to the lobby of the building. Beyond the guard booth at the end of the driveway they could see the white stone church gleaming in the moonlight. "Shvilli's taking us out for a drink," Cohen explained as they went out into the street instead of toward the parking lot.

They walked to the right, down to Jaffa Road, ducking into an archway that rose between a basement grilled-food restaurant and a newspaper and cigarette kiosk. From inside the arch, they could hear rock and roll competing with oriental music, and the tinkle and rattle of glasses and chatter. Three pubs, one beside the other, filled the alleyway that served as the downhill short-cut between Jaffa Road and the Government Press Office. The third pub in the alley was called Vodkalovsky. It was their destination.

Grobman, a Russian Jew from Moscow, kept seventeen different kinds of vodka stored in his freezer. Some were spiced with garlic cloves and lemon peels, others had parsley and small chili peppers floating at the bottom. The pub menu listed platters of smoked fish and raw onions and green peppers. Every table had a loaf of black bread and a large bread knife shared by all at the table. Many of the Russian Jewish intellectuals who had come to Jerusalem in the seventies had made the restaurant and bar into a collective living room.

There was nothing quite like it in Moscow or Leningrad, but it was nonetheless Russian, heavy chaired and dark walled. It was a place that few sabras or tourists entered; they felt too out of place as the language swirled about in shouts or sudden sobs. It could be a crazy place, especially when Grobman broke his own rule about not drinking while working. Sometimes he'd get drunk enough to climb a table to recite futurist poetry from the twenties, from memory.

The last customer was gone, and Grobman was at the counter piling up receipts when they entered. Shvilli pointed to a corner table for Cohen and Levy, and approached his Russian friend, who had already told his wife Irka, who combined bartending and waitressing, to prepare three glasses and a bottle and a platter of smoked fish.

"Where have you been?" said Grobman, welcoming Shvilli. "We haven't seen you in weeks." They were speaking Russian.

"Occh, I am busy. So busy," said Shvilli.

"So. Who isn't busy? Who cannot be busy?"

"You!" said Shvilli in feigned astonishment and mockery. "You, Grobman, a natural parasite, you call being drunk all day and all night busy?" But then he quickly stated his business, his voice turning confidential and low. "Listen, my friend, do any of them ever come in here?"

"Them?" asked Grobman, looking up at Shvilli.

"*Tihushniks*. The silent ones. From back there. You know. Just up the street there's a church and . . ."

"Oh, Them." said Grobman. He glanced toward Cohen and Levy in the corner table. The two men had chosen seats that gave them a view of the entire bar, as well as the courtyard alleyway.

Grobman disappeared for a moment behind the counter.

When he rose he had a bottle in his hand. There was a large garlic clove at the bottom of the clear liquid. Shvilli looked toward Cohen and Levy. Cohen was talking, Levy nodding his head.

"Yes," Grobman confirmed. "Twice. Very tall, says very little. He made a point of ordering his food in Hebrew. Sometimes, you know, they are very stupid, not believing we can recognize them, even here, where it smells different, we can smell them. I can smell their stink from across the room. I came here to get away from them, and they find me here. But here they cannot touch me. Here they cannot touch me, and I can touch them if I want. Do I want? No. I don't care. They cannot touch me anymore." Grobman drank the vodka, slammed the glass on the table, and offered a drink to Shvilli.

"Was he alone?" asked Shvilli.

"The first time alone. Maybe a year ago, very late at night. I said nothing. The people at the next table, Maya, the writer, you know, and one of her boys, she notices him and gets up and goes to another table to get away from him. Everybody notices. He drank his vodka, and then after a while, he leaves."

Grobman poured another round and continued.

"The second time he had a girl. Long dark hair, good looking. Young looking. But hard to say how old. Maybe twenty-five, maybe thirty-five. Good looking, you know. Nice tits," said Grobman. He glanced toward his wife. "You know I pay attention to these things, I look." He smiled and added, "And I remember. But I am always loyal to my Irka. Even when I am drunk and hanging all over someone else's wife, I am loyal to my Irka."

"What was she like? How did she behave? When was this?" asked Shvilli.

Grobman had his own priorities. "I remember all this because of the organ, that creep. It was raining, so maybe three, four months ago. Early winter. Anyway, she was nervous. Very nervous. Kept looking at his watch. They only stayed a little while. I never saw her again," explained Grobman.

"A Jewish girl, a Russian girl?" Shvilli asked. "What language were they speaking?"

Grobman thought for a moment. "Maybe Jewish, nice dark hair, oval face." But then he added, "Maybe Russian—she was very obedient towards him. He ordered for her. She drank, too. Not like an Israeli girl."

"What language were they speaking?" Shvilli asked, pressuring his friend.

"I don't know. He leaned close to her, whispering to her. Maybe Russian, maybe Hebrew. Who knows." Grobman shrugged.

"She didn't have a watch?"

"No, I remember, she looked at his."

Shvilli turned to look at Cohen and Levy. They were watching his conversation with Grobman, and he nodded at them, nodded perhaps too exuberantly, because Cohen shook his head slightly, raised a finger as if to signal a reminder, and Shvilli nodded again, this time barely moving his head, a blink of a nod.

Grobman was saying, "Eh? C'mon, Shvilli, you my friend, here I have a friend a cop. There, you tell me one day I have a friend, one of them, a cop, I laugh in your face. Here we have Jewish cops. Our cops." Grobman laughed. "So tell me, why you looking for him? Don't the secret police do that?"

"Look, Grobman," said Shvilli, suddenly serious, ignoring Grobman's questions, conveying with his intense stare a danger and a certainty that stilled even Grobman's natural joviality. "Maybe he'll be here again. Maybe he'll even show you my picture. You listen to me good. You don't know me. You understand. He asks you about me, shows you a picture, asks about a Russian cop, you say, 'I dunno. I don't know Russian cops.' Be tough, but you don't know me. Okay?"

"You going to get him?" asked Grobman.

"Maybe we have to get him, I don't know. Maybe. But you don't tell anybody. You understand. Irka the same thing. Not a word. You don't know me." Shvilli finally drank the vodka Grobman had poured for him, gulping it all down, gripping the edge of the bar as the warmth spread through his lower back and up his spine, rushing over his head like a blanket of snow.

"Irka," Grobman called. His wife came over, wiping her hands on a towel. "Listen, you see him? You don't know him."

Irka looked at Shvilli. He nodded. She looked back at Grobman and nodded, then leaned over the counter and kissed Shvilli on the cheek. He blushed and said, "Remember. You don't know me. Not until I tell you it's okay." She nodded to him and went back to rinsing the narrow shot glasses in which they served the vodka.

"And one other thing," Shvilli added. "You see those men I came in with. You see that young man. He'll walk by every night. If somebody comes in and asks if you know a Russian cop, you say nothing. But later, you nod when you see that young man, and he'll come in and talk to you. But if nobody asked about me, then you just shake your head and you won't see him again. You understand?"

Grobman said yes and poured another drink for Shvilli, who took it back to the table where Cohen and Levy waited.

"It's okay," said Shvilli, "but listen. Alex has a girl. Or he had a girl. A young girl, good looking even. That's not in our files. What girl?"

Cohen poured out three glasses of vodka and raised his own, resting his raised forearm on his elbow. "Something for you to find out," he said, toasting Shvilli's mission.

He shot the vodka down his throat and slowly lowered his arm, bringing the glass down like a short skinny balloon gracefully floating to rest on the table. "Now we start the next stage," he said, and then coughed, as the vodka continued to work on his body. Shvilli laughed. Levy stood up. Shvilli reached for Levy's untouched vodka, drank it, and waved farewell to the Grobmans.

Levy was the last one out the door, and as he stepped across the threshold, he turned to look at Grobman. The Russian nodded once and then Irka called him so he looked away for a moment. When he looked back, the young detective had evaporated into the darkness, and in his place was a lean man, wearing a gold-green vest over a T-shirt.

The man was peering into the bar, an expression of curiosity and wonderment on his face, but Grobman assumed it was the expression of a new tourist in town. "We're closing," Grobman shouted out in Hebrew, and the goateed foreigner walked away, lifting his sack onto his shoulder.

20

A JEEPLOAD OF BORDER PATROLMEN pulled up in front of the small house owned by the convent gardener on the northern outskirts of Bethlehem.

An officer followed by two soldiers climbed out as the driver waited. Another soldier ran toward the back of the house while the officer led the others to the front door of the house and banged on it.

A long nighttime silence followed. The lights of the Jerusalem night sent a dull glow into the sky to the north, defining the blunt profile of the ancient hills. Finally, as the officer continued to bang on the door, a light broke through a window.

"Police," shouted the officer in Arabic.

"One moment, one moment," a man's voice shouted back. "I'm coming, I'm coming."

The officer counted under his breath to ten and then nodded to the two soldiers, who leaned together against the door. When the lock gave out, the soldiers rushed into the living room with its plain sofas and chairs and bare floors.

To their right they could see four children's faces, staring up at them from a dark room. The officer smiled at the children.

"Where's George Hamdiya?" the officer said in a loud voice. The children stared back with fear and hatred.

A short, slender man rushed from the corridor. "I am George Hamdiya," he said, obviously frightened. Like a matron, he clenched the lapels of his bathrobe. His feet were bare, and he seemed to be shivering.

"Get dressed. We're taking you with us," said the officer.

"What for?" asked Hamdiya. "What did I do? I do nothing. Nothing."

"My orders were to bring you in. If they want, they'll tell you when you get there," said the officer.

"Can I put on some clothes? When will I be back? Where are you taking me?"

"Put on some clothes," the officer said. He motioned his soldier to stand out of the way, to let the Arab pass. He ignored the other two questions.

"How will my family know where I am?"

"They'll be informed."

Half an hour later, Hamdiya was in the lockup at the Russian Compound, where the overnight police guard smoked a cigarette as he filled in the forms. Cohen watched over his shoulder. When the long ash fell from the guard's cigarette, Cohen blew at it until it was dust in the air.

"Give me the papers and bring him in here," said Cohen.

"The papers are supposed to go to the duty sergeant in the morning," said the guard.

"I'll take care of it. Now get him," said Cohen, taking a cigarette from the guard's packet on the table.

Cohen grimaced as he heard the rattle of the key, the sliding screech of metal on metal as the iron door slid open. Each sound was as familiar to him as the sound of his own voice, familiar from the job and familiar from the years long before the job.

Hamdiya's footsteps and the guard's routine cursing of Arabs and officers drove away the memories.

"Take off his cuffs," Cohen ordered. The guard raised an eyebrow. "We're supposed to keep the Arabs cuffed," the guard said.

"Take them off," Cohen demanded, his gruff authority over-whelming the guard. The man took a set of keys from his desk drawer and, yanking on the cuffs, pulled Hamdiya closer.

Hamdiya rubbed his wrists.

"Come with me," Cohen ordered the gardener. They stepped

out of the lockup building and started across the courtyard. "I know you speak Hebrew," said Cohen. "That will make this easier. Come. I'll make you a cup of coffee."

Hamdiya nodded jerkily. He had never been arrested, though many times he had stood in the sun or the rain, at dawn or at dusk, with other Arabs stopped at police or army roadblocks at the entrances and exits from Jerusalem. Sometimes he had not been able to go to work because there were curfews, and sometimes he had not been able to get home until late at night because of the roadblocks.

"I'm not terrorist," he said to Cohen as they walked through the parking lot. "I don't throw stones and my children don't throw stones."

Cohen snorted a short laugh. "I know, George, I know. You're a good man, George, a good man. Never in trouble. I asked. Never in trouble. Your cousin in Dahaisha, that's another story, isn't it George," Cohen added.

"I don't know what he does, I'm not . . . how you say?" said Hamdiya, pausing as he searched his memory for the Hebrew words, "responsible for him."

Cohen led him across the courtyard to a small office where he had already set up a kettle with hot water and two glasses with coffee and a bowl of sugar.

"How do you like your coffee, George?" asked Cohen. "Lots of sugar? That's how I like my coffee, but the doctor says it's not very good for me, all the sugar. The cigarettes, the coffee, none of it is good for me. This job isn't good for me, not like your job. You have a healthy job, don't you George?" Cohen knew he was talking as much to reassure himself as it was to ease the gardener's fears. "You have a clean life," Cohen continued, wanting to drive every bit of patronization out of his voice, "I'm not saying it's an easy life. But it's a good life. Simple."

Hamdiya didn't understand all the Hebrew. But Cohen expected that. He was testing Hamdiya's Hebrew, seeing how complicated a vocabulary he could use with the Arab.

"Listen, George," said Cohen. "I have a problem and you are the only one who can help me. It's a terrible thing what happened to those sisters, isn't it?" Hamdiya looked at him blankly, and

Cohen felt he wasn't getting through. "The women from the convent, George. The two women," Cohen explained, as gently as possible.

George crossed himself. "Bad, bad, yes, very bad," said the gardener. He looked down at his coffee, away from Cohen. Tiny bits of coffee grounds floated on the surface of the hot water. George took a wooden match out of his pocket and stirred the coffee with it, collecting the coffee grounds. Cohen did the same with his own match.

Suddenly George looked up from the coffee. "I didn't do it," he said. His voice quavered, but his eyes were confident. For a moment, Cohen saw a kind of serenity in the man's eyes, a serenity that the old detective envied.

"No, I didn't think you did," said Cohen, gently. "In fact, we know you didn't. You were at a wedding that night, weren't you. Your neighbor's daughter was married. You went to sleep very late and in the morning you still went to work."

George looked at Cohen in astonishment. "How do you know?"

"We know a lot of things, George," said Cohen. "We have to know things. But there are some things we don't know, and that's why we need your help."

"General Cohen," said the gardener, "you are very big. I am very little. What can I do that such a big man needs help from such a little man?" There was suspicion as well as flattery in the Arab's voice.

"George, do you want us to catch the person who killed the sisters?" asked Cohen.

"Of course, you must catch," said George.

"Then we need your help. We need that you don't go to work. For two days. No more. Starting now. You'll be okay. No handcuffs, I promise. Two days. Here, I'll pay you for the days," Cohen opened his wallet and pulled out two 100-shekel notes. "It's even more than you usually make, no? It can buy you a lot of food for your children. I know it's not easy. But it's the only way, George. The only way I have. But George, you have to be here."

"But my family," the gardener asked, "what will they think? They will think I murdered the sisters."

Cohen scratched at his arm. "No, I promise, George. Nobody

will think such a thing. Because this is a secret. A very big secret, and if you help me keep this secret, just do this, it can help us find the person who killed the two sisters." Cohen wanted to believe it. He was telling the truth, but even he could hear the uncertainty in his voice.

George raised his coffee to his lips, keeping his eyes on Cohen. Cohen felt the rash on his arm but stayed perfectly still, waiting for the Arab's answer. There was no need for Hamdiya's agreement. Cohen could have left him handcuffed in the cell, a murder suspect against whom no evidence would be found, released after two days of questioning, another victim of politics. But for his own sake, Cohen needed the gardener's compliance. Without it, Cohen felt, there would be more sleeplessness long after the forty-eight hours. Cohen longed for earlier times, when survival was a guiltless instinct and not a calculation that he made with his conscience.

"Okay," said the gardener after a long pause, looking up directly to Cohen's eyes.

"Thank you, George," Cohen said gratefully.

He took the gardener back to the holding cells, making sure the guard followed the instructions to give Hamdiya a separate cell.

Shvilli and Levy were waiting for him. "It's on," Cohen said. "He says you should be there right after dawn. Sister Elizabeth always meets him at the gate. Today she'll meet you instead of George."

Shvilli grinned. Ever since Cohen had anointed him for the job, he had gone unshaven, practiced his Arabic with a stutter that he had perfected to guarantee frustration for anyone who asked him a question. He was wearing his oldest pair of trousers and was sockless in a pair of old shoes that he had found in the station's lost-and-found department. He was ready to play the part Cohen had written for him.

"Now let's hope the next part works" said Cohen. He was tired, but it wasn't only physical exhaustion. It was something else, something more painful than lack of sleep. He thought of Ahuva and how she had learned to move her hands over his shoulders, untying the knots that gathered under his skin. He thought of her body and suddenly in his mind, he saw the long legs of the dead young nun. He rubbed at his temples.

"Drop him off at the top of the hill," he said to Levy. "You'll walk from there to the convent," he said to Shvilli.

Levy picked up his keys from the desk, and Shvilli followed him out the door. Just before they closed the door, Cohen called out.

"Shvilli, remember," he said, "forty-eight hours. And just be careful."

Shvilli grinned. "I promise. Careful." And he closed the door.

Cohen settled into his chair, turned on the Walkman and fit the earphones snugly. He scratched at his arm as he listened to the *Requiem,* eyes closed, leaning backwards, until he dozed off in his chair.

21

THE JANGLING PHONE jerked Cohen awake. He glanced at his watch. Hamdiya had been in his custody three hours; Shvilli had been at the convent for one.

"Nu?" asked Yaffe.

"Nu what?" answered Cohen.

"The gardener. Is it him? What about the gardener?"

Cohen was quiet.

"Avram? You there?"

"Yes."

"So, I'm asking," said Yaffe. "What's with the gardener?"

"What gardener?" asked Cohen.

"Don't do that to me, Avram. You know damn well what gardener. The convent."

"We're holding him," said Cohen. "As you seem to know," he added, hoping to make Yaffe say how he knew about the gardener, without asking him directly.

"Alex called."

Cohen bolted upright, his knuckles whitening as he clenched the phone. If Alex knew about the missing gardener, he must already have encountered Shvilli.

Yaffe continued. "It's wonderful news. Wonderful," he exclaimed. "The prime minister will be ecstatic. It saves his trip."

"What trip?" Cohen asked, "what are you talking about?"

"I'm really not supposed to tell anyone, but I suppose now

there's no reason not to tell you. He's going to Europe. He has a meeting with the Soviet foreign minister."

Cohen suddenly understood why the PM had taken such an interest in the case. And he felt a hot flush cross his face as he realized that within forty-eight hours, unless Shvilli was able to learn the real killer's identity, the prime minister's delight with the police force's efficiency would turn to ashes. He stayed calm as he answered Yaffe's enthusiasm with his usual cynicism for anything Yaffe regarded as important.

"Yes? You think he can bring me a new Walkman when he comes back?" Cohen's machine had fallen off his lap while he was asleep, and he was scanning the floor for the batteries as he listened to Yaffe.

"Avram, be serious. You know what the PM wants to say at that meeting? I'll tell you what he wants to say. He wants to say that the Jerusalem police have solved the case of the murdered Russian nuns, so if they want to send diplomats, if they want to resume diplomatic relations, then we can guarantee their security."

"So?" said Cohen, trying to keep Yaffe talking while he calculated the risks to Shvilli's safety, and to his own, when the truth came out about the gardener's arrest.

"So up here," said Yaffe, meaning the fifth floor at headquarters in Sheik Jarrah, "they've been saying, 'What's the matter with Cohen?' And I've been telling them that you're fine, not to worry. And you've proven me right. You see, I'm on your side."

"So what are you worried about?" Cohen asked, not at all sure that Yaffe was on his side.

"I'm worried because you didn't let me know about the gardener. You should have known that I'd have to report to the PM's director general, I have to tell the church people something."

"Tell them to hire a new gardener," said Cohen, thinking fast.

"They did. That's how they found out. The gardener apparently got a message to a friend to go to the convent. Strange, no? Of course, it's hard to say nowadays about loyalties. It would have been proper if I heard it from you, of course. But it was Alex who contacted me."

"Good for him."

"To hell with you, Cohen," said Yaffe.

"You too, Yaffe." Cohen hung up and leaned back in his chair.

"It's begun," he said to himself, just as Levy stepped through the door as the phone call ended.

"What's begun?" asked Levy.

"The pressure," said Cohen. "If Shvilli doesn't turn up with something, we'll be feeling the wrath of the gods."

"So what do we do?"

"We wait. There's one piece of good news. Shvilli's in. Alex bought the cover story. So we'll wait and we'll work. On this," he said, slapping the fat folder of the grenades case onto his desk. It had come in during the evening before, while Cohen handled the matter of Hamdiya and Shvilli.

They were down to the final one hundred grenades, last recorded being loaded onto a truck for delivery to a paratrooper regiment responsible for the western sector of the security zone in southern Lebanon. There were twice as many names on the list as there were grenades missing. Attached to the list of names were photocopies of the munitions request form, signed illegibly by the commander of the regiment, and the delivery form, signed illegibly by the driver and the regimental commander's signature upon taking delivery. Ehud's scrawl at the top of the first page pointed out that the regimental commander had been killed a week after the delivery date by a Hizbollah suicide bomber who rammed his explosives-laden Mercedes into a truck carrying twenty-five Israeli troopers in the narrow zone established after the withdrawal from Lebanon. Twelve other soldiers were killed in the attack. "Go easy on them," Ehud's note ended. There were two hundred names on the printout, which listed name, rank, serial number, home and work address, telephone numbers, and special skills.

The search for the identity of the dead beggar had led nowhere. Levy's girlfriend had combed the Yad Vashem archives, trying to match the number to a name but to no avail. Nobody had stepped forward to claim the body, so right after the autopsy the *hevra kadisha* burial society had found a plot for the dead man in a distant corner of the huge Givat Shaul cemetery on the western outskirts of town. The national insurance institute would pay for the burial. Cohen had the beggars of the downtown triangle city rounded up for questioning about the dead man, but that too had led to nothing. There were only twenty of them, no less fixtures of the street than the lampposts. Almost all were harmless lunatics, while the rest, already resentful of the authorities, all said they had no idea why anyone would murder him. They knew him as one of the silent beggars.

"He never spoke to anyone," said the man who rain or shine sat with a plastic box filled with coins across the street from the main post office. "Not even to himself." Still, the beggar's file was attached to the folders of the nuns' case, an aspect of the case that troubled nobody except Cohen.

So they worked through the morning, dividing up the list among available detectives, contacting CID units throughout the country, according to the addresses of the reservists, for questioning. It was tedious work, made worse by the anticipation of the outcome of Shvilli's mission. Each time the phone rang, Levy would grab it before it finished the first ring. Each time Cohen would slowly raise his head from the paperwork and look questioningly at his aide. Each time Levy would shake his head. They were waiting for Shvilli and praying.

22

HE WAS OUTSIDE Sister Elizabeth's office an hour after his arrival. She had accepted his cover story. From the ladder where he had started the paint job on the building, he had heard her make the phone call.

"The gardener's been arrested," she said. There was a pause. "No. I don't know why. A friend of his showed up this morning to replace him. No. No. He seems retarded."

Shvilli smiled.

"I gave him a painting job." There was another long pause. Shvilli strained to hear, frozen on the ladder beside the half-open window, just out of sight of the nun.

She spoke again. "I can't believe that George . . ." And again there was a pause. "He's drunk. As usual," she said with disgust in her voice. Shvilli guessed she was referring to the archimandrite. "I'll be here."

When he had heard the clunk of the receiver on the phone, he had quickly resumed his work. He was on the ladder when Alex showed up less than half an hour later.

"You. Butros. Come down here," Alex commanded.

Shvilli climbed down slowly, carefully placing the paintbrush on the tin cover of the paint can on the ground before moving, eyes downcast, toward Alex. He walked deliberately, hoping that his effort to appear absolutely innocent appeared to Alex to be the effort of a man trying extra hard to do his job precisely.

"George's wife sent you?" Alex asked.

"Ye-ye-ye-yes."

"What did she tell you?" Alex asked.

"Geo-Geo-Geo-Geo"

"George," said Alex impatiently.

"Yes."

"George said what?"

"To-To-To-To-"

"To come here. Yes. Yes. But how did he tell you? The Israelis came for him. Why?"

"Do-do-do-n't kn-kn-kn . . ."

"You don't know. How did he tell you? The Israelis came. Took him away. How did he let you know to come here?"

"I-I-I-I wa-wa-wa-was there."

"When?"

"L-L-L-ast n-n-n-n . . ."

"Last night?"

Shvilli nodded. He could feel the sweat on his brow and wondered if Alex had noticed it, but he was grateful for Cohen's anticipation of the questions. He hoped the answers Cohen had chosen would be as wise.

"What were you doing there?" Alex demanded.

"Geo-Geo-Geo-Geo-Geo-Geo-"

"Enough. All right. That's . . ."

Shvilli kept up his stammer, knowing that the disguise had worked.

Alex gave him one last piercing look. Shvilli smiled and shrugged. Alex walked away angrily, around the back, into the building, to Sister Elizabeth's office. They talked in low voices for a few minutes, and then Alex came out again, shot one last glance at Shvilli, and headed for the parking lot.

When he heard the van's engine start, Shvilli climbed back up the ladder, waiting for his opportunity.

By early afternoon there was nothing more that they could do on the grenades folder, so Levy took charge of the routine paperwork that seemed to flow constantly into the office. Rutie came in almost every hour with a new stack of paper. Progress reports on cases, carbons of patrolman reports, all the information that was gathered by the police during the day flowed into Cohen's office. The files and folders of ongoing cases were piled on the table, the top of the filing cabinets, even the floor.

Cohen's forearm was itching terribly, and he was exhausted. "I've been sitting in this chair since yesterday," he grumbled.

Levy carefully offered his boss a recommendation that Cohen go home and get some rest. "If we haven't heard from him by now, he won't be calling until tonight," the junior officer tried. "I can handle things here."

Cohen thought for a moment. "All right. I'm going," he said, looking at his watch. "I'll be back at eighteen thirty." He rose wearily from his seat and left the room, heading across the main hall to the back staircase leading to the parking lot. Levy turned back to the paperwork.

Cohen didn't head for home. Instead of turning right at the Old City Walls as he came out of the Russian Compound by City Hall, he turned left. He put the Mozart *Requiem* into the tape player and drove past the Damascus Gate to the old road eastward from Jerusalem to the Dead Sea.

The road began in a valley at the foot of the Mount of Olives, where the White Russian Church had its own convent and onion-domed church. Yaffe had been assigned the White Russian angle, but he'd turned up nothing. Because of the politics of drunken archimandrites and diplomats in Paris, there was no connection between the two churches. But in Jerusalem, the Red and White church dispute was chaff in the political wind.

The road moved quickly up past the church and along the edges of the cemetery from where, it is said, the dead will one day rise. Then it was all downhill to the Dead Sea, through the potholes of neglected Arab neighborhoods and past the road-stand wicker salesmen and broken down cars stripped for spare parts. Cohen watched carefully for the potential ambush, a cluster of kids at an intersection could turn into a hailstorm of rocks thrown at an Israeli car. Police cars, marked or unmarked, were no exception. He could have taken the new highway that cut over the Mount of Olives, but he loved every quarter of the city, and as far as he was concerned, Bethany was no less Jerusalem than Rehavia, Abu Dis no less than Nahlaot.

Since the rioting had begun, the new four-lane highway that

bypassed all of the populated parts of East Jerusalem—and the stonethrowers—had become a popular road. But Cohen preferred the old route. He liked the way the city suddenly gave way to the desert at a Bedouin encampment of dead cars and black goat-hair tents, the last sign of settlement before the steep decline into the Jordan Valley.

Cohen sped down the long hill that led to the Jericho inter-section. As he swept past the left-hand turn with its backpacking tourists and soldiers heading north up the Jordan Valley to Galilee, a lazy army roadblock calmly waved through the morning traffic heading for the Dead Sea. Cars with the telltale black-on-blue license plates of Arab residents of the territories would be stopped, but the white-on-red plates of Cohen's car identified him as a police car.

When the eczema rash on his arm first began to appear, he was religious about the trip to the mineral-rich waters, which sev-eral doctors had said he might find soothing. But soon Cohen lost control of his schedule. He was unable to clear away a regular half day for a lazy afternoon on one of the rocky beaches, unable to run to the sea every time he felt the aching itch.

Sometimes he had gone to the sea with Ahuva. Feeling ad-venturous they took impromptu midweek morning drives down to the Dead Sea, seeking out secluded beaches anywhere between the plains at the foot of Masada and the potash works at Sodom. They walked slowly through the lush natural gardens of Ein Gedi until they found a place to picnic, alone, away from all their city mem-ories. Sometimes they would take lunch at a small restaurant in Jericho, eating chicken baked in a garlicky sesame sauce. The wait-ers carried the trays over tiny stone bridges to the tables in the shade. He thought of her, wondering why she didn't call, wishing she were already back.

The *Requiem* on the Walkman was over, and Cohen took off the earphones. He was speeding past the sea on his left, rush-ing past a burned-out Jordanian tank left as a reminder of the Israeli push through the territory twenty years before. There was no breeze, and the long fingerlike leaves of the towering kibbutz plantation palms were as still as the mountains to his right. A few kilometers past the second public beach, empty of vacationers that weekday, he pulled over to the side of the road.

Cohen stripped in the shade of the bulrushes, wearing only his sneakers in case of sharp stones. Then he walked to the edge of the water and stepped in, wincing as the sharp salty water eased into a scratch on his leg, groaning as the water rose and covered his arm. Once covered with water up to his throat, he leaned backward. The water lifted him, his head seemed to rest on a pillow of water, and his feet were raised by the buoyancy so that without effort he floated on a perfect bed.

He lay like that for almost half an hour, closing and opening his eyes to the sharp sunlight, floating slowly in the heavy water. He walked back to his clothes, occasionally bending to heft handfuls of wet clay that he rubbed over his arm and bare chest. The gray and black streaks of mud dried quickly, and he dipped again, rinsing off the dried mud. When he reached the beach where he had left his clothes, he stood naked at the water's edge, bending and lifting great chunks of the clay out of the water and rubbing them into his skin. Soon he was a gray-and-black statue, lying large and heavy on the beach beneath the sun.

He listened to his thoughts, to the rumbling dangers of the political pressure, to the voices of the cases of the present and the past. He could hear the voice of his wife and the voice of the child he had made but could only imagine. He could almost hear the voices of his parents, and when he winced, remembering momentarily the voices from the camps, the clay cracked on his face like a parched desert cracking into millions of lines. To settle his thoughts, he chose Ahuva's voice to hear. He remembered the first time they had been together alone, a year after her appointment as the youngest judge in the country, when he had breached all protocol and asked her to dinner, and he had first heard her laugh.

The laugh merged with the lapping water at the beach edge, and gradually all the voices and thoughts and noises of his life gave way to the whisper of the tiny waves falling heavily over his feet. He stayed that way for almost an hour until suddenly the crunching crush of car wheels on the gravel on the road above him snapped into his consciousness. He rose, bending at the waist, the effort sending the blood rushing through his body and for a moment causing an exquisite drunken dizziness. He slid into the water, rinsed the dry clay off his body, and was dressed by the time the tourists, led by an Israeli guide, stepped through the bulrush wall onto the beach.

An hour later he was at the outskirts of town, his mind made up. He had changed the situation by sending Shvilli into the convent. The risk was great, but he was in control again.

23

THE STARLINGS were returning from Africa, on their way to Europe, and filled the convent's treetops with great orchestras of singing. Shvilli whistled with them as he worked, deliberately overwatering the paint so that the wall needed several coats, keeping him in and around the building. Other nuns walked past him, tittering like the birds about his presence or silent as the ghosts of the two dead nuns. But he ignored them, concentrating on his goal: Sister Elizabeth's office, at the end of a narrow corridor just off the dining room.

Cohen's instructions were to listen, but aside from the one phone conversation between Sister Elizabeth and Alex, Shvilli had heard nothing except the starlings, and the wind in the olive trees.

Two nuns at work in the kitchen off the dining room shared only their humming, and from the mother superior's office he had heard only the occasional rumbles from the ancient filing cabinet. Alex had disappeared after the brief encounter early in the morning. So Shvilli worked on the painting, waiting for his opportunity.

It arrived when the mother superior came out of the building clutching a prayer book. "That's fine," she said, looking up at him on the ladder. "Really, it's enough here. Why don't you take a break for food and then go on to that building over there?" She pointed out the next building in the compound. She smiled at him. "I'll be back later on, to see how you're doing," she said, and carrying her book clutched to her chest, she hurried down the path toward the chapel with the red tiled roof that Shvilli could see from the ladder.

He waited until she was gone and then picked up the paint bucket and the plastic bag with his food and headed into the building through the outside door that led to the storeroom. He left the paint in the closet and carefully moved down the narrow hall until he could see the two nuns, past the dining room, in the kitchen. They were peeling potatoes, dropping the clean spuds into a huge vat on the floor. Their backs were to him.

He moved quickly, one stride into the dining room, heading for the corridor beyond. But his left shoe had a bad heel, worn down so badly that one of the nails in the sole scratched the floor. He grimaced and froze. To him, the squeal of the heel had been the loudest sound he had heard all morning. He looked across the room, waiting for them to turn, waiting to run, remembering the stutter, remembering the role he was playing and not the reason he was there.

But the women continued their humming, a song he was sure he recognized from his childhood but couldn't name. He tiptoed the last two strides across the room to the corridor leading to Sister Elizabeth's room, and once beyond any accidental view from the dining room, he bent quickly and removed his shoes for the last few steps to the nun's door.

It was closed. He reached for the handle offering a silent prayer. It was unlocked, and he moved inside soundlessly, closing the door behind him, squeezing the handle tightly as he slowly let it drop its aging latch in place.

He went first to the window, making certain of a secondary escape route. From the window overlooking the tiny terrace, he turned to the desk. Except for the phone and a collection of crucifixes sculpted from olive wood lining the edges of the broad wooden surface like a fence, it was bare.

He was sweating, and he practically leaped to the file cabinet, thanking God again when he discovered it was unlocked. Wincing with each creak of the wooden drawer, he looked down into the top one. He looked for the names—Helena, the daughter, Miriam, the mother, or Alex, the *tihushnik,* the silent one whose voice had made Shvilli sweat.

Nothing in the first drawer.

He moved to the second. He lifted slightly on the handle, to ease the weight of the drawer on what he imagined to be the rusting ball bearings. From beyond the door he could hear the humming stop, and again he froze, holding his breath. But then the humming resumed, and he returned to his search.

By the time he heard the rolling bottle at the back of the bottom drawer, he had leafed past every folder in the four drawers and was ready to quit. Every nun in the convent had a file. Except the two dead nuns.

Disgusted, he reached for the bottle, as much out of thirst for at least a partial reward for his effort as curiosity about Sister Elizabeth's taste in liquor. It was a cheap cognac. Disappointed, he nonetheless uncapped it and took a long pull, wondering what he could try next in order to learn more about the dead nuns and about Alex.

He sat Arab-style, squatting with his knees in front of him, sitting on his heels. And when he reached to return the bottle to the very back of the drawer, he felt one last file, lying down, instead of standing like all the others.

It seemed empty, but when he opened it he saw that it contained two pages of tiny Cyrillic script. After reading the first few lines, his disappointment turned to incredulity, and then to fascination and eagerness. Shvilli focused on the two pages, wondering if he should take them, trying to memorize them. He read as fast as he could. Beyond the open window, the starlings chattered loudly in the trees.

The humming from the kitchen suddenly ceased, replaced by voices. Shvilli hesitated for a moment, considering whether to take the document or to put it back in its place in the folder beneath the cognac bottle.

He slipped the papers back into the folder and replaced it in the back of the drawer under the bottle, closing the drawer as quietly as he could before jumping to his feet, grabbing the shoes.

Sister Elizabeth's voice came from beyond the door, asking the nuns in the kitchen if they had seen the gardener. Shvilli went directly to the window, taking one last look around. His plastic lunch bag was on her desk. He strode to it and dashed back to the window. He climbed over the sill, and then, with one hand holding onto the sill, he used the other to pull the window closed behind him, before dropping twice his height into the garden. He scuttled to the end of the building, pressing himself against the wall. He had a choice.

He looked cautiously down the path toward the parking lot. Two nuns were sweeping a flight of stairs that jutted off the path up the hill. He looked in the other direction. Elizabeth's head was sticking out the window, luckily for Shvilli, in the other direction. He ducked back and thought. Straight downhill through the woods? The sweeping nuns would see him. Brazenly out in the open, as if he were innocence itself? Elizabeth would see him. Up the hill to the highway to Hadassah?

"But-ros," he heard the nun call out in a searching tone.

It was the only clear way. He pulled on the shoes and dashed across the terrace upwards, heading for the four-lane road that he knew was two hundred meters above, past the thick woods and brush of the mountainside.

24

IF NOT FOR the childlike drawing in the lower right-hand corner of the standard form filled out by the overnight patrol team covering central Jerusalem, Levy would have scanned the page and then sent it onwards through channels. But the sketch, drawn by a Jerusalem patrolman sent to Nahlaot to investigate a predawn complaint about a screaming woman chased by an unidentified man, was of a man with a goatee.

"We've got something!" Levy shouted, raising the piece of paper in the air like a trophy. He studied it once, twice, three times. The complaint came from one Rahamim Aboudi, a fruit and vegetable vendor in the Mahane Yehuda market. He told Patrolman Sasson that he was washing up to get ready for work when he heard the first scream. When the screams continued, he went to the window to look outside.

The report said that was when he saw the tourist girl. "A pretty *blondinit*," Sasson had quoted Aboudi as saying. According to the report, Aboudi saw the man run past a few seconds later. "A hippie," the report quoted Aboudi as saying about the man chasing the blond girl. "Long hair and a funny beard," Aboudi had said. It was here in the report that Sasson had drawn the face. The report went on to explain that Rahamim Aboudi did not know the girl's name. But it said he believed she lived in Nahlaot. Aboudi's address was in its proper place on the form, alongside his ID card number.

Levy looked at his watch. It was 4:30. Cohen had been gone an hour. He tried calling Cohen at home, but there was no answer. He called Rutie into the office.

"Keep calling the commander every ten minutes until I get back," he ordered. "Tell him I've found a lead to the hippie and that I'll be back by 5:30. Tell him I tried phoning but there was no answer."

Levy ran down the marble stairs and out the front door; past an uncovered Roman column that lay desolate in an exposed pit in the fenced garden of the police headquarters; through the parking lot past the gleaming white church. A right put him onto a short street that led to Jaffa Road. From there it was a five minute brisk walk up and down the hills of the main street of downtown Jerusalem to Mahane Yehuda *shuk*.

A block before the *shuk,* he crossed the street, cut three blocks through an alleyway and then into the warrens of the neighborhood. He found the section of Nahlaot described in the report he clutched in his hand and searched for Aboudi's address. Nobody was home. He began knocking on doors, seeking someone who knew a *blondinit* tourist girl. No one answered—until the fourth door.

An aging woman, her face as wrinkled and hairy as a fig, her hair covered by a paisley bandana of bright oranges and reds and greens and yellows, stared down at him from an upstairs window.

"Auntie," he shouted up, "the blond girl who lives down here, have you seen her?"

"What?" the woman shouted down.

"The foreigner, the girl," Levy shouted upward. "The tourist girl?"

"I don't know. I know nothing," the woman answered. She pulled her head inside the window.

"Where the hell have you been?" Cohen exploded, when Levy returned to the office. "I told you to wait in case Shvilli called!"

"The hippie. The hippie's been spotted," Levy began to explain.

"I don't care if the messiah's been spotted on a white donkey, you were supposed to stay in the office in case Shvilli called. We have a man in the field. Alone. We're the only ones who know he's there. You can't leave him like that."

"There was a report," Levy tried again to explain, "a hippie, with a goatee. And a knife. In Nahlaot. I made a decision."

"You could have sent someone else. Anyone. Our man was out there and you abandoned him." Cohen's fury was devastating to his aide, yet Cohen knew that Levy had done what Cohen himself had done by putting Shvilli into the convent. He had gambled. Levy was wrong to leave the office, but the lead was important. Cohen softened his tone. "What did you find out?"

Levy handed over the patrolman's report. Cohen scanned it, immediately recognizing its importance. "What did you do?"

"I found Aboudi at work in the *shuk*. I went over his statement with him. But he had nothing to add. I left my card everywhere. In the shops, with the old people on the benches. I covered the top of the neighborhood, four streets in each direction from Aboudi's house on Abulafia Street. I left my card, asking people about the *blondinit* and the hippie. If she shows up, we'll hear about it. I think we should do a door-to-door search in Nahlaot."

"We can't close down neighborhoods with a curfew like the army in the territories," Cohen said impatiently.

"He's dangerous. And he's out there," Levy argued.

Cohen was silent, thinking about how to solve the problem. Levy interpreted the silence as an opening.

"I know it's him. I know it," Levy insisted. "I can feel it. A chase in the middle of the night. A knife. It means something, I'm sure of it. And God knows what he's going to do next. We have no missing persons reports from Nahlaot. I've combed them all. I've asked for hotel registrations, cheap hotels—the Old City pensions, the Petra, places like that. Places where the hippies stay. I know it's him. He's the one. I'm sure of it." Levy was adamant.

He was about to continue when the phone rang.

Cohen reached for it before Levy.

"Cohen."

"Chief, chief, I've got it. Proof. Alex. The nun," Shvilli was breathless from running.

"Where are you?" Cohen demanded.

"The hospital. Hadassah Ein Kerem."

"Are you hurt?" Cohen asked, worried about his man.

"No, no, I'm at a pay phone. Near the entrance."

"What about Alex? What nun?" Cohen asked.

"They had an affair. Can you believe it? A nun and a *ti-hushnik*," Shvilli exclaimed. "The dead nun. Helena."

"Stay there," Cohen ordered. "I'm coming to get you."

Levy had already gathered up his keys by the time Cohen hung up.

"What did he find out?" Levy asked as they rushed down the stairs.

"Alex and Helena. They had an affair," said Cohen.

"So he killed her?" Levy asked incredulously.

"That's what Shvilli thinks."

When they reached the parking lot, Cohen went past the car, telling Levy to pull around in front of the lockup. Cohen went to the four iron stairs that led into the cramped building containing the holding cells.

"Itzik," he said to the sergeant at the desk, "that Arab I'm holding, George Hamdiya, get him for me. Now." Cohen slapped the papers down on the table.

The sergeant moved quickly. He had heard from the shift man before him that Commander Cohen had a special guest in the lockup, and the urgency in Cohen's voice left no doubt that Cohen wasn't interested in conversation.

In two minutes Hamdiya was walking down the narrow corridor. "Well, George," Cohen said smiling. "It looks like you can go home already."

The Arab looked into Cohen's face. "Did you find the man who killed the sisters?" he asked.

"Maybe, maybe," said Cohen, "don't worry. You can go home. Here," he added, reaching into his pocket, "take some money. Take a taxi. But George," Cohen said, "don't go to the convent today. Wait until the day after tomorrow."

"But . . ."

"No buts," said Cohen.

Hamdiya blinked once and looked at the open door that led to the sunshine in the parking lot. Cohen nodded, and Hamdiya hustled out. The desk sergeant presented Cohen with a set of forms to be signed.

"A *shtinker,* eh?" the sergeant asked with disdain, as Cohen passed the forms back.

"No," said Cohen. "A gardener." He turned on his heels away from the perplexed guard and out the open door. Levy was waiting for him.

"Use the siren," Cohen said, getting into the car. Levy smiled and leaned forward to the switch as Cohen reached out the window with the revolving blue light for the roof of the car.

25

SHVILLI WAS WAITING for them by the entrance to the parking lot of the hospital. He was on his toes, practically dancing by the time Levy wheeled the car up to him. Shvilli jumped into the car and immediately began rattling off what he had learned.

"Alex and the daughter were having an affair," Shvilli began. "Or at least that's what Sister Elizabeth says. She wrote a letter," Shvilli explained, "a year ago she wrote it. It's addressed to 'His Holiness,' I guess that's the bishop. Anyway, listen to this. According to the letter, at first they used to take long walks, they were often together. But then they began going in the car alone and returning only late at night. According to the letter, she keeps civilian clothes in his rooms. They've been fucking."

Levy had turned the car around in the parking lot and was driving slowly along the road back to the city.

"Tell me from the beginning," Cohen ordered.

"Just like we planned," said Shvilli. "I went there early and said, 'My friend George asked me to come to work instead of him.'" Shvilli recounted his experience, relishing the success. "I stuttered a lot, they didn't ask any questions. Alex came later, he saw me working, and asked where I came from. The stutter, it worked beautiful. Sister Elizabeth. She told Alex I was retarded. I heard her say so on the phone. But she's the dumb one. Keeps such a thing in her filing cabinet."

"You got into her filing cabinet?" Levy asked, impressed.

Cohen could hear the jealousy in Levy's voice. "The chief told you not to do anything like that," Levy continued. "He said to listen, to look. Not to touch . . ."

"Quiet," Cohen commanded.

Levy fell silent. Shvilli sat arms folded, pouting in the back seat.

Cohen turned back to Shvilli, "Continue," he ordered.

"So I painted the walls, just like Sister Elizabeth said. Chief, I like this gardening business. It's nice. Quiet."

Cohen laughed.

"What's so funny?" Shvilli asked, offended.

"Nothing, nothing," said Cohen. "I was just imagining you as a gardener."

"Anyway," continued Shvilli, "I had an opportunity. She was in her office all morning. I saw her through her window. She even waved to me when I was painting." He laughed again, remembering.

"Get to the point," said Cohen.

"And she went out. To prayers, I guess. I got into her room, nice and quiet. And I found it. The letter. She wrote a letter. Like a report, as if to report this matter to the bishop. I found it. It was the last file in the cabinet. Hidden," he said, remembering the search. "She hid it. And I found it."

"She obviously didn't hide it very well," Levy added, his jealousy of Shvilli's success now obvious.

"There are lots of details," said Shvilli, ignoring Levy's comment. "But that's the important thing. They were having an affair."

"Let me decide what's important," said Cohen. "Continue."

"Alex and Helena, the daughter, they were doing it someplace," Shvilli repeated.

"So?" asked Cohen. "Why does that make Alex the killer?" He was being deliberately obtuse, forcing Shvilli to carry the logic through to all its possible meanings.

"So? So?!" Shvilli was astonished by the question. "A nun and a *tihushnik!* KGB! This is something that if Moscow finds out, everybody's in trouble. Chief, you don't know these people. I know these people. You don't understand how powerful Alex is for them. He runs their lives. He controls them. He can do whatever he wants with them, and they can't complain. Maybe he forced her? Maybe.

Maybe not. He's supposed to be above it all and there he is with this woman. A nun! It's very serious. Very serious."

"Why didn't she send the letter?" Cohen probed.

Shvilli shrugged. "I don't know."

"Maybe he found out about it and before she had a chance to send it, he stopped her," Cohen suggested, half to himself, half to the two junior detectives.

"That's it," Shvilli said, ready to grasp any theory that fit into his view of Alex as the killer. "He found out, and he's got something against her. That's it," Shvilli said. "Chief," he continued in as formal a tone as he was capable, "it will be my pleasure to do this. Arrest him."

But Cohen doubted the theory he had proposed. If anyone, it would have been Sister Elizabeth whom Alex would have targeted, if he had found out about the letter.

"Not yet," said Cohen. "I want to hear more."

"He has answers. I'm sure he has answers," Shvilli insisted.

"I'm sure he has answers to a lot of questions," said Cohen, shifting in his seat. "That doesn't yet make him a murderer. What did you find out about the mother and daughter? Why did they keep the fact she had a daughter secret?"

"Listen to this," Shvilli said, enthusiastic about every detail he had learned. "The mother was the woman of a very big hero of the war against Fascism. A general. One day, Stalin sent this general's men to take their hero away. Stalin, he was crazy, thought everyone was against him. So the mother, she sends her baby . . . this is maybe '51, '52—to her family in Lithuania, and then the mother goes to the church, she says she want to become a nun. She's been here a long time, and all the while she's been trying to get the daughter here."

"Why wasn't the daughter on the mother's visa application?" Cohen demanded. The pieces weren't fitting. But he pressed on with Shvilli, hoping that there was still some detail that would focus the picture for him. He realized he was sweaty and rolled down a window to the dusk falling over the city.

"Who knows?" Shvilli shouted. "Maybe she wanted to hide the daughter from the *tihushniks*. Maybe she wanted to hide it from us. It doesn't matter, what matters is she was twenty-seven, maybe twenty-eight years old then. She comes with Alex. At first, they kept it a secret. But a year ago, Sister Elizabeth finds out. And Chief. That scrap of letter you showed me. I understand it. The father in the letter. It's a priest. He made the arrangements for getting her to Jerusalem." Shvilli sat back in the seat, satisfied with himself. "Unbelievable. A *tihushnik* and a nun. Unbelievable." He noticed the Calder stabile ahead. "We're going there now? Yes? Let's go. We've got him."

Levy was slowing down. "Which way?" he asked Cohen, pulling over to the side of the road. To go into Ein Kerem, he'd have to make a left turn. To return to town, he'd have to stay in the right lane.

Cohen remained silent until Levy came to a complete stop.

"This report obviously didn't say that Alex killed the nuns," Cohen said.

Shvilli admitted the file made no mention of the murders. "She wrote it last year," he said, defending himself as much as he was defending her. "Chief. They had an affair. This is something they aren't supposed to do. This is a very big secret. Maybe she wanted to end the affair. Maybe she wanted to make it public. Maybe he wanted to end it and she didn't want to. Maybe . . ."

"Why did she save the letter?" Cohen asked. "Why would she save the letter?"

"To blackmail him?" Levy suggested.

"Then he'd definitely have reason to kill her," Cohen said.

"So he didn't know about it," Shvilli suggested.

"Then why save it?" Levy asked.

"In case of . . ." Shvilli tried, but he couldn't come up with a reason.

Cohen set aside the mystery of the letter for a moment. "The beggar?" asked Cohen, trying to put together the pieces. Like a split screen in the cinema, Cohen's memory divided the two scenes. The pool of blood from the single wound in the necks of the nuns, the shallow multiple wounds of mutilation on the face and body of the beggar.

"You're the one who doubted it was the same killer," Levy protested, reading Cohen's thoughts. "The one who killed the nuns had to be very strong. The one who killed the beggar didn't have the same kind of strength that Alex has."

"All right," said Cohen. He pressed his feet to the floor of the car, trying to stretch his cramped body, as if by doing so he could fit the facts into some comprehensive theory that could explain all of it. "The beggar was killed by someone else. Maybe. But the letter. Why didn't she send the letter."

"Maybe she did," suggested Levy, "but it turned out to be not such a scandal."

Shvilli broke in, as furious with Levy's suggestion as he was enthusiastic about his conviction that he had solved the case. "I'm telling you," Shvilli insisted from the back seat. "You don't understand. You don't understand these people." He held up his hand, and ticked off fingers with the next two words he spoke. *"Tihushniks.* Nuns." He held up the other hand, and matched one finger to its partner on the other hand. "A nun marries Christ." He held up the first finger he had ticked off and threw out his final point. "Not a spy."

Cohen rubbed absentmindedly at his forearm beneath his jacket as Shvilli continued.

"KGB," Shvilli was saying. "You think the KGB would allow their man to get involved in something like that! What do you think? That *glasnost* means the KGB has changed? Yes, okay. Gorbachev. He's great. Wonderful. But Alex and Helena. This is very dangerous for both of them. They're in trouble with their bosses. A nun having an affair. An agent getting personally involved with a charge. Alex was worried about it being known. He had to do something to prevent it from being known. He had to do something."

"Elizabeth had the file," Cohen repeated, feeling dizzy by the circles of the argument. "She was the one who could tell the story. If anyone, Alex should have killed her." He took a deep breath of evening air.

"When she wrote it, he didn't know that she knew," tried Shvilli.

"But if she knew about the affair, she would have said something, she would have somehow let us know after the murders," said Levy.

"Not if Alex knew about the letter and got to her somehow," said Cohen. "Or if she believed Alex wasn't the killer."

Shvilli lost his temper at the suggestion Alex didn't kill the women. "What are you saying?" he shouted, punching the back seat in anger. "No! Alex must have something on her! It was him!"

Cohen turned for the first time to face the Russian detective in the back seat. The look in his eye was enough of a reprimand for Shvilli to fall silent, embarrassed by his outburst. "I'm sorry," the Russian apologized, and then quickly went on, "Look, Chief, I'm sure of it, I'm sure he's the one," he said apologetically.

"But what was the murder preventing? Who was threatened by the existence of the affair? What's the motive?" Levy argued.

"Obviously nobody was threatened, as long as the affair was kept secret," Cohen said thoughtfully. "But what if Helena was pressuring to go public? What if Helena wanted more than a secret affair?"

"It would be very dangerous for Alex," said Shvilli, leaping on the explanation as proof of his conviction that Alex was the killer. "If he wanted to go away with her, he could be sure the KGB would find them."

"He could have defected," suggested Levy.

"No," said Cohen emphatically. "I heard the head of the Mossad. They'd only be interested in him if he doubled. He doesn't have anything to offer them otherwise. He's just a baby-sitter and he knows it."

"Just my point," said Shvilli. "He's just a hood, muscle with enough brains to take watch over a bunch of nuns. Or kill them."

Levy interrupted with another thought. "Alex didn't know about Sister Elizabeth's letter. If he did, he would have made sure it was destroyed."

Cohen shook his head. "Not if he was convinced he had succeeded in silencing her."

"Then if he killed the nuns, why didn't he kill her?" Shvilli asked, suddenly confounded by the permutations.

They sat silently in the car for a long minute. Cohen rubbed absentmindedly at his arm, watching the passing headlights of the cars on their way to the hospital. He patted his shirt pocket for a cigarette, pulling out an empty, crumpled pack. Shvilli's hand extended from the back seat over Cohen's shoulder, offering a cigarette. Levy's fingers tapped on the steering wheel.

Cohen could hand the whole matter over to Shmulik. Let the Shabak break their heads on the problem. If it was Alex, it was their problem. And the grenades case was burning on his desk. The list of suspects had finally begun to shrink instead of grow. He could begin to see progress there. He shook his head and took a deep drag on the cigarette. No, it was his case, his problem.

"We're going to talk to Alex," he announced. "But I don't think he's the killer . . ."

Shvilli began to protest.

"Quiet. But he's going to have to talk to us now. If he had this secret, maybe he has others." He motioned for Levy to pull the car over to the left lane, to make the turn into Ein Kerem. After the light changed, he gestured for Levy to pull the car onto the embankment below the Calder sculpture. "Okay," he said, "let's go over it again." For almost an hour, they sat in the car, planning their approach, trying not to fall into dizzying circles of questions that led only to more questions instead of answers.

26

THEY FOUND HIM JUST inside the gate, shouting at Hamdiya.

"You!" said the KGB officer in Arabic, recognizing Shvilli as he got out of the car.

"Me," said Shvilli in Russian, with a broad grin.

Cohen shook his head sadly at the gardener. "I asked you not to come here until tomorrow," he said.

Hamdiya tried to offer an explanation, but Alex interfered.

"Commander Cohen," Alex said forcefully, "I demand an explanation."

"So do I," Cohen shot back. "And you're going to provide it."

"I don't have to talk with you," Alex said. "And you," he said, pointing to Hamdiya, "you're fired."

"I'm not so sure that you'll have the authority for that anymore," said Cohen. "It wasn't his fault. Blame me." He turned to Hamdiya. "Don't worry. It'll turn out all right. You won't lose your job."

"What are you talking about?" Alex's eyes moved from Cohen's leathery face to Shvilli's gold-toothed smirk.

"I know about you and the girl," said Cohen.

"What girl?" asked Alex.

"Helena, Natasha," barked Shvilli, "your girlfriend, you bastard."

Cohen snapped his fingers for silence. But he was pleased with Shvilli's outburst. It went as they had discussed. Shvilli's threatening volatility would energize the interview. He knew how to make the sparks fly.

No matter what their relationship, Cohen reasoned, the letter implied that there had been some kind of emotional bond between Alex and the nun. Alex had remained cool since the start of the case. To break him, Cohen was relying on surprise, on catching Alex with emotion. Alex had already shown himself vulnerable to the approach. Cohen remembered how Alex's eye had twitched when Cohen mentioned that he and the nun had arrived in Israel together. The relationship had been important to Alex. Maybe even important enough for murder.

Shvilli's taunts of Alex broke into Cohen's thoughts.

"I don't know what he's talking about," said Alex.

"I think you do," said Cohen.

"I don't have to talk to you," said the KGB officer, dispassionately. "I talk with Yaffe."

"Not yet," said Cohen. "Maybe afterwards. Right now, I think you have to talk to me. Yaffe doesn't know what I know. Not yet."

"What could you possibly know?" Alex asked haughtily.

"We know about the girl," said Cohen. "It makes you our only suspect. I'm sure you understand what that means."

"You're wrong," said Alex. "You don't know what you're talking about. I warned you. I told you not to make assumptions."

"Tell me, then," said Cohen, almost gently. "You tell me what I have wrong. You have an affair with the girl. She's a nun. I don't know how it started. But I know how it ended."

He watched for a reaction. Alex shifted his weight, but his face remained impassive. "You know," Cohen added with sorrow in his voice, "A lot of murders are between lovers." He paused. "Or former lovers."

"I know nothing about your killer," said Alex. "I have nothing to say about it."

"But you know a lot about the dead nuns. Especially Helena. Too much, perhaps. Tell me," Cohen added with what he hoped was the slightest touch of insinuation, "what did you call her? Helena? Natasha?"

"You have no right to interrogate me," said Alex, defiantly.

For Cohen it was the first hairline crack in Alex's defenses, an admission that someone did have the right to interrogate him. But it would take a lot more leverage to widen the crack as far as Cohen needed.

"That's not exactly correct," said Cohen, allowing patronization to creep into his voice. "You have immunity. So maybe we won't be able to bring you to court. But even without diplomatic relations, we can let your bosses know about your indiscretion. I imagine that the very fact that we found out will be enough to make them angry. Not with us. With you."

"I have nothing to hide," Alex said. Cohen added Alex's left hand, clenching and unclenching, to the list of signs that he was on the right track.

"Fine. All the more reason why you shouldn't mind having a conversation with me."

"You're crazy, you know that," said Alex, suddenly lightly. "I didn't kill those women. I don't know what you are talking about, 'a girl.' What girl?"

Two nuns stepped out from behind a tall cypress tree that cast a shadow over the parking lot. They watched silently, their round pale faces expressionless beneath the black hoods.

"I don't think you want to have this conversation here, do you?" said Cohen, nodding toward the two nuns. "I know I don't want it here," Cohen continued, his voice gentle and prodding. "Come," he suggested, "we'll go over there." Cohen pointed to a small clearing in the woods just beyond the road outside the convent.

Cohen turned his back on Alex and began walking to the clearing. Shvilli kept his eyes on Alex, waiting until the KGB officer moved.

Cohen waited in the shade of an olive tree as gnarled as his face. "Look, we know you had this thing with the nun," said Cohen, as Alex approached. "I'm a Jew. For me, a nun is just another woman. Religious, but just another person. I don't believe in saints."

"What do you want, Cohen?" Alex asked, his impatience betraying a nervousness that Cohen was seeking.

"Well, it's my experience," said Cohen, waving Shvilli back, "it's my experience that most people have secrets, and if the secret is important enough, they're ready to kill for it. Sometimes they're even ready to die for it."

Cohen sat down on a large root that bulged out of the ground beneath the tree. He patted his pocket, and Shvilli ran over with a cigarette. He smiled at the junior officer and then waved him away again. When Shvilli began to protest, Cohen held a finger to his lips. Shvilli backed away, his eyes on Alex, who was standing arms crossed in a pose of defiance, in front of Cohen.

"You see, Alex, I have this theory," said Cohen. "I don't know how the affair began, but you were caught in it and she was caught in it. So you kept it secret. But she was getting ideas about leaving the convent, about you leaving the KGB. You thought about sending her back to Moscow. But these nuns never leave Jerusalem voluntarily, do they?

"I'll bet she even talked about *glasnost,*" he continued. "About freedom. She wanted more, that's all. And it worried you, didn't it? You tried to convince her to leave things be. Maybe you even cut off the relationship. But she was tired of secrets. She wanted to live freely in the West. She fell in love with you, that's all. Alex, I'd guess you even fell in love with her, too. But when she said she had decided to expose the whole business, well . . ." He left unsaid the obvious, watching for Alex's reaction.

Alex scuffed at the dirt with his shoe, glancing toward Shvilli, five strides away. Shvilli took a step forward. Levy put his hand on Shvilli's shoulder and whispered into his ear. Shvilli relaxed.

"We were friendly. That's all," said Alex, coldly.

It was the crack, widening. "You're beginning to contradict yourself," said Cohen. "I imagine you know what I think when someone begins to contradict themselves."

Cohen pried further, his tone becoming more friendly. "So you took long walks and talked late into the night, discussing what? *Glasnost?*"

"Politics, yes, that's right, politics," said Alex, leaping for Cohen's offered hook.

"Probably," Cohen chuckled. "But there was more to it. Wasn't there?"

"He told you all this?" Alex said with contempt, pointing toward Shvilli. He turned back to Cohen. "He hates the Soviet

Union. So he invented this. He spoke to no one here. I know. As soon as he was missing, I asked. No one told him anything. He's inventing."

Shvilli took a step forward, his fists raised. Cohen glanced toward Shvilli, and the boxer's pose melted away.

"Alex, I'll tell you the truth," Cohen continued. "The prime minister would love to be able to tell your foreign minister that the murders were the work of the KGB. I have the pieces that can make it seem so. All I'm asking you is to prove me wrong. But you'll have to do better than calling names. Talk to me, Alex. Give me the cooperation you promised from the very beginning."

Cohen waited for Alex to answer. Shvilli was still ready to punch out at Alex's pride. Cohen waited for Alex, and Levy was a silent witness, taking notes in his yellow, palm-sized notebook.

The KGB man remained quiet, the tree speckling his white shirt with the shade of the slender silver leaves.

"I figure it's all over for you, Alex." Shvilli's voice was gleeful.

"You don't understand these types," Shvilli said shrilly to Cohen, his posture ready to attack Alex. "You don't understand them. You think you can sweet-talk him, and he'll tell you everything you want to know. But all they know is force, strength, who's stronger. I'll tell you something, *tihushnik*, we're the strong ones here. We're in charge here." He danced forward, fists up. Alex stepped backwards and into a martial arts pose.

"That's enough, Shvilli," said Cohen, pleased with the performance. Levy touched Shvilli, and the former boxer relaxed.

Alex held his tense posture for another long second.

"Come on, Alex," said Cohen in a mocking tone. "Don't be ridiculous," he added protectively, knowing that with the right tone he could make the final breach. "It's over," he said softly, slowly approaching Alex. "I'm just waiting for you." He reached up to put his hand on Alex's shoulder.

Alex looked away from Shvilli to Cohen's haggard face.

"I didn't kill them," he said. His body slumped slightly, and Cohen knew he had won. "But you're right. We were in love and it was impossible. You see, we really did talk about *glasnost*. But I believed and she didn't. She said, 'Glasnost is only halfway to the West and we're all the way here.' She wanted to defect, to give up our pasts and start a new future. We talked about it all the time. She tried to convince me that I was wrong. I tried to convince her that she was wrong. But we never fought about it. We had an impossible love and then it was over."

"When?" asked Cohen.

Alex sat down on the boulder where Cohen had been seated. "When she was dead," he said, bluntly.

"So who killed them?"

Alex shrugged. "I don't know. I'm sorry. I really don't know."

"Why haven't you done any of your own investigation?" Cohen asked.

Alex lifted and dropped his shoulders again. "What could I do? All I could do was pretend that I wasn't in pain."

"You must have heard from Moscow," Cohen insisted. "They must have asked you what you were doing to find the killer. They must have asked what kind of security man you are, if two nuns under your protection are killed."

"I lied," said Alex. "I told them I was investigating right-wing Zionists." He looked up at Cohen. "I followed your investigation and told them it was mine."

"What are you going to tell them now?" Shvilli taunted. Cohen hushed him, asking another question.

"Did you ever run into a hippie on the hill? He has a beard like this," said Cohen, stroking at his chin. "A goatee."

Alex shook his head, no.

"A hiker," Cohen prodded.

"There are lots of hikers here," said Alex.

"Did you know that Sister Elizabeth knew about the affair?" Cohen asked.

Alex looked up astonished. "She knew?"

Cohen nodded. "She wrote a letter, but it seems she never sent it. She hid it. Why wouldn't she send it?"

Alex was completely deflated. "She's a good woman," he said, ignoring Cohen's question. He looked toward Shvilli. "She believed you." Alex laughed ironically. "She felt sorry for you." He offered Shvilli a smile. "You were good, I thought you were an idiot."

Shvilli grinned.

"She thought you needed Christ," Alex added sadly. He turned back to Cohen. "I don't know why she didn't send it, but I can guess. She was embarrassed by the fact that a nun under her supervision had broken her vows, and she was afraid because it was with me."

"So why save the letter, if she wasn't going to send it?" Cohen asked.

Alex laughed lightly. "She saves everything. Everything. She's obsessive about it. But what difference does it matter now?" he asked, his voice flat and deflated of all its strength. "What's going to happen now? Please, tell me. What happens now?"

Cohen considered Alex's explanation of Sister Elizabeth's letter, realizing that the Russian was right. It no longer mattered why she saved it or didn't send it. Not to Alex, and not to him.

"I don't know what will happen," Cohen said honestly. "I've wasted a lot of time on you. A lot of time. If I had known all this three weeks ago, it would have saved a lot of effort."

"I wanted you to find the killer," Alex persisted. "But I couldn't tell you."

"I understand," said Cohen. He stood up, his back painful. "That's it."

"What's going to happen to me now? Who are you going to tell?"

"I'll have to prepare a report. Other people will decide."

"You have to help me, Cohen. You have to help me." He was speaking to Cohen's back, as the detective walked slowly toward the car.

Levy strode ahead to start the engine. Cohen opened the passenger door to the car. Shvilli walked past the KGB officer, deliberately brushing him with his shoulder. Yanking open the back door of the car, he got in.

Cohen closed his door and rolled down the window for a last word. "You didn't help me, did you Alex? Maybe if you had helped from the start, I could help you. But now? I don't know. I still have a murderer to catch. I'll do what I have to do." He turned to Levy. "Let's go," he said.

All the way down the hill, until Alex was no longer in sight, Shvilli sat twisted in the back seat, staring out the window at the KGB officer standing alone in the small clearing outside the green gate of the convent. Cohen stared straight ahead, wondering how long it would take for the jackals to begin to bray.

27

COHEN HAD HOPED FOR A PAYOFF that would solve it all neatly, satisfying both himself and the prime minister. Instead, he had laid a trap for himself, and as he worked on his report about Alex, he wondered if he'd have to chew off one of his own legs, like an animal desperate to be free of a hunter's trap.

It was long after midnight before he finished his report, sending drop copies to the Shabak, the Mossad, army intelligence, and the fifth floor. After handing the copy into the teletypist in the basement of the station, he drove slowly home, taking the long route through Talbieh, through the tiny tree-lined streets that cut between Gaza Road and Jabotinsky Street.

He found himself in front of Ahuva's building. She was not due back for another week. He thought of calling her hotel, telling her all about the trap he had set for himself. But it made him feel weak at a time when he needed to feel strong. He took his foot off the brake and cruised home, the police radio in the car as silent as the streets.

The next morning, he gave instructions to the police spokes-man. "All avenues of investigation remain open," the spokesman was to tell reporters who asked. "A suspect was briefly held, but after clarification of his alibi, was released. No charges are expected to be pressed against him." As usual, the spokesman complained that he couldn't do his job properly without more information, and as usual, Cohen reminded the spokesman that he worked for the police, not the press.

From the spokesman he went to his office. "The inspector general called," Rutie said. "Personally. He wants to talk with you."

"I'm sure," Cohen said. He felt tired as he reached for the phone and began to dial.

"IG, please," Cohen said, when the fifth-floor secretary answered. "Cohen, CID Jerusalem," he told her when she asked who was calling.

A long half minute later, the *Mafkal* was on the phone.

"Avram, how are you?" The IG's voice boomed down the line. Cohen held the receiver away from his ear.

"Fine," said Cohen, feeling the ache in his neck begin to creep stiffly up the back of his head. He had drunk himself to sleep again the night before.

"Good. Listen, that's some report I found this morning on my desk. Avram, you've made some big waves with that investigation. And it seems strange," he continued, fumbling as he searched for the words, "it seems strange that you didn't clear it with us, with the Shabak, with anyone, before you did it."

"You wouldn't have let me," Cohen said matter-of-factly. He had known the *Mafkal* since they had been to police academy together as rookies. Mordechai's greatest talent as a policeman had been to know which cases won promotion and which cases caused careers to reach dead ends. He had risen past Cohen in the hierarchy almost a decade earlier, never understanding that Cohen never wanted to move to the fifth floor. That was the ambition of people like Mordechai and Yaffe and even Levy.

Cohen had a thought. "Give Meshulam my regards," he said, guessing that Yaffe was behind the phone call.

"How did you know that . . ."

"Just a guess," Cohen said.

"Yes, well, he did come in this morning quite upset. Really, Avram. You could have at least let him know. He's the one who has to handle the problem now."

Cohen sighed. "Mordechai," he said, "if I had let Yaffe know, it would have been the same as letting the convent people know."

"Yes, well, maybe. But that's in the past now, isn't it. You see, the prime minister . . ."

". . . is going to meet the Soviet foreign minister next week," Cohen completed the sentence.

"How'd you know that?" Mordechai asked.

"Because that *shvantz* sitting across the desk from you told me, that's how!" Cohen shouted.

Cohen could imagine the *Mafkal* suddenly feeling very tired, sitting with Yaffe. Cohen smiled, thinking about Mordechai wishing that he could already be an ambassador in Venezuela or Costa Rica, someplace where the Jews were rich and would take care of him well, and there wouldn't be too many decisions but a lot of honor.

Cohen decided for him. "Mordechai," said the detective, his voice suddenly soothing and calm, "I don't want to ask for a favor . . ." There was silence on the line. Cohen's knuckles whitened as he clutched the phone, waiting for Mordechai's answer.

"A favor," the *Mafkal* repeated back to Cohen. "Today's Thursday. The PM's going next Wednesday morning. You have until Tuesday morning," he said.

"Till Tuesday evening," said Cohen. He could hear Yaffe saying something in the background. Mordechai was caught between Yaffe, his current ally, and his loyalty to the past. Cohen had gambled on the past loyalties for the favor and was pleased when he won his bet with himself.

"All right," the *Mafkal* said. "Until Tuesday noon. After that, no promises."

"Thanks, Mordechai. I owe you."

"No. We're even, Avram. This made us even. I owed you a big one and this was it."

Cohen swiveled in his chair to look out the window to the magistrates' building, thinking about how Jerusalem, like all cities he supposed, was run favor for favor. He heard Levy come into the office.

"We have until Tuesday," Cohen said, without turning around.

"And then?"

"We'll cross that bridge when we come to it," Cohen said. "So much wasted time," he muttered to himself, "so much wasted effort." He swiveled to face Levy. "How'd it go last night?" he asked. Levy had spent the evening walking Nahlaot's alleyways and courtyards, hunting for blond tourist girls and bearded hippies.

"Nothing, not yet. I planned to go back this morning and continue."

"Get on it," Cohen said. "The hippie's all we have left as a lead."

"Have they said anything to you about Alex?" Levy's voice contained a consolation that only added to Cohen's pain over the wasted efforts aimed at Alex.

"Not yet." Cohen winced as he rubbed the back of his head.

"Are you all right?" Levy asked.

"Fine, fine," Cohen insisted impatiently. "Get going." He swiveled his chair around again so he was facing out the window.

Levy took a new notebook out of the cabinet and headed for the door. "Are you sure you're all right?" Levy asked again.

"Just close the door behind you," Cohen ordered, rejecting Levy's sympathy.

He ignored the ringing phone and the pain beneath his skull. He was concentrating on the fork in the path before him, aware of the chase behind him. Through the window he could look across the compound parking lot to Ahuva's courtroom. He rubbed at the ache of his itching arm and, after a while, turned back to the folders on his desk.

It was dusk when he looked up from the notes and lists he had distilled from the reports that had come in from all the CID departments in the country. They'll put it on my tombstone, he thought. "He made notes and lists."

There were now nearly two hundred names of soldiers who had both access to the grenades and some known relationship with criminal elements. He leaned back in his chair for a moment and then yanked open the bottom drawer, rummaging in the back for the bottle of Extra Fine cognac, the cheapest available. But when his fingers found the bottle, they froze. He didn't need the drink. He withdrew his hand and, picking up the open folder in front of him, leaned back in his chair and read.

A little past 2:00 A.M. during the long night alone on the second floor, he walked down the two flights of worn marble stairs to the basement where a lone radio dispatcher worked the graveyard shift, taking the calls that came in and sending patrol cars through the dark and empty city streets. In the dispatcher's room there was always a kettle of hot water and a jar of black powdered Turkish coffee.

The dispatcher, Rotem, had been in the job as long as Cohen had been CID chief. He had a gravelly tenor that kept calm no matter how urgent his message and an obscure wit of Talmudic passages. But most important, he had the peculiar talent needed by all vehicle dispatchers, an ability to keep a picture of all the city's streets in his mind. Cohen hoped that one day the police could finally afford a computerized electronic map of the city, but he doubted that Rotem would need such a map in order to do his job any better.

As Cohen came in, Rotem was leaning back in his chair, smoking a cigarette.

"Hello, Rotem," said Cohen.

"Avram!" said Rotem, "what despair or operation so secret that even I can not know about it brings you to the harem of the radio and the telephone?"

Cohen laughed. "Coffee," he said, pointing to the twenty-liter boiler on a rickety wooden table in the corner.

"You are always welcome, always welcome," said Rotem. A call came in as Cohen went to the kettle. He could hear Rotem speaking to a patrol car officer. "From where you are take your second right. That will be Shivtei Yisrael. Then your first left and again a left, and," said Rotem, glancing up at the clock on the wall in front of him, "by the time you get there, thirty-eight will be waiting for you." Thirty-eight was the radio code for the bomb squad van that patrolled the city around the clock.

Cohen tried calculating in his own mind thirty-eight's position in the city. "The second alley off Helene the Queen Street," he tried.

Rotem let go of the microphone and pushed himself along the counter, swinging around in the swivel chair to face Cohen. He took a deep drag on his cigarette and slowly nodded his head. "You could do this job, if your own is getting problematic," Rotem said. "Keeping you awake at this time of night . . ." He exhaled a cloud of blue-gray smoke. "Troubles?"

"It's just the work, nothing more. Just the work," said Cohen.

Rotem sighed. "The work. No work, no flour. No flour, no Torah. Yes. I do mine and I finish and go home and I wake up and visit my grandson when he comes home from kindergarten." He noticed Cohen's surprise. "You know I have a grandson, Avram, you were at the *brit*."

"I'm sorry Ya'acov. Yes, of course, I was there."

"Are you all right, Avram?" Rotem asked, concern in his voice. "Are you all right?"

"Tired. That's all. Yes, I'm all right," said Cohen, but he knew he wasn't. Luck had become his temporary religion, and its demand of faith ate away at him even as it propelled him forward.

"You look as if you need some sleep," Rotem said, ready to accept any explanation that came from Cohen.

"Sheer luxury," Cohen said, grinning as he lifted the Styrofoam coffee cup to his lips.

"Avram, we all have to sometimes say enough is enough. We all have to admit we're human," Rotem said. "Why don't you get some sleep?"

"You tell me, Rotem," Cohen answered with his own question. "Haven't you had enough night shifts? Why don't *you* say enough is enough."

Rotem sighed. "Avram, a man can live with a woman for twenty years and know nothing about her. You've been smart to stay single."

"Trouble at home?" asked the detective.

"The trouble is that it's not at home. It's at someone else's home," Rotem said, swiveling back to the switchboard as the phone rang. "Police," he said. He listened for a moment and began speaking. "Don't touch anything. Don't move anything. I'll send a car, but it may take some time. Now. Your name. Your address . . ."

Cohen waited until Rotem finished sending a patrol car to the burgled apartment. "Rotem, could you do me a favor? I'm going up to the archives. Do you know the switchboard number up there? Twenty-two. Call me at 5:30. I think I will lie down for a while."

"No problem," said Rotem, making a note on his pad. Another call came in, and he slipped a cigarette out of the packet on the desk before picking up his microphone.

Cohen went up the five flights of stairs from the basement to the archives. Beyond the last set of floor-to-ceiling shelves was a simple cot. He laid himself down, fatigued, and was asleep almost immediately.

When the phone rang, he reached for it out of a deep dream. The darkness of the night beyond the window confused him. He had expected dawn light through the window when the wake-up call came from Rotem.

"Avram," said Rotem, "Sorry to bother you. A call for you. They say it's urgent."

"Okay, okay," Cohen mumbled, straining to aim the dial of his watch into the pale light coming through the dusty window. He had slept barely twenty minutes.

"Commander?"

"Yes?" Cohen answered, uncertain of the voice.

"I think I have something. I know I have something."

"Daniel?"

"Ein Kerem! A prophet! A leader with followers! They're planning an operation!"

The panic in Daniel's voice shook Cohen awake. "Daniel, where are you?"

"I'm following them, I'm following them," the undercover agent's whisper was full of urgency, but his message was unclear to Cohen.

"Daniel, calm down. Now tell me, are you in Ein Kerem?" Cohen repeated, trying to offer composure to the youthful policeman.

"I'm following them. I stopped. A pay phone. I don't know his name, I'm trying to find out. I'm following. I'm on it."

"Daniel. Where in Ein Kerem? What's in Ein Kerem? Who's name?"

Daniel's whispers became even more urgent.

"I don't know. I'll know tomorrow."

"What time? Where?"

"I have to go. Follow. Meet me. The *Kotel*. In the morning."

"Daniel, wait!" called Cohen. For a moment he could hear the sounds of the street beyond the phone booth. He thought he heard a siren but wasn't sure whether it came through the phone or from the city beyond the compound. He called out to Daniel again, but the line was dead.

Cohen could still hear the siren, distant across the city or perhaps in his mind. Who was moving? Why Ein Kerem? He lay back on the cot. Just for a moment, he thought, before going out to find Daniel.

When the phone rang again, he was sure it was Daniel calling back. But it was Rotem with the wake-up call.

The bomb squad had the luxury of a shower, and Cohen went down to their squad room, taking a razor from his desk drawer. He shaved automatically, using hand soap for foam and the cold water of the single-tap sink. But as he wiped his face dry with the towel from the rack, he found himself staring into his own eyes. There were black circles beneath them. He stood that way for a moment, the towel pressed to his face, his fingertips just below the circumference of darkness above his cheeks. He heard someone walking down the corridor outside the bomb squad office and quickly finished before striding rapidly up the stairs back to his office.

Levy was unlocking the door to the office when Cohen reached the landing.

"You're early," Cohen called out to his aide, who was clutching copies of the morning newspapers under his arm, holding a cup of coffee in one hand and his briefcase in the other.

"You've been here all night, again," Levy said disapprovingly. "You've got to get some rest," he said.

"I slept," Cohen said, brushing aside Levy. "Stop worrying about me."

"I can't help it. I worry."

Cohen shook his head, hiding a smile of appreciation from Levy. He opened the door and they entered, Levy dropping the Friday weekend newspapers onto the desk before putting down his coffee and briefcase.

"Daniel called," he told Levy. "He had a confusing message about Ein Kerem, something about a prophet. I don't know. Before he could tell me anything he hung up."

"He's panicky about everything. Maybe it's the thing with his father," Levy said, picking up the *Ha'aretz*. The other morning newspaper, *The Jerusalem Post*, lay underneath.

"I'll find out this morning. He asked for a meet."

Levy scanned the front page of the newspaper, speaking as he read. "I was planning to go back out to Nahlaot today, look for that girl," said Levy. As Cohen reached for a second file, he saw the headline, just above the front-page fold of the *Post*.

Spy, Slain Nun in Secret Affair was played across five columns. Cohen stood up to reach across his desk for the paper. A stack of files fell to the floor, startling Levy, who was surprised to see Cohen grabbing for the newspaper instead of the scattered folders.

Cohen read standing up. Someone had leaked his report on Alex. There was nothing about Shvilli, but the story covered both the love story between Alex and Helena and the way Cohen had mentioned the syndrome as a possible element in both the grenades case and the murders.

By the third paragraph Cohen was already naming in his mind the possible sources for the report. Yaffe. Shmulik. Mordechai. Someone on the fifth floor. Someone in the prime minister's office. Someone had leaked the story about Alex and Helena to the *Post*'s crime reporter, Benny Lassman.

The story jumped from the front page onto the back. Lassman's quotes were almost directly lifted from Cohen's report, but couched in journalese.

> Sources close to the investigation indicated that the still-at-large—and still unknown—murderer of the Moscow-run convent nuns might be suffering from a mental illness that the authorities have been reluctant to speak about, known as The Jerusalem Syndrome.
>
> The Post has learned that the illness has been diagnosed in more than 100 patients in the last year. In its most acute form, it involves self-inflicted violence or random violence. According to psychologists working with the security services who have treated such cases, the violence is often directed against people or institutions regarded as religious symbols by those afflicted.

Cohen tossed the paper to Levy and grabbed *Ha'aretz*, searching for a similar story in the gray pages of the paper. But Lassman had a scoop.

Cohen slumped into his seat, covering his eyes with his hand. Levy read carefully. "Who could have done this?" Levy asked, astonished. For a moment, Cohen looked at Levy through his spread fingers, wondering if his loyal lieutenant might have tried to forge a shortcut to Cohen's chair. But Levy's fury was no less than his. "I'm going to call him. Lassman. We'll make him tell us who leaked it," Levy said.

Cohen shook his head. "It doesn't matter now who leaked it. I'll be blamed," he said wearily. "And the last thing we need is to be accused of trying to get a reporter to divulge his sources."

Levy looked at his boss with incomprehension. "Nobody on the fifth floor wanted word out about the syndrome," he said. "You told me yourself it's something the government doesn't want to hear about. But this? Why?"

"Well, it had to come out, didn't it," said Cohen. He couldn't deny he was pleased by the report, even though it had damaged him personally. At least the truth about the syndrome was coming out. But he also had to calculate the potential losses and benefits to the investigation. It all depended on who leaked the story. Yaffe could have done it by accident. Cohen knew that Lassman was clever enough to put pieces together if he got part of it from Yaffe. Anyone on the fifth floor trying to put Cohen away could have leaked it, and from Mordechai all the way down the floors of national headquarters, there were people who would be happy to see Cohen gone. The prime minister's office could have done it for political reasons that Cohen might never understand.

"It could help us," he said suddenly.

"How?" Levy asked.

Before Cohen could answer, the phone rang. It was Nussbaum.

"Commander Cohen?" the cabinet secretary asked.

"Yes."

"The prime minister would like to see you."

Cohen looked at his watch. It was 6:30. "Now?"

"In half an hour. At the residence."

"I'll be there," said Cohen, and hung up. He rose from his chair and reached for his uniform, hanging from a peg in the corner. It was wrapped in a dry cleaner's plastic bag.

"I've been called to an audience," Cohen said.

Levy looked at him quizzically. "How can the story help us?" he asked.

"I'll be back later on. Hold on here. There will be more phone calls. Tell them I'll be back by nine. Don't worry," Cohen said,

"It may work for us. It's going to stir things up. It will make things happen. It could create opportunities for us. If we're allowed to continue." The phone began ringing. "See what I mean," he said, as he closed the door behind him, leaving Levy to the ringing telephones.

Only after Cohen was gone did Rutie come in with the message from Aboudi, asking for the officer, Nissim Levy, to call the fruit and vegetable man in the Mahane Yehuda *shuk* behind Nahlaot.

28

T HE POLICEMAN ON GUARD outside the walls of the house on Balfour Street recognized him and smiled. But Cohen had to wait for the secret service bodyguard to okay his entrance to the Bauhaus-style residence.

While he waited, he gazed across the street. On the narrow sidewalk across the street, three sleeping bags were curled up in front of a low wall of posters demanding that the prime minister begin peace talks with the PLO. Separated by a metal police barrier, four more demonstrators, already awake, sat glumly beneath a poster with Ben-Yehoshua's face, demanding that the government deport Arabs. A car passing the two tiny demonstrations paused in front of the sleeping protesters. Cohen scowled when he heard a curse on the demonstrators' mothers spat from the driver's window of the sedan before it sped away, only to stop short half a block away at the red light of the intersection. Cohen looked at the policeman, who shrugged, as if to say "What do you expect?" Cohen turned away from him just as the security man came down the three stairs to the electric gate. The security man checked Cohen's ID and nodded to the policeman. There was a click, and the narrow gate swung open.

Inside the small lobby, Cohen was wordlessly directed through open French doors to the living room. "Where's Nussbaum?" Cohen asked, his voicing dropping naturally to a whisper in the wood-paneled room. The guard silently shook his head.

As the detective waited for the prime minister, he moved slowly around the room, looking at the book titles on the shelves and then at the four works of art on the walls.

Two were Chagalls, and two were Tichos. Chagall painted the prime minister's childhood in the Pale, Cohen thought. Anna Ticho etched visions of the empty Judean mountains that filled the prime minister's rhetoric. Cohen could hear the noises of the household as he moved about the silent room. There was a clatter of silverware from the kitchen, the sound of water running in a basin. A phone rang somewhere upstairs in the living quarters of the house, and Cohen could hear a woman's voice answer the phone and then call out for the prime minister, using his last name, the way she had always done since they were in the underground together. They had been together for more than fifty years.

The prime minister surprised him. "Mr. Cohen," said the familiar voice behind him.

Cohen turned, snapped to attention, and saluted.

"There's no need for any of that. Coffee or tea, perhaps?" asked the prime minister, motioning to a secret serviceman doubling as a valet who had materialized at the double doors separating the living room from the hallway.

"Black, please. Sweet Turkish," said Cohen.

"Please sit down, Mr. Cohen," said the prime minister, taking his own seat in an overstuffed arm chair with wooden handles and a faded rose pattern. Cohen immediately noticed that the prime minister was using mister rather than rank. He knew that it did not bode well for him.

"Now, Mr. Cohen. I'm sure you know that I spent almost ten years hiding from the British police. Sometimes they were very close, sometimes they were very, very close. But they never caught me. Perhaps it was because God didn't want them to catch me. Perhaps history didn't want them to catch me. But over the years I have come to think that it was simply that I was smarter than they were. My reasons for being here were better than their reasons."

The security man returned with a tray, and the prime minister fell silent for a moment, taking his glass of tea, waiting for Cohen to take his tiny cup of coffee. Then the bodyguard disappeared again silently and the premier resumed.

"Several times they should have found me. I was in their hands and they didn't know it. I must admit," he said, "that because of my experience, I have never really thought very highly of policemen. But now we have our own policemen. And you know what the poet said."

Cohen understood the reference. "One day," Bialik had written early in the century, "we Jews will be normal people, with our own prostitutes and our own policemen."

He smiled at Cohen and continued. "I've been told that you are the inventor of a certain saying. Correct me if I'm wrong. It goes 'The problem here is that half the people don't believe there should be Jewish policemen and the other half don't believe there are Jewish criminals.' " The premier clasped his hands and held them on his chest. "I liked that, when I heard it."

"I have said that. Yes," Cohen admitted, chagrined.

"Well," continued the premier, "I must admit, I still find it hard to believe that a Jew can be a criminal. But I want very much to believe that Jewish policemen can be better at their jobs than the British policemen were at their jobs."

Cohen longed for a cigarette, wishing the prime minister would get to the point that he was expecting and dreading.

"Now, I begin every day with a cup of tea and the newspapers. Usually the newspapers are full of mistakes, full of half-truths." He sighed, as if pained by those mistakes. "What can I do, this is a free country. A democracy. But this morning, what I read in *The Jerusalem Post* made my eyes go black. It was bad enough when I had to read in your report about this matter of what you call the syndrome."

In his report after questioning Alex, Cohen had included a final section outlining his views on the direction of the investigation. He wasn't surprised that the PM saw his report—both the Mossad and the Shabak reported directly to the prime minister.

"But to see it in the newspaper!" the prime minister was continuing, astonishment as much as anger in his voice. "This was too much. Jerusalem is our eternal capital, and yet you blame our possession of Jerusalem for some psychological theory that cannot be proven?" There was disdain in his voice as he said the word "psychological."

"I did no such thing," Cohen broke in, to defend himself.

"Sir," Cohen added, clipping his deference with protest. But the prime minister waved a hand at him.

"Please, let me finish," said the prime minister, clasping his hands together again in his lap. "I have been told that you knew I was in negotiations with the Soviets. These are very important negotiations, and they were threatened by the murders of the nuns. It was embarrassing to us. Now I read things that embarrass the Soviets. I do not want to embarrass them right now." He paused, holding up one hand momentarily, as if to study his fingernails. "In the past, yes, I have wanted to embarrass them, and in the future, perhaps, I will want to embarrass them. But right now, no, I do not want to embarrass them. But for some reason, you do want to embarrass them. And me. And Jerusalem itself." The prime minister's eyes were enlarged by the thickness of the spectacles and stared directly at Cohen. The eyes blinked once, and suddenly Cohen realized that he was being given a chance to speak.

"Sir," he said, "I had nothing to do with that story this morning. I was as shocked by its publication as you were."

"I have been told that you were probably behind the leak," the PM said matter-of-factly. He ignored Cohen's protest. "That doesn't matter now," the PM continued. "You had no reason to put your man into the convent without permission. You went behind the back of the security services. Behind my back." The prime minister's tone was accusatory.

"There was no other way," Cohen defended himself.

"It was not your job," said the prime minister, his voice rising from its low deliberate levels to a higher pitch of attack. "It was not your decision," he said firmly.

Cohen suddenly wondered how he could have been so mistaken about the PM's condition. Shmulik was right, Cohen thought, he was right to warn me about the PM.

"Such operations are conducted by the General Security Services," the prime minister went on, "under my authority alone. Such a violation of diplomatic immunity is not done by the police. You can infiltrate the underworld, you can infiltrate the criminals. But not foreigners with official standing."

Cohen could feel his face flushing red, the heat spreading across his cheeks as thoughts raced through his head. Ahuva was right. I felt responsible for it all. But it wasn't my responsibility. It was his. He's right. I should have given it to Shmulik. I should have let him break his head on Alex. "About the syndrome, sir," he said, using the opportunity of a pause in the PM's speech. "It's real, sir. We see it all the time. Sometimes it's silly and pathetic. But sometimes it can be dangerous. Very dangerous. It's not our possession of the city that causes it. It's the idealization of the city, and it's a genuine psychological phenomenon. Rohan, Goodman," he began, ticking off the names of madmen who since 1967 had personal visions that led them to arson and murder on the Temple Mount.

"Philosophy and psychology," mocked the prime minister. "That's all. It is cheap for you. But for a politician it can be very expensive, Mr. Cohen. For us."

"It's real. And every year it gets worse," Cohen persisted, wondering if "us" meant Israel or the prime minister and his coalition.

"You mean every year I'm prime minister," the older man said sardonically. "So, it's my fault? My illness, my crime?"

"No, of course not," said Cohen.

"So what would you have me do?"

Cohen was silent. He wanted to tell the premier that he should have been the first to condemn the sabotage attempt on the Mount, that no matter what his concerns about diplomacy, his first responsibility was to prevent insanity from spreading in the city. But the years as a servant of a system in which the prime minister's office was the symbol of its highest authority stopped him. He strained against the discipline of his profession, knowing that he was right about the syndrome, and that there was no way he could persuade the prime minister.

"I never told you not to investigate," the premier said, interpreting Cohen's silence as concession and returning to the immediate concern. "I asked you to be discreet, I asked you to keep us informed."

Cohen had to protect himself from the frontal assault. "Until he came out safely," he asserted, "I had to keep the secret of the presence of my man inside the convent."

"Yes, yes, I understand that. But I do not understand why you could not wait. Why could you not wait until I had conducted my talks?"

"Because . . ."

"It doesn't matter," the prime minister interrupted with a deep sigh, waving his hand like a sultan dismissing a servant. "It's too late now. Too late," the prime minister said. "For now. Maybe later. Maybe for my successor."

"Mr. Prime Minister," said Cohen, wanting to vindicate himself, feeling victimized by the report in the newspaper and regret about the trap he had laid for himself. He attacked to defend himself. "I did not leak that story to the newspaper," he repeated. "In fact, when I saw it this morning it did cross my mind that the leak could have come from your own office." He said it without defiance, but forcefully, and once said, he felt better.

"Really?" the PM answered sarcastically, discounting out of hand the idea that any of his loyalists would so betray him, not surprised that the police officer who had given him such trouble might believe such a libel. He continued with the same sardonic tone. "Perhaps now that you have discounted this Russian, you intend to accuse the chief rabbis. What was it in that report on this so-called syndrome? *'Religious justification for xenophobia . . .'* Or perhaps you would like to question me?" Again the prime minister quoted from the report. " *'Extremist rhetoric from official authority figures . . .'* "

Cohen knew the end of the quote by heart: *"can be interpreted by the susceptible as a legitimization of extremist action . . ."*

He realized the prime minister was attacking him with the same rhetorical blades used against the impotent Knesset opposition. But he chose to take seriously the question about other possible suspects. "There are several possibilities still open to us," he said, hoping that the PM wouldn't ask for specifics and he'd have to explain that all he had was a missing hippie and rumors of a prophet. "We're still trying to discover the truth in this matter."

But the prime minister waved his hand. "That's very reassuring, Mr. Cohen. And I'm sure you will be successsful," he said, with a tinge of disdain. "But you have already trod in places where maybe you were seeking truth, but in the end all you found was something small and sordid and something that has made my truth impossible—for now."

"What do you want from me?" Cohen asked coldly.

"Oh, now, it doesn't matter. With this story in the newspaper, it doesn't matter. Now it is too late. Too late."

"Mr. Prime Minister, sir. With all due respect, I have no interest in this matter except finding the murderer," said Cohen. "Yes. I have regrets. And I have no doubt that I will have regrets again in the future. But I took my actions with only the interests of the public's safety in mind."

The prime minister smiled for the first time since the conversation began. "And I don't have the public interest at heart?" he asked in a mockingly outraged tone, slapping his palm to his chest in an expression of surprise. "Who are you," he asked rhetorically, again his voice rising to higher levels of attack, "to think that you know better than me what must be done for the public interest? A policeman. That's all you are, a policeman. Enforce the laws, Mr. Cohen. Stop meddling with psychology and philosophy."

Cohen felt that he had nothing left to lose. "My job is to enforce the law, to discover the truth."

"Ah, the truth," said the prime minister. "Tell me, Mr. Cohen. What if this truth you are searching for turns out to be a bad truth, a truth that could harm the nation? Harm our people?"

Cohen thought for a moment. "Then the nation's leaders must be strong enough to repair the harm." It was his final defense, a direct attack on the prime minister himself. The leashes formed by three decades on the police force had given way. It surprised him as he said it, and it astonished him that the prime minister, too, seemed surprised by Cohen's answer.

"Yes, that is correct," said the prime minister. "That is correct." He seemed to sink into the pillows of the chair, closing his eyes as if to rest. In the silence, Cohen could hear the aged man's breathing, a slight raspy snore.

"Is that all, sir?" Cohen asked softly after a long minute of silence had passed.

"One last thing, Mr. Cohen. When I met you at the first meeting, that day, I didn't make the connection. But because of this affair, I have had questions asked about you. And I learned that you are the same Avram Cohen whom I once admired."

"Excuse me, sir?" Cohen was thrown completely by the statement.

"There was an Avram Cohen who came here right after the war. He had been a youth in a camp. It was said he survived three years in a camp. Some said it was impossible for a person to survive that long. But I knew that there would be such survivors, that for the same reason God would not allow me to be captured by the British, he would allow a few to survive the camps. Now I learn that you are this same Avram Cohen from Dachau."

Cohen said nothing, holding his hat in his hand, wishing he could get out of the overheated room.

"So you tell me, Mr. Cohen, was this what it was all about? Did you survive so that one day you would be responsible for harming the state by allowing such lies to be spread about our people."

Cohen began to speak again, but the prime minister waved a hand at him. "Go, conduct your investigation. It is on your head."

Cohen rose from his chair and put on his hat. As he stepped out of the living room he turned back to the prime minister. "Sir, I survived the camp because I was strong, because I was not ready to die, because it was my life and I would do what had to be done to save it. I am not proud of everything I did to survive. But I am proud that I survived. I did what had to be done. Just like you in the underground. Surely you cannot be proud of all that you did, even as you take pride in the accomplishment. And surely you know that God had nothing to do with it. Nothing at all. You, of all people, should know that."

With that, he saluted and turned on his heels, not waiting for a response. He strode the three steps to the front door, down the stairs, and into the garden pathway to the gate. The policeman on duty pressed the button to open the electronic gateway just as Cohen's hand pushed at it.

Only in the silence of his car, lighting a cigarette, did he drive out of his mind the long wheezing sigh that had whispered behind his back in the prime minister's living room. The sigh had been deep and terrible, and for Cohen it had a rhythm as repetitive as the clicking rumble of the iron wheels of the cattle cars on the tracks.

29

A S ALWAYS, Cohen felt uncomfortable among the praying believers, unable to duplicate their fervor. But he loved the Wall itself. He felt as though the massive stones laid thousands of years before were part of him. He liked the way the shrubs grew wild and graceful from the cracks between the stones. As he crossed the huge plaza in front of the wall, he watched birds swooping out of their nests in those shrubs, catching warm currents that sent them flying higher than the golden and silver domes of the mosques above the wall. He strode to the wall, the early morning sun in his eyes making the wall into a shimmering mirage of warm gold until he stepped into the chill of its long morning shadow.

He found Daniel beside the fence that separated the praying men from the women.

"Ein Kerem. Ein Kerem," the excited young undercover man whispered as soon as Cohen appeared beside him. He was dressed as he was the last time Cohen saw him, his black trousers dusty, the white shirt gone gray. His beard had thickened, Cohen noticed, and his red eyes had the look of sleeplessness and anxiety.

They each faced the wall. Daniel held a small prayer book. Standing side by side, they slowly swayed back and forth as they spoke. To the rest of the people in the plaza, they looked like two men in separate worlds, each privately conversing with God. But instead of murmuring the prayers, they whispered to each other.

Cohen ignored Daniel's first words. "How's your father? What happened?" he asked.

"I saw him, I followed him. I couldn't help myself. He went into this shul, a little one with a good rabbi. My father went into this rabbi's yeshiva and he sat down and was reading Psalms, and I don't know why I did it, but I sat down across from him. At first he didn't recognize me. I knew the psalm. Number 91. *'Thou shalt not fear the terror at night or the arrow in day.'* "

Cohen forced himself to listen with patience.

"I recited it," Daniel said, "and he looked up at me, and I looked at him, and then, like *tzwie alter kaker yids,* we were crying," Daniel summarized. "I promise, it's okay. Nothing for you to worry about. But I'm worried. I didn't tell him I was still in the police. I told him I was doing penance. I'm doing penance, I swear, that's how I feel."

"Are you sure you're okay?" Cohen asked, knowing well how an undercover man's cover story can turn into lies to his family and friends that he himself finally believes. He watched carefully for Daniel's response.

"Yes, yes, I'm sure. I'll be seeing him later, we're meeting, and it seems okay now."

"All right," said Cohen, turning to his reason for being at the Wall. "What about Ein Kerem?"

"I went to Ein Kerem. Last night."

"Nu," said Cohen.

"They call themselves kabbalists, but they aren't really kabbalists. They're real nuts. They call their rabbi a prophet. They call themselves *kohanim* and *levi'im.* Like ranks. *Levi'im* serve the *kohanim.* They're making plans for the Third Temple."

"A lot of people are making plans for the Third Temple," Cohen said, disappointed.

"These are different. They're crazy. And this leader, this one they call the prophet. He's dangerous. I'm sure of it."

"Go on," said Cohen, curious but not expectant.

"A whole group, they've gone completely crazy. They hold meetings. In Ein Kerem. Only they aren't prayers. It's madness."

"What do you mean?"

"They have their own prayers. And they *do* conduct sacrifices. I saw it with my own eyes. On a hilltop, near Ein Kerem. A scapegoat for their sins, a heifer for purification. They're really crazy. They all carry knives, and they do whatever he says. He's the prophet. And he says he's going to anoint the High Priest after they destroy the abominations on the Mount."

"So?" said Cohen, impatiently, "There's a bunch who want to lay the foundation stone for the Third Temple on the Mount. What makes him so different?" But he was already wondering if instead of the nuns' killer, he was moving closer to the grenades.

"He's preaching Armageddon. That's what he's teaching. It's his prophecy, Armageddon. He's not talking about praying up there or putting up the flag on top of the dome. He's talking about wiping out the abominations to make way for the Temple. He's crazy, I tell you, but they listen to him. He says he's the connection to the future, to the messiah. He embodies the connection, he says, and they believe him. I've been following them. And last night, I followed them to Ein Kerem. They have a cave there. I couldn't get too close. They would have seen me. It's a few kilometers past the village."

"Okay," said Cohen, thinking out loud. "So far we have some followers of a somewhat crazy rabbi who likes midnight hikes to Ein Kerem. What makes them so dangerous?"

"The people in the neighborhood say he's been to jail. That's where he became religious. The rumors say he went in ten years ago."

"Why didn't you say so before?" Cohen asked, suddenly more interested. "What's his name?"

"The prophet," said Daniel, "that's all I know. Some people call him the prophet, the rabbi. But some people call him the *meshugenah,* and a few call him the *meturaf,* the madman."

"What did he go to jail for?" asked Cohen, trying to remember a ten-year-old case involving someone who had turned religious in jail. He ran though mental lists of names of those convicts he knew who would have enough charisma to keep a gang in line.

"Nobody seems to know. Not in the neighborhood. All they know is gossip. About drugs. Sacrifices. The born *haredim* make fun of the newly repentant, so there's a lot of gossip. He gets driven around a lot in an old Ford Escort—I have the number for you," Daniel said, folding a piece of paper tightly into a knot.

He touched the wall, moving his fingers over it as gently as any of the praying men. His fingers found a crack in the wall stuffed with knotted paper wishes offered to heaven. He continued whispering, as if still reciting psalms, as he placed the tightly folded paper into the tiny crevice. "One of his followers, I overheard him talking with one of the others about *nafas*. They call it the spices of the Lord. And I saw at least one pistol."

Cohen pretended to be placing his own message to heaven in a crack in the wall but instead plucked Daniel's note out.

Cohen raised an eyebrow at the mention of the pistol and the drugs, and Daniel noticed, emphasizing the madness of the group. "They sacrificed this goat," Daniel repeated, "and then the heifer. He recites these prayers, I'm telling you, there aren't any prayers like that. Not any that I know of. About seeing lights, and salvation and vengeance on those who live in darkness. They wear special robes woven from pure linen and according to the rules for making the priests' clothing."

Cohen was more impressed with Daniel's report of the group's interest in drugs than he was with yet another group trying to speed up the messiah's arrival. "Drugs. We can check that out. But what's the connection to the nuns?"

"They hate the *goyim*," said Daniel. "That's the point. They say that the Christians stole Jesus and that the Moslems stole the Temple Mount."

"Half the people in Mea Shearim hate the *goyim*," Cohen said, his interest fading.

"But they don't talk about doing something to get rid of them," Daniel insisted.

"What have they done?" Cohen asked.

"I don't know the details. But something, they've done something. I'm sure of it. I don't know what. I heard two of them talking about the grenades at that antiwar rally. One of them, this Yossi, he's closer to the prophet, he said as if it was perfectly normal, 'The people at the rally deserved it, that's what the prophet says. It's part of the process.' "

"Anything about the grenades on the Mount?"

" 'The prophet sees it as part of a plan. He says it's the start of the job we're supposed to finish.' That's what I heard," Daniel said.

"What kind of job?"

"I don't know. You said Ein Kerem. I listened for Ein Kerem. This is what I learned."

Cohen dug into his memory. Who did he send to jail ten years ago and who turned religious? Mostly they started with a kippa in court, especially if they couldn't afford a suit and tie. Some stuck with the transformation. Surely he would know this person, for Jerusalem's criminal underworld never numbered more members than a mid-sized yeshiva. Some gang leaders were as powerful as any rabbi able to impose his will on his followers. He wanted to meet this religious outlaw with a criminal past. He was certain they would be old acquaintances.

"Tell me, Daniel, what does he look like, this leader?"

"Well, he's in black when he's not in the robes. Black coat, trousers, hat. White shirt. And I saw him only from a distance. Tall, a full black beard. And there's something about his eyes. He always wears sunglasses."

Ovadia. David Ovadia. Of course. Cohen knew him. Ovadia's eyes were a giveaway. One dark brown, the other a shockingly light green. His favorite mask had always been a pair of dark glasses. Before Cohen sent him to Ramle, he was Jerusalem's most powerful and dangerous drug dealer, controlling his gang on puppet strings made of violence. Cohen had tried and failed to prove Ovadia's tactics included murder. A key witness disappeared before the trial, and for all those years, Cohen had kept the file in his office, occasionally able to open it for a few weeks when a tip would come in or a rumor would be whispered in the city. Cohen had climbed down ravines and stood beside abandoned wells, watching men digging in sand dunes, looking for Danny Amsalem's body. Little Danny was going to testify against Ovadia. Cohen had even once sought a civil engineer's expertise on whether it would be possible to excavate a cement pillar beneath Jerusalem's tallest office building, because of rumors that Danny's body had been mixed into the cement. The engineer said it would be impossible. No body had ever turned up, and without it, there was no proof of murder, no charge to bring against Ovadia. The conviction was for manslaughter. Cohen had hoped to get him for premeditated murder as well as drugs, but all he had when he went into court was Ovadia using a knife to defend himself against an angry competitor. The ten-year sentence was the maximum penalty for the crime.

So, ten years ago, Cohen had sent Ovadia to Ramle. And now he was out, Cohen thought, with ideas about God and a new gang ready to do whatever he asked of them.

"You know him?" asked Daniel, interpreting Cohen's stillness.

"I know him," said Cohen. "We once wanted him for conspiracy to murder. All we got him on was manslaughter. It was the eyes, that's how I recognized him when you described him. One brown, one green."

"No, that's not it," said Daniel, shaking his head. "He's blind."

Cohen's knees seemed to turn to water for an instant. "Are you sure?" he asked Daniel, reaching to the Wall for support.

"That's what I understood. That's what I saw. His men lead him," Daniel reiterated.

Cohen turned away from the wall to think. A group of early morning tourists stood just outside the deep shade of the Wall. The tourists were photographing the Wall. A few had entered the prayer area where photographs were not allowed on Shabbat or the holidays. But it was Friday morning. Shabbat was more than a dozen hours away.

He looked back at Daniel. "Can you show us the way to the cave?"

"I don't know," said Daniel. "It was dark. I followed from a distance. I was scared. And sir, I'll tell you the truth," he added, apologetically. "I want out. Seeing my father. It made me think. I wanted out, but I promised you this. Now I need time to think. About my life. About my future."

Cohen wasn't surprised. He knew the feeling of being alone and afraid in the dark. And ever since their last meeting, he had expected Daniel's resignation. Fear had overcome the undercover man. At least he was wise enough to ask to be released, Cohen thought.

"You'll be fine. I'm sure you'll be fine," the old detective whispered. "And you've been a great help to me. A great help. Ovadia. A prophet. Ha!" he laughed. "If you want to come back, you can, you know that. I won't call this a vacation or sick leave.

Between you and me, we'll know what you're doing. But you've got to let me know, in a month or so, what you plan to do. You have to decide."

"I know. I will. I promise," said Daniel.

They stood silently for a moment. "I've got to go," said Cohen. "Good luck. Let me know what happens," he said, touching the wall once again, and then, in the manner of the religious, he moved backwards one step, still facing it. Then he turned and strode through the wide plaza to the Dung Gate parking lot where he had left his car. All the way, he kept his hand in his pocket, clutching Daniel's note with the license number.

As he drove out the ancient gate, he began using the radio to issue instructions to Rutie, Levy, and Deputy Commander Menachem Shahar, chief of the Jerusalem drug squad. Once onto the route that rounded the Old City's exterior walls, he flicked on the siren to cut through the traffic on the short ride back to his Russian Compound offices.

30

HE FOUND THEM IN HIS OFFICE, squared off like two tomcats in the *shuk*. The veins on Shahar's shaved head were pulsing with anger as he stood behind Levy's chair. Levy was behind Cohen's desk, his fists clenched and pressed to the table like a sumo wrestler about to take off. They were both sweating despite the light chill in the air.

"What's going on here?" Cohen demanded as he walked into the office.

The two officers began speaking at once. But with one glance from Cohen, Levy immediately deferred to Shahar, the more senior officer.

"Your man here says that he gave me a memo about a hippie, drugs, and Ein Kerem," Shahar said accusingly.

"And here's the carbon," Levy said, slamming his fist on a folder open to the orange copy that a memo writer keeps in his files.

"I never saw it," said Shahar. "I never got it."

"I gave it to you," Levy said, teeth clenched. "In person. In the corridor outside your office. I said, 'Here, this is important, this is urgent,' and you glanced at it and said you'd get back to me."

Shahar threw up his hands. "Fifteen times a day, someone bumps into me in the hall and says something," he shot back. "He says it was three weeks ago." That was directed at Cohen, and then Shahar turned again to Levy. "Do you know what my caseload was in the last year? Mud and coffins aren't the only thing the army brought back from Lebanon."

Levy bowed his head slightly.

"I know what's going on," said Cohen, a sop to Shahar, and then he continued, "and I'll know more, if people tell me what's going on," a warning to both subordinates in the room. "Why didn't you tell me about Ovadia before," he continued, aiming the dart at Shahar. "The hippie, that's something else. Memos get lost. You had no reason to make a connection. But Ovadia, out of jail. Blind. Running a rabbinical show? I would have wanted to hear about that. Why didn't you keep an eye on Ovadia when he got out of Ramle?" His tone was a prosecutor's driving in for the kill.

"This is the first I hear of some connection between Ovadia and Ein Kerem," said Shahar, trying to deflect Cohen's accusations. "I'm as surprised as you are."

"Daniel tells me that he's running some kind of show out there in Ein Kerem," said Cohen, "that he's preaching Armageddon and getting rid of abominations on the Temple Mount. What else do we have? When was he blinded?"

"Four years ago," Levy started, looking down into the file, "a second-rate hood, let's see . . ."

"Ya'acov Amsalem, from Lod," Shahar interjected.

"Little Danny Amsalem's cousin," Cohen added, his mind focused on all he knew about Ovadia.

Levy glared at the drug squad chief, but Shahar continued. "Amsalem was sent in for six years on armed robbery. He attacked Ovadia, nearly drowned him in a bucket of bleach. Ovadia can't tell when the sun is shining even if he's staring right into it."

"Why did Amsalem attack?" Cohen asked.

"According to the prison service report, Amsalem flipped out. He thought Ovadia was the devil. But Ovadia was clean. He made a big thing out of forgiving Amsalem, didn't even complain. Amsalem went into solitary for a year."

"He was trying to take revenge for his cousin," Cohen reckoned.

"And when he came out," Levy said, holding a page from the

folder, "he became one of Ovadia's followers. He had a dozen in jail, and when he got out last year, he found himself another dozen."

"Ramle reservists," added Shahar, referring to recidivists at Ramle prison, the toughest and most cramped of the country's jails. "They're in and out of there as often as I have to go to the army for reserve duty."

"Ovadia always found ways to persuade people to go do his bidding," Cohen said. "But he has changed in one way, that's for sure," added Cohen. "The David Ovadia I know would have arranged for someone to do Amsalem. All right, we'll keep that in mind. Now, what about a guide to the caves in Ein Kerem?"

"The Preservation of Nature Society promised us a guide to the area," said Levy. "It will take a little time before he's here."

"So what happened?" Cohen asked Shahar. "Ovadia became something of a rabbi, something of a saint? A righteous one? Eh?"

"It began toward the end of the trial," the drug squad chief said. "He said he understood."

"Understood what?" Cohen asked.

"He told the judge he understood where he had gone wrong. He started with a kippa, but within a week he was wearing *tzitzis*. He was inside for eight years. Good behavior chopped a third off the term. It didn't hurt that he worked as a teacher inside. He never was stupid."

"I remember," Cohen said impatiently.

"God knows what happened to him. And when I say God, I mean God. He's very deep into it. He has political support. Some refer to him as an example of successful prison rehabilitation. He's considered a good influence, because he's religious. For a while, he had a kind of traveling yeshiva in the southern neighborhoods. And he has a patron. An American, born in Syria, very rich. And this American, well, he makes donations, and he's connected to . . ."

"Bloody politicians," Cohen spat. "All right, nowadays what do we know about his followers? Daniel named someone, a Yossi. And he gave me this," Cohen added, handing to Levy the slip of paper with the license plate number that Daniel had given him. Levy immediately picked up a phone and dialed the vehicle registration department.

Shahar looked into the file in front of him. "The street says that there are a couple of girls, too. Ovadia apparently has an explanation. Biblical, I mean. For the girls."

"What kind of explanation?" asked Cohen.

Shahar shrugged. "Biblical, you know, Abraham had two wives, why not him? That kind of thing."

"Nissim?" Cohen turned to Levy, who was just hanging up the phone.

"The car belongs to Yossi Hadass, no outstanding tickets, a short record, no convictions. Oh, the Nature Preservation Society guide is supposed to be here by ten. Another . . ."

"Twenty minutes," said Shahar.

"People come and see him for blessings," Shahar said, continuing to leaf through the file. "Some think he's a saint. I don't know about drugs. He's always been careful. And he's protected. The American. Politicians. I'll tell you the truth, Avram, even if we find something going on in Ein Kerem. Drugs, I mean. We'll get him, and he'll be out in five minutes."

"All right," Cohen said after a moment of thought, "it's obvious that the blindness means that Ovadia didn't do the nuns. But he has some real power over his men. One of them might have done it. We'll go up there. If we're lucky we'll find some *nafas*— if we do, that could turn into a connection to the hippie in Ein Kerem."

"There's something interesting here," said Levy, still studying the files. "After Ovadia got out of jail, he spent a lot of time sitting in his brother's shop. His brother's a butcher." Levy looked to Cohen. "We interviewed him. Nothing turned up."

Shahar was reading from a separate file. "About six months ago, the American got up the money, and the Religious Affairs Ministry gave them backing for a *yeshiva* in the Moslem Quarter."

"Bloody politicians," Cohen repeated. "Let's see those files," he ordered. "I'll look at them while we wait for the guide. Meanwhile, you two figure out what happened to the memo."

"In all the confusion," Levy said abashedly, "I didn't get a chance to tell you. Aboudi contacted me right after you left the office. One of his sons came up with the name of the girl and an address. Marie. She hasn't been at her flat in more than a week."

"Put a man on her house," Cohen ordered, "and have Ovadia's

brother, the butcher, picked up. Pull out his statement from when we were questioning butchers."

Levy and Shahar passed their files to Cohen. He picked up the first of the fat files that the police had accumulated over the thirty-five years of Ovadia's life. During twenty-five of those years, Ovadia had been known to the police. Rutie stepped out of the room from her corner. She came back a little while later carrying a tray of coffees.

A few moments after she entered, the phone at her desk rang. She picked it up, listened for a moment, and handed it to Shahar, who began ordering his men into position for the trip to Ein Kerem, the arrest of the butcher, and a watch on the address in Nahlaot that Levy gave him.

Cohen looked at his watch. He turned on the radio. The five beeps announcing the ten o'clock news bulletin began almost immediately. It included a short item reporting on Lassman's story.

A moment later, the phone rang. Levy picked it up and, as he passed it to Cohen, said, "Alex. He's already called twice this morning while you were out."

"Cohen," said the detective, taking the phone.

"I'm dead," said Alex. "That story. It will get me killed. You've killed me."

"I didn't leak that story," said Cohen abruptly. He had sympathy for the KGB officer's plight but no time for argument.

"When I read it this morning I was sure it was you."

"No. It wasn't. I'm sorry. I reported to the people I was supposed to report to. But I didn't leak that story." Cohen's voice was cool, but he had hopes he could yet learn something from Alex.

"Mossad? Shabak? Who?"

"I don't know," said Cohen. "Yaffe?" Cohen tried, no less curious about the source of the leak.

"He's foolish enough," Alex said, making Cohen smile. "You know, it's funny," the Russian continued, "I didn't want to defect, and now I may have no choice. I'm ruined in Moscow."

"Maybe I can put in a word for you," said Cohen, but he could hear the uncertainty in his voice. Neither the chief of the Shabak nor the head of the Mossad had seemed particularly impressed by Alex's credentials.

"I'm not supposed to have a conscience," Alex was saying.

"I'm not supposed to be a human being. You, you're the one who's supposed to have a conscience. You. A Jew. Survivor of the fascist death camps. You're the one who should have the conscience. So now you have to help me."

"I'm still hoping you can help me," said Cohen, softly but forcefully.

"I want you to make an announcement," Alex demanded. "To say it wasn't me."

"I can't do that," said Cohen.

"You can do anything you want!' Alex said, his voice rising. "You've got to help me! You're the only one who can help me!"

"That's probably true, Alex," said Cohen. "But I can't help you if I don't have a real murderer."

"What do you want from me?"

"There's not much you can do for me now," said Cohen. "Unless you could deliver the real killer. That would help."

"Cohen, I don't know who did it! I don't know!"

"You said you used to take walks with her. In the valley. Did you ever come across any caves? Or any signs of animal sacrifices?" Cohen tried. The question had sprung into Cohen's mind, and when Alex fell silent for a moment, making Cohen hold his breath, the detective was certain he had guessed right.

"Listen, Cohen," Alex said, his voice suddenly calmer. "Maybe I can help you. Maybe. But you have to help me. You help me. I maybe can help you."

"I told you, Alex, I'll do what I can. But first you tell me what you know—and why you didn't tell me about it a long time ago."

There was a long silence at the other end of the line. Then Alex spoke. "There is a cave. A long walk westward from the convent just below the ridge. Somebody is using it as a storage space."

"For what?" Cohen asked.

"Hashish. A lot of hashish. Sacks. In canvas bags. And something else."

"What?" Cohen demanded.

"There was an open case of ammunition," Alex said. "And some other crates with IDF markings."

"Did you open them?"

"No."

"I don't believe you."

"It's true. I saw the hashish. I saw the open ammo box. That's all. I didn't conduct an inventory. I was there only once. Maybe half a year ago. I saw a fire burning up there. I was curious. I went up in the morning. It looked like someone had barbecued some whole animals. I saw the opening to the cave. I looked. That's all. I looked."

"Why didn't you let us know?" Cohen demanded, furious. "Why didn't you warn Yaffe?"

Alex snorted. "Cohen, despite *glasnost,* despite all the talk about warming relations," he said with the same self-confidence that Cohen remembered from before the truth was out, "I assure you, my job never has included shutting down your underworld."

Cohen felt like he was going to explode. The rash on his arm felt like it had spread all the way up to his biceps. His back was aching, his head pounding.

"Maybe if you had made it your problem, maybe if you had helped us, you wouldn't be in the trouble you're in now," Cohen said, clenching his teeth to prevent himself from raising his voice.

"So now I've told you," Alex said contritely. "I'm sorry. Okay. I'm sorry. Now, I helped you. You have to help me."

Cohen sighed and fell silent. He had promised. All the remorse he felt about Alex's predicament had evaporated in the glare of Alex's admission that he had known about the cave and its contents. But he had made a promise. "I'll talk to someone," Cohen hissed. "I'm not promising anything else."

"Shabak? Mossad?"

"You'll know who if they want you," Cohen said, businesslike. He rubbed at his arm.

Alex grasped at Cohen's promise. His voice changed again, going lower and calmer. "I will meet your friend wherever and whenever he wants. But it must be today. Otherwise, I am dead. I tell you, dead."

"I'll see what I can do, Alex. But don't hold your breath."

"Cohen, I'm counting on you," Alex was shouting down the line as the detective hung up. His voice echoed in Cohen's mind.

Levy and Shahar were silent, watching him. "I promised him," Cohen said, as much to convince himself as to explain to Shahar and Levy, who had listened in silence to his end of the conversation. "He knows about the cave. He saw hashish and some ammo boxes."

He dialed Shmulik's number. "He wants to defect," Cohen said as soon as Shmulik got on the phone. "He's helped me out a little bit, and now he wants to defect."

"Are you kidding me? You've already screwed up the PM's meeting with the foreign minister. You want to completely fuck it all? Besides," Shmulik said, "you went behind my back. Why should I help you?"

"Because we're on the same side."

"It doesn't look like it from here," Shmulik shot back.

"Look, Shmule," said Cohen, "I promised him I'd do what I can. He's given me some information that fits into some other information. Something that might lead to the grenades on the Temple Mount. Maybe other things. Maybe even the nuns."

"What did you tell him?" Shmulik asked, with resignation.

"That I'd speak to someone."

"Did you mention me?"

"Of course not."

"I don't know," said Shmulik. "I don't know what we'll be able to do for him. The prime minister will have to decide."

"He won't have much time," said Cohen.

"Who? The prime minister or Alex?" asked Shmulik.

"Both," said Cohen. "Look," he added, "I'm sticking it into your hands. It's up to you."

"You should have put it into my hands a long time ago," said Shmulik. "For your own sake."

"You're probably right," Cohen admitted reluctantly.

"How did he help you all of a sudden?" Shmulik asked suddenly.

"He was a second source on something."

"About the nuns?"

"Maybe. I'm not sure yet."

"And you believed him?" Shmulik asked with incredulity in his voice.

"I don't have much choice," Cohen admitted.

There was a silence as Shmulik thought. Cohen grew impatient. "Shmule, he was a second source. He confirmed without my asking. I believe him," Cohen reiterated. He counted another three beats before Shmulik answered.

"We'll talk to him," Shmulik decided. "Maybe he can walk into the American consulate. I don't know. He'd be useful if he wasn't burnt. But with his story blown? I doubt it. So, tell me, who the hell leaked that story?"

"I don't know," said Cohen. "Frankly, I wondered if it was you."

Shmulik laughed. "I was sure it was you."

"Well, I'll worry about it later. I've got other things on my plate now," Cohen said. "Talk to whoever you have to talk to about Alex. Do what you can."

"You worried about him?"

"I was. But not anymore," said Cohen. "If you can figure out what to do for him. That's fine. If you can't ... well, frankly, I don't care."

"Where the hell is that guide?" Cohen demanded as soon as he was off the phone.

Levy looked at his watch. "He should have been here ten minutes ago."

"Nissim, how long has that girl stayed away from her flat?"

"Since the night she was seen running from the hippie."

"Rutie. Contact all the hospitals. The entire country. And check with national headquarters for all reports of unidentified bodies found since then."

"We get copies of all reports of unidentified bodies," said Levy.

"Do it," Cohen ordered. "I saw today what can happen to a report. Who knows what else we're missing because of ill winds," Cohen ordered. The ill winds had scattered the pieces, and now they had brought them together. Cohen fell silent, watching Levy and Shahar work the phones. He heard a siren starting up just outside the compound.

There was a knock at the door. Before Cohen could call out, the door opened.

"Nobody said come in, but nobody said stay out." The voice was as raspy as it was high-pitched, as if the vocal cords had been sunbaked dry. "They tell me I can find Commander Cohen, here. You can call me Gingi. Everyone does. From the Society for the

Preservation of Nature. I was told you needed an expert on Ein Kerem caves. So, here I am."

Cohen almost burst out laughing. In sandals, shorts, and a blue pullover shirt half-tied at the neck by a shoelace, the balding redhead, with his leathery sunbeaten skin that made guessing his age impossible, with his sergeant major's British-style mustache, and a sloppy, but nonetheless efficiently military bearing, the Gingi looked like he had stepped out of a recruiting poster for Jewish pioneers in the twenties.

But as soon as he unrolled the map that he carried under his arm, Cohen could see that the Gingi knew his way through and around the wadis and hillsides of Ein Kerem.

"There's only one set of caves that could work as a real shelter for a group of people and which is less than five minutes by car from the bottom of Ein Kerem. That's what the message said. Find the caves five minutes by car from Ein Kerem. It's here," said the Gingi.

He was pointing at a spot on the map about two kilometers from the nearest road and about three kilometers due west of the center of the village.

Cohen studied the map. "Okay, that's five minutes by car. How far is it by foot? To here?" Cohen's finger pressed down hard on the cartographer's symbol for the convent.

The Gingi scratched at his head, said, "Just a minute, let me see," and mumbling to himself, traced his finger along the ridges he could recognize in the wavy concentric circles of the army-issue map.

"If he knows the way, it's not far, but he has to be careful to stay on the ridge. If he goes into the valley, it becomes twice as long." He looked up from the map. "I'd say about twenty minutes to half an hour, on fast feet from the caves to the convent. Slow feet? As long as an hour. Why, what happened at the convent?"

"None of your business," Levy growled.

The Gingi shrugged. "Okay. I'm ready to go. I'll take you."

"You'll tell us how to get there," Cohen growled.

"Look, commander," said the Gingi. "I was with Arik at the Mitla. I was with Mota when he took the Temple Mount. I was with Raful on the Golan in '73. I was . . ."

"Your war record is not under discussion," Cohen snarled.

"The point is that there's nowhere you could take me that I haven't already been in more trouble or danger. The point is that you won't be able to get to these caves unless I take you."

"Why not?" asked Levy.

"Because if you knew how to read a field map the way a map should be read, you'll see that the caves aren't even marked. And once you're out there, you could wander up and down the mountain looking for them without ever finding them. I can show you and I will show you," he said triumphantly.

Levy looked at Cohen, Cohen looked at the Gingi. He was standing as tall as he could stretch himself, his eyes barely level with the top of the four-drawer filing cabinet beside him.

"We are not playing commando here," Cohen said sternly to the Gingi. "I know how to read a map. We need you to show us a way to the cave without being seen."

"Fine. Fine. Whatever you say. Like I told Yanosh in Beirut . . ."

"Look, Gingi," Levy spoke up. "We're sure you've had a wonderful career as a soldier and a guide and a scout and whatever. But do me a favor. Not today. Some other time you can tell us your life story."

The Gingi wasn't at all insulted. "Fine, fine. Whatever you say. You ready to go? I don't have all day, you know."

"Maybe he's crazy, too," Levy whispered to Cohen as they led the way to the car in the parking lot. Shahar went in a second car, backed up by four of his toughest junior officers. On his way to Ein Kerem, he'd detour through Nahlaot, making certain that his man was already posted outside the missing girl's flat.

"Completely," said Cohen, "completely crazy." They both laughed. The Gingi ignored them, getting into the back seat.

As soon as Levy pulled out of the parking lot, the Gingi started giving directions. Cohen shifted in his seat and turned around. "All right, look, Gingi. You're coming with us to show us how to get to those caves. We don't need you to tell us how to get to Ein Kerem. I'll tell you when to start giving directions."

"Fine, fine. No problem," said the Gingi. He sat in the back seat humming to himself for the rest of the ride.

They drove all the way through Ein Kerem, past the turnoff to the Spring of the Grapevine and its own cave, past the turnoff to the convent, past the Baptist Church, the Anglican Church, and the Lutheran Church, past the tea house, the crafts shop, and the grocery store across the street from the bus stop, and then down, deep into the valley on a road that, once out of the residential part of the village, changed from two lanes to one.

As they came around a sharp bend in the road that dipped as well as curved, the Gingi said, "Stop." Cohen looked around. To the south was a steep hill. To the east was a valley that stretched for more than a kilometer and then climbed up more than five hundred meters to a ridge occupied by an air force radar installation and, farther down, by a mental hospital.

"We wait here," said the Gingi.

"I'll decide where we wait," snapped Cohen.

"Don't you want to wait for your other man?" asked the Gingi.

"Who is this guy?" Levy said, rolling his eyes.

Shahar's car arrived a few moments later. He was with two other plainclothesmen.

"How do you want to do it?" Shahar asked Cohen.

Cohen turned to the Gingi. "When we get to wherever it is you're taking us, is there some way we can approach without being seen, so we can see exactly what's going on there before we go in?"

"Sure," said the Gingi. "Why didn't you say so? But you have to turn off your walkie-talkies. If anyone's up there, they'll hear you from a long way away."

Levy made a gesture with his two hands, as if he were wringing the neck of a chicken. Shahar almost laughed. Cohen stared up the hill.

"*Nu?*" said Cohen. In the tone of his voice was the patient exasperation of expectant waiting.

"*Nu* what?" asked the Gingi.

"Are we going or not?"

"Sure, sure, this way," and the Gingi got out of the car and started marching down the road.

Cohen and his men followed a few paces behind. "Do you think he knows what he's doing?" Levy asked his commander.

"Does anyone in this country know what they're doing?" Cohen answered, and then, as if for good measure, he added, "Except us, of course," and smiled at Levy.

"Shouldn't we be going in with more men? And more backup?"

"Nissim, Nissim, my job is to catch killers, not kill them or get killed by them. First I want to know what is going on there. Then I'll decide. No guns. Not until I say. So far, we're far from needing any guns. We're out here on a nice road, in full view of anyone up there." He pointed to a new housing development going up on the slope of a mountain to their east.

"Not for long," said Levy. Cohen looked down. The Gingi was about to disappear around a sharp bend.

"He's as fast as a goat," said Levy.

"More like a muskrat," said Cohen. As they trotted up to the sharp bend, they heard the Gingi's shout. He was above them, pointing to a place to climb upwards into the forest. Cohen was more interested in the beat-up orange Escort, parked a hundred meters ahead just off the road in a small grove of fir trees.

"That's the same car Daniel mentioned," said Cohen. Shahar left a man behind to keep an eye on the empty car.

They climbed for twenty minutes along a twisting turning path that led them along an old shepherd's trail and then up through an abandoned olive grove. "This grove," the Gingi began, "used to belong to a sheik, but when Allenby came to Jerusalem . . ."

"Oh, shut up already," Shahar snapped at the guide. The Gingi shrugged.

"Yes, sir," he said, offering a lazy salute. "Anyway, we're here."

"What do you mean, here?" asked Levy.

"This is the place. Look." The Gingi pointed southward. The olive grove was on a terrace, and they were at the northernmost end. The western side of the terrace tilted down, the boulders and rocks that once held it up now fallen and woven into the dirt of the hillside. The eastern side of the terrace seemed to be carved out of the rock of the mountain. And at the far northeastern corner of the terrace, through the thick and thin branches of the ancient trees, Levy had a glimpse of a clothesline hanging between two trees. There was a faint smell of smoke in the air.

"I could get closer," said Levy. "See what's happening inside."

The Gingi offered to show Levy a way up above the cave. Cohen nodded, and the two men headed up the eastern wall of the olive grove terrace. Cohen reached into his shirt pocket and took out a cigarette. He lit it and immediately put it out, signaling one of Shahar's two men to do the same. "If we can smell their smoke, who's to say they can't smell ours."

31

COHEN HAD TOLD LEVY to keep out of sight and to report back on what could be seen at the cave entrance. Levy climbed directly behind the Gingi, using the same handholds on the rocks, grabbing shrubs and tree trunks for leverage as he pulled himself up the steep hillside. They moved almost silently, and then the Gingi stopped, scuttled to his right and crept belly down onto a small ledge above the cave. Levy started to follow.

And the ledge collapsed.

The Gingi fell almost directly into the small campfire in front of the cave. Levy heard a bellow and two sharp cries. He scrambled down, finding the Gingi, outraged by embarrassment, on top of a naked man. Shahar's three men ran through the grove into the clearing, guns drawn. The scene in front of the campfire made them all burst out laughing, and they were still laughing when Cohen and Shahar ran into the clearing. Cohen signaled to Levy to pull robes off the line for two girls, kneeling naked and afraid, a few meters away, and turned his attention on Ovadia.

The blind man was squatting, clutching a dirty white linen robe around him. He was speaking into the confusion as if he had it completely under control. "I understand, I understand," Ovadia was saying, "and you can also understand. If you studied the true ways of our people, if you learned the true ways of this place, then you, too, can be one of the pilgrims." His voice had the rhythm of a seer's, and it perturbed Cohen that the blind man had found

Cohen's face without having heard his voice, without even knowing yet the identity of the people who had crashed into the clearing.

He remembered a different David Ovadia, a younger man. When he was jailed, Ovadia was a thirty year old with the swagger of a teenager.

Now, Ovadia seemed ageless. There were white strands in his beard, but his face was smooth, without a single crease of age. Yet even blind, he still had the same hypnotic eyes. He wasn't wearing his glasses, and his eyes were the same as Cohen remembered them: one dark brown, the other light green.

"You've changed, David," said Cohen with almost gentle mockery.

The blind ex-convict seemed to listen to Cohen longer than the detective spoke. And then he smiled. "It's Avram Cohen," he said, pulling the robe's open collar around his neck, his smile revealing a front row of prison dental work.

"I hear you're a prophet nowadays," said Cohen.

"I am the Lord's servant," said Ovadia with confidence.

Cohen sat down on a large boulder, facing Ovadia, who squatted Arab-style, his buttocks on his heels, his forearms balanced on his knees. There was a small pile of charred bones in the center of a circle of stones. The entrance to the cave was the height of a short man, partially hidden by a thick stand of wild mustard. Without taking his eyes off Ovadia, Cohen motioned to Levy and Shahar to check the cave.

"I see you've been barbecuing up here," Cohen said lightly.

"We are re-learning our forefathers' ways," Ovadia said patiently, ignoring Cohen's taunt. "We are assuming our responsibilities." He had long fingers, and he gestured gracefully with them as he spoke.

"Yes," Cohen said derisively, "you've always been a responsible sort. Responsible for murder."

Ovadia bared his teeth again with his smile, ignoring Cohen's baiting tone.

"We have to return to our old ways, the old ways before the thieves who called themselves Christians stole the messiah from us." He spat when he said Christian, "and before Ishmael climbed down from the trees."

"That's quite an interpretation," Cohen said. "I bet the rabbis just love that." He mocked and insulted, a provocateur at work.

"The rabbis," Ovadia scoffed. "They are full of fear. I teach this and I teach the way to salvation without fear."

Cohen realized he was leaning forward on the boulder, elbows on his thighs, trying to find sight in the blind man's hypnotic gaze. "You fear me, for example," Ovadia said. "I can hear it. I can see it."

Cohen shook loose his stare. He had been momentarily entranced by the darkness behind the mismatched eyes and had to force himself to look away. He *was* afraid. He leaned backward and laughed, freeing himself of the fear. As the roar settled into a chuckle, he realized as he wiped his eyes that it was the first time since entering the clearing that he had taken his eyes off Ovadia.

Before either of them spoke again, Levy came out of the cave, lugging an army-issue duffel bag. "There must be another fifty of these inside there," he said, dumping the canvas bag onto the ground. Dozens of hand-sized jute bags shaped as ovals poured out at his feet.

"Well, well, David," Cohen chortled at Ovadia, "now who's afraid?"

Ovadia was silent for a moment and then spoke heavenward. "I follow the laws of God as brought by Moshe down from Sinai." He began reciting the Ten Commandments. "I am the Lord thy God . . ."

"And thou shall deal drugs?" asked Levy angrily, tossing a handful of the sacks at Ovadia's feet.

Ovadia halted his recitation. "No spice is forbidden," he said. "Yehezkel ate mushrooms. He had his visions. I have my visions. He saw the dry bones come to life. I see other visions. A Temple on the Mount, the Holy of Holies rebuilt. And my *cherubim* showing loving vengeance on the abominable. Even upon you, Avram Cohen." He spat the name.

Levy lunged toward the blind man. Cohen raised a palm to stop him. Ovadia held his face heavenward and began a recitation of prayers known only to him and his followers.

Cohen turned Levy away from the blind man. "What about weapons? Did you find anything?" he asked his lieutenant.

Levy shook his head. "But Shahar's still counting."

"He's not going anywhere," Cohen said, pointing toward Ovadia, who was still reciting. "Find out what you can about them," Cohen said, gesturing toward the two girls. "I'm going to take a look inside."

He walked to the entrance of the cave, stepping past the wild mustard, and ducked into the darkness.

Shahar's flashlight was propped on a ledge where candlewax had formed stalactites dripping down the wall. The cave's walls had been whitewashed, but streaks of black marked the places where smoky candles had been lit and relit. The flashlight beam was aimed toward the back, and Cohen could see Shahar's shadow shrinking and growing on the far wall of the cave. "Any weapons?" Cohen asked, as he moved down the chamber toward Shahar. The cave was shaped like a funnel, narrowing until at the very end it was barely half a meter high, forcing Cohen to his knees as he went past the piled duffel bags to the end, where Shahar briefly hefted the last of the canvas bags in his search for weapons crates.

"No weapons. Sorry. That's it. We'll have to empty all the duffels to be sure, but I haven't found any materiel. Just the hash," said Shahar. "I've got something to show you. Outside in the light."

Cohen took a last look around in the cave and turned to follow Shahar out. "Look," said Shahar, studying the inked stamp on one of the hashish sacks. It portrayed a cedar tree, the symbol of Christian Lebanon. Shahar read aloud. "Bravery, for the Glory of the Lord," he said. "Now look." He sliced it open with a small pocketknife he kept on his key ring. "Cherry red," he said, and then sniffed at the hash. "South Beka'a," he added. "And look," he said, turning the sack of hash over in his hand, "inside, there's another stamp. 'For Allah and his Prophet.'"

"So? What does it mean?" asked Cohen, impatient.

"It means that the people who produced it from the plants are Shia. In the Beka'a. But the people who handled it after it was packed are Christian. The stamps are like tax stamps. As the *nafas* is transported through an area controlled by a militia, they take their cut, either in drugs, weapons, or cash. When they take it in drugs, they put their own stamp on it. Whoever is supplying him, the last Lebanese to touch it were Christian."

Cohen picked up the empty duffel bag Levy had dropped. "These are IDF issue," he noted, dropping the bag and turning to Ovadia.

"We have a lot to talk about, David," Cohen said.

"I am not afraid of you, Mr. Cohen," Ovadia said, "I know nothing of what you may have found. I'm just a blind man, following God and led by mortals." He fell silent, grinning when he realized that he had silenced Cohen.

A blind man with the demeanor of a religious innocent who had found God could easily be deceived by corrupted followers. Cohen could already imagine the defense attorney at the remand hearing.

Levy interrupted his thoughts. "The girls are runaways. Over sixteen," the legal age of consent. "From Bet Shean. Ovadia kept them as concubines. 'Like King Solomon,' they say."

Cohen shook his head sadly. "Have one of Shahar's men take them down to the cars. Get a crew up here to collect everything." He looked around for the Gingi, calling out to the redheaded guide. The Gingi was beyond the clearing, headed up the hill.

"Get back here," Cohen commanded.

"I wanted to see the press. There are remains of a First Temple olive press up there," the Gingi explained as he returned.

"Are there any other caves in the area, places where more of this could be hidden?" Cohen asked.

The Gingi shook his head.

"What about that press?"

"It's just a round hole cut into stone," the redhead explained.

"Doesn't matter," Cohen called out to Levy, who was speaking into his walkie-talkie at the edge of the clearing. "I want a search of the area. Up and down the hill and ridge. Get a Border Patrol team up here." He turned to Ovadia.

The walkie-talkie whistled for a moment and then came the voice of the policeman Shahar had left behind to watch the orange Ford Escort on the side of the road at the bottom of the hill. "Have apprehended individual who approached car," the walkie-talkie sputtered.

Cohen confirmed the message and turned to Ovadia. "Who is it? Yossi Hadass? Who else is in the area?"

But Ovadia had fallen silent.

Cohen sighed. The breeze was warm, coming out of the east. It carried an occasional sound down the valleys that emanated from Ein Kerem. From far away, Cohen thought he heard a church bell from the village, or perhaps a bulldozer blade clanging against a rock. He had hoped that Alex's information about weapons in the cave would prove to be true, that it would be tied together neatly like in a Hollywood movie. But the drugs were too easy. Ovadia would be out quickly. Weapons would be too scandalous for the politicians to protect Ovadia. But the blind man would have people who could lead him out of the drugs case.

"David, David, who's going to be with you?" Cohen began, "you . . ."

Suddenly there was a shout from the other end of the grove. It was Levy, who had stepped out of the clearing and into the grove to send his messages for reinforcements. He called out again almost immediately, "Halt, police."

Cohen shouted "Go!" to Shahar's men, who pulled out their pistols, Desert Eagle .457's, from their shoulder holsters. They took off in the direction of Levy's cries.

"The only thing you're missing right now," said Cohen to Ovadia, "is that one of my men gets hurt by somebody coming to see you. Where are your followers?"

"Nobody will be hurt today. Not even you. I prophesy this. I know," said Ovadia. He was calm but alert, his blind eyes aimed directly at Cohen.

"Who is it? Who were you meeting here?" Cohen shouted, losing his temper at the self-satisfaction of the ex-convict.

Ovadia retreated into silence.

Levy's shouts rang out, instructing Reuven and Shahar, "That way, he went that way!"

And then Reuven was shouting back, "I don't see him, I can't see him!"

The hunt on the hill drew Cohen's attention for a moment. But then he was questioning Ovadia again.

"The nuns, David, the nuns, who did the nuns?"

"God," said the bearded blind man, looking heavenward. "Through his messenger. I only wish I could thank him," said Ovadia, grinning, "for ridding us of abominations." He seemed to be listening to the sounds of the chase, breaking branches and stones falling in tiny avalanches. The noise became fainter with every passing second.

Cohen remained calm, also aware of the fading chase, the

distant sounds. But he was concentrated on Ovadia. "David," Cohen said, his voice suddenly gentle. "You can tell me. You know me, don't you, David. You remember me. You can even trust me. You give sermons and lead prayers and it's just another way to hold a gang together. It's just another gang, isn't it David? You're still dealing, David. All your repentance, all your return to the answer, and you're still dealing. Just another street kid with bigger balls than the others." Cohen wanted to smash his head into Ovadia's face beaming with the inner convictions of sanctity.

"Poor Mr. Cohen. You don't understand, do you? But you will. I promise you, Mr. Cohen. You'll understand."

Levy's voice came from above. "It was him, the hippie!" Levy shouted down to Cohen. "He got away. But it was him. I'm sure of it!"

Ovadia's smile changed slightly, his lower lip trembled.

"Who is he?" Cohen demanded. "You set it up, didn't you? You had the nuns murdered. Why! Why?!"

The blind man's face had a natural grin that only added to his mockery of Cohen. "A hippie? Mr. Cohen, you make me want to laugh. I have friends, and yes, I have students, pilgrims to our holy cause."

"Who is he? You son of a whore. Who is he?" Cohen lashed out.

"Who? I saw nobody," the blind man gloated.

"The hippie. A goateed foreigner. A tourist. He gets his *nafas* from you, doesn't he? He comes here to get his *kef*. What's his name? His name? His name!"

Ovadia smiled. "I know many people. Some are foreigners. Hippies, you want to call them, so be it. That really is an outdated word, Mr. Cohen. Just for your information. But at least they understand what you don't understand, Mr. Avram Cohen. They understand that sometimes that which doesn't make sense can be the most sensible thing of all."

Cohen fought his impulse to hit the blind man. Disgusted, he turned away, calling to Levy and the other policeman to return.

"We have you for the *nafas*," Cohen snapped at Ovadia. "Those two girls better be as old as they say or we'll have you for rape. And we'll find that hippie. You can count on it."

"I count only the days until the abominations of the Mount

are gone, the trespassers in the holy city are eradicated and the Temple is restored to its place."

"Cuff him," Cohen said, as Levy tramped back into the clearing with Shahar and his three men behind.

"It won't be easy for him going down the hill handcuffed," said Levy.

"Good," said Cohen with a vengeance.

He gave Shahar instructions to post two of the men as guards until the Border Patrol unit arrived. "And let's get the mobile lab here. Maybe they can find something."

The long walk back to the car at the bottom of the ridge was no victory parade for Cohen. Ovadia clung to his stoic silence, not once complaining as branches slapped back at his body and the thistles caught on his robe.

It was almost two in the afternoon by the time they were back in the office, Ovadia in a solitary cell in the lockup, Yossi Hadass spouting names and addresses of Ovadia's followers. But as Cohen expected, Hadass was saying nothing yet about Ovadia except that he was a great teacher, a seer of the future, promising the powers of priesthood to all who obeyed his commandments.

32

BENNY LASSMAN always went to *The Jerusalem Post* building late on Friday afternoons, before Shabbat began. There was no newspaper to put out for Shabbat mornings, so the building was abandoned on Friday afternoons except for a lone security guard outside the main entrance.

It was Lassman's time for straightening his desk, combing through files that had piled up, typing up notes.

The thick sheaf of phone messages from the morning that he found in his mailbox didn't disappoint him. The prime minister's spokesman and the national police headquarters spokesman had both called twice. Half a dozen foreign correspondents had left messages asking him to call back. They all wanted to know his source for the story.

When the phone rang on his desk, he tried to ignore it. He'd choose who to call back first. But the caller was insistent, and the phone's ringing became annoying.

"Lassman," he barked, finally ending the ringing torture.

"Mr. Lassman? Mr. Benny Lassman?" It was a woman's voice, hesitant and tense.

"Yes." Lassman answered.

"Are you the same Benny Lassman who writes about the police?"

"Yes," said Lassman. "Who are you?"

There was silence on the line.

"Hello?" Lassman called down the line. "Hello? Is anyone there?"

"I think, I think someone is trying to kill me," the voice said.

"You should really talk to the police," Lassman said in the patronizing tone he reserved for paranoid crazies. There were half a dozen such calls a week, along with the occasional death threats for reporting what the anonymous letter writers were convinced was serving the interests of the country's enemies. "I'm not a body-guard," he added, and was about to hang up when she seemed to read his mind.

"No, don't hang up, please, don't hang up. I'm not crazy. It's taken me all day to work up the courage to call you. I'm so afraid. So afraid. He's trying to kill me."

"If you think someone's trying to kill you, go to the police. I really can't help you," he said, more gently, still unconvinced.

"I can't go to the police," she said firmly. "I have my reasons. I can't. And I'm not crazy," she insisted. "He really is trying to kill me." She paused and then, as if it would convince him, added, "I've been hiding for almost a week."

"Look, lady, whatever your name is. You have to tell me more than this if you think I'm going to be able help you. Who's trying to kill you? Why?"

"He thinks I know. But I don't know. I mean, I don't know anymore what I know. He came, the other night. I told him I wanted him out of my life, but he came and he had a knife . . ."

"Hold on a second," Lassman said, "You had a fight with your boyfriend, so you call me? I don't write a Lonelyhearts col-umn. I'm a police reporter. Look, I really don't have time for all this, really."

"Please, please. Yes. It's true, he was my boyfriend. Once. But I don't know what it's about. Maybe it has something to do with drugs. He always has drugs."

"Did he say why he wants to kill you?" asked Lassman.

"He says it's his message. He has to deliver a message, and when I saw what you wrote today . . . I thought you know the police, you could talk to them. Tell them about Clay. Clay at the Ein Kerem inn."

The mention of Ein Kerem made Lassman straighten up in his chair. For the first time since she called, he was curious. "What about Clay in Ein Kerem?" he asked.

"That's his name. Clay. Oh God, he's going to kill me."

Lassman was silent for a moment. "Look, you're going to have to trust someone. You say you can't talk to the police. Okay, you're talking to me. But you have to trust me. Now, who is Clay? What does he do at the Ein Kerem inn? What's your name? Why are you telling me this?"

"I'm afraid of him. I'm hiding from him. I'm sure he's looking for me," she said. "He was my boyfriend. Sort of. I left him. I was afraid. He collects knives," she added, as if to apologize for her fear. "He . . . please, please help me." She fell silent.

"Knives?" Lassman asked.

"Yes. He stole two from my kitchen that night. I had to run away. And he has more knives. I know. I've seen them."

Lassman took a deep breath. Knives. Ein Kerem. The nuns. "Listen, you'll have to tell me some name. I have to know what to call you. I'll tell you what. We'll meet. Where are you? In Jerusalem?"

"Yes," she said.

"Well, where would it be convenient for you? I'll go anywhere you say. Right now would be fine. You can tell me the whole story, and then, well, then we'll see what to do." He was speaking urgently, the questions he wanted to ask her were piling up in his head.

"It will be all right," he said, shifting his tone from urgency to compassion. "Really. Where can we meet? I could pick you up and we could go someplace safe. Out of town. Or my place. It's safe. Really, you can trust me. You'll tell me your story, whatever want to tell me, and maybe I'll ask a few questions. But you'll be safe with me, I promise."

She was silent for a moment. "Come on, come on," Lassman mouthed silently into the mouthpiece.

"I haven't been out in days," she said. "He might be watching. The police are looking for him. They're looking for me. I'm sure of it."

"I'll pick you up. I'll come in my car and collect you. You'll be safe. Okay? And then you can tell me everything."

Again she was silent for a moment, and he suddenly felt like falling to his knees and begging, or slamming the phone down and forgetting the entire conversation.

"Okay," she said. "I'm on Tverya Road. Number 14. In Nahlaot."

"Great. I'll be there in ten minutes," said Lassman.

"I don't have to tell you my name if I don't want," she said, seeking confirmation of the conditions of the interview.

"Not if you don't want to," he said. "Not right away. First we'll talk a little. We'll see how you feel. I promise. I'll leave right now. You just hang up the phone and be ready for me. I'll make sure nobody's watching. Can you see into the street from where you are?"

"Yes."

"Watch for an open green jeep. I'll honk twice."

"Okay," she said. "Okay, I'm waiting."

Ten minutes later, he turned down Tverya Road. She was tall, slender, and pale, and even before she climbed into the jeep, he could see her eyes were green.

"Mr. Lassman?" she asked, as he pulled over and looked at her.

"Get in," he said, "and call me Benny."

She smiled, a small, hesitant smile, and climbed the step into the jeep. She was wearing a pale blue cotton skirt and a paler green blouse that matched her eyes. As soon as she was seated, he started driving.

"We can go to my house. Nobody will see us there. Or we can go to the forests. We can go to a restaurant out of town. We can go wherever you want."

"Whatever you think is safest," she said.

"My place, really," he said, shifting into second gear after making a right hand turn at the top of the steep hill. "You're Scandinavian, no?" he asked as he jammed the shift into third gear.

"Denmark," she said.

"How long have you been here?"

"Seven months."

"I'm surprised I hadn't noticed you. It's a small city."

"I only came to Jerusalem a few weeks ago," she said, "I was in Ein Kerem a lot. At the inn."

He drove fast, the wind making any more conversation impossible, the streets almost empty as Shabbat approached. "We'll be there in five minutes," he shouted, and she nodded, one hand clutching the rollbar for balance as he took his twisting shortcuts through the city to Abu Tor, where Lassman lived in a Crusader wine cellar built into the side of the hilltop overlooking the Valley of the Scapegoats and the Old City.

He parked on the top of the hill and led the girl into the garden that overlooked the city. In his garden, Lassman always felt like an eavesdropper on the city. He could see an old truck spewing exhaust smoke as it made the steep climb out of the Valley of the Scapegoats just outside the walls. He was used to the reactions of newcomers to his house. She lingered at the place where the sight suddenly came into view.

"It's the best view of Jerusalem in the city," he said, halting on the path in front of her. "You can see the people on the Temple Mount," he pointed. In the plaza of the Western Wall he could see black-coated *haredim* at the foot of the wall.

"You must be very rich to own such a place," she commented as he led her to a wicker table and four chairs in the shade of a solitary cherry tree in the middle of the lawn. Flower beds framed the lawn on each side, except for a gravel path that stretched the length of the house and a waist-high stone wall that lined the far edge, preventing anyone from falling down a short cliff into the backyard of the neighbor's house below them.

"I'm afraid I'm only the house sitter here," he said. "I take care of it for some rich Americans."

"It's beautiful." She bit at her bottom lip, tightly nodding her head when he suggested something to drink.

He went into the house to get cold coffee from the fridge.

"I'll only be able to help you if you tell me everything. From the beginning," he said, returning with the tray of drinks.

She hesitated before turning away from the view. "My name is Marie," she began. "I came to Israel seven months ago. I went to a kibbutz as a volunteer. I stayed there four months and then went to Eilat. I was in Eilat two months, and then I came here. I heard that there was work at the Ein Kerem inn. I went and saw the woman, Tsipi, and she gave me a job. I was to be a waitress in the restaurant and clean rooms. She gave me a room, but then

I met Navah and she had this room she could let me have, this lovely room with a dome. I ate at the restaurant and Tsipi pays okay, and I earned tips. I thought I would stay a while. I liked Ein Kerem."

"It's a pretty place," said Lassman. "But it's too far from town for my taste."

"Yes, but it was nice. Anyway. Clay works at the inn."

"Clay?"

"His name is Clarence—Clarence Chandler—but he calls himself Clay. He says that it's because 'man is made from dust, and when clay dries it is dust.' " She recited, as if it were a lesson she had memorized.

"Where's he from?"

"America. He says his mother was an Indian," said Marie. "I suppose I believe him. I don't know. He says he's a warlock. That's pretty ridiculous. I didn't think so when I met him. But I was stoned so long with him, I believed everything he said. He's always stoned. He has hashish all the time. Lots of it."

"Marie," Lassman asked, "what makes you think he wants to murder you?"

"Well, you see, he wanted me. And I liked him then, too. So we went to bed a couple of times. But he started wanting me to do strange things, not just sex, other things. He does sacrifices. He wanted to paint me with blood. I didn't want . . . I ended it. But now, sometimes he seems, well, he seems very powerful."

"He's very strong?"

"Powerful. He does magic. Little tricks. He can make fire appear in the palm of his hand and not burn him. He has something, I don't know how to explain it. I was attracted to him. He has beautiful eyes, I thought. Dark. Very mysterious. But then I saw they had nothing in them. Nothing except craziness. Anyway, we went for walks in the hills, and he talked about God and Love and the Earth and Our Mission and the Devil and it was very persuasive. He eats hashish. I told you that—he eats hashish. When I was with him, we ate hash all the time.

"And then, the other night, he came to my room and he said he had to hide, that the police were after him. I said, okay, for a day, but you have to go, and he did go, and I thought everything was okay, but then he came back, and this time he was really crazy, he said that I know something about him and that I'm helping the police find him, and then, and then . . ."

"It's okay, it's okay," Lassman said, putting his arm around her.

"And then he pulled out this knife. He wanted to mix our blood. He said it was his tradition for making sure of our trust and that the prophet himself said it was a good tradition. He wanted to take the blood from, from, from . . ." She began to weep, clutching her hands together in her lap.

"It's all right now," Lassman said, trying to soothe her. "It's all right now. Really. What did you do when he pulled out the knife?"

"What do you think? I ran. To Navah's. He ran right by me. I was inside the stairwell, and he doesn't know Navah or where she lives, so he ran right by me. Navah let me in. I've been at her place ever since. There was nothing for me to do. She brought me the newspaper. I don't know Hebrew. She brought me the *Post*. I saw your story. That's why I called."

"Why didn't you call the police?"

"My visa, it's expired. I'd be in trouble. And the drugs. That's really why. My visa expired so I couldn't leave the country. But I'm afraid of the police. Because they'll know I took drugs."

"Nonsense. If you help them, I'm sure it will be okay. And the visa problem? That's nothing, really, a small fine. Who told you it meant you couldn't leave?"

"Clay," she answered, wiping at her nose with a tissue Lassman brought her.

Lassman smiled at her and reached out for her hand again. This time she smiled back.

"It'll be okay. Don't worry. I think you have to tell what you know to the police. I know them, and I can set it up. I know the man in charge of the investigation. He's a good man, and you can trust him."

"Navah said I could trust you," Marie smiled.

"Don't go jumping to conclusions," he said, and smiled. "Meanwhile, you wait here. Enjoy the view. I'll call Cohen. I'll bet he'll come here to meet you."

Marie stayed in the garden, watching the Old City's evening lights turn into bracelets of jewels across the hilltops. Half an hour later, Cohen was sitting in the garden with her.

They talked for more than an hour. As the night air grew chillier, they moved indoors.

When she finished and Cohen had exhausted his supply of questions, he asked her to sign the witness evidence form. Levy had transcribed her testimony almost word for word and translated it into a dozen handwritten pages.

As Levy went over her testimony with her, Cohen wandered through the huge living room, looking at the pictures, pausing long in front of an icon similar to the one he had seen in the nuns' room. It's not just us, he thought. Everyone wants a piece of the city. They think it will bring them God.

"Is it over now?' asked Marie, her voice interrupting Cohen's reverie. "Am I safe?" she asked, as she used Lassman's ballpoint to initial each page and sign her full name and passport number to the first and last of the pages.

Cohen walked over to her and reached out his hand as if to shake. Instead, he touched her gently on her cheek, comforting her and grateful. "It's okay. I promise you it's okay. We're going to find him before he hurts anyone else. But you may have to see him one more time. In court. If it's him, he'll go to court and we'll need your testimony."

"Do I have to do this? Can't I just go?"

"I'm sorry," Cohen said, offering his apologies as his only compensation for her fear. "You have to stay. Now, we have to find somewhere safe for you to stay. Nissim," he said, "get me Rutie on the phone. She's my secretary," he explained to Marie. "You'll like her, I promise."

Lassman whispered something in Marie's ear. She looked at him for a moment and nodded. He grinned and before Levy could finish dialing, Lassman said, "She's staying with me."

Cohen looked at Marie. She nodded. Lassman beamed.

"Lassman," said Cohen, "I want to talk with you. Privately," he added in Hebrew.

Cohen stepped to the glass door, slid it open, and walked through to the edge of the garden. Lassman followed. Cohen was leaning against the stone wall that defined the terrace. Lassman stood beside him.

"It's difficult not to look, isn't it," said Lassman. Cohen nodded.

The two domes on the Temple Mount and the Western Wall below were lit up by strong lights; the wall around the Old City was a hazy golden yellow. The blue light of a patrol car winked on and off as a reflection on the wall as the car made its way up the hill from the Valley of the Scapegoats to the Jaffa Gate.

"She'll be safe here," Lassman said with more confidence than Cohen wanted.

"We don't have him yet. I'll be going to see Tsippora at the inn, but from what Marie says, we may not find the Indian at the inn."

"What are you trying to say?" Lassman asked.

Cohen continued looking down at the city. He liked Lassman. The reporter could have gloated about bringing the girl to him, but he hadn't done so.

"You want to play knight in shining armor, rescuing the damsel in distress," Cohen said sardonically.

Lassman began to protest.

"You want to play that, you should know that you aren't going to be able to publish any of this. Not until I give my okay," Cohen said.

"You can't . . ."

"I can," said Cohen. "But it's for your own good. The Indian reads the *Post* and the last thing we need is him reading that he's a suspect. It's also the last thing you need, if he decides to come after you."

Lassman started to protest. "Why would he come after me?"

"Let me spell this out for you, Lassman," said Cohen. "If he's anything like the ones before him, this Indian, this Clay, is carrying a message that he has to deliver. Don't ask me what that message is. It might be that he's the messiah. It might be that all of us are supposed to go to hell. What worries me is that if the girl's remembering well, the Indian is a fan of yours. You heard what she said, 'He reads everything about the nuns.' He doesn't read Hebrew. That leaves you. He may have a message for you. If I can't find him anywhere else, at least now I know where he might show up."

"So, what do I do? What do we do?" Lassman asked.

"Not much. Pretend you're on a vacation in a nice house with a beautiful view in a foreign country. And hope that while you're sipping your drinks on the veranda, the view doesn't blow up in your face."

"How long?"

"Until we catch him. Or he shows up here. I'm putting a guard here."

"What makes you think he'll show up here if I don't write anything in the paper."

"That's exactly why he might show up. He'll miss you. He'll want to know why you aren't writing. He'll want to see you. And that, my friend, is why if you two are going to insist on staying here, I'm putting a guard on the place."

"I guess I don't have much choice, do I?" said Lassman.

"No. I'm sorry. Not much of a choice," said Cohen. Lassman turned away and went back to the house.

Cohen looked out again over his city for a moment and shivered in the spring chill, wondering about the connection between the Indian and Ovadia.

33

WELL, THAT'S IT," said Levy as he and Cohen drove down the steep hill that led away from Lassman's house.

"Not quite yet," said Cohen.

"Why not?" Levy was surprised. "We have the girl's statement, it ties in with the hippie. He's a hash-head and Ovadia has the hash. It all fits together. We go to the inn and pick him up."

"I wish it was that simple. First of all, we don't even know that he's there," said Cohen. "But the truth is, it doesn't all fit. There are too many maybes." He thought out loud, testing theories, permutations of possibilities. "I'm sure Ovadia had something to do with the nuns. I don't know how, but I can feel it. He's playing it too calmly. The Indian at that cave. It must mean something more. We can press charges for the hashish. But he's right. He'll be out *chick-chack*," said Cohen, snapping his fingers. "We have him for possession of marketable quantities. What's that worth? Three years? He went in for ten years with nothing suspended. Okay, he's a recidivist. The judge will have to take that into consideration. But he hasn't told us anything, and except for his presence at the cave—not inside the cave, mind you—we have nothing against him right now that we can bring to court. With a good lawyer, we won't even be able to keep him past the weekend. You'll see. Sunday morning we'll ask for remand, and we'll be thrown out. We don't even have him for selling. He has something planned for all that dope. I want to know what he has planned. And what's the connection between him and the Indian? Just the dope? Religion? What? And where in hell are the grenades that Alex told me about?" The questions overflowed in his mind, but he was feeling good. He was in control again. "The connection between the Indian and Ovadia," said Cohen. "That's when it'll be over."

"Maybe Alex was lying," Levy suggested.

"Maybe," said Cohen. "But I don't think so." He slapped the dashboard with an open palm. "Damn the Americans. They could have taken Alex. But Shmulik said that they said it was too expensive for too cheap a product."

"What does that mean?" Levy asked.

"According to Shmulik, his market value simply isn't worth the price. He can't be trusted, and he doesn't know enough. The Americans aren't interested enough to pay for a new life for him. And you know what's happening to our budget." Cohen drummed his fingers on the plastic of the dashboard. "Shmulik could have taken Alex and listened to his story about the grenades. But the PM said no, leave Alex alone. No, it's not all over. Not until we have this Clarence Chandler. And not until we have those grenades."

But even then it won't ever be over, Cohen realized, not as long as everyone wants Jerusalem for their own. His thoughts shifted to the investigation itself, to its details and its regrets.

A truck pulled out of a side street, and Levy had to brake to avoid an accident. "Pay attention to the road," Cohen commanded.

Levy had crossed the road to Bethlehem, heading past the city's tiny train station and turned left, and then another squealing right-hand turn up the hill into Talbieh. It was Friday night, and the streets were almost empty as Shabbat entered Jewish Jerusalem. He steered quickly through the twisting curves of the hillside neighborhoods, speeding through the last flash of a yellow light about to turn red, racing along the empty boulevard between the Kirya and the Ramat Gan campuses of the university and the museum.

Tsippi saw Cohen opening the front gate and rose from her chair at the lobby reception desk. She greeted him arms outstretched, expecting a kiss. He leaned forward and pecked her cheek, as she pecked into the air behind him.

"Avram Cohen! Avram!" she exclaimed., "it's been a Finnish winter since you've been here. What's the matter? You don't like my food?"

Cohen's laugh boomed across the patio, startling the well-dressed diners enjoying Tsippi's Mediterranean cuisine in the dining room off the lobby.

"You know I love your food. And you also know that on a policeman's salary, this is not exactly the kind of place I can eat every week."

"For you, a discount. A big discount. Let's say fifty percent."

"That's very generous, Tsippi. Very generous. Does it include my guests?"

"As long as they are young and attractive, like that young man," she said, nodding past Cohen toward Levy, who stood a few steps behind the detective.

Cohen took her arm and leaned toward her, nearly whispering. "I have to speak with you. Privately."

Her eyebrows arched, and she motioned with a short fat finger to beyond the lobby. "You've always been welcome in my bedroom," she smiled, making Cohen remember both of them as much younger, when she still had a figure and he was a young bachelor.

"It's been a long time, hasn't it," he said.

"I won't say too long," she said.

The bedroom was in the back of the first floor, with a large picture window that Cohen remembered facing onto a backyard rose garden terraced into a slope behind the hotel. The large unmade double bed was covered with food magazines and cookbooks, while on shelves that stretched from floor to ceiling on three walls, more books were lined up and piled. "Your library continues to grow," he noted with pleasure.

"When are you going to have some time for them?" she asked, knowing that he found almost as much pleasure in reading about food as preparing it.

"One of these days," he said. "I promise."

"Promise me that when you find the time, you'll show me how to enjoy food as much as you without getting fat like me," she said.

He heard a thin plaint in her voice, along with levity.

"Tsippi," he declared with a wink, leaning forward to peck her with a kiss on the cheek, "you're looking wonderful."

She waved a hand at him, disbelieving his flattery. "Enough," she said. "What did you want to talk about?"

"You have someone working for you. He calls himself Clay."

"Cosmic Clay," Tsippi laughed. "He smokes so much *nafas*, it's a wonder he knows his name. He works in the kitchen. Washing dishes. Takes out the garbage. He has a room, out there," she said, pointing out the window toward a one-story stone building at the southern end of the garden. "What did he do?" She flushed visibly. "Oh my darling. What excitement. What is it? I can do it. Yes, really. Tell me all about it."

"You tell me, Tsippi," Cohen said, keeping up the diminutive, coaching her with intimacy. "Tell me whatever you know about Chandler."

"Actually, he's been away for a few days. He took some time off."

She noticed the disappointment in his face. "But he has his things here," she added eagerly. "He has to come back. I really don't know where he went. I owe him some money, and as I said, he left his things here."

Cohen raised an eyebrow.

"He's okay," she said, summarizing, "He's kept his word for as long as he's been around. He'll be back. As long as you don't pay much attention to the other stuff."

"What other stuff?" Cohen jumped at her remark.

"Typical stuff. They catch a whiff of religion and the next thing you know, they're talking about God or the Devil. Things like that. He's a bit weirder than most, I admit. I found him once slaughtering a chicken in the yard behind the workers' cottage. He said it was a sacrifice. I told him to pay for his own sacrifices."

"Do you keep your workers' passports?" Cohen asked.

"Until they leave me, unless they need it for something special, like renewing a visa or something. It's as much for their security as it is for mine." She moved to the small desk next to the windows. Cohen stepped away as she approached, knowing she would brush against him with ideas that he didn't have.

"Oh, damn. I don't have his," she said, a moment after opening the drawer. "He said he needed it, because he had to make some arrangements and needed it for identification."

Cohen's face fell.

"But what a foolish cow I can be," she added brightly. "Here, I have his particulars. I write those down in my book. Let me see, hold on, I'm looking. Right. Here it is. Clarence Chandler. U.S. passport number D059773, issued in San Francisco. Birthday, June 17, 1955. No wife, no dependents. Passport issued three years ago last month. Due to expire in another seven years."

"Clarence Chandler," Cohen mumbled as he copied the woman's notations. "No picture?"

"Sorry," said Tsippi.

"I want to arrange a sketch," he said. "Someone will come by and you'll describe this Clarence Chandler."

"Okay. Fine. Remember, he calls himself Clay. Says it has to do with being made from mud. I called him Clarence once, and it made him furious. Clay, that's his name."

"What does he look like?" Cohen asked.

"Well, he's handsome, if you like the Mephisto look. He's not that bright, but he's not really stupid either. The girls—at least the naive ones—like him. They seem to think he's sexy. He's lean. Wiry. I told you about the *nafas*. You know I don't care, as long as he does his work. And he does. He's helpful around the kitchen. He knows the restaurant business, knows meat, knows . . ."

"What do you mean, he knows meat?"

"He's good with a knife and a slab of beef. He knows how to cut up steaks, cut ribs, you know, that sort of thing."

Cohen looked out the window at the one-story building that housed Tsippi's workers.

"Has he ever been violent? Done anything . . ."

"No. Yes. How can I explain it? He can be very docile, I guess. Maybe that's the *nafas*. You know. But sometimes, yes, it's true, sometimes you can see something else in his eyes."

Cohen moved toward the door. "He may have tried to kill one of the other people you had working here. A Danish girl named Marie."

"You've seen her? Tell me, how is she? I heard she had the flu. That's why she hasn't been around. Come to think of it, that was the same day that Clay went away. You know, for a while they were an item. Clay and Marie."

"Not anymore," Cohen said grimly.

"Is she all right?"

"She'll survive. She got away from him before he could hurt her. She'll survive."

"It's not just about her, is it?" Tsippi guessed from Cohen's tone. "There's something else, isn't there?"

"You don't need to know, you don't want to know," Cohen said, and then, before she had a chance to argue, he grinned quickly. "All you have to do is let me know the minute he arrives, without letting him know you let me know. And you have to keep him here until I get here. It's that simple, Tsippi."

"Simple," she said, doubt in her voice.

"Simple," he said, with a shine in his eye, trying to dispel her doubts. "Now, I want to see Chandler's things."

As Cohen started for the door, Tsippi spoke from her place at the desk. " 'Murder,' you said. You didn't say which murder. Who is this Clarence Chandler, who is this cosmic Clay I have in my hotel? Tell me Avram, you can tell me."

"He may be someone carrying around a flame just looking for a stick of dynamite. And I don't have to tell you how dry the tinder is here."

"I don't know when he's coming back," said Tsippi.

"That's why I have to count on you to keep him here if he shows up."

"I'll show you his room," she said grimly.

She led the way in a darkness illuminated by the moon and the lights from the dining room to the three one-room cottages that were in back of the inn. As she walked, she picked a key from a large ring on which, it seemed, there were dozens of keys, and when they reached the second cottage, she stopped and opened the door.

It took him barely five minutes to learn what he wanted to know. Clay Chandler, also known as the Indian, had not left his knives behind.

He asked Tsippi for a phone that he could use in private, and she suggested the one in her bedroom.

He made two calls, first to Ehud and then to Shmulik, asking them to meet him. As usual, Ehud was enthusiastic, ready to be at Cohen's within the hour. Shmulik was more difficult, complaining that he had Friday evening plans.

"There's an FBI officer here. I met him last year in Washington and he's taken a vacation here, so I promised him dinner."

"Shmule. It can't wait. I promised to keep you informed. That's what I'm doing. And I don't have a lot of time. I've found the hippie. He's connected to Ovadia. I need your help."

An hour later the three men were sitting in Cohen's living room.

"Okay," Cohen began, after offering drinks. Shmulik took a whiskey to match Cohen's cognac, but Ehud asked for juice.

"We have a name for a suspect in the nuns. And something else. Ovadia. He's an old buddy of mine." He turned to Ehud. "He had some hash. A lot. From Lebanon. It started in the Beka'a and it moved through Christian hands."

"So?" Ehud asked.

"You've got some people who have been trading weapons for dope?" Cohen asked.

"We think so."

"Have your people confiscated any drugs?"

"Yes."

"What kind?"

"Hashish."

"Yes, but what identification? What's the source?"

"I can find out," said Ehud.

"Do that," said Cohen.

Ehud leaned forward to take a sip of his juice.

"Now," Cohen ordered, handing over the phone on the table to his right to the army intelligence officer.

Ehud looked over the glass at Shmulik. The Shabak officer nodded. Ehud took the phone and began dialing. "And Ehud," Cohen added, "get me the army records of these people." He tossed over a folded list of names of Ovadia's known followers, as gleaned from Yossi Hadass.

"Shmulik," Cohen continued. "Clarence Chandler, also known as Clay. He did the nuns. I'm sure of it. He's on the loose in the country. He has his passport. We've put his name into the border computers, and we're checking hotels. I don't know if he has any money, though he may have a lot of drugs, which he could turn into cash if he has the contacts. Put your boys on the name. This is serious syndrome."

"It's not my case anymore," said Shmulik.

"What do you mean?" asked Cohen, astonished.

"The nuns are no longer my case. As long as it looked like it had something to do with the fact that they were Russian, it was my case. Now, it's just a murder case for you to handle."

"Nonsense," insisted Cohen. "The Indian and Ovadia are connected."

"With Alex out of the way, it's no longer a counterintelligence case. Maybe we could have used him in place, Avram. Now, he's gone. He's on his way back to Moscow. He was ordered onto the last flight to Frankfurt today. Our men watched him leave."

Cohen looked into his glass as if searching for something. He took a drink, extinguishing a small flicker of shame.

"The grenades. Ovadia's connected to the grenades," Cohen said, "and the Indian's connected to Ovadia. It's all connected."

"There's more interest in Islamic fundamentalists and what they're planning than there is in Jewish fundamentalists," Shmulik said bluntly. "You know that. It's reality, Avram. Reality."

Cohen thought for a moment, swirling the amber liquid in his glass. "For now, just give everybody the name, the description."

"All right, I'll help with that," Shmulik conceded.

"I might need some sound thieves in Ovadia's yeshiva," Cohen added, upping his ante.

"For that, we'll have to wait and see. The religious affairs minister is furious about the arrest. He says it's harassment of the religious. Unless you find the grenades, you'll be nowhere fast."

"How do you expect me to find the grenades," Cohen exploded, "if you don't help. I need the surveillance, and your people are the best." He turned the glass in his hand, calmer, waiting for Shmulik's answer.

"When the time comes," the Shabak officer said, "we'll assess again and decide."

"It is time. That's what I'm telling you."

"Maybe you'll get the remand," Shmulik offered.

"I'm not holding my breath," Cohen said in a low, vehement tone. Both men fell silent for a moment. Ehud's voice on the phone was low, apologetic about disturbing the people he was calling at home on Friday night.

Cohen changed his tone. "I had hoped the Americans might want him," he said, thinking again about Alex.

"After you found out what you did? And it was published?"

"I did not leak that story!" Cohen insisted.

"You were with Lassman today. At his house."

"You're watching me now?" Cohen asked suspiciously.

"Lassman. When the story came out, we wanted to find out where he got it. The tap's been on his home phone since this morning."

"What about the newspaper office phone?" Cohen asked.

"The PM wouldn't allow it," Shmulik complained.

Cohen guffawed. "The protector of democracy," he said sarcastically.

"We thought about your phone, as well," Shmulik confessed, "you went behind our backs."

He said it lightly, but it released all the tension that had built up in Cohen.

"All right, all right," Cohen protested smacking his palm onto the table.

Ehud looked up from the pad where he was jotting notes, listening to someone on the other end of the line. "Did I miss something?" he asked, but Cohen and Shmulik ignored him.

"I sinned," Cohen hissed at Shmulik. "I transgressed, I committed evil. I beg forgiveness. And now, I ask for help."

"It will be unofficial," Shmulik decided. "You understand. Your name is not exactly considered sanctified nowadays in the service. I'll be doing it for you."

"Unofficial, official, I don't care. Just get some sound from the yeshiva and I'm sure it will lead to the grenades," Cohen said.

"And I'll have to wait until after the remand hearing. It depends on what happens there."

"Fine, fine," said Cohen, already looking toward Ehud for the news he was bringing from the phone.

"A contact in Metzah," said the soldier, referring to the military police. "They say they have sacks. Cherry red, two stamps— Shia and Christian."

"Good," said Cohen. "Ovadia has the same. And I have a

source who saw weaponry along with Ovadia's *nafas*. I think Ovadia is responsible for both the grenade at the rally and the grenades on the Mount."

"Who's the source?" Shmulik asked.

Cohen took a deep breath. "I told you. Alex confirmed."

"He's no source, Avram, not anymore," Shmulik said, shaking his head.

"He told me he saw grenades in the cave where we found the hashish."

"He's completely untrustworthy. And he's gone. You're going to need more than that. Something else," said Shmulik.

Cohen didn't move his head. He was looking downward, as if in confession. He shifted his eyes to look directly at Shmulik. "We're looking for the connection. And if we find it, something that links Ovadia to the grenades," he added, now staring pointedly at Shmulik, "your bosses won't be able to hide behind their halos."

Ehud and Shmulik sat with Cohen for another hour. It was past midnight when they left. Cohen immediately called Levy.

"Meet me back at the office," Cohen said perfunctorily.

"Avram," Levy pleaded. "I'm in the middle of something."

"It's her, isn't it?" Cohen asked, referring to Levy's Holocaust researcher.

"Yes."

"You like her a lot, don't you," Cohen asked gently, thinking of Ahuva.

"Yes. A lot."

"Good," Cohen said brightly. "So marry her," Cohen said. "Marry her and make children and have a family."

Levy was silent.

"Forget it, Nissim," Cohen said, suddenly embarrassed by himself. "Have a nice time. I'll call you in the morning."

"If you need me, I can come tonight."

"No. It's all right. I'll manage."

He sat alone in his chair by the window, occasionally filling his glass. It had been a long Friday, one of the longest he could remember.

By next Friday, he thought, Ahuva would be back.

34

COHEN WORKED ALONE in his office all of Shabbat, preparing for the Sunday morning court appearance. Yossi Hadass had yielded the names of seventeen of Ovadia's followers, and Cohen poured over the list, comparing it to the names of soldiers who the army believed had access to the grenades. But six of the names on Hadass's list were common—there were two Yossi Mizrahis among the names Hadass provided, and another thirty on the army list. He needed more time.

Early Sunday morning, he watched from his window as Levy, handcuffed to Ovadia, led the blind man across the parking lot to the holding cells in the basement of the courthouse.

An hour later, Cohen made the walk himself. Ben-Yehoshua had organized a small but noisy demonstration in support of Ovadia, and Cohen had to push his way through the sweaty crowd that clogged the narrow doorway to the courthouse. "Down with police repression of the religious, down with police repression of the repentant." The chants echoed loudly through the long stone corridors.

Ben-Yehoshua spotted Cohen just as the policeman broke through the crowd into the lobby.

"You couldn't touch me, so you entrapped him," thundered the Knesset member. "You won't have him, either. You planted that evidence. Admit it!" Ben-Yehoshua was performing for the crowd, which quickly picked up on his slogan. "Stop police entrapment, stop police entrapment, free the repentant, free the repentant!"

Cohen could hear the clatter of hooves as three mounted policemen made their way down the parking lot to the demonstration. He shook his head silently and turned away from Ben-Yehoshua, whose laugh followed him up the worn stairs to the second-floor magistrate's courtroom.

Cohen could ask for fifteen days. If, at the end of those fifteen, he still wasn't prepared to bring charges, he could keep asking the court for permission to hold the suspect. He had the right to repeat the procedure for up to ninety days of remand. But he felt it was already a lost cause. The Sunday morning stories in the press, obviously planted by Ovadia's supporters, quoted political sources describing Ovadia as an innocent betrayed by a follower who had fallen back into the old ways.

Cohen could not bring Alex into court to testify about the grenades. Without Alex, there could be no mention of those suspicions. The courtroom was packed with reporters and friends of Ovadia and his followers.

"Do you have any evidence to show that he is selling these drugs?" asked the judge.

"None, your honor," Cohen admitted. "But in the past . . ."

"The past is irrelevant here," Ovadia's lawyer jumped. "My client went to jail ten years ago, but he has long since been reformed."

"You have confiscated all the drugs?" the judge asked Cohen.

"All that we know of, your honor," said Cohen. "An extremely large quantity."

"Do you have any evidence, any indications that he will try to leave the country?" the judge asked.

"None," said Cohen, feeling more on trial than Ovadia.

"Will you be able to find him easily if you need him for further questioning?"

Cohen had no choice if he stuck to the truth. "As far as we know, yes."

The judge turned to the defense lawyer, who had defended Ben-Yehoshua's people in the past and who had an unctuous manner that Cohen had always found offensive.

"Your honor," began the lawyer, "you have before you a blind man who has seen the light. A man who has devoted the last decade of his life to bringing wayward young men whose lives were ruined by crime and the circumstances of their immigrant parents to the safety of our people's traditions. He is no drug dealer. He has nothing but the best intentions for the people of Jerusalem. You can be sure that if he is released from custody, his only purpose will be to return to his students, to continue his educational efforts."

"And how do you explain your client's presence in the same place where the police found nine hundred kilograms of illegal drugs?" asked the judge.

"Your honor, the Rabbi knew nothing of those drugs. He surely could not see them. The officers have no evidence that he was using them or selling them. We do not dispute the presence of the drugs in the cave. But there is such a thing as coincidence, there is such a matter as chance. Yes, it is true that my client does lead his students into the fields. But did not Rabbi Yohannan Ben-Zakkai, indeed the great Rabbi Akiva, teach that there is a healthiness of the spirit in the teachings of nature? Is it a crime for this rabbi to teach his students that they should love nature? Is it his fault that he may have entrusted one of his students with too much faith, too soon?"

"Who is this follower?" the judge asked.

Cohen glanced over to Ovadia, sitting peacefully in the defendant's booth, his empty eyes locked on the judge's podium.

"I'm sure the police will be able to determine that if they stop harassing my client and turn to the real task at hand."

Cohen buried his face in his hands. Ovadia was being turned into a martyr. The reporters filled the benches of the courtroom, taking their rapid notes as the defense attorney's rhetoric sailed. The judge called on Cohen.

"Your honor," Cohen said, "it is this man's very abilities to lead people, his charisma as a teacher, that worries us; for he could easily use that influence to dissuade potential witnesses in the case. We fear he might try to suborn witnesses. We have still not arrested all the suspects in the case."

"But what has he done? Your honor?" asked Ovadia's lawyer. "What has he done that the good officers now believe he will try to cover up? All my client asks is to return to his yeshiva.

Cohen felt desperate. He couldn't tell the court about Alex's information about the grenades, for there were no grenades, nor any Alex to produce for a trial. He wanted to tell the court about the girls, to rip off Ovadia's mask of sainthood. But they had been of consenting age. The inadmissibility of the evidence of Ovadia's sexual proclivities frustrated Cohen.

He had only one chance, but it would mean revealing dangerous cards.

"Your honor," Cohen said, "we have reason to believe that the suspect is acquainted with another suspect not yet in our custody, whom we believe to be connected in some way with murders that took place in Ein Kerem some weeks ago."

"And what makes you believe there is a connection between these two men?" asked the judge.

"During our arrest, the other suspect was seen in the vicinity. We tried to apprehend him, but he escaped. Words spoken by the suspect indicated acquaintance with the . . ."

"That's a lie! A blasphemous lie!" came Ovadia's shriek. His outburst sent a rumble through the courtroom, reporters leaping to their feet for a better view. Ovadia's lawyer leapt to his feet as well, shouting objections.

"Reason to believe . . . we believe . . . indicated . . . these are not terms of sufficient evidence to deny my client his freedom."

The judge smacked his gavel once, twice, three times, calling for order. "The suspect will remain silent unless I ask him a question. The audience in the courtroom will be removed if there's another outburst." He turned to Ovadia's lawyer. "Continue, please."

Cohen wanted to storm out of the courtroom as the lawyer continued. "Does the esteemed police officer have a name for this mysterious suspect? Has he asked my client anything at all about this missing man?"

The judge peered down at Cohen. "Well?"

Cohen rose heavily from his seat for what seemed to him the hundredth time that morning. "Yes, we have asked the suspect about this missing man, but we have had no cooperation from the suspect. He has remained silent since his arrest. Indeed, it is his very lack of cooperation that motivates our request for a remand through the end of litigation. We believe the charges that we are planning to bring against the suspect are of the most serious nature."

"I appreciate your zeal, Commander Cohen," said the judge, "and perhaps even your frustration, but surely you understand that a missing, mysterious suspect, whose connection to the case in front of us now is at best tenuous, does not make for a very solid case. And a suspect has the right to remain silent, if he so chooses. I'm afraid I'll have to sustain your learned colleague's objection."

Cohen could feel the hot flush of anger spreading across his face. There was nothing he could do. The rest was all formalities.

Twenty minutes later, in the bright sunlight of the spring morning, the demonstrators cheered as Ovadia was carried out on their shoulders. The march would carry him all the way to his yeshiva, deep in the Old City Moslem Quarter, where—Cohen had no doubt—Ovadia's followers would do everything possible to make life miserable for their Arab neighbors in an effort to force them out of the quarter. In that, Ovadia and Ben-Yehoshua had a joint agenda and could rely on support from at least part of the prime minister's own Knesset coalition, acting in the name of the eternal undivided capital.

Cohen and Levy didn't stay to hear Ben-Yehoshua's speech congratulating Ovadia for proving that the ways of the religious and the God-fearing were the true ways of the nation.

"Great," Cohen mumbled to Levy as they marched out of the courthouse across the street from police headquarters. "All I needed. Ovadia and Ben-Yehoshua, together in the Moslem Quarter. Abulafia's going to need a lot of Border Patrolmen in town the next few weeks."

They walked in silence the two hundred meters across the parking lot, the ruckus of the demonstration slowly receding as it headed in the opposite direction, toward the Old City walls.

"We'll have to keep someone on him," said Levy as they walked into the lobby of the police station.

"Daniel still hasn't contacted me," said Cohen. "But I hope to hear from him." Pray is more like it, thought Cohen. Prayer is all I have right now.

But it wasn't all he had. Rutie met them halfway down the stairs. "The Indian! He showed up! He's at the inn!"

35

STEAM CLOUDED above the huge, eight-burner stove. Cohen ignored the cook and his helper. He concentrated on the man at the dishwasher, who was enveloped in the steam exhaled by the stainless steel machine. Tsippi had said Clay was wearing a golden-green vest over his naked torso.

He worked like a dancer, taking six or seven plates at once out of the machine. He pranced back and forth between the sink and the dishwasher, piling stacks of hot, clean plates on a stainless steel table between the dishwasher's position and the assistant cook's stand. After he emptied the machine into the clean racks, he flung the dirty plates into the slots of the plastic trays and filled the rest of the tray with wine glasses. He grabbed a half-full glass and downed the remaining wine in one gulp and then continued the dance, sending the wine glass to the dishwasher tray.

Cohen watched through a small window in the swinging door that separated the dining room from the kitchen. Levy was at his side.

"His back is to us," Cohen said.

Levy drew his gun.

"Not yet," said Cohen. "Put it away."

Levy reholstered the gun.

"I want to get the cook and his helper out of there before we go in. Just in case," Cohen said. Tsippi was seated at a nearby table. The breakfasters were gone and the luncheoners had yet to arrive.

"Find some excuse to get the other two out of there," Cohen asked her.

She rose heavily from the table and went to the door. Cohen and Levy stepped back. Pushing it open, she called out to the two men to come into the dining room, where she pulled them aside. They looked with astonishment at Cohen and Levy as she whispered to them.

Shvilli came into the dining room. "I've posted the Border Patrolmen," he said. "They've got every exit covered."

"All right," said Cohen, "let's go."

Shvilli took out his gun. "I don't want him to see any guns," Cohen repeated. Shvilli stood with his arms folded, the pistol hidden beneath a bicep.

"Look how Shvilli's holding his gun," Cohen instructed Levy. Levy adopted the pose, satisfying Cohen.

Cohen looked at both men, and once again through the windows of the swinging doors. "Let's go," he said, pushing the doors open and stepping into the kitchen.

The Indian's back was to him, and as Cohen took his second step toward the dishwasher's area, he raised his voice above the rumble of the dishwasher and called out, "Chandler, Clay Chandler?"

The man at the dishwasher turned around, clutching a broken wine glass in his hand like a shining clear awl, dripping water. Without a pause, without a chance for Cohen or his two men to react, the Indian shouted. The veins and tendons of his throat bulged as he lunged, the clear spike plunging deep into Cohen's belly, the other hand grabbing the back of Cohen's head for leverage.

"I can't get a clear shot!" Shvilli shouted behind Levy, who ducked and rolled to the floor tackling the Indian's legs, trying to bring him down. Cohen broke loose of Chandler's grip, the blood spreading across his white shirt. Shvilli aimed, but Levy was in the way, wrestling the Indian across the floor.

Cohen fell once against the counter, knocking a twenty-liter pot full of water onto the floor. He reeled backwards, hitting the shelves beside the dishwasher.

"An ambulance!" Shvilli called out, hoping the people behind the swinging doors could hear, still trying to take aim.

For a moment, there was a pause. Shvilli let out half a breath and fired, the bullet smashing through the Indian's shin; blood burst from the shattered leg.

But still the Indian fought, trying to wrench his hand loose of Levy's grip. They rolled across the wet floor, and Shviili ran up to them until he had the gun barrel up directly against the Indian's temple.

"No!" Cohen called out, but he was sure they couldn't hear his command. He had fallen to the floor after hitting the shelves beside the dishwasher. The pots and pans of the bottom shelf fell around him as he slipped to the ground. He held his hands to his bleeding wound, watching the fighting through the veil of steam billowing from the dishwasher. The shout made him cough, each heave of his chest seeming to turn into another pulse of blood. "No," he ordered once again.

Shvilli's eyes were bulging. He swung his aim from the Indian's head to the Indian's hand gripping the glass stem above Levy's head. "Stop," Shvilli cried out again, and then he pounded the gun barrel down with all his might, smashing the Indian's grip on the glass weapon.

The Indian screamed once and suddenly relaxed, unconscious on top of Levy.

"Avram!" Levy screamed, shoving the Indian's body away from him. He slipped and slid across the floor on hands and knees to his commander. Shvilli remained frozen in his semi-crouch, gun aimed at the still body of the Indian.

"You'll be okay, you'll be okay," Levy whispered into Cohen's ear as he tried ineffectively to cradle Cohen's body. He looked around for something to stem the bleeding, but there was nothing in sight. He tore at his own shirt, trying to get it off, to use it as a temporary bandage, discovering that the recently stitched wound in his shoulder had begun to bleed.

"I'm okay," said Cohen quietly, in the gentle voice he so often used to open a suspect, a witness, a cop with a problem. He looked down at the red stain on his shirt. A button had broken off, and he could see small dark hairs curling on the spreading red sea on his belly. Then he closed his eyes.

Levy clutched at Cohen's shoulders. "Stay awake, stay awake, don't close your eyes, stay awake," he said over and over again.

Cohen opened his eyes and smiled at Levy. "I hope that maniac Shvilli didn't kill him. I want to know why he did it. I want to know why."

Levy smiled back. "There's an ambulance on the way. Just stay awake. Don't close your eyes."

"Make sure he's alive," Cohen whispered, his voice hoarse. "Shvilli?" he coughed.

The Georgian's body relaxed. He bent to the Indian's body, pressing on the neck, looking for a pulse. It was weak, but regular. "He's alive, boss. He's just unconscious. The shock."

"You're bleeding," Cohen whispered to Levy.

"It's okay. I'm okay. Really." Levy answered, not sure which pain, his or Cohen's, caused the tears to well in his eyes.

Cohen smiled. Levy shivered.

"Listen," Cohen murmured. "A secret," he added, beckoning with his eyes for Levy to lean closer. "There's an airplane flight. Tonight. Expecting me to pick her up." He searched Levy's eyes for understanding. "Don't want her to worry."

"The judge," Levy said after a moment's thought. "I can leave a message for her with Marciano," he added, referring to the chief of the airport police station.

"No," said Cohen, emphatically, the effort making him cough. "She'll worry."

Shvilli's shouting, demanding to know if someone had called the ambulance, broke into their conversation. Tsippi snapped back at Shvilli, "It's coming, I called, what happened to Avram?"

She moved toward the doorway, as if to enter, and Shvilli stopped her. "Stay out of there," he tried to command her.

"Get out of my way," she blared, grabbing the tablecloth off the nearest table and rushing through the doors.

She threw the white cloth over Cohen and kneeled beside Levy. "It's all right, Avram. The ambulance is coming. It's on its way. Listen, we can hear it." In the distance, the wailing could be heard, echoing down the valley.

Cohen smiled weakly and tried to speak.

"No, don't say anything. You've got to conserve your strength," she said.

Cohen concentrated on the sounds. He could hear his own labored breathing, and Tsippi's voice. His eyes moved back and forth from Levy's face to hers, and then to the Indian. He could hear a bustle beyond the door and kept his eyes open as white-coated attendants took Levy and Tsippi's place around him and carefully lifted him onto a stretcher. But by the time the ambulance siren began to sound, his eyes were closed.

36

At FIRST LEVY, his shoulder restitched and back into a sling, and Shvilli, mourning his golden tooth knocked out in the fight, were alone in the chilly corridor outside the operating theater. They sat in the uncomfortable plastic chairs of the waiting room staring blankly at a wall of brass plaques naming all the contributors to that wing of the hospital. But after a few minutes, Levy lost patience with counting the names of American millionaires and began pacing the corridor. He was staring into the darkness of a glass window that in the daytime overlooked Ein Kerem's western valleys and at night reflected the fear in his face, when the *Mafkal* appeared with his entourage, including Abulafia, Yaffe, and a spokesman with a bouquet of flowers. Doctors bustling in and out of the swinging doors leading to the operating theaters ignored the officers.

Levy tucked in his shirt and turned to face the officers. It took him a few minutes to bring the *Mafkal* up to date. In Chandler's room, Shahar's men had already found the knives fitting the description suggested by the coroner as used in the nuns' murder. They also found a rucksack containing a dozen sacks of the same Lebanese hashish that had been found in Ovadia's cave. There was displeasure in the *Mafkal*'s eyes at that bit of news, but the inspector continued with his briefing. Chandler's leg and hand were wrapped in plaster casts, and he was under guard in a room a floor above, but he was refusing to speak with anyone except Cohen.

And Cohen was still in surgery with the doctors refusing yet to make any promises about a prognosis.

"We'll see about that," said the *Mafkal*. He stopped a nurse and demanded to see the chief surgeon.

Half an hour later, a green-suited doctor came out of the swinging doors. "He's very lucky," the doctor said, "No organs were damaged. But his stomach muscles were punctured badly. It's going to be very painful for him for a while."

Silently, Levy thanked God.

"How soon will he be out of there?" asked the *Mafkal*.

"Another hour. We've started sewing him up," said the surgeon. Levy felt dizzy.

"And how soon will he be able to go back to work?" the senior officer asked.

"It depends on his recuperative powers," the doctor said. "He'll sleep for a while, maybe as long as twenty-four hours. Maybe longer. Afterwards—it depends on how strong he is, how well he handles the pain."

"He's a strong man," the *Mafkal* decided, slapping Levy on the back before announcing in a loud voice that Cohen was out of danger.

"Now, I want to see this Chandler person," the *Mafkal* told Levy.

Levy led the way up the wide stairwell to the floor above, where a uniformed policeman sat outside Chandler's room. The policeman jumped to his feet as soon as he saw the olive leaf insignia on the inspector general's shoulders. The policeman opened the door.

"They gave him something to sleep," Levy explained as they peered into the room. The new plaster encasing Chandler's leg from hip to ankle was bright white in the darkened room.

Levy stayed in his place at the doorway as the *Mafkal* approached the bedside to get a closer look at Chandler.

Suddenly the *Mafkal* jumped backward. Levy rushed to his side.

Chandler was smiling, eyes open.

"Chandler," the *Mafkal* demanded, "why the nuns?"

But the Indian was silent, his smile a mockery of both men.

"You see," said Levy. "Nothing. All he told me was that he would speak only to Cohen. That's all."

The *Mafkal* thought for a moment and then motioned Levy out of the room.

"These drugs that were found in his room and in the cave. Are they absolute proof of a connection between Ovadia and the nuns?" he asked Levy.

"We've been at work on that connection from the moment we arrested Ovadia," Levy said, adding, "I'm sure it has been in Commander Cohen's reports."

"Yes, yes, of course," said the *Mafkal*. But again Levy noticed the worried look in the *Mafkal*'s eyes.

"We're still working on the connection," Levy said, trying to defend Cohen. "Now I definitely think we should continue. To prove that connection."

"He's a good man, Avram is," said the inspector general. "Don't worry, Cohen will be okay. And anyway, it's all over, isn't it? You'll all be due for promotions. You'll see." He looked at his watch. "It's late. I have to go. I want to let the minister know he can tell the PM that we've solved the case, that we found the murderer. In fact," added the *Mafkal*, pleased with the opportunity, "I'm going to call the PM myself. But I'll tell you something. I think it would only harm our cause if we start making a lot of noise about this drug connection to Ovadia. After all, the court released him."

The junior officer looked away from the *Mafkal*. "Bloody politics," he murmured.

"What's that?" the *Mafkal* asked.

"Nothing, sir. Just remembering something the commander once said."

An hour later, Levy followed the wheeled stretcher carrying Cohen's body the short stretch of corridor from the operating theater recovery room to the private room that the *Mafkal* had insisted was Cohen's due. Cohen's face was gray, and his skin was black and blue from the intravenous needles. Levy felt tears rising in his eyes. He blinked them away as he helped the orderly steer the stretcher down the corridor.

It was close to dawn when Levy sat down in front of a telephone in the drab staff room down the corridor from where Cohen was sleeping.

He could hear her fumbling with the phone in what he imagined to be the darkness of her sleep, before she answered.

"I guess you were working tonight?" she whispered into the phone.

Levy's anxiety about the phone call turned to an embarrassed silence.

"Avram?" she asked, perturbed by the silence.

"I'm sorry," Levy said, "My name is Nissim Levy. I work with . . ."

"I know who you are. What do you want?" But in the pause before he could answer, she understood. "What's happened to him? Where is he?" she demanded, her voice suddenly commanding.

Levy took a deep breath. "Hadassah Ein Kerem, post surgery," he said. "There's been an accident." He quickly added, "The doctors say he'll be all right."

There was a pause, and then she said, "I'll be right there," and hung up.

Levy held the silent telephone receiver in his hand for a long time. A nurse came in to make herself a cup of coffee. She said hello twice to Levy before he responded, and then, he carefully replaced the receiver, got up, and left the room. She watched him walk out, and a few minutes later, she brought a cup of black coffee in a Styrofoam cup to him where he sat in a plastic chair outside Cohen's room.

Half an hour later, Levy heard the slapping of Ahuva's sandals clicking down the stone tiles of the empty corridor.

"How is he?" she asked. The pre-dawn silence made them both whisper.

"He's going to be in a lot of pain for a while. His stomach muscles," Levy answered, looking up forlornly at her.

"He's in there?" she asked, nodding at the door.

Levy nodded. "He's asleep. They say he'll be asleep until tomorrow. That is, today. He's been asleep since the morning."

"When will he be out of there? When can I see him?"

He shook his head. "I don't know." He gave her his seat and leaned against the wall beside her. "They say he'll be fine," he tried again, seemingly trying to convince himself as much as her.

They remained silent a long time. But then she broke the silence.

"What happened?" she asked.

Levy shook his head. "A suspect, resisting arrest."

"Which case?" she asked.

Levy was startled by the question. He shot her a glance.

"Was it the case involving the nuns?" Ahuva guessed. "I've been away for a couple of weeks, but I know that it was an important case for him, a dangerous case, he said."

Levy nodded.

"Is it over? Is it done?"

Levy shook his head. "I don't know. The *Mafkal* thinks so. But you know the commander. He'll want to know everything. Only when he knows it all will he think it's over."

She sighed heavily. Levy let his body slump against the wall, until he was sitting on the floor. Again there was silence in the corridor. Levy broke it. "He told me he was supposed to pick you up," he said. "He didn't want you to worry. He said that if he weren't there that you would think he was working and wouldn't worry."

She nodded. "That's like him."

"But he told me," Levy said, trying to explain to himself, as much as to her, that there was some significance to Cohen revealing the secret of the affair. "So I had to call you."

"You already knew about us," she said.

"Yes, but it was an accident that I found out. And he never mentioned it, never said anything about it. As if I wasn't supposed to know because I wasn't . . . I don't know . . . old enough, or, or . . ."

"He loves you," she said bluntly. "He thinks of you as a son."

"He never says so. He never says anything."

"He said so today. When he told you he was supposed to go to the airport to fetch me and realized he couldn't, he was telling you something. That he trusts you."

"He was wounded. Maybe he didn't realize . . ."

"You know that's not true," she said softly.

They sat silently again until the morning sunlight began pouring through the eastern windows on the floor.

37

COHEN SLEPT through the morning, and by lunchtime, Levy made a decision. He made several phone calls and conferred with the doctor handling Chandler. Two hours later, Chandler was pushed in a wheelchair by a burly uniformed officer into the magistrate's court across the street from the Russian Compound police headquarters. Levy, his eyes red from sleeplessness and wearing the court-required black tie and jacket that he usually kept in the trunk of the police car, rose and summarized the case against Clarence Chandler, also known as Clay, also known as the Indian.

The judge had appointed a lawyer to handle Chandler's defense during the remand hearing, but after his own interview with Chandler, the court-appointed counsel realized there was little that could be done for the suspect. "My client," the lawyer said, "has no objections to the remand." Indeed, he said, Clay Chandler wanted to make a statement, "But only to Commander Cohen," said the lawyer, adding, "who I've been told is still incapacitated."

The judge looked down at Chandler. "Is there no other officer with whom you are ready to speak?" he asked in Polish-accented English, but Chandler sat motionless and smiling by the defendant's dock to his left.

"Your honor," said the defense lawyer, "my client has told me that he is ready to make a complete statement and that he does not deny any of the charges. But he will not say so in court until he has had a chance to speak with the disabled officer. And then he will want to make a statement which he says will clarify his actions. I believe that it is in the best interests of all concerned, including my client, that he be remanded to the Kfar Shaul sanatorium for observation."

"Do the police have any objection?" the judge asked Levy.

"None, your honor,'" Levy said. On the desk in front of him was a stack of the cardboard folders that had grown thick with paper during the investigation. On top of the folders was a plastic bag containing the two knives found in Chandler's room at the bottom of the sack full of hashish. The judge announced a short recess to write his decision, and everybody in the courtroom rose as he left the room via a door just to the left and behind the bench.

While waiting, Levy watched Chandler. He was leaning hunched forward like a cocked spring. But his eyes opened and closed with an intentional rhythm of long beats. Opened for a few seconds. Closed for the same amount. He was tapping his foot, keeping time, listening to his own voices.

The judge came out and read his decision. Chandler's lawyer leaned over to his client to translate. Suddenly Chandler came alive. "I saved the messiah, I saved the messiah," he screeched until his police escort pushed him in the wheelchair out of the room and down the corridor to the doors that led to the parking lot and the police van that would take him to Kfar Shaul.

Levy watched the van pull out of the parking lot and then went to his own car, to head back to the hospital. He heard Cohen's shouts before he saw him.

"I *will* walk out of here if I feel like it and I feel like it!" Cohen was shouting, his voice echoing down the hallway.

Levy was grinning as he entered Cohen's room. The officer was standing, his back arched slightly in a position dictated by the huge bandage taped over his belly. He was buttoning a shirt over the bandage and demanding from a pair of nervous nurses that if they wouldn't help him put on his trousers, he'd leave the hospital without them.

"There you are," Cohen snapped at Levy as the junior officer entered. "Here, help me put on my pants," he ordered, pointing to the trousers hanging from a hook on the pale green wall. Pointing made him lose his balance momentarily, and he grimaced with the pain as his torso naturally twisted.

Still, he issued his demands. "Where's the Indian? Where's Ovadia?" he shot the questions. Levy was frozen to his spot. "Well? Are you just going to stand there?" Cohen asked, "Or are you going to help me? Give me those pants!" Cohen's voice was raspy, and every movement was a ripple of pain across his face. Nonetheless, he was full of energy, wondering if it was the excitement of the chase or the pain killers he had been given when he woke.

Levy grabbed the trousers off the hook and passed them to Cohen, who had dropped into the single chair in the room, a high-backed lounger. "Pull them over my feet, I'll do the rest," Cohen ordered. Levy did as he was told.

"I'll get you a wheelchair," the inspector suggested as Cohen yanked at the pants, cursing as he struggled with the clothes.

"I can walk," Cohen said gruffly. "Chandler?" he demanded.

"He's been remanded to Kfar Shaul for observation. He says he'll only talk to you."

"That's fine. I want to hear what he has to say. Ovadia?"

"His yeshiva," said Levy, "in the Old City. Listen, we found the knives in Chandler's room. And hash just like Ovadia's."

"I know," said Cohen, "Shmulik was here when I woke up. I expected to see you. It would have been just like you to sit here waiting for me to wake up. Instead I had Shmulik." Again he grinned at Levy. "He told me you were handling the remand."

"I was here until the morning," said Levy, pulling Cohen's socks onto his feet for him.

"Yes. I know," said Cohen. "Ahuva told me." He watched Levy for a reaction, but the inspector merely nodded, as if it was the most commonplace matter for the two of them to refer to the woman.

"I called her," Cohen explained, "when I woke up."

"You don't have to explain," Levy said.

Cohen relaxed his struggle with the clothes for a moment, and Levy used the silence to change the subject, proud of Cohen's trust, embarrassed by its sudden intimacy. "Are you sure you're okay?" Levy asked, jamming the first shoe onto Cohen's foot. "We could wait another day or two for this. The doctors said you'd be asleep for twenty-four hours and would need a few days of recuperation. According to them, you should have been asleep another six hours at least and should be flat on your back."

Cohen ignored him. "What's the connection between Chandler and Ovadia?" he asked with a grin.

"The drugs, of course," Levy answered.

Cohen shook his head. "It may have started with that. But there's more. I can feel it. Here," he said, lightly touching his stomach. His smile was a wince. "Tell me again about Ovadia's yeshiva."

"His American patron bought him the building," Levy explained. "It was originally built by Jews, more than a hundred years ago, and the Jewish family lived there until 1939. They left it during the rioting and never returned," Levy explained. "And now Ovadia has the religious affairs ministry saying that he's helping to resurrect the Jewish presence in the Old City."

"Bloody politicians," Cohen mumbled. "They want an end to *intifada,* so they pour oil on the flames." He leaned back in the chair as if to catch his breath before continuing. "I have to get out of here. I have to stop him."

"What has to be done? Tell me, and I'll do it," Levy said.

"How many of his followers are we still holding?" Cohen asked, closing his eyes as he concentrated on his questions as an anesthetic against the pain.

"Three. But there's pressure to let them out. They're allowed to be with other probationers, if it's within the context of a recognized institution. Ovadia's yeshiva has recognition."

"The rest?" Cohen asked. He opened his eyes.

"With him," Levy admitted, "along with some of Ben-Yehoshua's people."

Cohen clenched his jaw for a moment and then took a deep breath.

"Okay," he said, pressing down with his hands, like a lever on the chair, to rise. "Let's go."

He walked slowly but confidently in his strength over the pain, certain of his intent.

By the time they reached the front entrance to the hospital, where Levy, using the authority of his police badge, had parked illegally on a sidewalk, Cohen seemed to have the wound under control.

"What are they saying on the fifth floor?" he asked Levy after finding as comfortable a position as he could in the car. His voice was hoarse, but there was no weakness in it.

"They say it's over," Levy said simply, as if it was a foregone conclusion that that's what the fifth floor would say. "The *Mafkal* was here last night, and when I told him about the Lebanese hashish in Chandler's possession matching the hashish we found in the cave, he wasn't too happy." Levy told Cohen about the *Mafkal's* suggestion that the hashish connection between Ovadia and Chandler be kept quiet. " 'Until there's harder evidence,' he said," Levy reported. "Nobody's interested in Ovadia. Except us."

Cohen's hand clenched, as if to test his strength. They don't like the connection, so they don't want to see it, he thought. The Indian. The syndrome. The Temple Mount. He wasn't sure himself what he was thinking. He was aware that the pain and the pain killers he had for it were combining to animate him in ways that he wasn't sure of. I've got to stop it, Cohen was thinking. But what can one person do to stop a plague, he asked himself.

He started at Kfar Shaul, the government hospital for the mentally ill.

38

THE BUILDINGS had once been a British army barracks, but now they were painted with childlike murals of animals and flowers. The colors had faded and the paint was peeling, and inside the administration building, the pale green walls were no less scratched and faded than the exterior walls.

An elderly secretary, protective of her boss until Levy flashed his police badge, buzzed an intercom and told the district psychologist's office there were two policemen to see him.

"Are they bringing someone in?" the psychologist asked. "If they are, give them the forms and have them wait. I'll be right out."

She looked at them quizzically. Cohen shook his head. "Tell him it's Commander Avram Cohen," said Levy.

She did, and a moment later the doctor opened the door to his office. "I didn't tell him everything," he said, apologetically. "I told him that we have cases. A few might even be extreme, but I told him to be careful about the word syndrome . . ."

"What are you talking about?" Cohen asked, using his right hand to support himself as he gripped the back of the wooden chair facing the secretary's desk. He held out his left hand to shake the doctor's offered right. The doctor was momentarily taken aback. From somewhere beyond the open window in the anteroom came the sound of hysterical laughter.

"That reporter. I didn't know he was a reporter. There was a party, and a bit of drink, and he got me talking . . ."

"Lassman," said Cohen, holding his laugh back lest it cause the ache to resurface in his belly. "That's not why I'm here. I want to see Chandler."

"Well, it's the syndrome, of course," said the doctor, relieved that Cohen wasn't accusing him of anything.

"Go on," said Cohen.

"We've had about fifty cases in the last month," the doctor continued. "That's a lot more than ever. It seems to be spreading. 'Syndrome,' of course, is a medical term, and I haven't published my findings yet, so I don't know if it should be used as easily as it has been in the last several days. Ever since that story in the newspaper. The fact is, I don't know what to publish. If only it was just the tourists, like this Chandler, who were affected. But it's all sorts now. Jews. Moslems. Christians. People who have been here all their lives. People who think they're prophets, people looking for prophets, ready to listen to anything that gives them the feeling that they possess the city."

Daniel's voice echoed in Cohen's mind. "Prophets. True and false," and Cohen wondered how it was possible to know which to believe.

"Anyway," the psychiatrist was saying, "He still says he's only ready to talk to you, but we've pieced quite a bit together. The messiah, it seems, has been born and is living in the city. A baby. His mother is dark, maybe Moroccan, it's hard to say, but the baby apparently is a redhead, and he quotes the prophecy about a descendant of King David. So . . ."

Cohen interrupted. "What about the nuns?"

"Only you. About that he says he'll only talk to you. He calls you Pilate. But he'll only tell you about the nuns."

"I want to see him."

The doctor spread out his arms. "Of course, of course."

He led them out the building and across a patch of weedy lawn. "We lost our budget for the gardening, so we have some of our patients doing the work," he explained apologetically.

"How are you holding him?" Cohen asked. There was the sudden backfire of a heavy transport engine moving slowly down the highway a few hundred meters away, below the asylum's wind-swept hill, to Tel Aviv.

"In a room to himself. Locked."

"Please, if you'll take us to him," said Cohen.

They walked along a narrow path of cement poured into a straight line across a flat lawn. Tiny white wildflowers dotted the green matte of the grass. The walk took them past a house full of the sounds of confusion and another full of the sounds of sorrow. The wind whistled, making shutters creak on their hinges, and a piece of tin roofing on a shed rippled with metallic tension.

Inside the building where the doctor led the two policemen there was a desk in a small anteroom, and then a barred door led to a corridor. The doctor signaled for the orderly at the desk to open the door.

"He's sedated," the doctor explained. The keys jangled in the lock. "Don't be surprised. There are no windows. The glass, of course. He could turn suicidal."

Cohen nodded, and the door opened.

Chandler was lying on the bed in the corner. "I have awaited you," he said, as Cohen stepped into the room.

"Without them," said Chandler, keeping his eyes on Cohen.

Cohen turned to face the doctor and Levy. The doctor shrugged. Levy shook his head.

"Without the doctor," said Cohen, "if you insist. The other stays."

"I know him," admitted Chandler.

"He stays."

Chandler looked straight at Cohen. There was a long silence, and then Chandler began to laugh.

"What's so funny, Clay?" Cohen asked.

"I did it. Someone had to do it, and I did it."

"What's that? Clay?" Cohen asked, moving slowly to the table and chair in the other corner of the room. It was only three steps, but still beyond Chandler's reach. Cohen was certain of himself but not taking any chances.

"It started because I was a witness," Chandler began. "But you know that," he added. "I witnessed the original sin."

"What sin was that?" Cohen asked, taking out a cigarette. He could see in Chandler's eyes his desire for a smoke, and he tossed the cigarette to the Indian. Levy stepped forward with a match and lit the cigarette. There was a moment when their eyes locked, but it passed, Levy stepping away when Cohen repeated his question. "What sin was that, Clay?"

But Chandler had his own way of explaining the incomprehensible. "It was enough that I was there. I saw the light," he said. "It was a moment of enlightenment, man. A ripe moment."

Cohen wondered where the words came from.

"A moment pregnant with the meaning of my mission in this life," Chandler was saying. "Just like Miriam, pregnant with the savior. But he's all right now, isn't he? The baby?"

"Yes, he's fine, Clay. He's fine. Tell me, were you, how do you say it? On drugs when you saw the sin?" asked Cohen, wishing he knew the slang in Chandler's American the way he knew the Israeli slang.

"You mean stoned? Man, I was ripped. Great dope, great stuff. Lebanese gold. You guys have got a great thing going with dope here," said Chandler.

"You took the dope from the cave?" asked Cohen. "How did you know to go there?"

"Sure, that cave where the prophet goes. Wonderful stuff, wonderful. And when I saw them, I had to act. Fast. I had to save the messiah, man. You understand. Don't you?"

"Sure, sure," said Cohen easily. "Clay, tell me, how did you meet the prophet."

"The blind one? He saw me. He's amazing. He could see me. I came to the cave, I followed them, and when I saw what they have in that cave, I was in heaven. All that dope. And he was there, and man, he was blind, but he could see me."

"Tell me, what do you know about the preacher? What did he tell you?"

The Indian cradled himself with his arms. "He told me I could serve God," he whispered. "I knew what was happening. I could see, he's some preacher, that one. I watched them at the cave. I saw him preaching. I could feel it."

"Did he tell you to kill the nuns? Did he suggest it as your mission?" Cohen asked again.

"I figured it out," Chandler said proudly. "But I knew it would please him. I wanted to please him. He let me have the dope."

"He told you that you could take the hashish?"

"Whenever I wanted."

"Why?"

"Because he could see me, he could see into me. And he's blind, man. He's powerful, powerful. Blind and he said he could see I was a pilgrim in search of truth."

"Could he see you in the convent, Clay? Was he with you?" Cohen was picking through the confusion with his questions.

"No, no, no," said Chandler. "He said they were the agents of devils, and I knew what had to be done. It was for me to do. Those women, they only pretended to be nuns. But I knew them for what they were," said Chandler.

Cohen leaned forward. "What was that, Clay?"

"KGB," Chandler whispered confidentially. "Russians. That's right. It said so in the newspaper." Suddenly his tone turned almost flippant. "But you knew that, of course you knew it. You must have known it. They're Russians," he added, in a low, conspiratorial tone. "KGB. That's right, the most evil of all the evil.

"I knew where the woman lived with the baby. The baby messiah. It was in the village, in the poor part of the village. She didn't have a husband. He was killed. But I found out, he was a carpenter once. Of course, I knew that it had to be that. It had to be, because the baby is the messiah. And those two, the KGB nuns. They were planning to kidnap the baby. I could hear them, at the bus stop, they were planning it. They were looking at him and they were planning it. I had to stop them. I was God's servant and God called on me to do it. He said, 'Protect my son, protect the Savior,' and of course I knew what God meant. There's so much to tell, and I'm telling you, because you're the man, the main man, Pilate himself. You know. You understand. I saw you. That first day and then whenever you came. I saw you come with him," said Chandler, gesturing toward Levy in the corner of the room. "And I knew that you were the one. I saw you talking with that kid, going into the cave at the fountain. I was inside there. I kept my personal stash inside there, with my knives. Aren't they beautiful, my knives? Yes," he said, looking up at Levy, who remained silent the entire time. "I know you have them." He turned back to Cohen. "But then you started coming every day and I was worried. I didn't know what to do. I didn't know then whether I could tell you, because I had to keep my mission a secret . . ." The last word was whispered, an alleycat's hiss.

"Tell me, Clay," said Cohen gently, "how often did you go to the cave? Every day? Every week? Only when the prophet was there?"

"I don't remember," Chandler said.

"Surely you remember, Clay. You were coming to get your *nafas,* your dope. Weren't you?"

"Great dope, that's great dope they have up there."

"Did you buy it from him?"

Chandler shook his head, back and forth, like a toddler refusing food.

"Did he give it to you?"

Again, Chandler shook his head, No.

"So, how do you know it is such good dope?" Cohen asked. "How did you get it?"

"I took it. It was there. I found it. I took it. He's a preacher, right? I don't need a preacher. I don't need someone to speak to God, because God speaks to me."

"That's fine, Clay, that's fine," Cohen said, humoring him. "But I have to understand, you do want me to understand, don't you?"

"Sure, I know who you are, you have to understand. You're in charge here, aren't you. So you have to understand."

"Okay," said Cohen, his stomach aching, his head aflame with pain. "What did you do with the dope?"

"I used it."

"Did you sell it? Trade it?"

Chandler stared at Cohen, amazement in his eyes. "There was so much. So much. I could take what I wanted. They usually weren't there in the daytime. I saw them at night, and when they would finish, I would wait until they were gone and go inside, to take what I wanted."

Cohen leaned forward in his chair. "What else did you see in the cave? What else did you take?"

Chandler pressed his head back against his pillow, suddenly silent and suspicious.

Cohen asked again. "There was something else in the cave, wasn't there?" he asked.

Chandler remained silent.

"You can tell me, Clay, you remember, don't you? You saw boxes and inside the boxes, you found something? What was it, Clay? What did you see inside those boxes?"

Chandler shook his head violently. "I had my mission, God's mission, to save the Savior from those two Russians. I took the hash. I didn't touch the other stuff. Not me."

"What other stuff? What was it?" Cohen pressed one more time.

Chandler turned his head toward Cohen and whispered, "Grenades. Hand grenades. Whoosh, boom," he whistled, imitating the noise he imagined of a grenade.

Cohen eased back in his chair, his stomach aching, his mind reeling. Alex and the Indian. He had two sources but only he could believe either.

"That's good, Clay, that's fine," said Cohen, and then he took the questioning around its circle again. "So what brought you to Jerusalem?" Cohen asked gently.

"God."

"Did he tell you to come here?"

"He brought me here. On the wings of a silver eagle," smiled Chandler. "That's the prophecy. On the wings of a silver eagle. That's the prophecy. For my mission. I didn't know what the mission was, of course, until I came here. And then I received the message. It was in the newspaper. The Red nuns. It was obvious. Especially after I spoke with the Prophet, especially after I told him what I saw.

"The baby messiah. A redhead, that's what he'll be, just like the Bible says, and like the Bible says, he was a son of David. That's right. His father's name was David. I know. I asked around. I did it all right. Just the way the message said. I knew when I saw the Savior and those Russians at the bus stop. They were measuring him. They were whispering about him, and then I realized they were whispering about me. They saw the baby messiah at the bus stop, and if I hadn't been there, they would have taken him. The Savior, I had to save the Savior. It was my mission."

"Who told you, Clay?" Cohen asked again, certain he was close to the answer he was seeking, suddenly knowing that Chandler would not give him the answer directly.

"God, of course. The cosmic coincidence."

"What coincidence?" asked Cohen.

"It was the same day. I saw the Savior, the baby messiah, and that same day, I didn't know what to do, but I followed the prophet to the fire on the mountain. It was God's will."

"So the preacher did speak to you," Cohen said adamantly. "He *did* speak to you."

"He told me to do what was right, what had to be done. I told him what I saw, and he said it was up to me to do what was right. To rid the Holy City of abomination."

"Did he tell you to kill the nuns?"

"He said I could do what was right."

"Did he tell you to kill the beggar?"

Chandler looked at Cohen, puzzlement in his eyes. He began to shake his head, accelerating the back-and-forth motion so that his stringy hair began to flay the air around his head. "No beggar, no beggar, no beggar," he said, "not the innocent. Only the evil."

"Yes, Clay," said Cohen, hearing it all, his mind reeling along the path Chandler's mind had taken, seeing darkness where Chandler had seen light.

Chandler looked up. There were tears in his eyes. "It was my mission," he bawled. "My mission. Everyone has a part. Everyone has their mission on the Lord's Day. On the day of the great sacrifice. And to prepare for that day, this was my mission . . . Mine . . . It was my mission! Mine! Mine!"

Chandler's voice was dry and cracked. Cohen raised his hand and pointed with his thumb at his mouth. It was a signal to Levy, who except for lighting Chandler's cigarette had stood silently by the door of the windowless room for the whole interrogation, to arrange for water. Levy opened the door and whispered to the waiting doctor.

"A few more questions, Clay, just a few more," said Cohen, suddenly wondering if Chandler was confessing to another crime that had taken place in his mind and had nothing to do with the two dead nuns lying on the floor of their cell, on a mountainside overlooking the valley where the Christians believe John the Baptist was born. Lassman had reported a lot of the details of the investigation—the two knives, the tracks leading out of the convent, the way the bodies were found—and Chandler could have read it all and known enough to convince anyone who wanted to listen that he was the killer.

"Did you hear any music that night?" Cohen asked. The *Requiem* echoed in his mind.

"Oh, man, there was such beautiful music. It was like a real church. Not that KGB fakery. Real church music."

"Was it in your head or was it really there, out there in the night?"

"Oh, it was real, man, really real," and Chandler had laughed suddenly, "really real," he said, enjoying the phrase, rolling it over and over on his tongue the way Cohen enjoyed a rich chocolate mousse.

The door opened, and Levy took the pitcher. Chandler stopped practicing his new phrase, "Really real."

He took the pitcher from where Levy had put it on the wooden table by the bed and drank from it directly, the water dribbling from the corners of his mouth.

"I followed them," Chandler said, as soon as he put down the pitcher. "They were tricky, they knew their business. I knew I had to be careful. To do what I had to do."

"Which was?" Cohen asked, as if he did not know the answer.

"Kill them, of course. To protect the baby."

"We can go," Cohen said to Levy. He rose, stiffly, and walked slowly to the door.

"Oh, Clay," he added, as he held the door handle, almost as an afterthought, "would you mind showing us exactly how you did it? We need pictures, we'll do it with a video camera. Nissim here will go with you, with another fellow who works with me. I'm afraid I'm still not fit for such a hike. It's something we do when we have a confession."

"I understand," said Chandler. "Sure, why not? We'll do it really real. Really real."

Even in the garden, beyond the closed doors of Chandler's room and the building itself, they could hear his laughter.

39

I DIDN'T UNDERSTAND half of what he was saying," said Levy as he walked slowly by Cohen's side to the car.

"He came to Jerusalem as a pilgrim, expecting to find the messiah. He learned the nuns were Russian and turned them into KGB or devils, take your pick. He met Ovadia by accident but fell for the whole show, starting with the hashish. Ovadia encouraged him to take action against the nuns. He didn't touch the grenades. And he wanted to tell me the whole story because as far as he was concerned, it was all a message he had to deliver and I was the one he was supposed to deliver it to."

"But why? Why the nuns? Why did Ovadia want the nuns dead? And who killed the beggar?"

Cohen shot a grin at Levy. " 'Armageddon and salvation, apocalypse and purification.' That's what he preaches. That's what he wants."

"Chaos," Levy said, following Cohen's train of thought. "He wanted chaos. But surely the nuns wouldn't give him that. And who killed the beggar?"

"The nuns were a sideshow for him. Just another little bit of action he set into motion and which he could tell his 'students' was part of his plan," Cohen explained, his eyes bright. "The beggar?" he added, "We don't know who killed the beggar. Maybe we'll never know. But the case will stay open. It's just no longer part of this case."

Levy fell silent for a moment, tapping out his thoughts with the car keys on the roof of the sedan. "So, is Ovadia crazy, too?" Levy asked. The sounds of a truck changing gears on the steep hill of the highway below them rose with the wind that swept in from the west.

Cohen leaned on the hood of the car. "Ovadia? Crazy? Maybe. But maybe not. He's always been the same, using people for his own pleasure."

"Well, he's been doing that," Levy acknowledged. "Chandler, the vermin. He's even using the religious affairs minister, getting that yeshiva in the Old City."

"He hasn't changed much at all," Cohen reiterated. "The only real difference seems to be that he figured out that if he calls it religion, he can get away with things. He's playing the saint, selling blessed water from a faucet."

"I still don't understand what he expects to gain from the chaos, the Armageddon."

"More pilgrims, more students, more converts to his cause. More power. People want easy answers, they want causes and missions and messiahs, prophets telling them that the chaos is temporary, that there's light on the way."

"But what does he want?" Levy asked, frustrated by his inability to comprehend Ovadia's motives.

"That's easy," said Cohen, opening the door to the car. "He wants to be the High Priest, the most powerful man in Jerusalem."

"Then he is crazy," said Levy.

"Maybe," said Cohen. "But there are a lot of people in this city who would agree the time has come for the Temple to be built and a High Priest to rule it. He's just one of the contenders, trying to improve his odds. And meanwhile, for the people who listen to him, he's already a very powerful man."

Levy started the car. "You must be tired," he said, as Cohen settled into the seat.

"I'm all right," Cohen insisted through clenched teeth.

"Home?"

"The office," Cohen commanded. "We have planning to do."

40

BUT HE *WAS* TIRED. The ache in his gut was ever present. The doctors had given him some strong painkillers, but he was afraid the pills would dull his mind, even if they relieved it from the ever present hurting in his stomach. He had suffered worse pain, much worse. But he was much younger at the time and could focus the pain back into the inherent revenge he would take upon his enemies in his very survival of their tortures.

Back in the office, answering questions, giving orders, preparing for the final move, the biggest gamble, he was in control of a hundred men. Inside his mind, he was alone with the thought of losing control.

The tinder had been kept damp, but each time somebody like Chandler appeared, it meant there was another little bit of powder too long in the sun, dry and waiting for the match that could set the whole city aflame. Chandler didn't even know that he had tried to do that. He had thought he was bringing salvation. Cohen wasn't sure that Ovadia acted with the same obliviousness to the repercussions of his actions. Armageddon. A false prophet can easily win his faithful, if he promises them the salvation he never gave them, Cohen thought.

He worried about what would happen when the policemen arrived at the yeshiva. The combined groups, Ovadia's and Ben-Yehoshua's, added up to more than a hundred people. They could put up a fight. The ruckus could draw a crowd, Arabs and Jews in a moment of familiar tension and the delusion that this ruckus, this fracas, this riot would solve everything, that the truth would finally be out in the open for all to see.

The TV cameras would arrive with their own hot lights, putting it all in a circle of bright lights and flames. The fighting would start in the alleyway outside the yeshiva, clubs and stones in hand, and it would spread throughout the Old City, into the Street of the Butchers, the carcasses a mockery of the wounded. It would fan out across the plaza in front of the Wall, encompass every church, spill out of every mosque gate.

It would rumble and burst, lavalike onto and out of the Mount.

And from the Old City that steaming passion and belief in a holy war over holy stones would stream into the parking lots and bus lanes, it would wrap itself around the thin bars of neon and rise into the top floors of the too-tall buildings in West Jerusalem. Into the kitschy shops of East Jerusalem it would roil and rumble, down the mountain wadis eastward into the desert the anger and hatred, passion and belief would rush, eastward and westward to the coastal plains and the sea, the lava of belief would embroil the whole land in the brightness of an unforgiving sun. Belief would overcome reason, faith would wrestle down knowledge. The detonators for the explosives were made of pride and prejudice, and the blaze was ignited by history, ancient and recent. Memory, collective or individual, ethnic or racial, was the great concussion, a wave shoving the combatants along, lifting the children and trampling them, pushing aside those who dared raise their hands to try calling out, "Wait, stop, no!" And other screams would rise, "Mine!" "Mine!"—each "Mine!" another claim of possession, another demand for exclusive ownership.

Cohen thought all this as he sat in his office, planning the raid on Ovadia's yeshiva, knowing that this was the nightmare of the entire city and that because of his job it was woven into his private nightmares.

Thus, into the deep and unforgiving darkness of the Old City before dawn, he led the men, hoping his belief in the truth was stronger than Ovadia's, hoping that he, and not Ovadia, would control the events.

41

"Y̲O̲U̲ ̲S̲T̲I̲L̲L̲ ̲D̲O̲N̲'̲T̲ ̲U̲N̲D̲E̲R̲S̲T̲A̲N̲D̲, do you Mr. Com-man-der Cohen?" Ovadia's lupine grin was aimed slightly to the left of the detective.

They were alone in Cohen's office. The pale early morning brightness of the sun was painful to Cohen's all-night eyes. Ovadia stared into the light that had begun to pour into Cohen's office through the huge windows behind his desk.

"It's just you and me, David. Just you and me. Make me understand."

"You still don't understand what happened, do you?" taunted the blind man.

"Why don't you tell me, Mr. Prophet," Cohen answered with no less sarcasm. "Why don't you tell me? What do you have to lose?"

"You think you've arrested me, you think it's all over. It's not over. Not at all. You know," he said, moving his head from right to left, "I remember this room. I remember sitting here with you. How long ago was it? A decade? You said to me that I was going away for a long time, that you figured you'd never have to see me again. Well, here I am. You see me. And you know what? I see you. I see you here," said Ovadia, tapping his forehead with a long, crooked finger.

"And what do you see?" asked Cohen. He felt a strange serenity. The raid had gone perfectly. The bomb squad officer had quickly identified the materiel they found inside the yeshiva as the missing Sidra 13 grenades. Cohen's gamble had paid off.

"I see a man who feels his place slipping away from underneath him," said Ovadia. "I remember you, ten years ago, so certain that you knew what was going on. But do you really know what's going on now? Do you understand what's happened? You think this city is yours. You think this city belongs to you people of progress." The sarcasm was thick and bitter, the statements were mockery to Cohen's ears.

"You people can own this city? Professors and politicians and the godless and the secular? It belongs to us, it belongs to us who believe. You don't believe, Mr. Cohen," Ovadia declared emphatically. "You don't believe, and you break the Lord's laws, and . . ."

"I believed I would get you. And I did, didn't I, David? I did get you." Cohen was leaning back in his chair, his hand resting on his painful stomach.

"But you *didn't* believe you would get me. I know you didn't believe that. And now you think you have me? Do you really think it matters to me if I am in jail or not? To my followers?"

"And how many followers will you have when we display those grenades?" Cohen mocked in return. "How many politicians are going to be able to help you then?" Cohen snapped. "Really, David, how many people can you fool?"

"It doesn't take very many to believe," said Ovadia. "Someone to carry a bag, someone to throw a grenade, someone to . . ."

"Someone to murder two nuns?" Cohen interrupted.

"Even that, even that. It takes very little, if the purpose is God's."

"How did you convince him?" Cohen asked.

"Truly, I did nothing. I let him take his *nafas*. He would have done it all without me. But I had no complaints. He fit into my plans. He fit into God's plans."

"You're ready to do a lot in the name of God, aren't you?" Cohen snapped.

"God demands a lot," asid Ovadia. "He has his laws, and we must obey them. He who doesn't obey is doomed."

"Which one of those brilliant students of yours threw the grenade? Which one put the grenades at the church? Who left the knapsack on the Mount?" asked Cohen.

"Oh, Mr. Commander. How naive you are. You still don't understand. It doesn't matter which one threw the grenade. It doesn't matter who left the knapsack on the Holy Mount. All that matters is that this time we failed. But believe me, we have time. We are winning. If you won't believe in the Lord, or believe in his law, then this is something you should believe."

"Why?" Cohen asked, no gentleness in his voice, yet the anger hidden by practice. "David, what good did it do to kill those nuns? What did you accomplish?"

"Accomplish?" Ovadia laughed, his face to the ceiling, his mouth wide open. "I proved even to the prime minister that all his temporal powers are meaningless. Only God's way is the way. And we, who own this city, we who know his law, we are the ones with the power."

"You're mad," Cohen exploded. "You're mad!"

"You don't want me to be mad." Ovadia smiled as serenely as Cohen had felt moments before. "If I am mad I will be no different than your hippie."

One of the wheels of Cohen's chair was broken, and the chair scraped the floor with an eerie squeal as he pushed it back from the table. Cohen remained silent and then rose silently from his chair, the pain in his gut a cocked spring of tension.

Ovadia's head moved back and forth, searching for Cohen. The anticipation in Cohen's body made every tendon feel taut, every muscle feel strained. Yet he remained silent, waiting, hoping, believing.

Fear grew on Ovadia's face as the silence lasted a full minute and more. Still Cohen waited, forcing himself to be patient.

There was a knock at the door. Ovadia jumped, turning his head to look to the sound behind him. Cohen remained silent. The door slowly opened, and Levy's face appeared at crack of the door. Cohen held his finger to his lips in a signal of silence. Levy nodded and backed away, closing the door behind him.

"What is it?" Ovadia asked, and still Cohen remained silent.

"Who's there?" Ovadia's voice rose. "Who's there? Why aren't you speaking?" the blind man asked, "why are you silent?"

Cohen's silence continued. Ovadia started to rise.

"Sit down," Cohen commanded.

Ovadia lapsed back into the wooden chair. His lips began to

move in prayer. "Blessed art thou, King of the Universe," he began, "who made me a messenger of his word."

"That's *your* prayer," Cohen snarled. "Not a Jew's prayer." And again he fell silent.

Ovadia repeated his prayer, deliberately and slowly.

Cohen walked slowly out from around his desk. Ovadia turned to his left, trying to follow the sound. He suddenly flinched in anticipation of an expected blow and began mumbling a different prayer. Cohen stepped directly up to him and for a long moment, Cohen looked down at the blind man.

Ovadia gazed blankly, the speed of his prayers increasing until they were one long mumble in which Cohen could no longer differentiate any of the individual words. Suddenly Ovadia stopped and began another prayer.

Cohen recognized it. The prayer for the dead. He smiled. "You don't say kaddish for yourself, David," he said. "You don't say kaddish for yourself." He spoke softly, with as much pity as contempt in his voice, and then walked past Ovadia, out of his office and into the bustle of waiting reporters, fifth-floor officers and Russian Compound staffers who had heard the news and wanted to be part of it.

He walked through the crowd, stopping only to tell Levy to put Ovadia in a lockup cell. He ignored Levy's whisper that the inspector general was on the phone and ignored Shvilli, who said that the suspects in the lockup were already beginning to inform on each other. Two tipped as responsible for the Temple grenades had named a third responsible for the grenade on the peace rally. He ignored Abulafia's outstretched hand of congratulations. And he ignored the cries of his name, from the reporters, from the policemen, from Ovadia himself, calling out, "Cohen, come back here, Cohen, I'm not done. Cohen!"

He was on his way home. He'd sleep, long and peacefully. And when he woke, he thought as he stepped into the bright white light of the city in the morning, he'd call Ahuva to make plans for a special dinner.

42

A FEW DAYS LATER, Cohen was at home on his sick leave when Schwartz, the operations commander for the Jerusalem police, knocked on the door. "I'm sorry to bother you at home, Avram," Schwartz said. "But there's something I'd like to talk with you about, if it's all right."

Cohen welcomed him into the apartment.

"Let's say there's a man," Schwartz began nervously. "An old man. A survivor. Like us. And he builds a new life. Far from there. But you know, it never goes away. You can never get away from it. But he thinks he does. And now, he comes here. To see Jerusalem one time before he dies. Avram?"

"I'm listening," said Cohen, his eyes closed against the bright light falling into the room, against the memories that never went away.

"I'm getting to the point, really I am," Schwartz said.

"I'm listening," Cohen repeated.

"He comes here, and he sees someone. From there. Someone as evil as anyone you or I knew in those places."

"Yes?" said Cohen.

"He wanted his revenge. How many years did he wait? How long has it been? Two generations? By the third, who will want revenge? A *kapo*. A *kapo*, Avram," Schwartz said, finally spitting the word.

"The beggar was a kapo," Cohen said, suddenly understanding

Schwartz. He snorted at the irony. "He came here as a beggar to do penance," Cohen murmured. "Such a holy city . . ."

Cohen remembered the *kapos* of his barracks. Some were chosen. Others volunteered. Some used their position of temporary safety to make it easier on others. Others took pleasure from the pain they helped to inflict. He looked up suddenly at Schwartz's expectant face. "Not you, Yosef, please, not you. You didn't kill him . . ."

"No, no, of course not," said Schwartz. "No. But an old man. He came in. He spoke Yiddish. He sat on the bench downstairs at the station. He was talking to himself, in Yiddish. He wanted to confess. He said it over and over again. 'I want to confess.' Nobody downstairs understood him. Who knows the *mamaloshen* anymore? The *haredim*. That's all. But I understand. So I listened. He called the beggar Shneiderman, 'I thought he was dead,' he said, 'I come to Jerusalem, I come here to the city of peace, and who do I see? Him. Shneiderman. The *kapo*. Ever since the camps, I have been able to live because I thought he was dead. If I were to let him live, how could I live. You know what he did?' That's what he asked me, Avram, and of course I knew. I know the *kapos*. So do you."

"So what did you do?" Cohen asked.

"Nothing. I sent him home."

Cohen sighed but remained silent.

"He was made crazy by it. He was made crazy," Schwartz insisted. "If I had known that this beggar was a *kapo*," he suddenly added with bravado, "I would have done it myself."

"No you wouldn't," Cohen said gently.

"He deserved it, the *kapo* deserved it," Schwartz said.

"Maybe," said Cohen, "probably."

"He's gone," said Schwartz, defiantly. "Back to New York."

Cohen put down the pen. He rubbed at the rash on his arm. "There was a *kapo*," he said, remembering. "He carried a stick. Not long. But hard." He covered his face with a hand. "There, then . . ." he said, his voice muffled by his palm. He paused, the memory of the clubbings as deep as the creases on his face. "It was the right thing to do. To kill them—if you could survive." And then he looked up. "But not here. Not now."

"I did what I thought was right," said Schwartz. "And I felt I had to tell you." He rose from the sofa, picking up his officer's cap.

"Why? Why did you wait until now to tell me?" Cohen asked.

"Because I was afraid you would tell me what you just told me. That I was wrong, that I shouldn't have let him go. But now I hear you might be leaving the force, that the politicians aren't happy with what happened, that maybe you're retiring."

"That's months away," Cohen said, "if at all."

"I thought you deserved to know. To know now, so that if there was something you wanted to do about it, while you still have the authority," Schwartz said, "I mean, while you're still on the force." There was apology in his voice, recompense in his attitude. He stood with his cap in his hands, turning it about, nervous and expectant.

Cohen rubbed lightly at his forearm, thinking about the beggar's mutilated face, thinking about all that the *kapos* did.

"You would have done the right thing," Schwartz added, trying to explain himself, seeking an answer from Cohen. "You're the Great Priest, after all," Schwartz added, with some embarrassment as well as flattery.

"What are you talking about?" Cohen snapped.

"That's what they're calling you nowadays at the office. *HaCohen Hagadol.* It's not a joke. Seriously. The secretaries, the junior officers. The senior officers, well, you know the fifth floor."

Cohen didn't like the title but appreciated the affection as well as the admiration that must have prompted the nickname. He ignored Schwartz's embarrassment. "You want to know what I would have done?" he asked.

Schwartz nodded.

Cohen walked to the window overlooking the garden. Suspect the cat was stalking a hoopoe bird resting on a low branch. Cohen leaned out the window and clapped his hands once hard, drawing the cat's attention and startling the bird into flight. He watched the bird disappear into the upper branches of the eucalyptus tree and looked back at the cat, washing itself furiously. He turned to face his troubled colleague.

"I would have arrested him," he said flatly.

Schwartz eyed Cohen with dismay.

"I would have asked for lenience and consideration, and I would have said that he posed no harm to society and that justice would be best served by his release. But I would have arrested him. Because that's the truth, Yosef. And that's what it's all about. Even here. In this city. Especially here."